Benét Stoen

THE WARRIOR

S.D.G

Copyright © 2022 by Benét Stoen

ISBN: 9798841930143

Cover by Benét Stoen.

To Daisy–
This one is ours.

Also by Benét Stoen

His and Mine
I Am Write

The Royal Three Trilogy:
The Heir

The Warrior

PROLOGUE

ARTEMIS wasn't at all allured by the naked woman before him. She stood in the center of a pile of her discarded clothing, her long blonde hair falling in ringlets down to her narrow waist. Her smile was a flirtatious dare. But as she stepped toward Artemis, he held up a hand. She paused, for the first time looking unsure. He pointed to the connecting washroom in his chambers, and followed behind the young prostitute as she entered. A bath had already been drawn, and tendrils of steam coiled upward from the surface of the still water.

"Get in," Artemis said simply.

Uncertain, she did as she was told. She stepped into the tub and sat down, the top of the water just reaching her breasts.

Artemis leaned against the doorframe. He twirled his finger. "Go on."

The woman blinked at him, so he pointed at the bar of soap next to the tub. "Bathe." He was losing patience. This was taking too long. The sight of her confused face and unwashed body made his blood boil and his lip curl in disgust. How many men had she been with before coming here? How many hands touched her, and how many of those hands had been clean? None of them, Artemis was sure.

He wouldn't touch her until she was spotless.

For the first time, the woman's expression shifted from confusion to anger. Her cheeks pinkened slightly, and Artemis rather liked the sight.

"I'm sorry?" she scoffed. *"Bathe?"*

Artemis' eyes shifted around the room, bored. "Do you speak to all of your customers this way?"

She remembered her place instantly. Her expression cleared, though Artemis still saw the anger hidden in the creases around her dark blue eyes. Her flirtatious smile returned, painfully forced. "Won't you join me?" she asked in a low, husky voice as she leaned back in the water, exposing her chest.

The idea made Artemis' skin crawl. "No. Now, bathe."

The woman actually flinched, and Artemis rolled his eyes, having finally had enough. He lunged forward, too fast for the woman to react. He gripped the top of her hair with his gloved hand and hissed, "I said *bathe.*" He shoved her head under the water. The woman flailed, gasping for breath once Artemis pulled her back up again.

"I'm sorry," the woman choked, "I'll do what you ask, I'm sorry."

7

Artemis released her, letting his hand trace the side of her face. Hope blossomed in her eyes, but turned quickly back to fear when Artemis' expression hardened to anger. He supposed it wasn't truly the woman's fault; no one understood how filthy they really were. No one sensed the buzzing of dirt and grime around their bodies, like a swarm of tiny, invisible gnats. No one but Artemis.

He felt all of it.

No matter what he did, there was no escaping it. He should have known better.

He pushed her head under the water again, but this time he didn't let her up. She thrashed impressively, much stronger than she looked, but Artemis' hands clamped around her throat, pushing her down, down, down, until the back of her head slammed against the bottom of the tub.

He held her there until she stopped thrashing. Until she didn't move at all. Then he let go, taking off his now soaked gloves and dropping them into the tub.

His body would allow him to wait for the right one; he didn't need her as badly as he needed her to be perfect. To be cleansed.

But people simply refused to see their own contamination.

Artemis scrubbed his hands in the wash basin, above which hung a narrow mirror. His pulse was too fast in his ears, and he let out a long breath as he rinsed his hands. He stepped back into his chambers, and had barely finished changing into a clean, dry shirt before there was a pounding at the door. Someone down the hall was shouting, too far away for Artemis to decipher their words.

He closed the door to the washroom, then smoothed his shirt and tucked his arms behind his back, spine straight, expression calm. "Enter."

Two guards burst in, eyes wide with fear they made no effort to hide. Artemis concealed a sneer. "What's happened?" he asked, feigning surprise and concern.

"You have to come, sir," one of them panted. "Queen Morgeoux is in a right state— one of the patrols found her outside the castle. She's asking for you."

Artemis' eyes widened. Could it be... was it done?

Artemis crossed to his dresser and took out a clean pair of black gloves, slipping them on before putting on his long black coat and allowing the soldiers to lead him to the High Queen's chamber, though there was no need; even if Artemis didn't know the way, he could have simply followed the screaming. It got louder as they approached, multiple different voices shouting multiple things at multiple frequencies. Artemis' stomach turned; he experienced the abrupt desire to cover his ears. But he had to see her; had to know if...

Queen Morgeoux was huddled in the corner of the room, her rail-thin body curled in upon itself, her usually so carefully styled blonde hair a tangled nest of snarls and dirt and leaves, as though she'd run through a forest. A filthy cloak was tangled around her, and her feet, Artemis noticed, were bare, crusted with dirt and bleeding in places from long cuts. She was also screaming— no, *howling*— furious and panicked like a wild animal, the sound only growing louder when a servant tried to venture nearer. Morgeoux slashed her arms through the air, fingers curled like claws.

The servants turned toward the door as Artemis entered, their expressions instantly changing to relief.

"They found her outside," a particularly hysterical-looking servant woman gasped.

"Get everyone out of here," Artemis snapped. "I'll see to her." When they just stood gaping at him, he added, "Now. Can't you see you're frightening her even more? Get *out*."

They scattered like cockroaches, leaving Artemis alone with the queen, who wrapped her arms around her head, long fingers gripping the roots of her hair, her body quaking with violent shivers.

Artemis knelt before her, head cocked pensively. "What happened, Morgeoux?" he asked, voice calm, though his pulse knocked hard against his chest.

Her head snapped up, eyes wild and demented. But recognition flashed across her face when her eyes met Artemis' and her arms lowered. She dragged in a breath, her eyes wide and unblinking. She opened and closed her mouth, but nothing came out. Artemis gripped her arms, helping her to her feet. When he was certain she would remain upright, he smoothed his gloved hands down her hair, freeing a few stray leaves tangled in the golden mane. He brushed away her tears with his thumbs. "There, there," he soothed. "Now, what's happened?"

"She... fell," Morgeoux gasped. Her voice was raspy, as if shards of glass speared her throat.

"Who fell?" Artemis struggled to keep his voice from sounding too eager. He stroked her hair as gently as he could, despite the cold adrenaline flooding his system. *Please... please let it be...*

"I didn't mean to," Morgeoux gasped, her face contorting in misery as a sob stole her breath. "I didn't know. I couldn't... I couldn't stop..."

Artemis gripped the queen's shoulders until she looked up into his face. "Morgeoux," Artemis asked calmly, "Did you kill Andromeda?"

Her wide blue eyes went strangely blank as she finally, slowly, nodded her head.

Artemis' head suddenly grew light. It had worked.

His face stretched into a smile as Queen Morgeoux turned away, hand against the bedpost for balance as she slumped forward. With hands that trembled slightly, he reached into one of the many pockets of his coat and extracted a small bottle of amber liquid, and the silk handkerchief from his breast pocket. He let the liquid drip onto the silk, then in one swift motion he covered the queen's mouth and nose with it. She started, her skeletal fingers gripping Artemis' wrists reflexively. "There, there," Artemis crooned over the sound of Morgeoux's muffled scream, "You won't remember a thing in the morning."

When she slumped backward against him, Artemis pocketed the cloth and lifted Morgeoux around her shoulders and under her knees. He laid her gently on the bed, arranging her hands so they laid over her stomach, the picture of peace.

He sat on the mattress beside her, watching her with something akin to wonder. He did it. The High Queen was powerless against him, in every conceivable way. She had signed the decree to outlaw Magic, and now she'd killed her own sister. He needed only to speak, and she would obey.

He reached a hand toward her, letting his fingers trail through her tangled locks. His beautiful, powerless pearl.

He stood, and left her alone once more.

The hallway outside the bedroom was empty, save for a single servant, arms crossed, shoulder leaning into the wall, waiting.

She straightened when Artemis stepped in front of her, her face expectant. Artemis' eyes swept the hallway, making sure they were alone, before procuring from an inner pocket a teardrop-shaped glass vial so small Artemis could conceal it in a closed fist. Its contents was entirely translucent, making the vial appear empty. He handed it to the servant. "Same as before," he told her in a low voice. "One drop in her tea."

"Yes, sir," she said, tucking it into her apron pocket.

Artemis expected her to leave, but she seemed to be waiting for something. Annoyed, he glared at her. "You'll get your coin," he snapped, "now be gone." She dipped her head quickly and scurried away.

Artemis waited for her to disappear, then made his slow and easy way out to the castle grounds.

*　　*　　*

THE lake's waves lapped rhythmically, hypnotically, against the gravel shore. The lake looked beautiful from a distance, but Artemis found upon closer inspection it smelled distasteful, like fish and salt, and the wind blowing across the water's surface was bone-chilling in the early morning air. Gritting his teeth, he watched as two soldiers walked along the pebbled beach, eyes scanning the water, searching for bodies.

"Over here!" one of them shouted.

Artemis shivered. He managed to keep from running, instead gliding purposefully to where the men waited on the other side of the water.

The sun was just beginning to rise over the tip of the steep cliff above, and in the pink and gold light, Artemis could see two bodies lying side by side, their feet inches from the lapping water.

He stopped once he reached them, peering down at the woman. At Andromeda. If it wasn't for the blue tinge to her lips, her still chest and the pool of dried blood under her skull, he would have thought she was only sleeping. The physician at her side, however, more obviously suffered a fall, broken limbs set awkwardly. Someone had moved him. Both of them.

"Who moved the bodies?" Artemis asked, not tearing his eyes away from Andromeda's gray face. He knew the answer before the soldier beside him spoke.

"The Third Queen's guard, sir. Patrol saw him run west from here."

"Have they apprehended him?"

"Not yet, sir."

Angelus. Artemis had humored Andromeda's taking in that stray child all those years ago. He rather regretted that now.

"Sir..." The second soldier's voice wavered slightly. His face was pale, his eyes wide, fixed to Andromeda's body. To her flat stomach. "What happened to—"

Artemis glanced at the soldier standing beside him, who drew his sword. The other soldier was so transfixed by the queen's corpse he didn't seem to notice. Artemis nodded, and the soldier's sword slashed clean through the other's neck. His head hit the ground, along with the rest of him, neck spewing crimson.

Artemis smiled at the remaining soldier. The soldier smiled back, doubtlessly dreaming of the handsome sum Artemis promised him.

Reaching into his coat, Artemis stepped toward the soldier, as though about to pay him then and there. The soldier never saw Artemis' blade, didn't understand what happened until he was on his knees, hands covering his slit throat. While he still knelt there on the pebbled ground, Artemis, with a grimace of disgust, cleaned his blade on the soldier's arm, before raising his leg to kick the man squarely between the eyes. If he died before he hit the ground or not, Artemis did not know nor care. No one— *no one*— could know the nature of the Mother Queen's death.

With a sigh that fogged the cold air in front of him, Artemis knelt beside Andromeda's gray, blue-lipped corpse. His smile warped into a gritted grimace as his gloved fingers trailed over Andromeda's stomach.

"You were always a clever girl," Artemis mused. He bent lower, until his lips were inches away from her ear. She smelled like the lake, like blood, and like death. "But it didn't save you in the end," he whispered, "Now did it?"

He could have kicked Andromeda, spit on her, thrown her back into the water with a lead weight shackled to her ankles so her remains could decompose at the bottom of the lake for all eternity; she deserved it, for making a fool of him these last months. But no... he still needed her for one last task. If Artemis couldn't use her for her intended purpose, her corpse could still prove useful. Atremis did not believe in being wasteful.

He took off his gloves and pocketed them, then smoothed his hair back with his fingers as he got to his feet again and crossed to where the two dead soldiers lay. He considered for a moment, then, with all his strength, kicked the severed head toward the lake. It arced impressively before it hit the water with a satisfying splash.

He looked down at the gore on the tip of his boot. *Gods damn it.* They were his favorite pair.

*   *   *

ARTEMIS hummed as he made his way to the throne room, an old song his father used to sing before he died of the coughing sickness. He hadn't been a Lawmaker long, Artemis replacing him at only eighteen years old. The song's exact tune escaped him after so many years, but he remembered a few verses.

The lake was under guard. The queen's body and that of her physician had been covered from prying eyes. No one was to go to the lake, under any circumstances, until Artemis could move the bodies discreetly. It had been hours, and still Andromeda's guard remained unfound. He wasn't worried; nothing stayed hidden from Artemis for long. The stray would be dealt with, just like he'd dealt with everything that had gotten in his way thus far.

He was still humming when he entered the throne room, the large wooden doors closing loudly behind him. The Lawmakers were already assembled, a few pacing, a few sitting, but they all wore the same restless shock on their faces.

"Artemis!" Batilda gasped, rising from her seat at the round table set up for meetings of the powers. "Is it true? Gods, please tell us this has all been some kind of mistake! A misunderstanding!"

Artemis blinked at her birdish face calmly. "I haven't the slightest idea what you are talking about."

"The queen!" Loren bellowed. "Her Majesty Andromeda, is she dead?"

"Ah," Artemis sighed. "That. Tragic business, really."

Batilda gave a soft scream, clapping her hands over her mouth.

"What happened?" Loren demanded. He was a large man, fat and muscular at once. A piece of his morning porridge seemed to have gotten caught in his gold beard.

Once Artemis saw it, he couldn't stop staring at it.

"Assassins from Resh?" Loren continued.

"Don't be ridiculous," Samina snapped. She appeared the least shocked of everyone, or perhaps merely the least concerned. "Why would Resh assassinate the queen? They've wanted nothing to do with us for years."

"Lawless?" Batilda suggested, still looking dazed.

Artemis finally dragged his eyes from Loren's beard, his gaze falling on Batilda. "That will be the public story, yes."

All eyes turned to him.

"S-story?" Batilda stammered, voice barely audible. "Is it not the truth?"

Artemis shook his head.

"You know what happened?" Loren was glaring at Artemis incredulously.

Artemis never liked Loren— he was hulking and loud and, apparently, an un-neat eater. These attributes combined tended to differ Artemis' amicability. But above all else, he was the only

16

Lawmaker who did not harbor a fear of Artemis. He supposed this was because Loren relied on his size to deter threats, underestimating how much more powerful a sharpened mind was than a blade or fist. Artemis, for the first time, smiled. Just as the massive cloaked figures barged through the doors.

The Lawmakers jumped and began backing toward the wall as the doors crashed open. There was no exit except the double doors, which were now blocked by massive forms nearly twice the size of a normal man.

Batilda's scream bounced throughout the room as the men drew back their hoods. Their eyes bulged, as though being squeezed slightly from their skulls, their hair missing in places and their faces riddled with stitches where their cheeks and foreheads tore before bones that grew too quickly. They wore no shirts, only the cloaks and brown pants that stopped at their knees. They breathed heavily, loudly, and hunched forward slightly, as though their arms were a heavy burden they carried. Drool dripped from their gaping, slack mouths. They were hideous in an unformed, not-yet-finished way, like newly hatched birds.

"What in all the gods' names is going on here?" Loren cried, his voice slightly higher than usual. His back was against the far wall.

Artemis relished the horror in his eyes. Pathetic, such a large man trembling in fear, eyes wide and terrified, porridge still caught in his beard.

Artemis slid a chair away from the table and sat down, leaning back comfortably. He turned to face the creatures. "Well?" he asked. "Go on."

With what looked to Artemis like relief, they dropped to their hands and knees, their distorted faces elongating as their bodies began to shift, bones cracking as they hunched forward, their spines stretching as if about to tear through their skin. They shot upright again, their faces completely transformed, the skin taking on a silvery hue, their pores opening to sprout hair across their entire face. One moment, they were men, and the next, in the time it took to lunge forward, they were enormous dog-like monsters, covered in thick, coarse, gray-black fur. They charged, all four limbs dashing across the ground, mouths stretching to reveal their bared, pointed teeth. They pounced like animals on their prey, wide jaws closing around throats and arms and legs, tearing through the Lawmakers' flesh like wet parchment.

The screaming was unending. It rose and rose like the crescendo of a temple hymn, reaching toward heaven like a sacrifice. A sacrifice of blood.

So much blood.

Artemis watched with some fascination as the veins of red slithered across the smooth floor, following him as he walked to the High Queen's throne. He sat down on the smooth wooden panel, letting his arms fall lightly over the armrests, the sides embroidered in carvings of intricate flower patterns and ropes of vines and tree roots.

When the last monster released Loren's throat from its teeth, Artemis smiled, satisfied. He rose, slipping a new, clean silk handkerchief out of his pocket. He crossed to where Loren's mangled corpse lay in a mess of blood and brains and intestines. Careful to avoid stepping in the mess, he knelt down to brush the stubborn food from Loren's beard. Then he tossed the handkerchief aside and moved toward the door, but Samina's twitching fingers caught his eye. She'd made it the closest to the door, and her hand reached for it as though she could bring it closer. Artemis peered down at her curiously, and her wide eyes met his. She gurgled, lips moving, trying to speak.

He turned to the creatures. "You missed one."

One of them stepped forward, clamped the top of Samina's skull in it's teeth, and relieved her head from her shoulders.

With a nod, Artemis led the way out the double doors, where a handful of guards waited. They were shaking, and Artemis could smell their sweat. His lip curled.

A pale guard asked shakily, "What are your orders, sir?" He did not address Artemis, however. His terrified gaze was locked on the pack of wolves that followed Artemis into the hallway. They walked on two legs, revealing muscular, human-like chests completely at odds with their wolfish faces and dagger claws.

The soldiers' surprise, their horror, was delicious. Artemis did not particularly care that these men followed him out of fear, unlike the Lawmakers, who simply followed power, and money, wherever it led. Some, perhaps, were with him because of greed, but Artemis didn't mind. They all followed, and that was what mattered.

"Have that mess cleaned up at once," Artemis said, never pausing his purposeful stride down the hall as he spoke. "And have a servant run me a bath. By the gods, it's been a long day."

PART ONE

CHAPTER ONE

THE sun was rising, and Angelus was running.

The scent of the lake still burned in his nose, his throat. His wet clothes clung to him, weighing him down, and the sound of running footsteps pounded in his ears, louder than his heartbeat.

The trees around the lake wouldn't hide him forever, he was reaching the end of the woods, and then there would be nowhere to hide. The hilts of the many daggers concealed in his vest punched against his chest and into his sides, reminding him of their presence. He'd shed his sword, his cloak, everything too heavy to run with. All that remained were the soaked clothes on his back, and the knives hidden on his person. There was nothing inside him but the need to run.

The wind picked up, chilling him to the bone. Summer had been so short, like it never existed.

"Spread out!" a soldier called from somewhere behind him. "Artemis wants him alive. Find him!"

He thought he was about two miles out from the castle, maybe more. How long had he been running? A searing pain tore through his side every time he breathed, but he didn't stop.

Heat flashed across his right arm, and Angelus lost his footing, hitting the ground so hard all the air left him. He turned over onto his back, clutching his bicep. An arrow protruded from a tree beside him, and he understood he'd only been grazed. He barely felt the pain; he was more aware of the hot blood oozing from between his fingers than the wound itself.

Blood. His was hot, but hers had been cold.

Blood, so dark red it looked black, covering his hands. Her blood. Her blood was still on his hands.

"He's here!" a soldier shouted, but where he was Angelus didn't know. The trees above him were swirling around and around, and every sound came from every direction.

Angelus rolled onto his stomach, dragging himself up to his hands and knees.

"Don't move!" shouted a man's voice from.... behind him? Angelus thought so. The creak of a bow being drawn echoed in the air.

Angelus was still for a moment. He could hear the soldier's companions making their way closer, but for now, they were alone.

Angelus didn't move. His hands, his bloody, bloody hands, were in the mud, so cold and thick against his skin.

He remembered her long, wet hair fanning around her in the water, the cold silk of her dress against his skin, the weightlessness of her body. Empty. She'd been empty before he could reach her.

23

Gone...

Dead.

Angelus didn't feel himself stand, didn't feel himself pull a knife from his vest, didn't feel it leave his hand when he threw it, burying itself in the soldier's throat. All he felt was fire, burning him from the inside. The soldier let the arrow fly, but it only managed to impale the ground a few feet in front of Angelus, before the soldier crumpled to his knees, then fell onto his back. He writhed on the ground, eyes bulging as he clutched his throat, blood spilling everywhere.

"There!" another voice shouted, and the remaining two soldiers emerged from the trees, swords drawn.

There was a single breath in which Angelus imagined what it would be like to surrender. For this unending nightmare to finally be over. It would be easier, wouldn't it? What was there for him now, with her gone?

Gone. Dead.

For a moment, the men were triumphant, until Angelus buried a blade between their eyes. The knives appeared in his hands, pulled from his vest, and then flashed as he hurled them through the air. His aim was perfect, and the soldiers fell, lifeless.

The forest went utterly silent, except for Angelus' panting breaths, and the gurgling from the, incredibly, still-living soldier on the ground. He tried to scream when Angelus wrenched the knife free, but he couldn't.

Angelus fell upon him, fear retreating in the wake of something else, something frenzied and fragmented, spreading like fire but as cold as ice, something that had lain dormant until that moment. Like a scream building in the throat, but it was inside his entire body. The writhing man's chest pinned between Angelus' thighs, he raised the bloodied knife. He brought it down on the man's neck, burying the blade deep, *deep*.

The lake, cold and silky against his skin, the smell of blood and salt, her limp body in his arms.

Angelus' vision blackened around the edges, tunneling until the dead soldier beneath him looked miles and miles away.

"Andromeda... Andromeda..."

The knife, still clutched in his bloody, numb hand, found a home in the soldier's chest, neck, arms, over and over and over again, until there was nothing but red.

She wasn't answering. Why wasn't she answering?

Screaming. The man was dead but Angelus still heard him screaming.

He touched the back of her head, and his fingers came away red.

Over and over and over.

"Andromeda!"

It was not the soldier who was screaming, he realized. Alone but for the birds startled into flight above him, Angelus was the one that was screaming.

CHAPTER TWO

ANGELUS didn't know how long he walked. His feet carried him numbly onward, one hand clutching the arrow wound on his arm, his legs heavy, but his chest weightless. There was nothing there to weigh him down, no lungs, no heart.

The cold breeze had long ago dried the blood on his hands.

And so he walked; down the endless, dusty road, eyes on his feet, unaware of anything around him. Until he found himself on the outskirts of the Imperial City. Even from a distance Angelus could see a crowd forming in front of the temple, a tremendous white pillar of a building, the doors curtained by banners bearing the royal family's crest; three crowns forming rings around the blade of a sword, behind which were crossed a scroll and a cluster of flowers, the images silvery against the red fabric of the banner.

Angelus stared at it, uncomprehending.

He moved off the road to avoid being seen, blending in with the trees of the small wood skirting the city's edge. He eased down into a sitting position, leaning against the trunk of an enormous oak tree. Gently, he peeled away the tatters of his shirtsleeve, examining the wound across his right arm. It was still bleeding slightly, but it did not appear to be deep.

From the trees, he could hear people as they passed by on the street beyond. "...a messenger from the castle," someone was saying. "Hurry, we'll miss the announcement."

The words took a long time to reach Angelus' ears, for him to understand what they meant. For a moment he didn't move. Then he got to his feet. He swayed, and grabbed the tree trunk to steady himself. He crept from the trees until he got as close as he could manage without being visible to the people in the crowd quickly growing before the temple steps.

"I bring grave news from the castle," a man's voice declared, loud enough to carry back to Angelus, though he couldn't see what was happening. He looked up at the tree beside him. There were multiple branches, perfect for footholds. His right arm flashed white hot as he pulled himself up into the tree, and he carefully made his way to the top, the familiar feeling of the rough bark and the green scent of the leaves penetrating the fog in his mind long enough to reassure him, to steady him.

He hid in the foliage, looking down on the city, invisible to the people below. He was just another shadow in the trees, silent and unmoving.

"There have been numerous attacks on castle staff over the last several weeks, all believed to be the work of the Wielder rebels, known also as the Lawless."

The *Lawless? They* were being blamed for Silla's death, for the chief physician's? He remembered, as though from another life, the man who had attacked Andromeda's carriage, who bled to death on the city street, his arm severed by a soldier.

"It is my duty to inform you that the destructive nature of these radicals has reached the royal family. An attack was carried out on the castle last night, claiming many lives."

The silent crowd tensed, and Angelus' vision started to tunnel.

"Our beloved Mother Queen, Andromeda, was found murdered by the Lawless."

Finally, the dam of silence broke. There were shocked gasps, wails, a woman's scream. Hands covered mouths, eyes went wide with shock. "No one is safe from those savages!" a man shouted.

"During the attack, the Mother Queen, as well as the Lawmakers, lost their lives despite the valiant efforts of castle soldiers to protect them. They were outnumbered, and were shown no mercy."

The Lawmakers were dead? How? When? Artemis. Artemis must have killed them. Which meant he had no opposition. With Queen Mayva missing, it was only Artemis and Queen Morgeoux left in the castle.

"The spread of the Wielders' unfounded hatred and rebellion against the laws of this country will not be tolerated," the messenger continued, his voice rising as the crowd hummed with approval. "A task force has been constructed to hunt the Lawless, and all those associated with them."

The crowd shouted questions at the messenger, but Angelus was far beyond listening. He leaned back against the trunk of the tree behind him, his legs hanging off either side of the branch he sat on. He wanted to stay there like that forever.

The fingers of his uninjured arm floated unconsciously to his chest, expecting to feel the smooth, familiar shape of his identification necklace. But it wasn't there.

His hand flew to his throat, seeking the chain. Nothing.

Cold panic flooded his entire body. His breathing grew rapid as he fought back images of dark water, the press of the cold, cold night all around him, the scent of blood and salt. He squeezed his eyes shut so tight stars floated in the darkness.

His hand clutched at his chest, no longer weightless, but heavy, and somehow run-through, like an enormous metal pole had been punched through his chest. The world started to blacken. But then he heard a soft crinkling, like paper, coming from where his hand pressed into his chest. He sucked in a full breath, let it out again, trying to regain control. He reached into the inside of his vest, fingertips brushing something stiff and smooth. Surprised, he gingerly freed the envelope of his inner pocket.

Instantly the world began to refocus.

Finn's letter.

"I want you to give that to Veronica. If something happens to me, there are things I want her to know."

Veronica. Images of her long dark hair swaying as she walked filled his mind, the surprise on her face the first time she saw him, though it had not been the first time he'd seen her. He'd known her face long before that.

He tucked the letter back into his pocket, against his heart. He pressed it into his chest as if it could warm him.

With hands still bloody, and his arm still bleeding and pulsing with pain, he climbed down from the tree, and headed west. To the village. To her.

He had nowhere else to go.

CHAPTER THREE

THE door to the house burst open, making Veronica and the children gathered around her jump as a boy came flying into the room, chest heaving, eyes wild.

"What is it, Sully?" Veronica asked, startled.

"Miss Veronica," he panted. "You have to come! There's someone on the road, he isn't moving!"

Veronica got to her feet, grabbed her cloak and pulled it on. "Stay here," she said sternly to the children still sitting on the floor beside the fireplace with the book they had been poring over, their faces growing pale. Martha, the youngest of the group, clutched her ragdoll to her chest as though to protect it, her eyes enormous. "It'll be alright," she added, more softly. "Mary." She looked at the small twelve year-old girl, the eldest of the children, as she opened the front door. "Make sure they stay inside. I'll be right back." Mary nodded, and Veronica jogged behind her six year-old student, who clearly got sidetracked on his way back from the outhouse.

Veronica's mind raced. Could it be Finn? Could he have come back? She banished the thought; she couldn't get her hopes up.

She almost tripped over Sully as he practically threw himself down beside the motionless figure of a man lying on the road that stretched behind the house. She knew instantly it was not Finn—this man's body was long and narrow, his straight hair as black as raven wings. Not a golden curl to be seen. He wore boots, pants, a thin shirt and a dark leather vest, all of which were filthy. The way his body lay, head pointed west, made Veronica think he must have come from the east, not from the village. Veronica knelt down to inspect him more closely. "Did he say anything?" Veronica asked Sully as she rolled the man onto his back. She pressed an ear to his chest, breathing a sigh of relief when she heard a faint heartbeat.

Sully shook his head. "No, he was just lying here."

Veronica looked him over quickly, trying to find an injury, then she noticed the blue tinge to his fingers. "Gods," she gasped. How long had he been there? She didn't see him that morning when she went to the village to collect the children for their lessons. She turned to Sully. "Go and find some of the older boys; I can't carry him by myself. Tell them it's an emergency." Sully was already running toward the field. Veronica took off her cloak, shivering slightly in the cold morning air, and draped it over the man. Summer only just ended, but autumn was already present in the early mornings, making the air cold enough that she could see her breath. "Wake up," she said, patting his cheek. *"Wake up."*

His eyelids twitched. His lips moved, but no sound emerged.

"You're alright," Veronica said, rubbing her hands over his arms, trying to create some heat. "Just keep your eyes open. Help is coming." She could already hear running footsteps getting closer.

The man was trying to say something, and Veronica leaned closer. "What?"

A gurgling, grunting sound vibrated through his throat.

Veronica frowned, shaking her head. "I don't—"

The man reached for the pocket of his mud-slicked vest, but Veronica stopped him with a hand on his arm. His hands, she saw, were covered in dried blood. His? Someone else's? "Later. We have to get you fixed up first, alright?" She began trying to shift him into a sitting position as Sully and two other boys arrived, taller than Veronica and covered in mud from working in the fields. They helped her get the man on his feet. He tried and failed to stand on his own, unable to keep his balance, and leaned heavily on all of them, Veronica taking one side and the two boys taking the other, his arms slung over their shoulders. Veronica's legs wobbled under the weight, but they half carried, half dragged him to the house.

"Sully," Veronica gasped. The boy stood a few paces away, wide-eyed. "Go and tell Mary to boil some water, and get all of the blankets out of the wardrobe in my room. Then tell the rest of the children to go home." She didn't need them watching a stranger die in their classroom.

Sully only stared.

"*Now.*"

He sprinted toward the house, faster than Veronica had ever seen anyone run. "Hurry," she told the boys.

33

They struggled forward.

All of the children were in the kitchen when they got there, Mary scurrying around them to get everything ready and barely avoiding several collisions. Sully had apparently only been half listening. "You children go home," she said quickly, easing the man down on a pile of blankets Mary laid out on the floor in front of the fireplace, then Veronica began to strip away his clothes. She unfastened his vest, thick and strangely heavy, and tugged it off him. His shirt was another matter, stuck to his skin with moisture, and she needed to use a knife to cut it open and tear it away. The nearly frozen fabric was sucking all of the warmth from his body, and as soon as his shirt was torn away, she tossed the tattered pieces of fabric aside and draped thick blankets over him, trying to preserve what bodyheat he had left. Before he was covered again, however, she made out a horrific scar across his left rib cage, a thick, raised smear of pink and white flesh. There was nothing clean about it. The wound had been messy, violent, and savage. Veronica only had a heartbeat to wonder what caused an injury like that.

Thankfully, the children had all scattered, and only Mary and the boys remained. "Where's the water?" Veronica called, pushing her long braid over her shoulder and out of the way. Mary scurried into the kitchen, returning with a steaming pot. Veronica poured the water into two clay bowls, gently easing the man's fingers into them. His eyes were open, but barely. His head lolled from side to side.

"What does that do?" Mary sounded terrified, but was trying not to show it.

"It will get the blood flowing to his fingers again." Veronica dipped a cloth into the steaming water, wringing it out slightly and pressing it to the man's forehead. "Hold this," she told Mary, who took the cloth with trembling fingers.

"What happened to his arm?" one of the boys asked shakily.

Frowning, Veronica looked closer. There was blood crusted along the man's right arm, nearly concealing a gash across his bicep. Veronica grimaced. The skin around the cut was flaming red and swollen.

Veronica rolled up her sleeves. It was impossible to tell how deep the cut on his arm was with all the dirt and blood, but it didn't appear to be bleeding heavily. "Get me the bandages in the kitchen and the alcohol in the cupboard," she told one of the boys, who jumped to his feet and returned a moment later with an amber glass jar and a roll of cloth bandages. Veronica beckoned him forward. "Hold his arm in case he jumps," she instructed, and the boy obeyed, setting the supplies down next to Veronica.

The man did jump, badly, as soon as the alcohol made contact with his skin. He shouted something unintelligible, swinging his other arm wildly and trying to sit up. His nostrils flared, his eyes going wide with pain and confusion.

"Shhh," Veronica soothed, trying to push him back down. His eyes locked on her, irises green like the first tree buds after a long winter. For a second, she was frozen. She'd seen those eyes before. "It's alright," Veronica said, shaking free of her shock, and guiding him gently back. "You're going to be alright."

He just stared at her, like he couldn't believe she was real. Perhaps he was feverish, hallucinating. She had little doubt then that his wound was infected.

"I'm going to make a poultice," she told Mary, starting to get to her feet, but the man's hand shot out, closing around her wrist.

"Don't," he gasped, Veronica barely making out the word. He squeezed her wrist so tightly it hurt. "Don't— Don't go." He could barely hold his head up, but his hand was like a vise around her wrist.

Veronica wrapped her other hand around his fingers. "I won't," she promised. She turned to Mary and instructed her to make the poultice. It was something they'd practiced countless times, and Mary dashed to the kitchen to fetch the supplies. She was learning fast; she would be Veronica's apprentice soon.

Veronica's apprentice. Veronica had just *been* an apprentice a handful of months ago. She should have been sitting in Mary's place, helping to gather supplies and watching as Finn's skilled and efficient hands did their work. He would have been able to save this man, there was no doubt in Veronica's mind. But all he had was Veronica, a small and frightened guardian barring him from death.

The thought of Finn sent a sharp jab through her heart, and she forced her focus to return to the injured man. She *knew* him from... somewhere.

His grip relaxed, but only slightly. She pried his fingers away and Mary returned with the poultice. He gave a sudden, violent shudder, and cried out like a wounded animal.

"What's wrong with him?" Mary asked, her hands shaking, face a bit green. Veronica wondered, in a distant, detached way, if she'd looked to Finn how Mary looked to her now when she'd first come to this house. Goddess, that had been so long ago.

"He doesn't have any other injuries I can see," Veronica answered, surprised her voice came out so calm. "It must be the fever. He'll be alright."

Her eyes fell to the man, or boy really— his sweat managed to clean away most of the dirt on his cheeks and brow, and Veronica could now see he was probably about her age. His breathing started to slow, though it still hitched and faltered. "Sleep," Veronica whispered to him. "You'll be alright. Just sleep."

And with what might have been relief, he closed his eyes, and obeyed.

CHAPTER FOUR

"PLEASE."

The word echoed inside Angelus' head. His whole body was on fire with pain, the back of his head pulsing, his face swollen and bruised as a fist crashed against his jaw. But the worst feeling was the certainty that after this beating, there wouldn't be another one. Because he was on his own now.

"You steal from me," shouted the man who held Angelus' shirt collar in his fist, while his other dripped with Angelus' blood, "I'll make you wish you'd never been born."

It was far too late for that.

"Please," Angelus begged. He was going to leave. His master was going to leave him behind. "I won't do it again. *Please.*"

"You steal like a stray," Resmond spat, "You get kicked like a stray. Don't you ever come back— if I see you again I'll kill you."

"Please," Angelus gasped again, even as Resmond's fist crashed into his stomach, leaving a bloodied impression of Resmond's fist in his ruined shirt. "Please, take me with you."

Face contorted with disgust, his master— former master— let go of Angelus' shirt, and it wasn't until he crashed to the ground that Angelus realized Resmond had been the only thing keeping him on his feet.

Resmond spat on the ground beside Angelus' face, and he could do nothing but watch as Resmond walked away, leaving him behind.

* * *

ANGELUS woke, though the pain from the dream, from so long ago, didn't fade. His entire body was stiff and sore, his right arm useless and leadened. Was he still dreaming? He didn't know. Everything around him was gray and unfocused. There was nothing but a faint smell— herbal, combined with something sweet. Raspberries. He recognized that scent. He'd only smelled it once, but he remembered.

"Are you awake?"

The voice was quiet, feminine. He blinked until his vision cleared somewhat, and he made out a face hovering above him. Veronica's long dark braid fell over one shoulder, her round, dark eyes tired-looking as she peered at him.

Dreaming. He was definitely dreaming.

His left hand rose, and she stilled when his fingertips grazed her cheek. Soft, just like he'd always imagined. His hand fell, arm heavy and weak.

Her head cocked slightly to the side, confused and thoughtful. "Who are you?"

He couldn't answer her. The world faded and blurred into black, and the smell of raspberries followed him into the dark.

* * *

WHEN he woke again, he knew immediately something was wrong. He was lying on a hard, cold floor, not the cot in the soldiers quarters he was used to. The ceiling above him was not gray stone, but wood, aged and sagging in places like a tired, aching spine. The smell was not of steel weapons and men packed into tight quarters, instead it was fresh and herbal, mixed with...

Raspberries.

He sat bolt upright, which he instantly regretted, and a blanket slid off his bare chest and revealed his bandage-wrapped upper arm. He surveyed the room slowly; it was small and cluttered with random objects, the walls partly made up of drafty windows with chipped and dented sills, little potted plants balanced on them.

Where am I?

The floor creaked, and Angelus' head whipped to face the doorway, hand flying to his vest for a blade, but remembered he wasn't wearing it. Panic seized him. Where were his knives?

His eyes locked on a pair of dark ones, round and molasses-brown, like a bear's eyes, too wide in the narrow face they belonged to, and he was instantly frozen. Veronica stared at him in surprise for a moment, hovering in the doorway like a mirage.

Finn's home. This was Finn's home.

Veronica blinked, her expression fading from surprise back to... not sullen. Something else, a sort of resigned regret, or tired sadness.

"You're awake," she said, though Angelus wasn't so sure.

It was impossible, her standing before him, speaking to him, crossing the room to where he sat and holding out a mug of steaming liquid toward him. His hands were clumsy as he accepted it.

She knelt down on the ground in front of him, tucking her skirt under herself. "Do you know where you are?"

He did, but he didn't understand *how*.

He glanced at his bandaged arm, and Veronica answered the unasked question. "You were injured. A child found you collapsed on the road; we carried you here. Do you remember?"

Angelus didn't respond, too lost in the gray cloud that was his memory. He recalled the trees, the soldiers chasing him. The Imperial City...

The letter.

Angelus' eyes scanned the room quickly, searching for his belongings. Veronica seemed to understand because she said, "Your shirt was ruined, but there should be one here you can wear. Your vest is in the kitchen, I was just about to clean it." She gestured to the mug in his hand. "Drink that, it will help. Your fever broke last night, so you should drink as much as you can."

Angelus peered into the mug, making no move to drink.

"My name is Veronica," she said, but of course Angelus knew this already. She didn't know that, though. "Can you tell me your name?"

"Angelus," he heard himself whisper.

"Angelus," she repeated, but like it was a question. Her voice dropped to nearly a whisper. "You've been here before, haven't you?" she asked.

His stomach hollowed. She remembered him. He had watched her from afar, his task to observe Finn, but Veronica had been his ghost, his shadow, impossible for Angelus to ignore. They only met once, and he hadn't spoken a word to her— he'd simply given her Finn's letter, all those months ago, and left. But she remembered. That day was the closest he ever got to her, close enough to catch her scent. Raspberries.

Angelus forced himself to nod, just once.

He was there for the same reason as last time, to deliver a letter. He wondered if this was to be his fate, carrying correspondences instead of delivering his own words.

"Finn... he's dead. Isn't he?"

Angelus' eyes were already on Veronica's, but they sharpened, shock forcing them to focus at her words.

The lake, cold and black. Blood. Finn's broken body. Her still chest—

The images swam up from somewhere deep inside, but he buried them, swift and silent.

How did she know? It was impossible. But her eyes had grown so sad, her expression thinning until it looked as fragile as glass, that Angelus couldn't doubt that she knew.

"Yes." He heard his voice, but didn't feel it, had no connection to it. "He is." The words stole the last of his energy, and now there was nothing inside him. Emptiness should have been bliss, peace, but it wasn't. There was just... nothing.

Veronica's eyes slowly drifted to the window, and she nodded, the movement so slight it was barely perceptible. She got to her feet, still nodding, saying nothing.

And then she left, and Angelus was alone.

CHAPTER FIVE

VERONICA had been watching Finn fall for weeks.

Her dreams were complicated things, balls of snarled knots not easily untangled, but occasionally something clear got through. The rustle of wind through branches, the smell of trees and water, night air in her lungs... the ground disappearing. Then falling. Then nothing.

Nothing.

Her dreams never just *ended* like that. She'd watched Finn— no, *been* Finn— standing on a ledge overlooking a moonlit body of water Veronica knew she'd never actually seen before, and then she was falling. She thought perhaps there was someone with her— him— but she wasn't sure. She didn't think she would ever forget the horrible moment that seemed to last forever of pure blackness before waking.

She'd had the same dream every night for twenty days. She counted. But the last night, the night before Angelus appeared on the road, it had all been crystal clear, as though she were actually living the scene, not dreaming it. She saw everything in bizarre, blinding detail, caught every sound, every smell. She felt hands grasping Finn's arm, nails biting into skin, sensed his fear as his eyes found the face of a young woman Veronica didn't know.

It was exactly like when she dreamt of the soldiers taking Finn away. The dream started out vague, slowly growing clearer and clearer, until the night before they came to take him. She'd woken with a sense of certainty something would happen that day. The scene played out precisely as it did in her dream, and she could only stand there, paralyzed, unable to change anything. Unable to save him.

And now he was dead. Replaced by a green-eyed man who barely spoke.

Angelus.

He had moved in and out of sleep for two days until his fever broke. Now, in the late afternoon of the third day, he slept soundly, not stirring even as Veronica wiped away some of the sweat on his face with a cloth. With the dirt and grime cleaned away, Veronica could better see the thick scar on his chest. The wound had needed stitches but didn't look like it ever received them. The skin stretched tightly over his ribs revealed the offset bones that must have broken and never healed properly. Whatever the cause, it must have been excruciating.

She covered him with a blanket, somewhat ashamed to have seen the mark, like it was supposed to be some kind of secret. She turned her attention instead to the sky, visible through the windows. She barely slept the last three days, but even so her body did not feel more fatigued than usual. She always felt as though she hadn't slept enough, it didn't seem to matter if she actually had or not.

Veronica allowed herself a heartbeat to drown in the exhaustion. Only a heartbeat. Then she turned her eyes back to Angelus, satisfied his breathing was even and slow. She moved to his wrapped arm, and made quick work of removing the bandage and poultice. The swelling and redness had faded, and now all that remained was the cut. She hoped this one wouldn't scar, though he bore so many perhaps it made little difference. She gently applied a salve to the injury, and then replaced the old bandage with a clean one before sitting back against the wall, her work finished for now. Her eyes wandered the length of the small main room Finn used to dry herbs in the summer, store dried herbs in the winter, and house overnight patients in all seasons. At that moment the room was being used for all three, glass jars of dried herbs lined up on a table against one wall, the windows and other surfaces occupied by potted plants, some still green, others losing the battle against the encroaching cold, while the floor was claimed by a pile of blankets, in the center of which Angelus slept soundly.

Finn... he's dead. Isn't he?

Yes. He is.

Her head tipped back against the wall, and her eyes drifted closed. She was so tired.

Yes. He is.

If she didn't open her eyes, then maybe the tears wouldn't escape.

When she did finally open them, she saw Angelus was awake. Watching her. She was frozen under his stare for a breath, then she straightened, getting to her feet. She wasn't sure how long she'd been asleep. "How are you feeling?"

He didn't answer. He just looked at her strangely. Like he didn't understand what she was saying. There was something far away about his eyes. They seemed... dim, somehow.

"Do you think you can eat something?" she tried.

He didn't say anything. His eyes drifted from her to the ceiling, as though she were too complicated to comprehend, and he needed to look away to something easier to process.

"I'll get you some food," she said.

His mouth opened, barely, and he whispered, "Don't trouble yourself."

A little surprised, Veronica shook her head. "It's alright." Then she added, "I don't mind," because that seemed to be why he was refusing. "I'll find you something to eat, then you can take a bath, get the rest of the dirt and blood off of you." She went to the kitchen, and scrounged up some bread and the last dregs of butter. The food was nearly gone, and Veronica averted her eyes from the bare pantry shelves. Later, she would think about it later.

When she returned, Angelus was sitting up, and he accepted the plate she handed him. He stared at it, and Veronica knew she was hovering but she couldn't help it. Eventually, he picked up a piece of bread and took a bite, chewing so slowly it looked like he wasn't moving at all.

Veronica left him to draw a bath, grateful for something, anything, to occupy her hands. She hoped Angelus hadn't seen her tears. She got the feeling he had.

AFTER moving the table out of the way, Veronica retrieved the wooden tub from the closet in the kitchen. She and Finn had used it for baths when the weather was too cold to bathe in the creek. Shawl wrapped around herself, she stepped into the chilly morning. The cold wind made her grit her teeth. The temperature could change so fast, going from humid summer to brisk early autumn overnight. As the day wore on it grew increasingly overcast, and she suspected rain wasn't too far off.

Picking up two of the pails from the pile next to the house, she trekked to the stream behind the house and filled them with water before taking them inside, and pouring the water into an old metal pot on the stove. She stoked the fire in the stove and let the water come to a boil. She repeated the exercise a few more times until there was enough water to partially fill the little tub. The routine was so familiar, Veronica was momentarily startled to see Angelus leaning in the doorway, not Finn. But, of course, she would not be heating water for Finn's baths again. She cleared her throat, gesturing to the tub. "It's ready."

Angelus remained where he was, peering at the water, as though the idea of climbing into it was the most taxing chore ever conceived.

The softness in Veronica's voice surprised even her. "I'll go get you some clean clothes. There's soap on the table."

She walked down the narrow hallway that housed her room and... Finn's room. It was the one place in the house Veronica had been avoiding at all costs. She stared at the closed door for a long time, and out of habit she found her fist rising as if to knock. Finn liked his privacy; she always knocked before entering. But Finn wasn't inside now.

Her eyes burned suddenly, her chest seizing, closing off her airway until she was choking. Angrily, she kicked the door.

It opened a crack.

It took a long time, too long, hours or centuries or a lifetime, for Veronica to open the door all the way.

The room was exactly as Finn left it, though now a layer of dust covered the bed, dresser, small desk and stacks of papers and books. They looked as sad and lost as Veronica felt, waiting for the return of an owner that would never come.

Veronica hadn't entered the room since Finn left. She had, perhaps, been holding on to some naive hope Finn would return, wishing for his room to remain as he left it.

The space was small and simple, tidy in a very Finn-like way; stacks of books appearing almost politely disheveled, the papers bearing his notes on herbs that were organized but impossible to read if you didn't understand the way Finn wrote, which was to say, the way he thought. Despite its not being occupied for months, the room still smelled like Finn; like warm spices and herbs, mixed with the subtle hint of lavender Veronica left in each room.

It was like he was *there*, in the room, his smell and presence occupying the space as though he were only hidden, not truly gone.

Gone.

Veronica moved quickly, wrenching open the rickety dresser and taking the first handful of clothes she found. She carried the clothes and a clean towel back into the kitchen, pausing when she saw Angelus. His back was to her, and he was so tall the water only came to just above his waist, his knees bent awkwardly to fit into the tub. His skin was clean, streaked with a few remaining bubbles of soap, and with the dirt and blood gone, Veronica could see the scar on his chest was nothing compared to his back. It was completely covered in slashes and tears and markings of every size that spanned across his entire back, over his shoulders and down his arms. His body looked like the canvas of a mad painter, the brushstrokes random and furious.

Veronica stared, shocked, even as he turned to meet her eye. She glanced away, and set the towel and clothes down on the table. The next pot of water was steaming on the stove, and Veronica poured it into a pitcher, setting it on the table next to the tub as Angelus rubbed some soap into his dark hair. She started to leave, but paused when Angelus made no move to pick up the pitcher.

She swallowed. "Do you... want help?" she offered.

He said nothing, his head hanging. She hesitated, then walked back to the table and picked up the pitcher. When he still said nothing, she slowly and carefully poured the water over his head and exposed skin. The water in the tub was pink with washed away blood. Though his face was surprisingly free of scars, Veronica noticed a small one behind his ear, nearly lost in his hairline, a little white line like a stream of water trickling down the back of his neck.

She set the pitcher down on the table and handed him the towel. "I'll get some fresh bandages, go ahead and get dressed."

When she returned with bandages and salve, Angelus stood in the middle of the kitchen, eyes on the ground, in pants that were just a little too short, the tips of his black hair heavy with water droplets. When he looked up, a few of them fell to the floor like raindrops. Veronica pulled out a chair from the table and gestured for him to sit.

"I can do it myself," he said. His voice was empty. "I've done it before."

Veronica's eyes scanned his scarred arms and torso. She hadn't realized until he was standing before her just how tall he really was. He towered above her, her eyes level with his chest. The angry scar across his ribs glared at her, stretching slightly as he breathed in, and shrinking when he breathed out again. Veronica shook her head, forcing her eyes back to his. "No, I will." What kind of physician was she if she let him do it himself? Finn would have been appalled.

To her surprise, Angelus sat down, less like he'd decided to and more like he was simply too exhausted to remain standing. The kitchen was warm from boiling the water, and the smell of raspberry soap lingered in the air. As Veronica stepped beside Angelus, she could smell it clinging to his hair and skin. It was strange for such a familiar scent to be worn by a stranger.

She picked up the jar of salve. "This might sting a little."

Angelus didn't say anything. As she gently spread the salve over the wound, his head turned slowly to watch her hands. Angelus peered at his wound, brow creased slightly, not as though he were in pain but like he was thinking, as Veronica wrapped his arm with a clean bandage. When she was finished, she helped him slip Finn's shirt over his head and thread his arms through the sleeves.

He said nothing, and neither did Veronica. The sky had grown dark, and lightning lit the horizon, white-blue snakes in the sky. Angelus' eyes followed hers, and his expression didn't change.

"You can stay the night," she said. "Wait out the storm." She took his wordless nod as thanks, and suddenly the idea of being in the house alone terrified her. She'd known, deep down, Finn was not coming back. But the little bit of hope that remained in spite of this was long gone.

"I'm going to bed," she said, though it was not very late. She couldn't get out of the kitchen fast enough. "Goodnight."

CHAPTER SIX

ANGELUS laid on the floor in the small main room of the house long after the storm began to beat against the roof. His body and mind were fuzzy and dulled. He did not feel tired, despite how late it must have been. With his eyes closed, he could imagine he was in a small black box, and nothing except the sound of the rain and the cold floor beneath him existed. At least, until a strange sound penetrated the dark. It sounded like... crying. Or, more specifically, the sound a person made when they were trying *not* to cry; the hitching of breath, the soft moan as the sob lodged itself in your chest, fighting its way out. He could have imagined it, but then he heard it again, coming from the kitchen. Angelus climbed numbly to his feet. A small light pulsed and flickered, a candle on the floor of the kitchen, in the light of which Angelus found Veronica sitting on the ground, crying, clutching a bleeding hand.

For a moment he just stared, but then he crossed the kitchen and knelt down in front of her, reaching for her injured hand, dripping blood on her skirt, and the dark pile of something in her lap. What it was, Angelus couldn't tell. Fabric of some kind.

She startled when his hand closed around her wrist, bringing her hand toward him. There was a cut across her palm, but it was shallow and not very long. She pulled her hand back. "It's just a scratch," she said hurriedly, wiping her eyes with the palm of her other hand. "I was trying to clean your vest and... I didn't realize those were knives in the pockets."

Angelus' eyes flitted to the fabric in her lap, only then recognizing it as his vest. For a second everything around Angelus slowed, sound fading to a distant echo. His vest. There were knives in his vest, and also something else. Something Veronica was supposed to have.

He turned and reached for the roll of bandages on the table Veronica had left there hours before. He tore off a strip and secured it around her hand. It was sloppy and probably too loose, and he wondered suddenly why he'd bothered. She, clearly, could dress wounds better than he could. But something about the purposeful movements of his hands brought a bit of clarity to his dull senses.

She swiped the backs of her hands under her eyes, but more tears quickly appeared. Something pricked at the inside of Angelus' chest as he looked at her from where he still knelt on the floor. "Are you in pain?" he asked. The cut hadn't appeared deep, but maybe it was worse than he thought.

She shook her head. "No— I'm fine. I just..." The fingers of her bandaged hand trembled as she pressed them to her lips.

Veronica's dark eyes found his in the candlelight, and a little sob escaped her mouth. The sound thudded uncomfortably against his breastbone. "I didn't... I didn't really understand what it meant until tonight, that he isn't coming back. I'm alone." The last two words sounded like an accident, like she hadn't meant to tell Angelus this, and they slashed across his chest, the pain startling and intense.

I'm alone.

Where before every sensation had been dulled, now he was too aware of his body, of the clothes against his skin that were not his. Finn's. These were Finn's clothes. He was wearing a dead man's clothes.

He started to stand, desperate to get out of that room as quickly as he could, when Veronica's eyes locked with his, and he couldn't move. "Did you know him?" she asked. "You brought his letter months ago... Did you..." She was trying so hard to stop crying, but tears still leaked from the corners of her eyes.

"I knew him," Angelus admitted. He didn't dare say more. One of his hands was on the ground, ready to push himself to his feet, but he didn't move. There was something he had to ask. "You knew he was dead before I came here. How?"

The emotion, the sadness, on her face seemed to retreat slightly. Her eyes looked a bit haunted. "I..."

Angelus held her gaze for a moment.

She took a deep breath, shaking her head. "I'm sorry I woke you," she whispered. She made to get up, but Angelus stood first, and without thinking he held out a hand to her. One of her eyebrows turned slightly quizzical, but she placed her uninjured palm in his and allowed him to help her to her feet. She weighed practically nothing, and for some reason it bothered him. She was so small. But her fingers around his hand were firm, and when she let go he balled his hand into a fist, as though to preserve the sensation. Or perhaps hide its effect.

She turned to go, but Angelus said suddenly, "Wait," a bit louder than he meant to. She turned to face him, surprised. He bent to retrieve his vest, taking the envelope out of one of the inner pockets. It was horribly stained with water, sweat, blood and dirt, but he gave it to her.

Veronica took the filthy envelope, frowning. "What's this?"

"He wanted me to give that to you," Angelus said. "If something happened to him."

She just stared at him. Then she blinked, as if coming out of a daze, and said, "Thank you," so quietly Angelus barely caught the words before she disappeared from the kitchen and walked slowly down the hall to her room.

Angelus stood alone in the kitchen, the swaying candle flame distorting his shadow so that it was too thin, too tall. She'd only gone into the next room, but Angelus felt infinitely alone in the house.

His task was done, his promise fulfilled. So why did he feel so much worse?

He picked up his vest from the floor, slipped it on, and blew out the candle.

*　　*　　*

VERONICA sat on her bed, staring at the envelope. For a moment, she didn't want to open it. It was a long moment that stretched

56

into another, then another. It looked as though it had been submerged in water, the paper wrinkled and stiff, and her fingers trembled as she opened it, the dirt and dried blood powdery against her fingertips. It was next to impossible to procure the folded papers from the envelope; moisture managed to blend everything together, and when she did finally free the letter, it tore, a quarter of the page falling away in a crumbling handful.

She knelt on the floor, trying to smooth the paper out on the ground, but it was no use. Even if the paper stayed intact, the words were so badly distorted that Finn's words were unreadable. A pair of lips sealed shut, never to speak again.

"No," she gasped, and realized she was crying. She couldn't breathe, she was underwater, she was drowning. A sob hitched in her chest, and she didn't try to fight it. The second page. The second page was perhaps still legible. She managed to peel most of it away from the first, but something was wrong. The handwriting wasn't Finn's. In the center of the page she could barely make out one simple line: *If you need help, find Mayva.* It was followed by a string of numbers Veronica thought might have been coordinates. Then at the bottom of the page, in smaller writing, *I'm sorry I wasn't strong enough.*

Veronica didn't understand. Was this another letter for her, from someone else? She picked it up, trying to see it properly in the slowly lightening morning sky— she'd stayed up all night again— and as her fingers passed over the neat, feminine handwriting, Veronica's skin suddenly burned. An image— no, a sensation, tied closely with images— burst to life in Veronica's body. Guilt. Horrible guilt, like a physical pain, a brick crushing her abdomen. And a face. Black hair, green eyes, a thin mouth that was... smiling. Just a little. Angelus. But a different Angelus, younger. His eyes were so soft, and Veronica felt so much in that instant, so many complicated emotions blurring into gray nothingness. But the guilt remained.

Veronica dropped the letter, gasping, clutching her chest. Her body was ice and her hands trembled so badly her palms *clap, clap, clapped* against her chest.

No, she thought. *Not now. I can't do this now.*

But her body never listened to her. In moments she was especially vulnerable, like when she was sleeping, or scared, or in pain, it found a way out, no matter how hard she fought it. The Magic.

*　　*　　*

BY the time Veronica emerged from her room and walked, a little unsteadily, into the kitchen, the rain had stopped, and the sun was only an idea on the horizon. For just a second, Veronica could believe it was any other day— she was up early, because she was always up early, and Finn would be coming in from his room soon. She would get the herbs ready for the patients, checking to make sure his satchel was well stocked with supplies for his housecalls.

For a wonderful second, it was any other morning.

But Finn's absence was not the only thing wrong with the house. Angelus was also gone. Not gone like he'd stepped out to wash up at the creek; gone like he'd never been there. Panic seized her, closing around her throat. When did he leave? How long had she been in her room? An hour? He could be anywhere.

Veronica tugged on her boots, not bothering to lace them properly. She was out the door and dashing across the lawn, trying to wrap her shawl around herself while clutching Angelus' letter in her hand. If he wasn't on the road leading to the village, she had no idea where to look. She needed to find him, to give him the letter. She didn't know why it was important, only that it *was* important. She still recalled the guilt dripping so heavily off the paper, like thick blood trickling from a wound.

Then she saw him. He was a tree on the horizon, long and dark and willowy, his arms like branches and dark hair like leaves swaying in the breeze.

"Angelus!"

He stopped, turning slowly to face her. Even from a distance, she could see shock on his face, disbelief. He looked entirely different from the flash Veronica glimpsed. What happened to him?

He made no move toward her, letting her run up to him, panting, and he stared at her. "Wait," she gasped. "This— this is for you." She held out the letter to him.

He took it, but didn't read it.

"It was with Finn's letter," Veronica said.

He still didn't read it, and Veronica thought she understood why. The same reason she hadn't wanted to read Finn's words. Whoever wrote that letter, or who he suspected wrote it, was gone now. This was their goodbye, and Angelus did not want it.

"Come back to the house," Veronica said, still breathless from running. "At least let me change your bandages before you go."

He glanced at the road, his expression impossible to read. Finally his gaze found her again, and he gave a small nod. The letter hung loosely in his hand as he followed Veronica back to the house. Their boots on the gravel road sounded like little explosions in the silent morning. Mist slithered across the ground where they walked, giving Veronica the odd sensation of stepping through a cloud. It was cold, but the sunrise was beautiful, taking its time turning the sky from blue to pale orange. For a breath, Veronica could forget the heaviness in her chest. But as soon as she became aware of its absence, it returned immediately, as though reemerging through a trapdoor. She was so accustomed to the squeeze in her chest that the pain had dulled slightly over the years. It used to overwhelm her, but it had grown familiar. Now, however, it was accompanied by something else, a hollowness deeper down. She thought of the ruined letter on the floor of her bedroom, words sealed in blood that didn't belong to the man who wrote it. She remembered the other letter, the first one Finn had sent her from the castle. She'd read it, once, and then thrown it away. She couldn't remember why. Had she been angry? It felt like such a long time ago. Now, she wished desperately that she kept it, that she could remember what it said, that she had found some way to respond, though he'd told her not to. What was the last thing she had said to him? She couldn't remember.

Veronica glanced back at Angelus, who walked a bit more slowly behind her, his eyes on the sky. His face was strangely clear, holding no expression, and he looked very young somehow.

When they reached the house, Angelus paused outside the front door, his brow furrowing as if confused.

"It's alright," Veronica said, holding the door open wider. "Come in."

His eyes met hers, then flitted away again.

He stepped inside, almost carefully, his eyes roving the walls and ceiling as though having never seen them before. Veronica supposed the first time he came through this door he'd barely been conscious, but it was still odd how closely his attention was fixed to everything, like he was trying to read some kind of message in the walls. She was abruptly self conscious of the shabby place; it was larger than the houses in the village, but it wasn't in much better shape. It was not messy, Veronica cleaned it religiously, but it was crowded. There was little free space, most flat surfaces occupied by potted plants, herbs in every stage of preservation, tools, and books stuffed with folded pieces of paper. It didn't look like Veronica's or Finn's space, but like their collective space, their personalities blending until it was impossible to tell what was Finn's and what was hers. To an outsider, it probably appeared random and cluttered, but to Veronica it was familiar. Or, it had been. Now the house felt impossibly big.

Alone. I'll be alone here. It was an empty, upside down thought, not quite real.

"Come on," Veronica said, a little too loudly, waving Angelus into the kitchen. "You must be hungry." He'd barely eaten anything since arriving. She waited for him to refuse, but he didn't, instead following behind her and taking a seat at the table when Veronica gestured to it. She started the fire under the stove and readied the tea kettle, and while it boiled she sliced bread and cheese and made a plate for herself and one for Angelus— though the idea of eating made her nauseous. She glanced at him periodically, but his eyes were fixed to his tightly clasped hands, fingers curling into knuckles, leaving little white blotches on his skin. The letter laid, face down, on the table.

"Here," she said, bringing him his plate. "Try to eat something?"

He glanced at the plate, but didn't reach for it. Veronica finished the tea and set a mug in front of him, then sat down on the other side of the table with her own plate and mug. For a moment she wasn't sure why she felt so odd sitting across from him, then she realized that Angelus had taken the chair she usually sat in. The chair beneath her was Finn's. Or was it hers now?

She tilted her mug sideways, watching the dark, fragrant liquid dip and swirl, something like homesickness floating in her chest. Glancing at the letter on the table she said, "Who is it from?"

Angelus didn't answer, giving no indication that he heard her.

She wanted to tell him how guilty the writer had felt, wanted to ask him who they were to him, but she couldn't. No one could know about her. Angelus might not have been like the soldiers she'd encountered, but he worked in the castle. Maybe he hated Wielders, just like everyone else did.

Angelus' only stared at the letter, making no move to turn it over to see the words written on it.

"You don't have to read it." She wasn't sure why she said it. She regretted her words immediately. Who was she to tell him what he did or didn't have to do? But he looked so... scared.

He turned his head in something between a nod and a shake. "Yes, I do." But he didn't reach for the letter. He got suddenly to his feet, striding to the front door and shutting it behind himself. Veronica let out a shaky breath. In silence she drank her tea, ate her food, then she got to her feet, gathered her soap-making supplies in a rusted cauldron and went out the backdoor. Angelus was nowhere to be seen, but Veronica didn't think he would go far.

She set down her supplies next to the small fire pit Finn made for her out of bricks. She arranged handfuls of dry grass and planks of wood inside the ring of bricks, then procured from her apron pocket a pair of flint stones to light the fire. She used to be afraid to start fires and insisted Finn do it every time she needed to make soap, or light the stove, but she eventually learned to do it herself. Now, the sight of a flame didn't immediately remind her of her family home, eaten from the inside out by orange, fiery teeth. It had taken nearly ten years, but these small fires no longer frightened her.

She struck the flint a few times before the dry grass caught, and while she waited for it to spread to the wood, she hung the cauldron from the hook attached to a four-pronged iron fixture that Finn hammered into the ground above the fire pit. Soap was one of the only things Veronica could make for trade in the village besides herbal remedies, and she grimaced at how little supplies she had left. Finn always traded his herbs for supplies in nearby villages, but now that would be Veronica's job. The idea of venturing out on her own made her stomach flutter with nerves. And when would she be able to go? There were patients in the village who still needed her to make almost daily trips to their homes to deliver remedies, and besides that she needed to keep up Finn's herb garden or there wouldn't be any remedies to give anyone.

She wiped her damp eyes with her shirtsleeve quickly, furious with herself. She couldn't cry anymore. It didn't help. But she was so tired.

With a sigh Veronica sat down next to the fire, pulling apart a strip of dried up lavender with her fingers and sprinkling the shriveled up, seed-like petals into the now bubbling mixture. Almost immediately the air around her smelled like warm lavender mixed with the musky scent of the melting fat and oils. Standing, she brushed off her skirt and walked to the creek where a cluster of raspberry bushes grew. Veronica didn't know who planted them, or if they were just wild bushes, but they'd been on the property long enough neither Finn nor Duvar had been sure where they came from. She gathered a few handfuls, sticking them in the large pockets of her apron. Despite the cooling weather, the deep red berries grew thick and fat along the shrubbery. She always waited until the last moment to pick them so their scent was strongest. Carrying them back to the cauldron, she dropped them carefully into the bubbling mixture. She stirred the contents with a long stick, the off-white mixture turning a soft purple-pink. Veronica breathed in the sweet scent deeply, and exhaled in a long sigh. The morning mist had dissipated, and the day was finally starting to warm. She shed her shawl and sat down on the ground again, drawing her knees to her chest. She still needed to weed the herb garden, and get another batch of remedies prepared and delivered.

I'll just close my eyes for a second, she decided. *Just for a...*

She started when the wood in the fire popped. She looked up and saw Angelus standing on the other side of the fire. Without saying anything he sat down. The sides of the letter were crushed slightly in his hands, and he stared down at the words as though they were written in a foreign language.

"Is "Mayva" referring to the Second Queen?" Veronica asked. She didn't really expect an answer, so she was surprised when he gave a stiff nod. She hesitated before asking, voice a little quieter, "Are you going to go?"

When she searched his face, she did not see the sadness she expected. His eyes darkened and dulled, as if his soul had disappeared. There was something empty, but also fragile about his face. A piece of glass with too much pressure applied to it— at any moment it would crack.

His face looked how she felt most of the time.

"No," was his short, hard reply. Certainty, but also something else edged that one word. Anger.

Veronica hesitated. "Where will you go then?"

His eyes met hers, and there was so much pain in them Veronica's breath caught. He didn't have to answer with words.

I don't know.

He had nowhere to go. She'd suspected this, deep down. The truth was evident by his very presence; this farm was the only place he'd known to go for help, despite the fact they didn't even know each other.

The soap in the cauldron bubbled, and Veronica got to her feet. The handle of the cauldron was warm to the touch as she grasped it to lift it free, but a large, long-fingered hand swallowed the handle. Surprised, she withdrew her hand as Angelus lifted the cauldron easily. She gave a quick nod of thanks, and picked up her basket of supplies, now dwindled to nearly nothing. As she watched him, an idea began to form.

"You... could stay here." She remembered his feverish fingers brushing her face, and she added quickly, not wanting her meaning to be mistaken, "I could use the help. There's too much for only one person." She ignored the twinge in her chest.

He hesitated, looking down at the fire like it could tell him the right thing to do. Then he took the letter and dropped it in the fire.

CHAPTER SEVEN

ANGELUS didn't know how Veronica managed on her own— there was a never ending list of chores, not to mention her physician duties that dragged her into the village at least once a day.

The morning was warm compared to the previous days. He and Veronica walked, arms laden with baskets of soap bars and remedies, toward the village. Angelus' world narrowed to the smell of autumn's approach, the crunch of gravel beneath his feet, and the hypnotic sway of Veronica's braid as she walked a few steps ahead of him. Nothing else felt real.

Veronica turned to peer at him. "Are you alright carrying that much?" she asked. "Tell me if your arm hurts."

Angelus nodded, though he would say nothing of the kind.

They reached the village, an odd little cluster of worn buildings and worn people that struck Angelus as both tired and sturdy. Veronica looked a bit like this village, and Finn had too.

Something about their faces was the same, drawn with the fatigue of survival that never touched those in the castle. Angelus' face looked like that once, before going to the castle. He felt a bit ashamed he'd forgotten. What else had castle life dulled inside him?

He followed Veronica into a metalsmith shop, where a gaggle of skeletal dogs sniffed around the base of the building, paying no attention to the people walking around them. Inside, Angelus expected to see weapons on display, and while there were a few, they'd clearly gone untouched for a long time. A few swords, axes, and a display of simple knives in leather sheaths were coated in a thin layer of dust. Most of the tables and wall space were occupied by tools, farming equipment, kitchen knives, and metal pots and pans. There was no one in the shop except for Veronica, Angelus, and the woman shopkeeper who waved goodnaturedly at Veronica when she approached.

"I hoped you would come today," the woman said, smiling. "I'll take the usual two bars."

Angelus stood by the door to wait. Out of habit, he peered out the window, eyes roving the streets carefully. He gave his head a little shake, chiding himself. Veronica wasn't in any danger here. She wasn't royalty in need of a body guard, as Angelus was accustomed to.

"Who's your friend?" the shopkeeper asked in what was clearly supposed to be a whisper, but the shop was small and her voice carried. Angelus stilled, though he wasn't sure why, listening for Veronica's answer.

"He's been helping me on the farm," Veronica said easily.

Angelus glanced at her, and caught a sympathetic expression on the shopkeeper's face. "I'm sure Finn will be alright," she said softly.

Angelus' eyes shot to Veronica's face, but she just nodded, returning the woman's kind smile, though it wasn't nearly as genuine.

So news from the castle hadn't reached the villagers yet. No one except Angelus and Veronica knew Finn was gone, and Angelus was forced to wonder what would happen when word finally trickled this far west. Artemis would have a carefully concocted story to feed them, of course, if the display in the Imperial City had been any indication.

No one will ever know the truth, Angelus thought. Something hot and unpleasant surged up from his chest and into his limbs, something dangerous, an instinct long buried. He was not going to tell them the truth— he couldn't, for one thing, without giving away his identity. But still, the idea of the truth staying hidden itched beneath his skin. He snapped his attention back to the shop, startled by his own thoughts. He was never touching anything having to do with the castle, with Artemis, ever again.

He watched Veronica trade two bars of soap for a few coins, sticking them into her apron pocket and thanking the woman.

The sight of the coins made Angelus pause. He frowned as they left the shop, and asked, "Didn't you receive any of the money from Fi—" he hesitated. "From the castle?"

Angelus didn't know how much the physicians in the castle were paid, but he guessed it was enough that Veronica wouldn't need to sell bars of soap for a few coins. Finn hadn't required money, not with all of the resources of the castle available to him, and Angelus made the arrangement himself for the money Finn earned to be sent to Veronica.

Veronica stopped, looking at him in bewilderment. "Why would I have gotten money from the castle?"

She hadn't, then. It should have been delivered to her every two weeks. The money either remained unsent, or was intercepted on its way to her.

Angelus shook his head. "Never mind."

They made a few more stops, Veronica exchanging the soaps for supplies, food, even some fabric, and the sight rested uneasily in Angelus' gut. This was what she needed to do to survive, to be able to feed herself?

"What's wrong?" she asked as they paused outside a small house.

Angelus realized he was frowning and quickly smoothed out his face. He shook his head. Her brow creased but she didn't press him.

"Here." She handed him her basket of traded goods. She still held one of the baskets of soap, only two bars remaining. She'd wrapped them in cloth, and tied it all off with a piece of twine. Angelus didn't understand why this extra touch was necessary, it didn't seem to make a difference what they looked like, but Veronica took care to wrap each one. "You head back to the house, I'll finish up and meet you there. You can start on the barn door."

He'd agreed to repair the hinges on the barn door, and he might as well start on it if she didn't need any more help. A piece of him was immensely grateful for these tasks, and to Veronica for offering them to him.

Adjusting the basket in his hand, he started back in the direction of the road leading to the farmhouse. A pair of border guards turned a corner and began walking toward him so quickly Angelus had no time to react. They passed him, one of them briefly catching his eye. There was a terrible second in which Angelus thought the man recognized him, but he kept moving without a backward glance at Angelus. The men walked intentionally in the direction Angelus just came from, and Angelus allowed himself to be relieved. Until he glanced back and saw where they were going.

Veronica, talking to an older woman, her back to the soldiers, didn't notice them until they were right behind her. She turned, taking a startled step back. One of the soldiers tried to grab for her basket and she pulled it out of his reach. He laughed, and his companion joined in. "Come on, Veronica," the first man chided. "Everyone knows you're in that house all alone, trading these little trinkets for food. All you have to do is come to the barracks with me one time and you'll have all the food you can—"

He was abruptly cut off by Angelus seizing his arm and hauling him backward, neatly catching the man's leg with his own and tripping him. He fell, landing on his backside, and stared up at Angelus, who towered over him, chest heaving. Heat bellowed through him— he was barely aware of what he was doing, thinking. He did not remember the decision to attack, did not truly feel his fist drawing back.

Two hands gripped his raised arm, and Veronica's face was suddenly in front of him, pushing him back. Angelus did not realize his vision had dimmed until it sharpened again, and sensation came back to him.

"Don't!" Veronica cried. She whirled to face the soldier, who had gotten to his feet. He was practically shaking with fury. "We're leaving," she said, though Angelus did not know if she was speaking to him or the soldier. He didn't appear to be listening, because he stepped toward them, eyes locked on Angelus'. A thrill tingled through Angelus' limbs, all the way to his toes.

Relief. Relief was one punch away.

But Veronica was still standing in front of him, one hand on his chest, pushing him back, and the other extended to the man advancing toward them. There was a hesitation in his stance, and for good reason. He was a full head shorter than Angelus. Veronica noted his pause, and she took the opportunity to grip Angelus' arm and pull him away. Angelus' eyes stayed locked on the soldier's as he allowed himself to be led away.

"You're lucky today, bastard," he called after Angelus. This was a lie of course.

Angelus took quick stock of the man's too-big uniform, his sword like an oversized toy at his hip. The border guards were the men no one knew what to do with, so they had the dirty jobs in faraway villages like this one so the castle could pretend they didn't exist. They possessed no dignity, and even less training. Angelus could have disposed of him easily, and the man knew it.

"Don't even think about it," Veronica warned, not looking at him as she hauled him back to the road. It would have been easy to break her grip and finish what the man started, to give him what he was begging for, what Angelus was all too eager to deliver, but he didn't. Fire crackled and popped inside him, but it started to fade the farther away from the village they got.

72

"What the hell was that about?" Veronica hissed. She seemed certain now that Angelus would not bolt back toward the village, so she let go of his arm.

Angelus was indignant. "You heard what he said to you." Gods, he was furious. But he didn't know *why*. He was just heat, charged and undirected, energy with nowhere to go. He should have punched the border guard. It would have been worth it to take the buzz out of his hands, his arms and legs.

Veronica shook her head. "It isn't worth getting arrested over." She sounded as angry as Angelus felt. But there was something else in her expression. It took Angelus a moment to place it. Fear. She was afraid of him. The thought sat uneasily in his stomach, making something cold and unpleasant expand in his chest, extinguishing all the heat inside him.

They reached the house, neither of them speaking, until Veronica pointed to the barn. "Go finish the door, I'll make dinner soon." Her voice still held irritation, and Angelus' anger had dissipated enough for him to feel ashamed.

Scowling, he went to the barn. If Angelus had not spent weeks watching Finn on Andromeda's orders, he would have expected to find animals inside, but he knew there would be none. There were stalls, as though animals might have once occupied the space, but nothing living could be found in the shabby, dark building. Cold air leaked through the gaps between the wooden panels of the walls, whistling faintly and blowing a fir tree and plum-scented breeze across Angelus' skin.

By the time he was finished, the sun was setting and his stomach was howling pitifully. As he replaced the rusted tools Veronica had given him to repair the barn door, the evening air cooled his sweaty back and brushed pleasantly against his face. His head was perfectly empty, just for a second. It was easy in this place to pretend the world beyond simply did not exist, it was too far away, leaving the barn, the house, untouched.

With so little sleep, and the crash from the adrenaline taking what little energy he had left, he sat down on the ground, suddenly exhausted. Back against the barn wall, he examined the door. It was slightly less crooked than before.

He must have fallen asleep, because the next thing he knew, a hand was on his shoulder, shaking him awake. He opened his eyes, startled. There was less light than before, the sun beginning to set, the west side of the barn glowing with the red-gold light, leaving everything else dark.

"Sorry," Angelus said, rubbing his eyes. He looked up at Veronica and...

And...

For a heartbeat, no, less than a heartbeat, Angelus was frozen. It was not Veronica crouching beside him.

Andromeda got to her feet, looming over him. Her smile was cruel, her eyes soulless. And in her hand was a belt, faded leather splattered with blood. Resmond's belt. He would know it anywhere. He was afraid of it as one could only be afraid of the thing that had killed you a hundred times before.

There was blood on her hands, on her dress. Angelus' blood. His back seared and screamed in agony, the memory of wounds burning across his skin.

"No!" Angelus cried, hands flying up to protect his face instinctively. "It's me!" he shouted, curling into a protective ball. The anticipation of the blow was always the worst part.

"Andromeda, it's me!" She wouldn't hurt him. That was what Resmond did. Andromeda was not Resmond.

Andromeda was not Resmond.

"Angelus!"

Angelus' eyes flew open, instantly awake. Veronica was throwing open the barn door, struggling slightly with the weight of it, before she ran toward him. He tried to stand, but his knees buckled and he crashed to the ground, flattening his palms against the ground to steady himself. He sucked in ragged, uneven breaths, glass shards raking across his lungs. He couldn't breathe.

A sound broke free from his tight throat, somewhere between a gasp and a moan, and the sound, the fact that he could make any noise at all, was a short lived victory.

"Angelus." Hands closed around his shoulders, but he couldn't move. He remained still, the world spinning around him. "Angelus," Veronica said again, shaking him. He stayed on his knees, one hand lifting to press against the pain in his chest. "Breathe, you need to take a deep breath. You're alright, just breathe. Slowly, yes, good, good."

He heard her voice but it was only noise. He couldn't understand her, and he couldn't speak to tell her this. Dark spots burst to life and floated around his vision, the world tilting and tilting... He pressed his hands harder against the barn floor, and the sensation of dirt digging into his palms and dead grass and dried up pine needles biting into his skin, the world began to feel real once more. He was tethered, he was not going to vanish, or float away. He could breathe, just a little. He became more aware of Veronica's voice, of her hands. Now that the world wasn't spinning, now that he could take a deep breath, he caught the panic in her voice, in her eyes. He still couldn't move, but he took deep, grateful gulps of air. His fingers prickled and burned, pain shooting through them like they were on fire.

"Are you alright?" Veronica gasped, her hands gripping his shoulders tightly, and that too helped anchor him.

He was so cold. His body spasmed horribly, thick, terrible shivers raking over his skin and strangling his muscles. He bit his tongue to keep his teeth from chattering.

"Can you stand?" Veronica asked.

He nodded, allowing her to help him up. It took a moment, but he finally got to his feet. Veronica held his arm, draping it over her narrow shoulders, helping him back to the house, nearly losing her hold on him as they stepped over the threshold. He did his best not to fall into the bed of blankets Veronica had made him before the fireplace, but it was a vain effort, his legs giving out as soon as he tried to bend them, leaving him on his hands and knees on the floor.

Veronica knelt beside him. "It's alright, here, lay down. Are you hurt?"

Angelus gave a jerky shake of his head. Heat was building behind his eyes and he shook his head again, harder, to clear it away.

"I'll get you something." She stood, and Angelus could hear her moving around in the kitchen. By the time she returned, Angelus managed to sit up, his back against the wall. She pushed a mug into his icy hands. "Drink this, it'll help."

He obeyed, not because he wanted to, but because he didn't know what else to do. He tasted chamomile and lavender, and felt the pleasant sensation of the warm drink traveling down his throat, through his chest and into his stomach.

"What happened?" Veronica whispered. The worry on her face was his fault, and he was instantly ashamed of himself. He couldn't answer her. She would think he was insane. Maybe he was.

"I'm sorry," he whispered. It was the only answer he could give.

*　　*　　*

IN the dream, Angelus could feel the wagon crash across the dirt road leading from the Imperial City to the castle, making his teeth rattle in his skull. He glanced sideways up at Resmond, who sat next to him, the reins of the horse hauling their canopied wagon full of goods wrapped around his hands. The crates of bottles of alcohol, all of which Resmond and Angelus had collected from across the continent, rattled dangerously behind Angelus.

"When we get to the castle," Resmond barked— everything Resmond said was a bark, an angry dog's snap of teeth and growl of vocal chords. "You keep your eyes down and your mouth shut. Do you understand?"

Angelus nodded. He was a bit surprised Resmond told him not to speak. Angelus never spoke. The wagon bounced uneasily down the gravel path, and when they finally arrived, Angelus' mouth fell open as wide as his eyes when he beheld the dark castle. Windows taller than Resmond's ship, tower heads scraping the sky and gray-black stone walls that were as beautiful as they were impregnable. It reminded him of an enormous, elegant spider, towering over insects caught in its web, ready to devour anything and anyone that ventured too close.

Angelus smoothed his palms down his shabby, too-small clothes, the cuffs of his pants little more than tangled thread, instantly self conscious. Resmond dressed slightly better, in newer clothes and polished boots, but Angelus wore what he always did; a ratty and stained shirt, faded and torn trousers that used to be Resmond's, and bare feet.

He'd been with Resmond for three years, traveling from place to place to procure and sell Resmond's imported goods, and in all that time they'd never been to the castle. One of the Lawmakers was purchasing wine Resmond had traveled far, far south to retrieve. Angelus glanced at the wrapped bundles and crates in the back of the wagon. Clearly Resmond intended to sell more than just a bottle of wine. Angelus was unsurprised. A Lawmaker, one of the richest people in Lavdia, was prepared to give Resmond money— he'd be damned if he didn't try to get as much as he could.

The gates opened for them, uniformed soldiers pulling open the prison bar-like fixture to admit them. Angelus shivered, though he wasn't sure why.

They stopped their wagon at the front of the castle, where two other wagons similar to Resmond's were already parked, merchants with their own goods to sell bustling around their wagons. Young boys, perhaps twelve, the same age as Angelus when he started working for Resmond, helped lift crates down from the back of the wagons. It was common for merchants to have one or more older children assist them in exchange for room and board. What was not common was for them to be treated well.

From a distance Angelus could see one of the boys was little more than a skeleton. That he could lift any of the merchandise from the wagon seemed incredible. He coughed wetly when Angelus and Resmond approached. Angelus looked away.

Resmond jumped down from the wagon, and immediately began giving Angelus orders. Clearly he wanted to appear in control in front of these other merchants. They would all be competing for attention and coin, and Resmond would not lose, not even these small games.

A tall, bulky man with a brown-gold beard greeted Resmond like an old friend, clapping a hand genially against his shoulder. A jeweled sword decorated his hip, and he was dressed in such fine clothes Angelus couldn't help but stare. He, along with three guards escorted Resmond and the other two merchants inside, as well as a couple of the boys. Resmond appeared to think better of taking Angelus with him, and instructed him to stay with the wagon.

Angelus nodded, though he was disappointed. He wanted to go inside; he'd never been in a castle before.

Angelus waited until the sky started to blush with the coming sunset. He shuffled his bare feet in the grass, leaning against the side of the wagon. Resmond had removed the covering, and Angelus tipped his head back against the lip of the wagon bed, the chipped wood grinding into his skull. He sighed, long and low. It was late into the summer, and the heat was a blanket over his skin, his shirt stuck to his damp spine, which itched with bites from the loudly buzzing insects hovering around the fruit in the wagon.

There was a soft breath behind Angelus, and he turned, standing up straight. The skeletal boy from before was on the opposite side of the wagon, having snuck up on it as silently as a rabbit. His wide, eager eyes drank in the treasures in the wagon, including a bushel of blood-red apples. The boy just stared at them, unmoving. He looked so hungry. Angelus knew the feeling.

His long fingers closed over the side of the wagon, and his knuckle bones jutted through his skin as though about to tear through. Angelus had never seen someone so thin in his life.

It was getting late— Resmond was still inside with the other merchants. No one was around, except a few soldiers patrolling the grounds, but not a single eye was upon Angelus.

He'd never stolen from Resmond, not once, no matter how hungry he was. Resmond whipped him for misbehavior— he'd never tried to imagine what he would do to a thief.

Somehow, the fear did not touch him as he hoisted himself up into the bed of the wagon, and picked up one of the apples.

Resmond would never know.

He held out the apple to the boy. His sunken eyes went wide with shock, and the disbelief on his face made Angelus feel a little sick. This boy, with his protruding cheekbones and humid cough, wouldn't live much longer. It was the end of summer, and Angelus knew with inexplicable certainty the boy would not see another one.

The boy took the apple. He didn't eat it, he just stared at it, cupping it in his bony hands like it was something priceless and breakable.

When he looked up, his smile was like a flash of sunlight on the water. Then his face suddenly turned to horror at the same moment something seized the collar of Angelus' shirt, dragging him back. He tripped over the side of the wagon, landing hard on the ground. Resmond hauled him to his feet, pulling their faces so close together Angelus' mouth was sprayed with spittle as Resmond demanded, his voice as deafening and terrible as thunder, "You think you can steal from me, boy?" He threw Angelus to the ground, and he landed face down in the dirt. He tried to get to his feet, but pain lanced through the back of Angelus' skull, swift and blinding. It hurt too much to scream, to make any sound at all. He could only curl into a ball, hands wrapped around his head, knees drawn up to protect his chest. One of the rings on Resmond's fingers dripped blood, and Angelus felt something hot and wet against his palms as he pressed them to the back of his head.

Resmond had his belt off and raised to strike so fast Angelus could do nothing except brace himself, but then something small and fast hurtled through the air, and the starving boy appeared between Angelus and Resmond, his hands up. "Wait!" he croaked. Angelus barely had time to understand the boy was protecting him, before Resmond was shoving him to the side, hard.

He fell, the back of his head cracking against one of the wagon wheels. The boy's eyes were closed, his body unmoving. Was he dead? Angelus wanted to scream, but his throat was too tight, all the air in the world trapped inside his chest, as Resmond bent down and yanked Angelus to his feet. And Angelus understood, by the look in Resmond's deranged eyes, that he was in for a world of pain.

CHAPTER EIGHT

VERONICA did not sleep very much. It was for this reason she didn't mind staying awake until Angelus fell asleep, and remaining at the kitchen table, candle illuminating the pages of a book she couldn't focus on, long after he drifted into slumber. She put a heavy dose of drowsiness-inducing herbs in his tea, and they appeared to be working. They didn't work on Veronica. If anything, they tended to make her more alert. It was both a relief and a nuisance to know she was the anomaly, not the herbs. She leaned back in her chair to look into the next room, but Angelus' position remained unchanged. He slept on his back, head fallen slightly to the side, lips parted and chest rising and falling. He would be asleep for hours.

She wasn't sure what to make of him. She'd been shocked by his display in the village, the seething anger that seemed to have come from nowhere. But, of course, she had no way to know if she should have been surprised. He could be anyone. And she'd invited him into her home, given him a place to sleep and a seat at her table. What if he was dangerous?

He didn't look especially dangerous, sleeping on the floor in the next room. He hadn't looked dangerous on the barn floor, either, mouth gaping as he tried to breathe but couldn't.

What ghosts, she wondered, hid in his shadow?

She got to her feet, being careful not to let the chair legs squeak against the floor, and walked to the doorway leading to the next room. The small fire in the fireplace crackled quietly, bathing Angelus' face in a soft orange light.

I'm sorry. That was all he'd said.

"I'm sorry," Veronica whispered back. She went to her room to try to get some sleep.

* * *

WHEN Veronica woke up, Angelus was already awake and working. Veronica could see him carrying pails out to the creek and filling them from the kitchen window. He was a dark wraith in the morning light, wandering along the water's edge. Veronica didn't think it was her imagination that he was not completely *there*.

By the time Veronica put her boots on and wrapped her shawl around herself, Angelus was standing before the door, buckets in hand. Veronica paused when she saw him, and closed the door quietly behind her before taking a step toward him. He was all stormy black hair and shuttered green eyes, and Veronica couldn't

83

help but remember his face in the vision. He'd smiled then, but now his face was the furthest thing from smiling.

"Are you alright?" she asked. It wasn't quite the right question, but there were no better words she could think of. He just stood there, not saying anything. This was more or less what Veronica expected, but she wanted to ask regardless. The answer should have been clear, but it wasn't entirely. Veronica nodded to the buckets in his hands. "You didn't have to do that," she said.

"You did it for me," he said, extending the buckets toward her.

Surprise loosened the tightness in her brow, and she accepted one of the buckets, using her free hand to open the door and hold it so he could enter behind her. She boiled the water, and Angelus disappeared outside so she could bathe. She had been putting off taking a bath for a few days, not sure she could do it comfortably with him around, but he seemed to be making an effort to show her his sharp edges were not a danger to her.

In the small tub, Veronica dipped her head under the water and held her breath for as long as she could before she finally surfaced. She needed to hurry if she was going to be ready for the children to come. It would be the first time they came for lessons since Angelus arrived, and Veronica had thought she would be nervous because of it, but she actually felt a little relieved. Teaching was the only thing she could do with her entire focus and attention, without her mind tugging her away.

The water in the tub was cold when Veronica got to her feet. Reaching for the towel on the table, she shivered as the air touched her bare, wet skin. She dried off and dressed quickly, braiding her hair and tying it off with the red ribbon Finn gave her years ago. It had been the prettiest thing she'd ever seen, and that was still true.

There was nothing particularly special about it, a plain dark red without any embroidery or decoration, but Veronica loved the color. She never asked Finn where it came from. Now she would never know.

After disposing of the water outside and cleaning up the kitchen, she pulled her boots and shawl on and started down the road to collect the children. She liked meeting them halfway down the road and walking back with them. It made her feel a bit better to know where they were; the border guards bullying village children was not an unheard of occurrence, and Veronica preferred to keep them in her sight whenever possible. Their parents had trusted them to her, after all. They were, for those few hours a day, her responsibility.

She glanced back at the house for a second, and made out Angelus' long, dark shape walking along the creek, a tree branch hanging from his grip, the tip trailing over the surface of the water. He was such an aimless ghost, when he didn't think anyone was watching. Veronica looked away.

Sully and Mary were already coming down the gravel path, waving excitedly when they saw Veronica, and her heart lifted. She wondered if perhaps her teaching these children was motivated purely by selfishness; they distracted her, and Veronica needed badly to be distracted.

Sully bolted forward and latched his arms around Veronica's waist, grinning up at her. Veronica smiled back, the unfamiliar expression rendering her face a bit stiff.

"The others are on their way," Mary said, pointing back the way they had come. Veronica could see the outlines of the other children in the distance. She turned back to Mary, watching her for a moment longer than was perhaps necessary, but she wanted to make sure Mary was alright after the fright of Angelus' appearance. Mary offered her a smile, and she knew her worries were unfounded. Veronica was glad these children were brave, but wished they didn't need to be. Despite their smiles, their upbringings were clear in their thin faces and worn clothes, their shoe soles holding on by threads. They looked tired, their eyes too old for children. Veronica was sure she didn't fare much better, but she was old enough it was simply life, not tragedy.

When the remaining students caught up to them, Veronica led the way back to the house. Mary walked closely next to her, and Veronica slipped an arm around her shoulders.

"Did that man survive?" Mary asked in a low whisper so the other children didn't hear.

"He did, thanks to your help."

Mary's smile was wide, and it strummed something in Veronica's chest. Why couldn't smiles like that exist all the time?

At the house, Veronica scanned the property for Angelus but didn't see him anywhere. The children filed into the house, too familiar with the place to need an invitation. They piled their muddy shoes outside the front door, Veronica being careful not to trip over them as she stepped inside.

"Get your supplies from the box by the fireplace," Veronica instructed, hanging her shawl on the hook by the door.

Once the children were settled with the book of poems they were reading from, Veronica sat down on the floor in their midst. The children took turns reading lines from poems, sounding out the letters with a level of care Veronica had been surprised to learn children could be capable of. She was so absorbed in the lesson she did not immediately notice the intruder in their company. Angelus stood in the doorway, leaning against one side of it with his arms crossed, watching them. His distance from her and the group appeared strangely intentional, as though he wanted to be forgotten. Veronica turned her eyes away quickly, but not before she caught his expression. It was oddly... blank.

After their lesson was over, the children dispersed to play outside for a while. The boys especially couldn't sit for too long, and they crashed out of the house and were howling at each other across the lawn within seconds. Veronica only then realized Angelus was no longer there. She hadn't seen him leave, and wondered how long he'd been gone. It was a little disconcerting how quietly he could maneuver around the house, disappearing at will and reappearing just as silently as he'd gone.

As she picked up the abandoned pencils and books on the floor, she heard a collective, disheartened "aww" from outside. A peek out the window revealed several of the children looking up at the barn's low roof, where their ball was stuck. Veronica frowned, though she was slightly amused. The broom in the kitchen might be long enough to reach it, so she fetched it and brought it outside. She arrived in time to see Angelus, who had appeared from nowhere, jump up to grip the edge of the roof, and as easily as a cat climbing a tree, hoisted himself up onto the roof and retrieved the ball. He tossed it down to Sully, who cheered, along with the other children. Sully kicked the ball toward them and the game recommenced as if nothing had happened. Angelus remained on the roof, sitting down and letting his legs dangle off the side. He observed the children with a mixture of fascination and wariness Veronica thought was warranted.

Veronica stopped directly beneath him, broom still in her hand. "Impressive," she said. "How did you get up there?"

Angelus shrugged, motioning for her to step back. She did, and he leapt down with barely a whisper of noise. They were suddenly standing very close, and she took another step back. He was wearing his vest, strange and new against the faded fabric of Finn's old shirt. His eyes were so unbelievably green, and with his lithe form and wild hair it wasn't really a stretch of her imagination to think he'd simply been created by nature, painted by the Earth Goddess in all of Her favorite colors.

She remembered when he came to her doorstep with Finn's letter, what felt like a century ago, though in reality had only been a few months. He'd looked like a soldier then, with a sword at his hip, but not anymore. Now, he was something different. Something Veronica thought might have been closer to the truth.

CHAPTER NINE

THE next morning, Veronica ventured to the village by herself. It was a quick errand, delivering a mixed herb concoction to a patient with a fever, and Angelus would probably still be asleep when she returned. Veronica wasn't keen on taking Angelus with her into the village— last time he'd managed to get into a fight, not to mention the terrifying episode that followed a few hours later. She didn't know if the encounter with the border guards had been what brought it on, but she would rather remain on the side of safety.

She opened the front door as quietly as she could, slipping out into the cold morning air that froze her lungs. The bright, cool autumnal weather was always painfully short lived, before the snow came and buried the world in a cold, white grave. Veronica so hated the winter.

As soon as Veronica reached the village, she knew something was wrong. There was a large group gathered in front of the metalsmith shop, the object of their fixed attention indiscernible to Veronica until she got closer, and caught sight of a man speaking. He stood at the center of the assembly, out of place in a royal guard's silver armor, addressing the crowd of villagers. He was flanked by a cluster of other soldiers, and one man wrapped in a cloak, hood obscuring his face, but even from a distance Veronica could tell he was enormously tall. Veronica could hear the first soldiers' raised voice, but was too far away to understand the words. A hand closed around her wrist and she turned. Rayn, the metalsmith's wife, was beside her. She squeezed Veronica's wrist, looking stricken. "Veronica, did you hear?"

Veronica shook her head, a lead weight pressing down on her stomach. Something terrible had happened. Rayn was pale, her eyes wide.

"Queen Andromeda," Rayn breathed. "She's been murdered, along with the Lawmakers. They're saying the Lawless are responsible. Veronica, do you think that's true?"

Veronica wasn't listening. One of the queens was *dead?*

The soldier unfurled a scroll of parchment and held it up high enough for those in the very back to see. Veronica's breath caught.

"This man is wanted for questioning by the High Queen's advisor. He is the Mother Queen's former guard, who disappeared shortly after her death. He is a suspect, and is most likely armed and definitely dangerous. A reward for his capture will be..."

Veronica didn't hear anything else he said. Angelus, utterly unmistakable, gazed out at the crowd with eyes drawn from charcoal. Veronica stared at the poster, uncomprehending, until she saw the border guard, the one Angelus had fought with, stepping up to the soldier holding the poster, eyes glittering, and pointed toward the road. Toward Veronica's home.

"Where are you going?" Rayn called after her as she started to retreat, creeping as quickly as she dared to the road.

Angelus was Queen Andromeda's guard. Queen Andromeda was dead. Angelus was a wanted man, and he was sleeping in front of her fireplace at that very moment. She broke into a run as soon as she reached the gravel road, the herbs in her pocket forgotten as she bolted back to the house, her sharp pants loud in her ears.

Angelus must have seen her coming down the road, because he was out the door and jogging toward her before Veronica reached the edge of the property.

"What's wrong?" he demanded, reading the panic on her face.

"They're looking for you!" Veronica was slightly shocked at how angry she sounded. But, after a split second of reflection, she realized she *was* angry. She was furious. She was also terrified. "Soldiers from the castle came to the village to find you!"

Angelus gripped her arm before she'd even finished speaking, leading her back to the house, glancing over his shoulder at the road. "Alright," he said, voice low. "They have no reason to come here. Just stay inside—"

"They *are* coming here!" Veronica said. "That border guard told them you were here!"

His eyes went wide. Then his grip on her arm tightened, turning painful, as he hurried her inside, practically dragging her through the doorway and slamming the door behind them. "Shit," he cursed under his breath as he brought her into the kitchen, "Shit— *shit.*"

Veronica stared at him as he began rummaging through the kitchen drawers as though searching for something.

It was a moment before Veronica could regain enough control over her breathing to speak. "He said you're wanted for questioning about Queen Andromeda's murder."

Angelus froze, his expression turning to clear glass; clean, transparent, and breakable.

And then she understood.

"She was the one who wrote you that letter, wasn't she?"

His lack of an answer was enough for Veronica to know she was right. Veronica had never seen the Mother Queen, but she was prepared to venture a guess she had long brown hair and brown eyes. Just like the woman in Veronica's dream. The woman who tumbled over that cliff with Finn.

"Angelus?" His name was a warning as much as a question. "What really happened to them?" Ice slowly crept into her veins, and she took a single step back from him. "Did... did you kill them?"

Something flashed across his empty face— anger. "No." The word was heavy and final in the way only the truth could be.

"Then why do they want you?" Hysteria was creeping into her voice, drowning her anger until there was nothing but ice cold panic left. "Angelus, what did you do?"

He said nothing, and Veronica stared at him as he grabbed Finn's old satchel from the chair it was hanging on, throwing out most of its contents, and began shoving things into it. A blanket Angelus had slept on and a loaf of bread disappeared into it before Veronica shook herself. "What are you doing?" she demanded, snatching at the bag.

He swung the bag out of her reach and opened a drawer in the kitchen. He grabbed an old canteen and a knife and shoved them into the bag. "I'll stay here, and you head into the forest. If they find me, they might not come after you."

It took a minute too long for Veronica to understand. The border guard's finger that had pointed to this place had painted a target on her back as well as Angelus'.

"You can't do this!" Veronica cried, her hands flying up to cover her face as though trying to keep her head from bursting apart. "You can't drag me into this!" She'd worked so hard to stay out of the way, to go unnoticed. This couldn't be real.

Angelus stepped in front of her, grabbing her shoulders and shaking her. He had to bend down to look into her face. "I'm sorry." His voice was terrible, low and rough and full of regret. "But you have to run."

He pushed her, not hard, but Veronica almost fell backward on her useless legs. He'd slipped the bag's strap over her shoulder without her noticing, and it suddenly felt unbearably heavy. This wasn't real. This wasn't happening.

Angelus freed a knife from inside his vest, holding it with the kind of familiarity that meant he knew how to use it, and that he *would* use it. "Go."

Veronica shook her head. "What are you going to—"

The front door crashed open, the metal latch snapping off the wood and landing on the ground with a thud.

Angelus dove for Veronica, pressing his hand over her mouth and shoving her into the broom closet, his body a wall against her chest as he slipped in with her, pulling the latchless door closed silently behind him. The only light came from a narrow gap between the floor and the bottom of the door, but it was enough to see Angelus' eyes boring into her, a warning.

Veronica nodded her understanding, and he lowered his hand from her mouth. There was no room for Veronica to move away from him, and her chest pressed against his so hard she couldn't tell what movements were her own breathing, and what were his.

"There's no one here," a man called.

Silence, then a deeper voice, raspy and rough, said simply, "He's here. I can smell him."

Veronica's eyes widened, and Angelus stopped breathing. *Smell* him? What was that supposed to mean?

"Search the barn," another man said, this one younger. "He could be hiding out there. There's nothing but fields and orchards for miles, if he ran he has nowhere to hide."

"And if he's hiding in the village?" a third male voice asked.

The younger man chuckled. "Artemis' orders are to bring him back, no matter what. Burn the village down if you have to."

Veronica started to shake, and Angelus must have felt it because he gripped her arms, squeezing so hard it hurt.

If they harmed the villagers, it would be her fault for harboring a wanted man.

My fault... my fault...

Tingling heat fluttered in her chest like butterflies on fire, reaching into her fingertips and down to her toes. It rose and surged with her panic, separate but simultaneous.

Not now, she thought desperately. She couldn't lose control. She wouldn't.

She closed her eyes, taking a slow breath in, then letting it escape without a sound. She could sense Angelus' gaze on her, but she didn't open her eyes. She needed to get herself under control, or they would be discovered.

The front door slammed shut, and Angelus held up a finger. They waited a few breaths before Angelus pushed the door open with his elbow, waiting, then stepping out into the kitchen. He was still holding one of his knives, and his eyes did a quick sweep of the kitchen before he grabbed Veronica's arm and pulled her to the back door of the house.

"Wait," Veronica gasped, pulling at his hand. "We have to warn the villagers."

"No time," Angelus said, his voice hard. He didn't look at her, just dragged her with him out the door, his eyes scanning the property. "I need to get you out of here. How can we get to the forest without them seeing us?"

Veronica shook her head, not because she didn't know but because her mind was taking too long to process his question. "Th-there's a plum orchard a quarter mile north of here. It leads all the way to the village." It covered several properties and reached nearly to the woods on the village's western edge.

It took her a moment longer to understand the rest of his words. "Get *me* out? What about—"

They both sensed it at the same time. Eyes on their backs. Veronica and Angelus turned in unison toward the hulking figure in the middle of the property, only feet away from them. His body, though massive and covered with what looked like fur more than hair, was human. Making his face all the more horrifying for its strangeness. It was not a man's face. It was a wolf's.

And then Angelus was shouting, *"Run!"* and they were running. Her hand trapped in Angelus', she bolted, running faster than she'd ever run before. She didn't know if he was leading her, or if she was leading, she only knew that *thing* was right behind them. When she turned her head back, she saw the creature, who had been standing on two legs, was now on all fours, and any scrap of humanity Veronica might have been able to detect was forgotten. He was all wolf. A monstrous wolf, two or three times larger than a real one. It was fear alone that kept Veronica from freezing. Its enormous hands were somewhere between a man's and a dog's, ending in hooked, talon-like nails that tore into the earth as it ran, sending clumps of grass and mud flying as it bolted after them.

There was nothing to hide behind, nothing to cover them in these wheat fields. The orchard. If they could get to the orchard, they might be able to hide.

"This way," Veronica managed to gasp, tugging Angelus' hand. He didn't question her, just kept running, letting her direct their steps.

The plum trees of the village's orchard were now discernable on the horizon, brown and green and purple masses waving their arms as though beckoning them forward. *Almost there.*

A thunderous roar boomed across the field, and something collided with Veronica's side, and she crashed to the ground, the air exploding out of her lungs. The sky, and the tips of the plum tree branches swirled round and round above her. Then the creature was over her, huge maw opening to reveal hideously sharp teeth.

But he didn't strike. Something streaked through the air, hurtling toward the beast and knocking it momentarily off balance. Angelus.

Veronica scrambled to her feet, and took off running into the trees. She didn't know where Angelus was, and she couldn't make herself look back. All she could do was run.

She sprinted through the narrow path between the rows of plum trees. She'd thought this orchard would provide enough cover, but seeing it now, her hopes vanished. The trees, tall as they were, looked like playthings the pursuing monster could tear apart easily.

We are going to die, Veronica thought.

Angelus appeared beside her, grabbing her arm and hauling her forward. "Come on!" he shouted. "Keep moving!"

There was a single beat where their eyes met, and Angelus must have seen the terror on her face, because he shook his head, as though answering a question. And then they were running again.

The sun was starting to retreat underneath the horizon, turning the trees above them into gray ghosts, formless heads pressing together as they peered down at them. Branches snapped and crashed as the beast chased after them, thick hide colliding with branches and snapping them like icicles.

Angelus led Veronica off the narrow path, ducking between trees, trying to go where the thing couldn't reach them. Another terrible roar rang out, too close, far too close.

"There!" Angelus gasped, pointing to the end of the row of trees. In the distance, Veronica could make out the beginnings of forest. They were almost there. But there was something else as well. Smoke. Thick black smoke like storm clouds sent to earth.

To her left, Veronica could see a portion of the village, the outermost farms, through the breaks in the plum trees. And they were on fire.

Castle soldiers and border guards alike shot flaming arrows into the fields of wheat and hurled burning torches through windows and into the barns. The shrieks of the animals mingled with human screams as they fled their burning homes and barns.

Burn the village down if you have to.

This was Angelus' fault. This was *her* fault.

"Come on," Angelus urged, pulling her forward. "Before—"

One of the soldiers, holding a bow and flaming arrow, turned toward the orchard, a slow and terrible grin lighting his face. He looked demonic, the fire's light turning his skin pale and waxy, his eyes nothing but dark holes in his face, as he drew back the arrow, and let it fly. Straight into the orchard.

Veronica screamed as the arrow flashed in front of her face, close enough for her to feel the heat, before the tip buried itself in the trunk of the tree next to her.

"Got you," came a low, raspy drawl from behind them.

The wolf creature stood on its two back legs, his yellow, slit-pupiled eyes hungry. He was a pillar of muscle, three heads taller than Angelus, his chest heaving in a strange, uneven way. Around his neck, straining against the thickness of his throat, was a silver chain, something small and green hanging from it. It was similar to the identification necklaces Veronica had seen soldiers wear. Angelus noticed it too, and his eyes widened.

I can smell him.

The necklace was Angelus'. They had tracked him.

The creature bared its fangs, thick drool dripping from its mouth.

"Run!" Angelus shouted at her, but this time it sounded different. Like he was speaking to her, only her.

The soldiers were running for them, and the beast merely stood there, grinning— could animals grin?— in triumph.

There was no way out.

"Go!" Angelus shouted, pushing her behind him and shoving her toward the end of the orchard and the border woods beyond.

She didn't move. They would catch her. She couldn't run anymore. The flaming arrow was eating the tree alive, the flames spreading up into the foliage and lighting the branches of the trees next to it. Plums sizzled and oozed thick, black-purple juice onto the grass.

Heat buzzed in her veins, but for once, her mind was clear, not clouded with panic. Something inside her, something primal and ancient and long buried, hummed in her chest.

Angelus held a knife in both hands, crouched like an animal ready to pounce. He couldn't fight them all.

"We've been looking for you," the soldier who shot the arrow said to Angelus with a grin. The beast and the soldiers formed an impenetrable wall around them. The burning trees crackled and popped.

Burning.

Fire.

Veronica felt it inside.

Putting a hand on Angelus' shoulder, she leaned forward and whispered, "Close your eyes."

He turned his face to her, bewildered, as she raised her hand and drew with a single finger the symbol she knew best, the one she promised she would never use again.

Fire.

Tongues of flame cut through the air until the symbol was burning in front of her, a perfectly round spiral, and it reminded Veronica of the sun. It hung, suspended, for just a second, then it exploded into a wall of fire and light. It covered everything, the beast, the soldiers, the orchard, the already burning house and barn beyond.

Her vision tunneled, and she drifted away into blackness.

CHAPTER TEN

TO Veronica, the space between blacking out and waking again was only a second. She was asleep, then she was instantly awake. It took her a long moment to understand what had happened as she stared up at the ceiling of a cave.

A cave?

She sat up, looking around. Angelus was sitting at the mouth of the cave, his back to her, a small fire crackling between them.

Veronica was too stunned to speak. She remembered running to the farmhouse, remembered the beast chasing them, remembered... fire...

Her airway constricted. She'd done it. She used Magic, purposefully, for the first time in almost ten years. And someone had seen her.

She got to her feet, nearly tripping over the blanket she'd been lying on— the one Angelus packed for her. Finn's satchel laid next to the blanket, seemingly undisturbed, though the tear in the side appeared to have grown wider, the contents visible through the gap in the fabric.

Angelus turned, getting to his feet when he saw her. She backed up quickly, fingers brushing the wall of the cave, yellow-orange in the firelight. Angelus' eyes widened, and he raised his hands as if trying to reassure an anxious animal.

"Where are we?" Veronica demanded.

"It's alright," he said, though Veronica didn't calm. "We're in the woods between Lavdia and Resh. I carried you here after you collapsed. No one followed us."

"How do you know that?"

He reached into his pocket and procured the necklace the wolf had been wearing, the chain broken and the glass cracked and blackened. "They were tracking me with this. That's how they knew to come to the village."

The village. Veronica swallowed. "What... what happened to the villagers?" She thought of Sully and Mary and the other children, of the houses and barns burning.

Angelus shook his head. "I don't know."

Veronica stepped forward shakily. "Take me back. I have to go back."

He shook his head again, and stepped between her and the mouth of the cave. He was impossibly tall, and though he made no threatening move toward her, Veronica felt trapped. "The village will be crawling with soldiers by now. You can't go back there, anyone who survived that fire saw what you did."

Survived. Survived *her.*

Did she kill those men, that monster?

Nausea shot through her, from her stomach to her mouth, and she could feel all the color leach out of her face, the heat retreating from her fingers and toes.

"It's alright," Angelus said again, and Veronica knew her panic must have been evident. Wasn't he going to ask her about her Magic? Wasn't he going to threaten to turn her in? "You're safe here."

"*Safe?*" she demanded, incredulous. "With *you?* You're the reason this happened!"

His eyes darkened— she didn't realize his eyes *hadn't* been dark until they were again— and he swallowed, his gaze drifting away from her to the cave floor.

"Angelus... If you don't want me to believe what everyone is saying about you, you need to tell me the truth."

He lowered his hands to his sides, eyes still on the ground. "Alright. But will you please stop looking at me like I'm going to hurt you? I'm not."

He sat down on one side of the fire, and after a breath of hesitation, Veronica did the same. She watched him over the top of the flames, his face shadowed by the tendrils of smoke.

"I didn't kill them," he began, voice flat and hard. "I was her— the Mother Queen's— guard. Finn was her physician. She needed his help to expose Artemis, the High Queen's advisor, as a murderer. But they discovered something else— he created that thing that chased us, and more like it, to hunt Wielders."

Veronica's heart stopped. She could only stare at him as he continued.

"Artemis must have found out she knew, or at least what she was up to. I think he had both of them killed. I was the only other person who knew what he was planning, and that's why he wants me."

She didn't want to believe him. But that was how she knew he was probably telling the truth. Whatever was hardest to hear tended to be the truth.

"So those... *creatures*... are hunting Wielders? Are hunting... me?"

His eyes flashed brighter than the fire, anger accentuating all of the hard lines of his face. "They aren't going to find you," he said, and the certainty in his voice startled her slightly.

Veronica shook her head to clear it. "We have to go back— I need to help them." Images of the children running from burning houses, into the waiting arms of soldiers, flashed across her mind, making her stomach tighten.

Help, she thought. They needed help, but what could she do? Nothing. They would be hunting her now, too.

Help...

If you need help, find Mayva.

"The Second Queen," Veronica said suddenly.

Angelus looked at her, brow creasing. "What?"

"Queen Andromeda told you to find her. Maybe she can help."

Angelus' expression darkened, the corner of his mouth twisting. "No one knows where she is," he said, with more bitterness than the words seemed to call for. "She's missing."

"But the coordinates in the letter— that's what those numbers were, weren't they?"

"I recognized it," he admitted. He dragged a hand through his hair and over his face, haggard and exhausted. "It's the location of a checkpoint in the mountains,"

"You know where it is?" Veronica asked.

He didn't answer, and Veronica took that to mean yes. She stood. "Take me there."

His eyes narrowed. "There's no guarantee you'll find her, or that she will help you if you do."

"Please," Veronica said. "I... I don't have anywhere else to go."

His face tightened, his eyes widening slightly, but then the strange expression faded. He got to his feet. "Alright," he said, so low Veronica almost didn't hear him. "I'll help you."

PART TWO

CHAPTER ELEVEN

VERONICA had never walked so much in her life. Angelus seemed to be able to walk forever at the same annoyingly fast pace, and Veronica fell behind more often than not.

They walked north— or, Angelus said it was north. Veronica couldn't tell— leaving her village farther and farther behind them with every step. She could *feel* the distance, like a tether straining tighter and tighter the longer she walked, threatening to snap. What happened when it did? What if she never got to go home again? The thought made her chest leaden, dragging her down as though her lungs were made of brick. She felt the ominous prickle of an episode encroaching, and she walked a little faster, as if she could leave that behind, too. She could fight it off for a while, but eventually, maybe after a day, she would have to hide from Angelus so she could...

She shook her head. She didn't want to think about it. Thinking about it only brought it on faster. She told herself her body was heavy because she was tired, her breathing rapid from climbing up steep inclines for three days. No matter what, she couldn't lose it now.

"Watch your step," Angelus called from a little ways ahead of her, just as her foot slid several inches to the left before she regained her balance. The grass was wet and slippery, and Veronica took a moment to catch her breath. She scowled at Angelus, who was moving easily through the damp grass and moss and slimy fallen leaves.

Sighing, Veronica picked up her skirt so she wouldn't trip, and stepped carefully between the mossy rocks. They were about the size of her feet and were indistinguishable from grassy mounds of earth. She wondered if the damp grass meant there was water nearby, and she opened her mouth to inquire, but instead let out a sharp yelp as she lost her footing. A hand closed around her upper arm, pulling her back up before she fully processed what happened.

She blinked up at Angelus, who raised an unimpressed eyebrow. She tugged her arm free. "Thanks," she said flatly.

She'd been right about the water. After a few minutes, she could hear the soft bubbling of a creek. She and Angelus both dashed for it, gathering handfuls of the icy water and gulping them down. Then Veronica filled the canteen from her satchel, screwing the lid on tightly. She peered around at the surrounding area; the trees were thick on either side of the stream, the tallest she'd ever seen. She'd never been this far north, where the woods grew wilder and darker the closer one ventured to the mountains.

The *mountains.*

They had always been nothing but hazy ghosts floating far away on the horizon. Now she was actually going to see them. The idea both thrilled and terrified her.

Angelus stood, wiping his mouth on his sleeve. "We should follow the stream as long as we can," he said. "I'm going to find wood for a fire. Stay here."

Veronica frowned but said nothing. She knelt beside the narrow stream, wetting her hands and washing away the dirt and sweat on her arms, her face and neck. Her reflection was terrible, flesh pale against the dark marks under her eyes. She avoided mirrors at home. She looked worse every time she saw herself.

She turned her eyes up to the sky instead. It was starting to get dark, and it reminded her of what would be coming tonight. It was getting closer. She took a deep breath. She would get through it. She always did.

Veronica got to her feet, brushing off her skirt. She was hungry, but didn't want to eat the single loaf of bread in her bag. It would need to last a long time. She started scavenging for edible plants. Medicinal plants were more her specialty, but she knew of a few edible mushrooms and roots.

By the time Angelus returned and built a small fire, she'd managed to find a few roots and washed the dirt off of them, though it did little to make them more appealing. She offered Angelus one, and it was merely a testament to how hungry he was that he accepted it. Veronica sat down on a flat boulder so smooth it was as though it'd been cut clean through with a blade, leaving a table-like surface.

"Is it safe to build a fire?" she asked. "Won't someone see the smoke?"

Angelus shook his head. "We're deep into the woods now. There are miles between us and the border."

Veronica should have been reassured, but a little shiver slithered up her spine. Miles away from the nearest village or house or border guard station. Miles away from *people*.

Veronica's eyes suddenly widened. Finn had hidden the Wielders who came to him for help in these very woods. She wondered where they were, if they were nearby, or if she and Angelus had left them far behind along with the village. She never accompanied Finn into the woods when he escorted those people, and he never told her where he hid them. It was safer that way, but there was also a bitter side of Veronica that didn't want to know. She never wanted Finn to go. She'd warned him over and over it was too dangerous, but nothing she said ever changed his mind.

Her heart ached at the thought of him.

But there was also a dark and secretive part of her that had wanted nothing to do with Wielders. They were like her in blood, but she felt infinitely different from them. Her Magic was not the blessing the others pretended it was. Magic was a curse, and Veronica was the only one who could see it. Even if she and Angelus could find their camp, which she very much doubted, the idea of the Sanctuary made her flesh crawl.

Angelus stretched his hands out over the fire. He looked cold and tired, but despite this he appeared... different. More alert, more awake. He was not the man she'd found on the road, nor was he the man from her vision. He was somewhere in between, or perhaps something else all together.

"Get some rest," he said. She could tell he wasn't happy to have been coerced into this trek, but she was still grateful, even if he did seem to resent her for it.

Veronica swallowed the last tasteless mouthful of root she managed to gnaw into a somewhat softer mass. The breeze tousled her hair, and long, cold fingers reached inside her chest, pressing down until her ribcage was made of glass, on the verge of shattering. It was coming. She couldn't fight it much longer.

"Alright," she agreed. She unpacked the blanket from her bag, laid it on the ground, and waited.

*   *   *

IN the dark of the forest, with the fire nothing but embers, the moon obscured by the trees, and Angelus sleeping soundly a few feet away, Veronica's body began to shake.

She pressed her hand over her mouth as she laid flat on her back, trying to stifle the sound of her lurching breath. Tears burned her eyes, and the cold numbed her fingers, but the worst part was the pressure in her chest, the rapid and uneven beat of her heart as though she were being chased, but her body didn't move, couldn't get away.

As her sobs became louder, she pressed her other hand over her mouth, trying desperately to mute her pathetic cries. She couldn't get enough air into her lungs; her head started to lighten. Once, during an episode, she'd passed out and Finn found her on the floor of the kitchen. He attributed it to lack of proper sleep, and Veronica readily agreed, too humiliated to admit the truth. She couldn't control her own body.

How she had wanted to tell him, how she wished someone knew, even if they could do nothing about it. She'd suffered all alone for so many nights for so many years.

She squeezed her eyes shut. She felt so unbearably small.

Hands abruptly gripped her shoulders, dragging her up. Her eyes flew open, and she registered Angelus in the dark, but she couldn't speak, couldn't explain.

He pulled her against him, tucking her head under his chin, his arm around her shoulders tight and warm. She wrapped her arms around his waist; she didn't care if he thought she was insane, she just needed something to hold onto, to keep her from floating away.

"It's alright," he whispered. His hard voice had softened slightly around the edges.

Nestled between Angelus' bent legs, one of his knees pressing into her spine, the pressure in Veronica's chest started to lessen. Her breaths came easier, slower, breathing in through her nose and out through her mouth. The crying ebbed away until there was nothing left but a silent stream of tears.

She waited for him to say something, but he stayed perfectly still, and Veronica relaxed slowly. She never realized how tightly coiled her body became until she started to calm, her shoulders sliding away from her neck and her legs turning to liquid as though she'd been running for miles. Her hands burned as the blood flowed back into them, prickling with bolts of lightning that made her grimace, and she bit her lip to keep quiet until the pain subsided.

She sniffed, wiping her cheeks with her palm quickly. "I'm sorry," she whispered.

"Does this happen to you often?"

Veronica searched the words carefully for judgment, for annoyance, but his tone gave nothing away. "Yes," she admitted. She couldn't meet his eye, so she kept her cheek pressed against his chest. "They've been happening since I was ten years old."

They were silent, the unspoken question, "*why?*" going unasked, but hanging in the air nonetheless. Veronica didn't know. She never understood, but she had to live with it.

"I'll get you something to drink," he offered, pulling away from her. For a moment, she wanted to tell him to stay, but she banished the thought. She unwound her arms from around him and sat silently, knees to her chest, while he fetched her canteen.

"Thank you," she said, not looking at him as she accepted the canteen and took a small sip. Her hands were trembling. She hoped he didn't notice.

She hazarded a glance at his face. Humiliation was starting to set in, and she wanted to curl up into an invisible ball. It was difficult to read his expression in the dark, but his eyes were on her.

"Sleep." His voice was uncharacteristically soft. "You don't have to be afraid."

When he said it, it actually sounded true. She had to remind herself that it wasn't.

CHAPTER TWELVE

ANGELUS stayed up the rest of the night, his eyes only leaving Veronica's sleeping form to scan the clearing occasionally. His muscles were taught with tension, ready to spring into a fight that wasn't there. Her cries had been so pitiful, like someone was hurting her. The adrenaline took hours to fade.

He'd been an idiot to only take one blanket from the house. It was thick, made of heavy gray wool, but with the nights getting colder, even with a fire they wouldn't last long. They needed supplies. He would need to find a village soon. Neither he nor Veronica had a single coin between them, and Angelus wasn't much of a thief, he never had been, but he would have to try.

As the sun began to rise, Veronica stirred, turning over and facing him. "I'm going to find a village," he told her from where he sat, back against a tree, arms folded against the cold. "We need more supplies."

She sat up. "Alright." She shivered, getting to her feet and picking up the blanket. It was wide enough she could fold it in half, laying on one side and folding the other half over herself, and she shook it out, grass and pine needles fluttering to the ground. She wrapped it around her shoulders, face pale and eyes tired.

Angelus stood, ready to leave that instant. "You should stay here," he said. "I'll be faster on my own."

Her eyes widened. She started to shake her head, but then stopped. "I... I won't slow you down. I promise."

Something in Angelus' chest flinched. She was so small, so breakable-looking. "Come with me to the edge of the woods," he finally said. "But I'll go into the village alone."

She looked relieved, and Angelus felt guilty for wanting to leave her behind. There was no real camp to pack up, so Angelus kicked the crisped branches left from the fire, and Veronica put down the blanket long enough to slip her satchel over her shoulder, then wrapped it around herself again.

Veronica managed to keep up fairly well, though Angelus did have to slow down a few times so she could catch up. Her face was still pale, despite the exertion and the sweat starting to bead on her forehead. Angelus was growing increasingly uneasy. *She just needs to eat,* he told himself. *Get her some food and she'll be alright.* He hoped.

They had trekked farther west into the dense woods than Angelus originally thought, which explained why there was no sign of pursuers, or anyone else for that matter. It took most of the morning to reach a place where the forest thinned, and the distant sounds of villages could be heard through the trees.

Angelus paused, and Veronica stilled beside him. "This is a good place for you to wait. I'll be back before sundown."

Veronica nodded, though she looked ill at ease. It was too risky to take her with him. He needed to get in and out as quickly as possible. He didn't think she would be recognized, but if he was caught he wasn't risking her safety. If he didn't come back, at least she would have a chance to get away.

He watched her duck under the low branches of a tree, disappearing beneath it and becoming nearly invisible wrapped in her dark blanket. Angelus didn't waste any time. He broke into a run.

I'm coming back, he thought. *I'm coming back.*

*   *   *

THERE was nearly a mile of green field between the edge of the woods and the village, and Angelus only slowed down when he reached it. The grass was long, swaying in the wind like thick green hair. It was long enough to brush his fingertips, tickling across his skin. The day was growing warm, and sweat trickled down his spine uncomfortably. The village before him was much larger than the one they'd left, mostly made up of squat brick buildings. A drinking town, Angelus could tell right away. There was a tavern on nearly every corner. By sunset the streets would be crawling with drunkards and those seeking to become drunkards. No one seemed to notice Angelus slip into their midst, the anonymous shadow of those around him.

As a child he'd never been a talented pickpocket, and he hadn't practiced since then, so he doubted his abilities too much to risk it.

But if he could find a food cart, or an abandoned inn room, he could probably get away with an armful before anyone discovered him. He took a moment to scan his surroundings. The streets were wide, and not terribly crowded. Going back the way he came wouldn't be difficult, but he still wanted to keep his other exit options open. There weren't any soldiers on the streets, so they were probably in the taverns. He'd just set his sights on a promisingly abandoned open air display of bread in front of a small bakery, when he heard a shout blair from somewhere up ahead, followed by cheers and the unmistakable sound of a fight turning bloody.

A chill like a sheen of cold sweat spread over his skin. It was something like fear, anxiety, but also an old, almost forgotten thrill.

Angelus didn't remember deciding to go, but he found himself walking toward the sound. He found the small crowd gathered around a makeshift ring of ribbon and planks of wood driven into the ground. Two men stood at the center of the ring, shirtless and sweaty, blood smeared over their faces and chests and knuckles. One of them swung his fist, colliding with the other man's face. It was as though he didn't even feel the blow. He charged forward, barreling headfirst into the other man's chest, pummeling his ribs with his fists.

Angelus surveyed the people watching the match, waiting to see... there. Coins changing hands, bets being placed and prize money being collected.

"You a fighter?" an older man asked Angelus, appearing beside him and having to tip his head back to meet his eye.

"How much if I win?"

The old man chuckled, but when he realized Angelus was serious, he pointed to another man holding a sack of coins. "Winner takes all," the old man said. He jerked his head toward the ring, where the shorter and wider fighter had his opponent in a headlock. He was turning an unsettling shade of blue. "That's Leon. No one beats Leon."

Angelus raised an eyebrow. The old man seemed to sense Angelus' thoughts. "It's your funeral," he said with a dismissive shrug. "You pay to play though, boy."

Angelus took one of his knives from his vest, shoving it into the old man's hand. He stared at it, at the tiny red jewels decorating the hilt. Angelus didn't know how much the knives cost, but they were from Andromeda, so he was betting a lot. He'd have it back soon enough.

The old man followed behind Angelus as he approached the man holding the prize money. The one in charge of the money was in charge of everything. "Put me in next," Angelus said, already shedding his vest and letting it fall into a pile of shirts discarded outside the ring.

The man looked Angelus up and down, sizing up his tall and narrow build, comparing it to Leon's solid, brick-like body. "You got a death wish, kid?" he asked, his voice almost lost in the crowd's sudden cheer. Leon had won. The other man was being dragged out of the ring by three people. "If you want to fight Leon after that, be my guest. Payment?"

The old man held up the knife. The other man gaped at it, shocked, then studied Angelus with new curiosity. He nodded slowly. "You're up in three minutes."

DESPITE the sunny day, Veronica was freezing. It wasn't unusual for her to be cold and exhausted the morning after an episode, but she didn't recall the effects lasting this long. It was worse because Angelus still wasn't back. He told her he would return before sundown, but that wasn't for another few hours, at least. What if he'd been captured? What if he was never coming back? What if he needed help?

She couldn't wait anymore.

Leaving the blanket and satchel safely hidden under the branches of the tree she'd sheltered under, she crept carefully out into the open. She could make out the sounds of civilization not far beyond, and she followed a footworn path to the edge of the woods. A field separated her from the village, and she breathed a sigh of relief. She was certain she could find her way back to her supplies, if she remembered this was the spot she came from. She looked around for a landmark, and saw a slender tree with leaves just beginning to change, a few bits of red scattered among the green. It was the only tree with red leaves. She would remember it.

She started toward the village, walking through grass almost as tall as she was, and her feet barely touched the street before a young boy, probably twelve, ran past her. "You'll miss the fight!" he shouted at her over his shoulder. "They've got a real animal in there!"

Veronica frowned, following after him at a slower pace, trying not to brush against the bodies crowding around, trying to see...

Veronica froze.

In a ring made of wood stakes and black ribbon, Angelus stood, shirtless and drenched in sweat, smashing his fists into another man's face. Over and over and over again.

Without his shirt, his scars were on display for the world to see, but in that moment they did not make him look weak. They were battle scars. *I survived once,* they whispered, *and I will do it again.*

Angelus was standing there one second, and then his foot was flying up into his opponent's jaw. He stumbled back, shaking his head, but Angelus gave him no time to recover. He buried his fist into the man's stomach so hard it sank past his wrist.

"Brass knuckles," someone beside Veronica said, "Had to be." For a moment she was confused, then she realized he was talking about the scar on Angelus' chest. *Brass knuckles.* That injury had been caused by a punch? One hard enough to break bone and tear flesh. Veronica's stomach rolled as she pushed forward into the crowd, ducking under arms and shoving bodies out of the way. "*Move,*" she gasped, winded, but no one was paying any attention. They were riveted by the fight before them. The only sounds were the cheering crowd, the crunch of knuckles against flesh, and the roar of Angelus' opponent. Angelus was silent, jaw clenched, eyebrows low. He bounced on his feet, light and ready, each blow calculated and devastating. His eyes were wild, lit up by something Veronica couldn't place.

Veronica gasped as Angelus ducked beneath a punch, the man's movement exhausted and desperate. How long had the fight been going on?

Angelus hooked his arm under his opponent's, turning his body, and as easily as if the man were a sack of grain, Angelus flipped him over his shoulder and onto the ground. Even over the cheer of the crowd, Veronica could hear the air burst out of the man's lungs. Angelus wiped sweat from his upper lip with his forearm, chest crashing up and down as he panted, but he was otherwise silent. His muscles were tight, his fists ready for when the man got up. A vein pulsed in his neck, and the green of his eyes was almost entirely swallowed by black.

That boy had been right. He was an animal.

When Angelus' opponent didn't get up, a man holding a heavy coin purse shouted, "Winner!" and the crowd screamed. Veronica pressed her hands over her ears, grimacing. She needed to get out of there, the crush of bodies pushing her closer and closer to the ring was overwhelming. She was painfully aware of how much shorter she was than anyone else in the crowd, and suddenly being trampled seemed like a very real possibility.

She tried to find a break in the crowd, anywhere to escape, but gasps from people in the crowd made her pause. Veronica turned back to face the ring and saw Angelus, walking to the edge of the ring, back turned to his opponent who had gotten to his feet.

"Angelus!" she screamed, her hands flying over her mouth and her blood seizing in every inch of her body. Angelus turned, momentarily shocked to hear his name, then he dropped into a crouch as the man swung a punch Veronica could tell just by watching carried the man's full strength. The punch missed, and Angelus shot to his feet, about to lunge for him, but several men surged forward to seize his arms, holding him back, while two other men did the same to his opponent. They hauled the two away from each other like dragging dogs from a fight, Angelus straining against his holders, while the other man, finally succumbing to exhaustion, allowed himself to be taken away.

The crowd surged forward, clapping and cheering for Angelus, and Veronica was nearly swallowed by the crush of bodies. She shoved her way to the front of the crowd, desperate to reach him. His eyes— he was a caged animal, cornered and frightened, and no one could see it.

His eyes found hers as soon as she broke free of the crowd. He was staring at her, and she stared back. The only thing tethering him was her gaze— his pupils were enormous, and he looked ready to fight everyone in the crowd, to devour them whole, expression trapped somewhere between predator and prey. But he didn't move, his eyes staying on hers. And Veronica understood the question there. *Are you afraid?*

Veronica stepped toward him, and closed her hand around his wrist. "Come on," she said, and the crowd parted to let them through. She guided him forward, and he paused only long enough to gather his shirt and vest from the ground, and swipe the bag with his winnings out of a stunned man's fist. He stood next to an old, white-haired man who offered Angelus a knife. His knife.

Veronica accepted it with her free hand, and they left the alley. Already two more fighters were making their way to the ring, and Angelus' victory was forgotten. She paused in the mouth of the alley, looking up into his face. His emerald gaze was blank, far away and unfocused. Something akin to fear, dread, tingled through her chest like a cold mist. "Angelus?"

His eyes found hers, but he was still miles from her.

"Are you hurt?" she asked. She realized she was still holding onto his wrist, but she didn't let go.

"I don't... know." His voice was tight, strained. Though the fight was over, his body was still tight as a bowstring, ready to snap. Was it her imagination, or was he shaking?

Veronica glanced around. "We need to get out of here." She pulled him forward, and he followed her down the street, both of them pausing when a man pointed at Angelus and said, "You can clean up in the back." He jerked his thumb over his shoulder, indicating a bar. A few other men were exiting the building, clothes stained with blood but their faces scrubbed clean and their hair dripping with water.

Veronica gave a quick nod of thanks. Angelus either hadn't heard him or wasn't able to form a response. The inside of the bar was lit by hanging lanterns, the rapidly setting sun staining the brick walls red-gold and casting long shadows across the floor. She led him to a doorway at the back of the building, on the other side of which was a small room with a table bearing a metal bucket of water and washcloths, bandages and splints and other things for quickly setting injuries until a real doctor could be found. She thought she should probably leave him alone to get cleaned up, and opened her mouth to say she would be waiting outside, but paused when she saw he was just staring at the water in the bucket, unmoving.

"Let me help," Veronica offered, stepping forward.

He gave no answer, but didn't protest when Veronica motioned for him to sit on the table. He sat, and Veronica stepped forward, carefully. She was very aware of how tall and strong he was, how she was nothing more than a flower to be crushed in his hand, but she stepped between his knees. With him sitting down, they were almost eye to eye, and he looked straight at her as she picked up a cloth from the table and dipped it into the tub of water. She rang it out and started to wipe down his torso. His chest went perfectly still, as though holding his breath.

"You were supposed to wait for me," he said after a moment. His voice sounded more normal, if a little thin.

"I know." They were alone in the dark back room, and despite there being people just outside the door, she felt like they were the only ones for miles.

"You shouldn't have seen that."

Veronica glanced at his face, then away again. She dipped the cloth in the bucket of water, saying nothing as she wrung it out and pressed to his chest again. "You were fighting for me, right?" she finally asked, keeping her gaze on her hands, unable to meet his eyes, though she sensed his blazing stare on her face. "For money?"

He nodded.

"Thank you."

He remained completely still as Veronica finished wiping off the blood, and set the cloth down on the table next to Angelus' leg.

"Is that how you got all those scars?" she asked, trying not to look at the one on his chest. "From fighting in rings like that?"

"Some of them," he admitted.

Her eyes flitted from his face to his chest, and hovered her fingers over the jagged scar there. "This one?"

He swallowed. His face was so close to hers, she could feel his slow exhale across her lips.

"We should go." Her voice dropped to a whisper though she didn't know why. "Someone might recognize you."

He blinked, as if coming out of a trance, and stood so quickly Veronica barely stepped back fast enough. Without a word, he picked up his shirt and put it back on, then slipped his vest over his shoulders and fastened it in the front. Then he picked up his winnings and Veronica followed him out of the bar, her heart an erratic monster in her chest, begging to be let out.

*   *   *

ANGELUS told Veronica to take the winnings and buy what they needed. Flint for starting fires more quickly than twigs, blankets, warmer outer gear if possible, another canteen, and food.

It gave Veronica a strange little thrill to carry the money around in her pocket. She was tempted to spend more of it, but she knew they had to save it. Even so, she loved how heavy her pocket felt. She'd never handled so much money in her life.

She left the shop with arms full of two thick blankets, a canteen, two new flintstones, and a sack of dried meat and bread. Coats had been the first thing she'd sought out, but just one would have cost the entirety of Angelus' winnings. Blankets would have to do. She found Angelus where she left him, leaning against the little shop with his arms crossed. The fewer people who saw his face the better, and he hung in the shadow clinging to the side of the building. His right leg bounced, practically vibrating with restless energy.

"Let's go," he said, straightening as soon as she approached. He took what she was carrying, pocketing the stones and tucking the rest under his arm.

Veronica cast a longing look at a tavern across the street, the scent of meat and spices drifting through the open door.

Angelus sighed, but thrust an arm toward the building as though to say, *Fine, go.* Veronica, her stomach empty, could have jumped in delight. Angelus must have sensed her excitement because his expression became a little less hard. He followed her across the street and inside the tavern. It was crowded, women carrying tankards of ale to customers flying through every open space between tables, but Veronica and Angelus managed to squeeze into a tiny table in the corner. The place was lit gold by lanterns that hung over the tables and bar, swaying slightly from long chains protruding from the ceiling. The sun had set, and the street outside sparkled with the lantern light shining through the windows.

"It's so beautiful," Veronica breathed.

Angelus' mouth quirked. "You're easily impressed."

Veronica scowled. "You saw my village," she said. "Pardon me for being excited to see something else for once."

They fell silent, both remembering the last time they had seen Veronica's village. Her heart panged, and she said a silent prayer that the children were safe. If they weren't...

A barmaid appeared beside their table. "Ale?" she asked.

Angelus shook his head. "Anything we can eat for this much." He gave her a handful of coins from his winnings.

She took the money. "Back in a moment." She disappeared into the crowd again.

Veronica turned back to Angelus, eager to change the subject. "Where did you learn to fight? When you were at the castle?"

He clasped his hands together, resting them on the table. "I... learned. On my own. Had to, it was the only way to get money."

Veronica cocked her head, waiting.

He glanced at her, then away again. "I lived in an orphanage for a while, but I was on my own after that."

Veronica swallowed. She realized she was mimicking his posture, her hands clasped on the table, and she quickly lowered her hands to her lap. "You... you fought as a *child?*"

He looked irritated, not with her but with the direction the conversation was taking. "There was a group of merchants that paid boys to fight each other. We got a share of the money they won in bets." He shrugged, as if it didn't matter. "It was a long time ago," he said, voice final, like a door being shut.

Not that *long ago,* Veronica thought. Angelus couldn't have been older than twenty. A year older than her.

"Still," Veronica said quietly. "You're really good."

Angelus shook his head, mouth cinching to the side as though he'd tasted something sour. "No better than a stray dog," he said, and Veronica didn't miss the bitterness. "That's all we were, after all. Worse, maybe."

"Stray dogs," Veronica said softly, "Are just dogs who haven't found a home yet. That doesn't make them worth any less."

Angelus looked at her, his brows drawing together slightly in confusion. He opened his mouth to say something, but the barmaid appeared again, setting down a plate of cheese and bread and bowls of broth. It was somewhat plain compared to what some of the others in the place were eating, but Veronica felt like a banquet had been laid out before her. Angelus' mouth turned up at her wide eyes, but he ducked his head so she wouldn't notice. She noticed.

"Eat up," he said. "We won't eat like this for a while."

He had barely finished speaking before Veronica picked up her bowl of broth and raised it to her lips. It burned her throat as it went down, forming a hot trail through her chest and into her cavern of a stomach. She tried to eat slowly, to savor the flavor and the feeling of having enough to eat, but it didn't last long. Too soon the food was gone, and Veronica gazed down at her empty plate and bowl regretfully. Angelus had the good sense to eat more slowly, and she tried not to stare at his remaining food as he ate.

"What happened next?" she asked.

Angelus wiped the corner of his mouth with his wrist. "What do you mean?"

"After the fights, for the merchants. Where did you go after that? To the castle?"

He leaned back in his seat, as if distancing himself from her questions. "I was hurt." It was not what he said, but how he said it— with a thudding finality, as though "hurt" really meant "finished."

She remembered the scar across his chest. *Brass knuckles.* She could picture it: the metal instrument, the blow, the blood, the broken ribs, the ruined skin, merchants cheering just like the crowd had been earlier.

"Then what?" Her voice was soft and careful.

"One of the merchants who watched the fights fixed me up. I couldn't go back out on the streets, not like that. So he became my master."

Master. Angelus had been a slave?

He must have noticed his slip, because his face hardened. He stood up, his food gone. "Let's go." He picked up their purchased supplies and made for the door.

Veronica followed him outside. The cold night air jabbed icy fingers into her exposed skin, and she shivered, wrapping her arms around herself. Despite the cold, she felt surprisingly pleasant, her stomach full and the taste of food lingering on her tongue. Angelus glanced down at her, then took one of the blankets he carried and draped it over her shoulders. He looked like he wanted to say something, but didn't.

They were walking back through the field separating the village and forest when Angelus stopped. Veronica maneuvered the blanket so she could turn to face him without tripping. "What?" she asked.

"Maybe you should stay." His words were quiet, fast and hard like he was trying to get them over with.

Veronica blinked. "What? Stay where?"

"Here," he said. "It's a decent enough place, not many soldiers. You could—"

The pleasant warmth inside Veronica disappeared. "You— you want to leave me here?"

It was because she was small, weak and slow. This was about her episode last night, about her disobeying him when he told her to stay hidden, for pressing him for information he clearly hadn't wanted to give. Stupid, she was so stupid. Of course he wanted to leave her behind. Veronica would have left herself behind if she could. She realized she was shaking her head and stopped.

"This might be the last safe place for you to stay. Once we reach the mountains, there's no going back."

"I know that." Veronica wasn't sure why she was angry, but she was. "But leaving me here isn't going to make me safer. Those soldiers saw what I was. I broke the law." And death was waiting for her because of it. When word of the High Queen's law, the ban on Magic, had reached the village, Veronica had been sure she felt her soul leave her body for an instant. She already despised her Magic— it seemed the rest of the country agreed.

Angelus shook his head, but Veronica continued, "If you don't want me around just say so." Hurt and anger amplified her voice, though she knew she needed to be quiet. She'd known this was a possibility. She should have been grateful he was telling her instead of simply leaving her in the woods.

Angelus' hands suddenly shot toward her, and for a wild moment she thought he was going to strike her, or shove her, but he only gripped her upper arms. "It's not like that," he hissed. "I don't want anything to happen to you. It's my fault you're in this mess."

Veronica's breath left her in a rush. She was so stunned she couldn't speak.

Angelus straightened, letting his arms fall to his sides. He sighed, and the last part of it turned into a laugh. A single soft, amused exhale. "Alright," he said, then nodded. "Alright. If that's what you want."

Perhaps she should have considered it. But the idea of him leaving pressed down heavily on her chest, a duller, softer version of the pain from last night. "It is."

He adjusted the supplies under his arm. "Well. Come on then." And he led the way back into the forest.

CHAPTER THIRTEEN

VERONICA wasn't asleep.

With the thrill of the fight and the victory of her first meal in days, she'd been able to forget, or at least ignore, the aches in her hands and legs, the cold that didn't dissipate despite being wrapped in the new, thick animal skin blanket. She was always restless at night, but this was worse. Restlessness and exhaustion fought for dominance. It was as though she was being told to run while strapped to a chair. She uncurled her limbs, flexing her hands and feet to coax some blood back into them. She sat up slowly, her stomach no longer pleasantly full but painfully nauseous.

Not another episode, she begged. But she did not sense the haunting dread, the shortness in her breathing or the lead in her chest that meant the overtaking panic was on its way. It was more like the previous episode had never really ended, not entirely. Her body hurt with how tired she was, while her mind was alert, her eyes absorbing every detail of the dark forest around her. She glanced over to where Angelus lay. He didn't stir or react to her movements, so she got carefully to her feet. She needed to walk, needed to get rid of some of the nervous energy humming through her. But she was so heavy, ladened by an invisible weight in her feet and arms. She dragged herself forward, walking slowly in wide circles around their little camp, until her knees began to wobble. Her hands found a thick tree trunk in the dark, and she leaned against it, slowly easing down to sit on the forest floor. She needed to get some sleep if she was going to have the strength to keep up with Angelus tomorrow, but the idea of sleep made her nausea increase. She would have nightmares, she could tell.

She sat in the dark for hours before crawling back to her blanket. She thought she heard Angelus turn over, away from her, but she wasn't sure.

Nightmares made of fire were there to greet her once she finally fell asleep.

*   *   *

VERONICA only felt worse when she woke up. The first thing she noted after the pounding in her head was that Angelus was gone. She barely had time to understand his absence, and to feel the fingers of panic pressing into her mind, when he emerged from a line of trees.

Looking triumphant, he said, "Come on, there's something you need to see."

Veronica got up, trying not to appear as miserable as she felt. She started packing up her blanket, but Angelus shook his head. "Leave it. Come on." Then he started back the way he had come.

Veronica followed. To her surprise, Angelus waited for her to catch up to him before walking further, and stayed by her side as they walked through an unfamiliar patch of forest.

"Where are we going?" Veronica asked.

"Almost there."

Walking so close to him, she hoped he couldn't tell how little sleep she'd gotten. She wondered if he had been awake last night. If he had seen her. The idea made her squirm with embarrassment.

A sound like faraway thunder was slowly getting louder, and Veronica frowned. There wasn't a cloud in the sky.

"There." Angelus pointed. Through the trees, she could make out a tower of white mist. A waterfall. Veronica gasped, her exhaustion forgotten for an instant. She had never seen a waterfall before. She'd read about them, but this was so much bigger than she'd imagined. The ledge the water cascaded over was wider than a house, and the water moved so fast and hard it appeared solid, like a strip of white-blue paint brushed over the rocks. She moved closer, large wet rocks jutting out of the earth all around the circular pool the fall emptied into. The water was perfectly clear in the pool, lapping at the base of the rocks around the pool, so much so that Veronica couldn't tell how deep the water was.

"I followed a stream for a while and it led here," Angelus explained. "I thought you might want to wash up."

Veronica had been doing her best to ignore the itch of dirt and sweat on her skin, but the idea of finally being cleansed of it made her lightheaded with relief. "Thank you," she said. She couldn't help a little bit of surprise leaking into her voice— Angelus had found the pool, he could have bathed first, but judging by his dry hair and the dirt on his hands, he clearly hadn't.

He nodded stiffly, suddenly irritated, but Veronica was starting to learn this sometimes meant he was embarrassed. She was beginning to find it endearing. "I'll stand watch." He turned away from the water, maneuvering through the rocks until he was a few yards away, then sat down, his back to her.

Veronica climbed carefully down the slope, holding on to the rocks for balance, though they were so wet and slippery they didn't offer much support. She shed her clothes and unbraided her hair. She set her clothes on a flat rock away from the water's reach, then lowered herself into the pool. The water was cold, and Veronica stifled a yelp, then a laugh. She dove under the water, muffling the sound of the waterfall crashing next to her. She opened her eyes, blinking away the initial discomfort until her eyes adjusted. The sunlight above reached into the pool, making the water sparkle around her. She swam down and touched the bottom of the pool with her fingertips, then shot toward the surface, sucking in a breath before diving down again. She turned over so she could see the surface of the pool, and it was so clear that if it hadn't been moving, Veronica would have thought she was simply looking at the sky.

She swam slowly around the pool, avoiding sharp-edged rocks. Her hair was a silky dark curtain floating around her, and she felt clean for the first time in days. She was content in that moment, and allowed her mouth to turn up in a small smile.

She wore herself out swimming, and dragged her body regretfully from the water. The day had warmed, and Veronica was only a little cold as she got out of the pool. Too wet to put her clothes back on yet, she walked between the rocks toward the water falling from above. There was a wide space between the water and the wall of rock behind it, and Veronica maneuvered closer, avoiding the spray of water but still getting misted. The water beaded on her skin like sweat.

Once she made it around the water, she could see strange shelf-like formations in the rock wall behind the waterfall, and realized they were enormous stairs, leading from the bottom corner of the wall up to the opposite top corner of the rock. Fascinated, she walked closer, wanting to get a better look. She lifted her foot to the first step, wondering who had carved them, and how long ago.

Her foot slipped, and instantly she was underwater. The waterfall slammed into her body, and she couldn't see, didn't know what was up or down. Lights danced in her vision, two pale yellow lights that waved in front of her. Her hands. They were her hands. And they were glowing.

She could make out the pool's bottom, the crashing water in front of her, and she swam backward until she could break the surface. She gasped, the water in her lungs clawing its way out in sharp, hard coughs that made her eyes swim.

Her hands were no longer glowing. But the pool was warm. Hot. Steaming. Tendrils of heat spiraled off the top of the water. Minutes ago it had been almost too cold to tolerate.

Veronica studied her hands, but they were the same cursed hands she'd always had, no inner light to be seen.

She was losing control.

*   *   *

DRESSED and mostly dry, Veronica made her careful way back to camp. Angelus appeared from the trees, startling her.

"There's nothing here," he said. "No sign of people that I could find. We should move our things here and set up camp close to the water."

Veronica made an absent sound of agreement. Her palms felt hot and slick with sweat, while the rest of her body was cold and clammy. "You should use the pool then," she said, trying to keep her voice normal.

He nodded. "Alright."

"I'll go get our supplies." She left before he could say anything more. She had to make two trips, even though they didn't have much, because her arms were shaking too badly to carry everything at once. With a heavy sigh, Veronica set the last of the supplies down on a flat piece of land near the pool. Her head pounded horribly, great throbbing pulses that traveled throughout her skull and down into her neck. She lowered herself onto one of the blankets. She was so tired. Her body ached and all she wanted to do was sleep. Her eyes drifted closed, lids too heavy to fight.

When she opened her eyes it was darker than it had been before, and Angelus, hair damp and flat against his head, was pulling his shirt over his head. There was a thin red line across his right arm, the remnant of the injury Veronica had treated. She didn't think it would scar, which was a bit of a relief. Before he tugged his shirt down, Veronica saw that around his neck was the silver chain with the ruined identification tag, the glass cracked and black. It seemed a dangerous thing to carry, to have against his skin. When he noticed her watching, he frowned. "If we're moving too fast, we can slow down."

Veronica blinked, unsure of what he meant. Then she realized he thought she was tired from traveling. She sat up, shaking her head. "I'm fine." It was a lie, and she could tell he caught it. He wasn't an idiot; she'd been slowing down for days, and now she was falling asleep in the middle of the day.

Veronica's brows drew together, her lips forming a question she wasn't sure how to ask. "Why... why don't you ask me about it? The... Magic." He knew it was there, he had seen it, but he had never once spoken of it.

Angelus frowned. "Why would you tell me anything about that?" The question was mere curiosity, no bitterness or sarcasm, but Veronica still felt stupid as soon as he asked it. He didn't care, that was all there was to it. That was a *good* thing, Veronica told herself. But it didn't feel good. It stung, just a little.

Angelus jerked his head in the direction of the waterfall. "I want to show you something." He started toward the water, not looking back to see if Veronica was following, but she was, and struggling to keep her balance on the wet rocks in the rapidly increasing darkness. With the trees so thick around and above them, night came upon the forest fast. Veronica stepped between two large, pointed rocks, the space between their bases barely wide enough for her foot to fit in. When she glanced up, Angelus' hand was stretched out to her. When his face wasn't stony, he looked unbearably young, the hardness around his eyes softening until he was almost handsome, in his wild way. She took his offered hand, allowing him to help her down the slope and onto flatter ground. He didn't let go of her hand, though Veronica was no longer in danger of falling.

He led her toward the waterfall, across the rocks on the pool's left side to avoid the spray of water. His hand was enormous, all calloused skin and long thin fingers that swallowed her small hand. His skin was warm, and Veronica was so cold that all she could think of was wrapping her other hand around his arm and curling into him.

She gave her head a hard, quick shake.

"There." Her eyes followed to where he pointed— the stairs in the rock Veronica had seen earlier. The memory made her hands ache, her stomach tightening as she recalled the pummel of the waterfall across her back, the moment of disorientation. Her hand tightened around Angelus' without her realizing it.

He didn't smile at her, but his eyes danced with amusement. "Scared of heights?"

"No," Veronica said immediately, letting go of his hand and crossing her arms.

"Good." Angelus started to climb. The stairs led to the top right corner of the rock, to where the water was coming from. The top of the rock was a fair distance from the ground, and Veronica decided she was not afraid of heights, she was afraid of falling and becoming a mess on the solid rock floor, or getting sucked back under the torrent of water. Angelus beckoned for her to follow, and Veronica grimaced.

"Be careful," she warned. "They're wet."

Angelus said nothing, just kept climbing, no hesitation or fear in his movements.

"This is what you wanted to show me?" she asked, annoyance creeping into her voice. "I saw these earlier."

"You didn't see what was at the top," he said.

Veronica sighed, but started to climb, being more careful where she put her feet this time. She stuck close to the wall, fingers gripping the rough rock. Below, the water reflected the remaining daylight, a hazy gray-purple mass shifting among the rocks.

Halfway up the rock, Veronica's pulse turned to thunder. This was high, higher even than the loft in the barn that required a ladder to reach.

A hand closed over her fingers that had been gripping the wall tightly. Her eyes met Angelus', and the usually hard green had softened into... something. Something warmer. "You won't fall," he said. "If you did I would catch you."

Veronica stared at him. Even as she leaned her head against the wall, her eyes stayed on his. Her heart was a caged bird in her chest, trying to escape.

Slowly, carefully, he pried her hand away from the wall, and led her up the remaining steps. She didn't look down, only watched his back as they climbed.

You won't fall.

He pulled her to the top, and Veronica gasped as she beheld a sky on fire. Orange and red and purple stretched out above their heads, lit by the setting sun, the rapidly shifting clouds making it appear as though the sky was breathing. The forest stretched on forever, a blanket of green, speckled with some red and yellow just starting to bloom. Mountains pierced the sky, black and green sleeping giants, except for the tips, which were dusted with white.

Water flowed in a white, misty rush over the ledge next to their feet, streaming from a long, narrow river.

Veronica had never seen anything like it. It was horrifying and bewildering and enthralling to know this place had existed long before she was born, and would still be there long after she died.

It was so beautiful, Veronica felt it in her chest like grief.

"Almost there," Angelus said, his eyes on the mountains.

That's where we're going, Veronica thought. *The Northern Mountains.* She was suddenly overcome with relief and gratitude that Angelus hadn't left her behind in that village.

How long they stood there Veronica wasn't sure, but when they started back down the stone steps it was almost completely dark, the last dregs of sunlight disappearing as soon as they descended the steps, the wall of rock blocking most of the light. The steps were wide enough for both of them to fit, and Veronica walked carefully between the wall and Angelus, who was himself something of a wall, dark and imposing... and solid, sturdy.

"Angelus?"

He paused, peering down at her. His features were barely discernible in the dark, and whatever Veronica had been about to say was forgotten. In the minimal light, the shadows somehow softened his face, and where she expected the usual hardness, there was a softness, an openness. He'd forgotten, for a moment, to look stony. The sight above them had distracted him. It had not, however, taken the sadness from his eyes. Veronica wondered if anything could.

His eyes found her face, confused, and a little surprised, and it made him look about ten years younger. He glanced away, his expression shuttering once more as he continued down the stone steps.

What an odd mystery he was, Veronica thought. Very odd indeed.

CHAPTER FOURTEEN

VERONICA slept heavily, for once, and still felt like she was half asleep as she packed up their things the next morning. Angelus took one look at her and without a word he removed the satchel and blanket from her arms, leaving her with nothing to carry.

"I can—"

"They're slowing you down. I'll carry them."

Veronica was too tired to argue. Maybe without the extra weight she would be able to move a bit faster.

"Can I have some food?" she asked. She wasn't hungry but she knew she needed to eat something, and so did Angelus.

Angelus fished the remaining bread they had taken from the house out of the bag, saving the fresher food for later. The corners of the loaf were spotted with mold, and she picked the chunks with white fuzz off as they walked, tossing them to the ground. She broke what was left in half and offered a piece to Angelus. He shook his head. "I'll eat something later."

The taste of the stale, slightly sour bread made her grimace. She struggled to swallow, coughing a bit at the dryness.

They were no longer climbing upward, but instead the forest floor appeared to tilt slightly down, the trees beginning to thin slightly and letting more sunlight in to illuminate their path. Veronica had to walk quickly to keep her balance on the sloping ground, and she was growing winded. It didn't help that a piece of the bread seemed to be lodged in her throat, making her cough again.

Angelus paused once the ground evened out, offering her a canteen. "We should stop here for a while," he said.

Veronica took a deep drink, trying to soothe her throat, but the itching tickle remained, and she stifled another cough. They couldn't have walked more than a couple of miles, so she knew he was stopping for her sake.

She sat down on the ground, the canteen pressed between her palms.

"Are you alright?" Angelus frowned at her from where he stood, leaning against the thick trunk of an oak tree. He was watching her face with drawn brows.

Veronica nodded quickly. "I'm fine." She cleared her throat to hide a cough.

"Your face is flushed. Do you feel sick?"

The problem was Veronica always felt sick so she wasn't sure how to answer. She didn't have to though, because Angelus stepped forward, bent down, and pressed his palm to her forehead. "Warm," he observed.

"I'm fine," she repeated, batting his hand away, annoyed.

"If we need to stop for the night—"

"I said I'm fine." Her words were harsher than she meant them to sound, but Angelus was unoffended. He said nothing, his eyes unconvinced, and sat down a few feet in front of her, elbows propped on his bent knees.

"We're near the base of the mountain," Angelus said. "We should reach it by tonight, or tomorrow at the latest."

Veronica nodded, not really listening. Her chest rattled as she inhaled, and she took small, slow breaths. She forced herself to her feet, and Angelus rose, much faster and easier than she did. There was a question in his raised eyebrow. She picked up the satchel from the ground. She would carry it herself.

Angelus' eyes lit momentarily with something akin to amusement, or respect.

"Let's go then," Veronica said.

Angelus picked up their remaining supplies and walked beside her in silence.

*　　*　　*

THE cough was beginning to worry Angelus. Veronica was pushing herself too hard— her cheeks were almost feverish, her eyes dull and exhausted. And the cough was getting worse. Angelus didn't have any medicine, he didn't know how to help her if something was wrong. They were nearly to the base of the mountain, and not far from there was a village. He'd never bought medicine in his life, but he prayed to the gods he had enough leftover money from the fight to buy some. She just had to make it there.

Veronica's shaky cough sounded behind him, grating against his ears. He should have made her stay in that village. She needed proper shelter, not a blanket on the cold ground out in the open air. That was probably what had made her sick in the first place.

She gasped behind him, and Angelus looked up sharply, only then realizing how long his eyes had been on the ground. Immediately he found what she was staring at: The trees around them had vanished, and laid out before them was a basin of earth with nothing but dark grass for at least a mile, maybe two. And at the edge of the field was the base of the mountain. Angelus' gaze traveled up, and up and up, to the tower of earth before them, trees covering every inch of it for miles.

The Northern Mountains. They had arrived.

CHAPTER FIFTEEN

THEY spent the night in the woods, and Angelus was up and ready to leave before the sun had fully risen. He was restless, anxious to reach the mountain village before nightfall; Veronica had coughed all night and couldn't sleep in the cold air again.

He hated to wake her, but they needed to get moving. He knelt next to her, placing his hand carefully on her shoulder. Heat radiated off her body, shocking in the cold morning air. Angelus' stomach fell. She was curled into a tight ball, and as her eyes opened, they struggled to focus on his face.

"Time to go," he whispered, hating himself for making her travel any further.

She nodded, and didn't protest when Angelus grabbed her hands and helped her to her feet. He picked up her blanket and wrapped it around her.

"We can find you some medicine in the village, it isn't far."

She didn't answer, just burrowed her face into the blanket. Angelus shouldered the satchel and tucked his blanket under his arm before leading the way to the field separating them from the mountain base. There was nothing around, not a house or border guard post or barn, nothing. The wind across the tall grass was cold, and Angelus knew the nights and early mornings would only get colder from here on out.

They moved at a painfully slow pace across the field. Angelus cast anxious glances at the sky, feeling the day trickling away from them. Veronica's breathing only worsened as the ground grew uneven, pitching upward and becoming steeper. He could hear it, even over the rustling grass. She suddenly doubled over, a wet, rattling cough bursting from deep inside her chest. Angelus practically ran back to her, shocked by how far behind him she'd fallen without him noticing.

Veronica straightened, wrapping her blanket tighter around her. Angelus draped his own blanket over her, but she gave no indication she noticed.

"You won't last another night without proper shelter," Angelus said, more to himself than to her.

"I can keep going," she said, voice hardly more than a whimper.

"No, you can't," he snapped, his voice rising. He knew this was unfair; it was himself he was angry with, not her. This was his fault, and he didn't know what to do. "You can barely walk."

He surveyed the road ahead of them, disappearing into the trees. The village couldn't be far. But she wouldn't make it, not in the dark, not when she was this sick.

"Alright," Angelus said slowly, nodding his head as he made up his mind. "Alright— Get on my back."

Veronica looked up at him. He couldn't tell if her eyes were red because she was sick, or if she was crying. "What?" she asked, her terrible shivers robbing the word of air.

"I said get on my back." He took the satchel and slipped the strap across his body, then knelt down in front of Veronica. "Now."

Her small hands found his shoulders, and when she pressed her chest to his back, he nearly gasped at her heat.

"Bring the blanket," he said.

"I can't hold it," Veronica whispered, her breath hot against his neck. "My fingers aren't... working."

Something inside Angelus' chest cracked, threatening to cave in upon itself. "It's alright," he said, slipping his hands under her thighs and standing up. She wrapped her arms around his neck, clumsy but careful. "It's alright," he repeated. He glanced down at the blankets on the ground. He couldn't carry them. There would be no surviving the night without them if he didn't reach the village in time.

He would make it. He had to.

"Hold on," he whispered. Veronica whimpered, wrapping her arms tighter around him as he started to run.

*　　*　　*

THE moon was Angelus' only guide. He was drenched with sweat, not just from Veronica's feverish body pressed against his back, but from carrying her up the mountain road, a seemingly endless stretch of worn footpath washed blue-black in the night light.

"Almost there," he grunted for the hundredth time. He was no longer sure if he was saying the words for Veronica, or himself at this point. Veronica was silent.

"Veronica?" he asked, forcing out the word.

She didn't reply. Her arms around his neck were limp.

Dread crept into his lungs, filling them with water. He paused on the trail, his legs trembling from the exertion. "Veronica," he repeated, louder, harder.

She jerked, her head snapping up as though she'd been sleeping. Angelus only had time to breathe a sigh of relief before she was writhing in his grip, trying to get free. He dropped her— he didn't mean to, but he couldn't hold onto her— and she fell to the ground. Angelus whirled on her in the dark. "Veronica? Veronica, it's me. It's Angelus—"

She scurried backward on her hands and feet. In the moonlight, her eyes were enormous silver orbs, full of fevered panic.

"Veronica," Angelus said, desperation stealing all the force from his voice. "Please. We're almost there—" He caught her before she could bolt, his arm sliding around her narrow waist and hoisting her up. She clawed at his arms, nails scraping across his skin, making him grit his teeth. He wrapped his arms around her, pinning her arms to her sides. She slumped forward like a puppet whose strings had been sliced through.

He swept her up, one arm around her shoulders and the other under her knees. Her head fell back, her neck exposed to the night. So vulnerable, so fragile; the image rested in his stomach like sickness.

"Hang on," he whispered. He didn't have any strength left to run. But still he ran. He ran until the lights of the village were visible, torches burning on the sides of stone buildings, lamp light flickering in windows like frantic, beckoning hands, telling him to hurry, *hurry*.

An inn sat at the edge of the village, windows alight and revealing people inside. He struggled with the knob on the door, finally throwing it open and nearly tumbling over the threshold.

"A doctor," he gasped to the startled man and woman behind the long counter, keys hanging from little hooks on the wall behind them.

"I'll find Avery," the woman said, running out the door Angelus had just come through. The man behind the counter grabbed a key and motioned for Angelus to follow him.

He led them up a flight of stairs, to the first vacant room, opening the door to reveal a narrow bed. Angelus laid Veronica down on it, her face screwed up in pain, whimpering softly. The sound raked red-hot talons across his chest.

"What happened?" the innkeeper asked, bending over Veronica and touching her face, turning it from side to side as though inspecting for injuries.

Angelus' hand was instantly around the man's upper arm, pulling him back, though he had no memory of deciding to do it. "No one touches her but a doctor." His voice surprised even himself. The man looked at him, shocked.

"Enough," a voice snapped from behind Angelus. A man in a white coat, a much older and less glamorous version of what Finn and the other physicians had worn in the castle, entered the room, a black bag in hand. The woman from before hovered anxiously in the doorway.

"Get him out of here," the doctor ordered the innkeeper, gesturing dismissively to Angelus as he opened his bag with his other hand.

"I'm not going anywhere," Angelus snapped.

"If you want me to save her, I need space and I need quiet. Get out *now*."

The innkeeper pressed a hand to Angelus' arm, pushing him toward the door. "She'll be alright," he told Angelus in a low voice. "Let the doctor work."

For a breath, Angelus didn't move. Then he pointed at the doctor, who met Angelus' unwavering gaze. "You will save her." It was not a question.

The doctor turned back to Veronica without a word, and Angelus allowed himself to be guided from the room. The door shut, leaving him with the innkeeper and the woman in the hallway.

"Is she your wife?" the woman asked. She had a weathered, kind face with a smile that matched.

Angelus shook his head. He was starting to get dizzy, his legs threatening to dispose of his weight. Every inch of his body hurt. He shouldn't have been able to run that long, that hard, while carrying another person. His body had momentarily forgotten its limits, but it was reminding him now.

"Can we get you anything?" the innkeeper asked. "If you want to wash up, there's a bathhouse behind the inn. It should be empty at this hour."

At this hour? What time *was* it? How long had he been running?

He had to get out of the cramped hallway, pressing in on him from all directions. He descended the narrow steps to the lobby and opened the door, stepping out into the night and letting the cold air wash over him. Legs shaking, he lowered himself to sit on the step in front of the inn's door. Elbows digging into his thighs, he let his head fall forward, hands pressing to either side of his skull. His whole body was trembling, and he couldn't remember how to stand.

Veronica's sweaty face, contorted with pain, was burned onto the insides of his eyelids. He wrapped his arms around his head, pressing his forehead to his knees. He rocked back and forth, back and forth.

His body was exhausted, but his head was alive and humming like a beehive.

This was his fault. He never should have agreed to take her to the mountains. He never should have gone to her village in the first place.

My fault, this is all my fault. If she dies—

He heard her cries inside his head, and sucked in a hard, sharp breath, a pain like a puncture wound opening his chest. *Just be alright,* he thought, *Please.*

Angelus struggled to his feet, needing to move, needing something to occupy space and time and his mind. Walking in the dark around the inn, he could see a stone building behind it, two small torches burning on either side of the doorless entrance. Inside, the floor was mostly made up of an empty, steaming pool.

It was similar to the bathing chamber in the castle, but much smaller, and free of soldiers and servants.

Angelus shed his clothes, leaving them in a filthy heap on the floor, except for the vest, which he brought with him to the edge of the pool and laid within easy reach. The water was hot, burning his sweat-slick skin. It wasn't until he sat down on the bench along the inside of the pool, that he remembered the chain around his neck. He picked up the cracked glass pendant between two fingers, the steam from the bath rendering it hazy and not quite real. Or perhaps that was just his exhaustion. He tipped his head back, letting it rest against the lip of the pool.

All he could do was sit. He didn't reach for the soap in a basket by the pool, or one of the brushes next to it. He never wanted to move again.

He didn't know how long he sat there, but he might have fallen asleep because the next thing he knew someone was clearing their throat in the echoey bathhouse chamber.

Angelus' eyes flew open, turning to face the innkeeper, who held a pile of folded clothes. "I'll take your clothes and wash them," he offered. "You can wear these."

"How is she?" Angelus asked.

"The doc's still with her," he said.

Angelus nodded slowly, letting his gaze fall to the water. He could make out his pale legs under the steaming surface, distorted masses Angelus felt entirely detached from. "Leave the vest," he muttered. When he looked up, the innkeeper was gone, along with Angelus' dirty clothes, the pile of clean clothes sitting on a shelf of towels and brushes.

Angelus ducked under the water, scrubbing his hands through his hair and over his face. He surfaced, reaching for a bar of soap. It smelled like wood and moss, and Angelus thought of Veronica's homemade soap, her scent of raspberries and lavender. That scent was entirely hers; he would never be able to smell raspberries and not think of her.

After he had finished washing, was dry and dressed in the pants the innkeeper had brought him, he walked barefoot, boots, vest and clean shirt in hand, back to the inn.

The woman was alone behind the counter, and offered a smile when Angelus entered. "You can go in now," she told him.

Did that mean she was alright? He walked as fast as his sore legs would allow, opening the door to the room he had taken Veronica to. She was asleep on the bed, tucked beneath the blankets with a damp cloth covering her forehead. Her chest rose and fell slowly, but easily.

The doctor was packing up his supplies. He glanced at Angelus when he heard him approach. "I'll be back in the morning to check on her," he said, fastening his bag closed. "The fever broke. She needs rest now."

Angelus said nothing, only watched her sleeping form. He was silent as the doctor left, casting Angelus a sideways look as he left. There was something of a question in his expression, but Angelus ignored him, letting the door fall closed once the doctor was gone.

He sank to the ground next to the bed, barely keeping upright as he watched her. He lifted his hand, stretching it toward her as though to touch her, but thought better of it and only laid his hand on the bed beside her. He leaned his forehead against the mattress, letting relief and exhaustion wash over him.

He was just starting to doze off when he felt Veronica turn in her sleep, and something brush against the top of his head. He froze, unable to move as her fingers twined in his still-wet hair.

"You smell good," she whispered. Her hand fell away, and when Angelus looked up, she was asleep again, curled on her side around the place where Angelus' hand still rested. He slowly slid his palm to rest over one of her hands, and tumbled into sleep beside her.

CHAPTER SIXTEEN

RESMOND dragged Angelus to the stables. He couldn't regain his footing, and his heels made tracks in the dirt as he kicked wildly, his hands clutching Resmond's fist, which was clenched tightly around the front of Angelus' shirt.

"I'm sorry," Angelus gasped. "Resmond, I'm sorry, I'm sorry! Please don't—"

"Shut up," Resmond snapped. There was no one in the stables, and the only eyes upon them belonged to the horses. Resmond shoved Angelus into an empty stall and slammed the door behind him. It was just the two of them in that tiny space, and Angelus had never been so afraid in his life.

He scrambled to his knees. "Please," he begged, too scared to cry.

The first punch hit him like a tidal wave, drowning him, dragging him under. There was nothing but pain, nothing but the taste of blood in his mouth and the explosion of heat across his jaw. He opened his mouth to free his tongue from between his teeth, and Resmond seized his shirt collar, pulling him up, before he hit him again.

"You steal from me," Resmond roared, "I'll make you wish you'd never been born."

He hit him again.

"Please." He could take the beating, he could take the punches and the lashes. It had always been so much better than the alternative, than being alone. He couldn't take going back to the streets. He couldn't take being alone again. "I won't do it again. *Please.*"

"You steal like a stray," came Resmond's voice from the hazy, dark shadow the world had become, "You get kicked like a stray. Don't you ever come back— if I see you again I'll kill you."

Resmond's fist collided with Angelus' stomach. "Please." Angelus wasn't sure if he had spoken aloud. "Please, take me with you."

Resmond let him fall, and spat on the stable floor. Angelus heard the squeak of the stall door opening, and he struggled to focus his fading vision. He could barely make out Resmond's form, walking away from him, leaving him behind, before the world disappeared and there was nothing.

There was nothing.

*   *   *

ANGELUS woke up to sunlight shining on his face, and his back aching from sleeping so long bent over the side of the bed. He told himself it was for these reasons his eyes were burning, and he quickly wiped the moisture away with the back of his hand.

It was early, the sunlight bathing the little room in a pale yellow-blue glow. Veronica slept soundly, lips parted and her breath expelling in soft, low puffs.

Angelus straightened, standing up and stretching. His leg muscles seized, but he ignored the stiffness. His clothes, freshly laundered, were folded on the end of the bed. His vest still laid on the ground next to him where he had left it. He counted the knives to be sure. They were all there. He dressed silently, fastening his vest over his shirt, the weight of it reassuring over his shoulders. Leaning against the window frame, he could see the narrow space between the inn and the shorter building beside it, a few people carrying baskets of laundry or walking toward the bathhouse milling about.

Angelus looked back at Veronica, her expression clear, her coloring healthier. With a full night's sleep, he could think more clearly now. He knew what he needed to do.

He began packing up the satchel, stuffing it with everything he would need. He was finishing this task alone. It was his fault Veronica was here, his fault the soldiers had attacked her village. He would find Mayva on his own, and bring her back. Veronica couldn't handle this journey. She would be safer here.

A soft knock rapped against the door, and the woman from last night entered, bearing a tray of fruit, cheese, and two cups of tea. She set it on the end of the bed and smiled at Angelus. "I thought you might be hungry. There's enough for her when she wakes up."

Angelus nodded a stiff, uncomfortable thanks. He was starving, but didn't reach for the food.

"Avery should be here soon," she said, eyes falling to Veronica, who still slept quietly. "How was she through the night?"

He was sorely tempted to ignore her, but he forced out a reply. "Fine." The woman's smile softened with relief.

Angelus reached into the satchel and fished out a few coins from his winnings and offered them to her. "This should cover the room."

The woman shook her head. "No need. Happy to help."

Angelus fought a scowl. If she didn't want his money, she must want something else. "What is it you want then?" he asked, folding his arms, instantly on guard.

The woman shook her head again, confused. "Nothing." There was pity in her eyes, and Angelus hated it. "Some people just want to help," she added. "Not everyone wants something from you."

Angelus stiffened. The woman left without another word.

Hungry as he was, he didn't want the woman's offered food. He had to eat though, especially if he was leaving soon.

He ate the cheese and some of the fruit as fast as he could, then adjusted the satchel on his shoulder and picked up one of the spare blankets from under the bed. It would have to be enough.

The door opened again, and the doctor appeared, closing the door swiftly behind him. He was older than Angelus, maybe thirty, his dark hair already showing some gray. Tension radiated off of him, his eyes alert and his movements hurried.

"What—"

"You have to go," the doctor, Avery, the woman had called him, said quickly. "There are soldiers on their way here. Someone must have seen you come here last night and recognized you from the wanted posters."

Angelus' stomach plummeted. Avery had known who he was? But why not turn him in? Why warn him they were coming?

"Don't worry," Angelus bit out, "I was just leaving."

Avery's eyes narrowed, his gaze flicking from Angelus to Veronica, to the bag of supplies on Angelus' arm. He shook his head. "You can't leave her here. She's stable, for now, but she needs help I can't give her."

Ice shot through Angelus' limbs. "What are you talking about? I thought she was sick with a fever."

"She was. But the fever was only a symptom."

"Of what?" He was standing very close to the doctor all of the sudden. Angelus was taller than Avery— he was taller than most people he encountered— and glared down at him.

Avery glared right back. "Her Magic is making her sick. I'm guessing she's been sickly for a while, and it came to a head last night?"

Angelus had the doctor's coat in his fists and was slamming him into the closed door before he had even finished speaking. "If you tell *anyone*—"Angelus hissed, but Avery cut him off.

"I won't. I came here to warn you, didn't I? I'm a friend to people like her." Angelus didn't miss his exclusion, but it didn't bother him. Angelus didn't have friends, nor did he need them. "There is a village a few miles from here, they can help her. She needs a Wielder doctor, one skilled in healing Magic. I can't do any more for her."

Angelus slowly loosened his hold on Avery's coat, though he didn't let go completely. "What's happening to her? Why is she like this?"

"I don't know. I've only read about sickness like this, I've never actually seen it before. But the doctor in the village I told you about can help her. You need to get her there, and fast. She won't last long if she doesn't get the proper help."

Angelus released him, stepping back. "How do I find it?"

Avery took a folded piece of parchment from the pocket of his robe and shoved it into Angelus' hand. A map. "Follow the mountain road on the north side of the village. When you see a tower with a green flag, you're there."

Angelus glanced at Veronica, still sleeping despite their noise. "How do I get her out of here without being seen?"

They glanced in unison at the window.

Avery raised an eyebrow. "Can you make it?"

Angelus scoffed, and Avery smirked. "I'll leave it to you then. I can distract them, but hurry."

He started toward the door, but Angelus said, "How did you know? About her Magic?"

Avery looked at him over his shoulder, his smile knowing. "Blood always knows its kin." And then he was gone, disappearing into the hall and out of sight.

Angelus crossed to the bed, shaking Veronica's shoulder. "Wake up. We have to go."

She slowly opened her eyes, squinting at him. "What's wrong? What's going on?" She sat up, and Angelus went to the window, opening it and peering down. Alone, he could make the climb easily. But Veronica...

"We have to leave," he said, taking the blankets off the bed and rolling them into a ball. When the alleyway below was clear of people, he tossed it down.

"What are you doing?" Veronica demanded, pushing him out of the way to see the pile of blankets now laying in a heap on the ground.

"Soldiers," he said by way of answer. "You need to climb down."

Veronica turned a wide-eyed gaze upon him. She shook her head. "No— no, I can't—"

"Yes you can," he said, grabbing her shoulders. "It's easy, just don't look down. There's a window right beneath this one. It's like climbing a ladder."

"No it's not!" she cried, and Angelus winced at her raised voice, glancing at the door. How long did they have until the soldiers came to search the inn? A few minutes? Probably less. "My legs aren't long enough, I won't make it!"

Angelus chewed his lip, stifling a frustrated groan. She was probably right, she was too small.

"Get on my back."

Her eyes grew impossibly wider. "What— No!"

"Veronica, get on my back *now.*"

Her face was pale, her eyes enormous and terrified.

"It'll be alright," Angelus said, his voice softening a fraction. "Trust me."

*   *   *

THEY barely made it out the window before the door crashed open, and heavy footfalls thundered through the room.

Angelus' arms screamed as he clung to the windowsill, Veronica clutching his neck, nearly choking him. He could feel it— at any moment, a soldier would look down through the open window and find them, or they would be spotted from the street outside the alley. But the footsteps began to fade, the soldiers leaving the empty room just as noisily as they'd entered it, and moving further down the hall.

As soundlessly as he could, he stretched his legs until his toes brushed the top of the window below him. His instinct was to jump, but if he landed on Veronica she would be crushed beneath him, and if he misjudged the distance to the ground, he could break his legs, or something else. He had to reach the bottom of the next window, then maybe Veronica could jump.

"Don't scream," he whispered, his straining muscles stretching his voice thin.

Veronica stiffened, and her arms squeezed around his neck so tightly Angelus couldn't breathe as he let go of the window sill. They were falling for only a second before Angelus caught the sill of the window below them. He couldn't help a strained grunt as he arms threatened to tear free of their sockets.

"Can you jump down?" he gasped.

He felt Veronica nod. Her arms slipped from around his neck, and then her weight disappeared, and Angelus' breath left him in a rush of relief. He let go, falling the remaining few feet to the earth. He scooped up the blanket bundle still on the ground, and gestured for Veronica to follow him. He glanced around the side of the inn, then snatched his head back when he saw three soldiers standing outside the inn's front door, attentive eyes sweeping the streets around them.

A hand closed around his arm and he whirled, ready to strike, but froze. The woman from the inn, holding a cloth bag in her other hand, stood next to him. She let go of his arm, pressing a finger to her lips and beckoning for Veronica and Angelus to follow her to the back of the inn.

Angelus hesitated, just for a second, before following. He grabbed Veronica's hand, not wanting to be separated, and she didn't protest. Her hand was impossibly small in his. They wouldn't touch her. He would die before they touched her.

The woman led them behind the inn, pointing to a narrow path that connected to the wider road leading away from the village. "That way," she whispered, shoving the sack into Veronica's hand. It smelled like fruit, and fresh bread.

He met the woman's eyes. "Why are you doing this?"

She gave him a smile just as knowing as Avery's. "Some people just want to help." The same words she had said to him earlier.

Wielders and sympathizers, working together.

She pushed them toward the path. "Go," she breathed.

With only a glance back at the woman, Angelus tugged Veronica forward. She turned and whispered, "Thank you," to the woman, before turning back and allowing Angelus to pull her to the road.

They reached the end of the path when Veronica jerked to a halt. Angelus whirled. "What?"

Then he saw it. A thick tree trunk with a square of parchment nailed to its center. *WANTED* was emblazoned in thick black letters across the top, above a charcoal drawing of Angelus' face, unmistakable with its flurry of black hair and thick, angular brows.

These posters would be all over the kingdom soon, if they weren't already, chasing them up the mountain.

Veronica let go of Angelus' hand to grab the poster, ripping it free from the nail and crumpling it. Then she turned to him, eyes fierce. "Let's go."

Angelus obeyed.

CHAPTER SEVENTEEN

"I don't need another doctor."

Angelus struggled to keep his voice from rising with annoyance. "That doctor said you need help from someone in the next village. We're going."

Veronica, who sat on the forest floor with her knees to her chest, watched Angelus lay out the food from the bag the innkeeper's wife had given them. There was a loaf of bread, dried meat, apples, and plums. If they ate a small meal every day, they would have enough for a week, maybe more if they were careful. He extracted a knife from his vest and cut the apple in half, offering one to her. She took it, but didn't eat, though they had been walking all day without pause and she must have been starving.

"I'm fine," she said again. "It was just a fever—"

"It wasn't," Angelus said, harsher than he meant to. "The doctor said your Magic is making you sick. There's a Wielder in the next village who is supposed to be able to help you."

Veronica's eyes lowered to the ground. She looked irritated and embarrassed, and though her color was better than it had been only a day ago, she was still pale. "I don't want to see a Wielder doctor," she muttered.

Angelus bit into his apple. "Why not?" His patience had thinned to virtual nonexistence.

She rested her chin on one of her knees. She didn't answer.

"We're going," Angelus said with finality. He wasn't repeating last night. Not ever. She couldn't be left to get that sick again.

They ate in silence, the midafternoon light turning the wooded mountain road pale gold. After a while, Veronica said, quietly, "Thank you."

Angelus looked up, eyebrows drawing together. "For what?" His voice still held a note of impatience.

Veronica swallowed. "Helping me." She gnawed on the fingernail of her thumb. "For... carrying me. I don't remember last night but... I can put two and two together."

Angelus didn't say anything, cleaning the apple juice off his blade on a patch of grass.

Veronica tilted her head, watching him. "Why didn't you leave without me?"

Angelus stilled, unable to meet her gaze.

"I make everything harder for you. Why didn't you just leave after you took me to the inn?"

Angelus swallowed. That had been the plan. But the doctor's warning rang in his ears. *She won't last long if she doesn't get the proper help.*

"Do you wish I had?" he asked, trying not to sound hurt but it bled out.

"For your sake, yes," Veronica replied softly, speaking more to herself, Angelus thought, than to him.

"My sake isn't what's important," Angelus snapped, getting to his feet. He was done with this conversation.

Veronica's eyes widened, and to Angelus' horror, filled with tears. She exhaled slowly, pressing her forehead to her knees. She looked so small, curled up like that.

"I wish I was stronger," she said quietly, voice strained with the effort of not crying.

I'm sorry I wasn't strong enough.

Angelus shook his head, a single, hard jerk to clear it.

Veronica looked up at him, and for a breath, her sad, dark eyes were a little like—

He stood. If Veronica wasn't strong enough, he would make sure she didn't need to be. "Come on. We need to keep moving."

*　　*　　*

ANGELUS had forgotten how spread out the mountain villages were from each other, and it only reinforced the impression of walking up an endless hill, any destination merely a desperate idea instead of reality.

But gods, it was beautiful.

As he walked beside Veronica on the path, he observed the changing leaves above them, the tops of the trees leaning down over the road as though tired, dozing off to the melody of his and Veronica's footfalls. It made his heart ache. How badly he wanted to melt into those trees and disappear.

"Are we lost?" came Veronica's voice from behind him.

His mouth cinched to the side, and he slid his gaze to her. "No." He glanced down at the map Avery had given him. It was old, outdated, but the main roads should have been the same. The problem was Angelus didn't think the main roads were safe enough to travel, and instead was attempting to maneuver through the forest. He was not lost, just... uncertain.

"Let me see the map." Veronica appeared beside him, reaching for it.

With a dry snort Angelus held it out of her reach. She made an annoyed sound and jumped up in an attempt to take it from him.

Angelus paused. Slowly, he turned his head to look down at her. His eyebrow was arching in the same slow way his mouth was forming a twisted grin. He held the map higher, purely for the pleasure of seeing her scowl with indignation. She made another grab for it, and Angelus' teeth flashed behind his smile.

"Angelus!" she protested. Then she coughed, covering her mouth with a fist.

Guilt immediately replaced his amusement. Her face had paled, but she kept walking, hand over her mouth to muffle her coughing.

After a while, Veronica's arm brushed against his, surprising him. He watched her, frowning. She looked a little unsteady on her feet. "Do you need to rest?" he asked.

Veronica shook her head, but the movement was more confused than it was final. Angelus stopped, touching her shoulder. "Veronica?"

"I said I'm fine," she snapped suddenly, though she hadn't said anything, her voice surprisingly loud and firm. "I don't need the herbs to sleep, Finn. I told you that. They don't help."

Angelus stared at her, even as she continued walking. He matched his steps to her angry, forceful ones. "We need to stop. You pushed yourself too much. Your fever must have come back."

Shit. He glanced around wildly, as though the village they sought may have materialized on the horizon when he wasn't looking. But there was nothing except trees.

Where are we?

Veronica tried to shove his hand away, nearly losing her balance. Angelus grabbed her shoulders, steering her toward the trees on their right. "Come on, sit down—"

"No!" she shouted. She was furious, her eyes blazing but unfocused. All at once her face contorted as if she were about to cry. She stretched her hands out in front of her, staring down at her palms. "I don't want to burn," she said, voice already the better part of a sob. "I don't..."

"Veronica." Angelus took her hands, and Veronica slowly looked up at him, shocked, as though her hands bore some contamination she couldn't believe he would touch. "Veronica, you're not going to burn. I'm going to get you help, alright? I promise."

She sucked in a breath, and for a moment she was herself again. "Angelus," she gasped, eyes and voice desperate. "I don't— I don't know what's happening to me."

171

"It's alright," he promised, and, without thinking, pulled her to his chest. She wrapped her arms around his waist, trembling against him. She was terrified and he could do nothing to fix it. He hated it, he hated himself for his uselessness. He thought, sudden and fleeting, but banished it just as quickly, *Finn would know what to do.* "Don't be scared. We're almost there." He had no idea if that was true. They could be minutes away, or hours. *Days.* "Almost there," he repeated, stepping away from her. "Can you walk?"

Veronica nodded, and Angelus let her lean on him as they walked. She clung to his arm, nails digging into his skin, but he said nothing.

"I'm sorry," she whispered.

Angelus shook his head. She was silent. "Veronica?"

Her grip on his arm disappeared as she crumpled in a heap on the forest floor, so fast Angelus couldn't catch her. He dropped what he was carrying, picking her up and shaking her. "Veronica— Veronica, can you hear me?"

She didn't answer. Her eyes were closed, her face slack and body limp.

"Veronica." He shook her again, then pressed his ear to her chest. A heartbeat thudded faintly like the wings of a dying bird. Her skin appeared gray in the fading sunlight. Angelus' heart was erratic, loose somewhere in his chest, crashing and falling.

Hands and breath unsteady, he took the blankets and wrapped her in them, then shoved everything else into the satchel. There was a gaping tear in the side, the contents threatening to spill out, but there was nothing to be done about it. He picked her up, tucking her head under his chin.

He didn't know what to do. He didn't know how far away help was, he wasn't even sure *where* exactly they were.

"Veronica," he breathed. "Veronica, you're going to be fine."

She didn't answer.

CHAPTER EIGHTEEN

THE guards on the tower saw Angelus before he saw them. Angelus couldn't see anything except the ground in front of his feet, could feel nothing but the weight of Veronica's body against his chest.

Faraway voices shouted indistinctly. Blurry figures ran toward him in the dark, one of them carrying a torch that bathed the black surroundings in a soft orange glow. Angelus made out the foggy image of a green and black flag hanging from one of the towers, and it swam before his eyes, formless and indistinct.

Then they were trying to take Veronica from him. "Doctor," he managed to say. "Help her."

As soon as Veronica was lifted from his arms, his legs gave out and his knees crashed to the ground. He didn't feel the pain. His body was completely numb from the cold.

"You're alright," someone was telling him, grabbing his arms and trying to hoist him to his feet, but it was no use. Angelus couldn't stand, much less fight off the encroaching blackness. He heard more running, shouting, before it all faded to nothing.

*　*　*

"...not a drop of Magic. He can't be trusted."

"He was traveling with one of us. He brought her to us. That counts for something. We should listen to what he has to say."

"And the girl? Has she said anything?"

Angelus' eyes flew open, and sunlight stabbed them like needles. He hissed, raising a hand to shield his eyes as he sat up.

A hand closed over his shoulder. "Careful," a deep male voice warned. Angelus blinked rapidly to adjust his swimming vision, until the man's face was clear. He had a long graying brown beard and dark eyes, his skin tanned and aged with sun.

"Where am I?" Angelus demanded, trying to swing his legs over the side of the bed so he could stand up, but the man pushed him back firmly. "Where's Veronica?"

"Your friend is fine," the man said. His voice was low and calm. "You're in my village. My name is Rom, I'm a doctor. Do you remember coming here last night?"

Angelus did, somewhat. He looked slowly around the room. It was small, with close-cropped walls and a low ceiling. There was a vase of flowers on a small table in the center of the room, bright white daisies with egg yolk-yellow centers. There was a dresser next to the bed, and Angelus understood he was in someone's bedroom.

"This is my home," Rom said calmly. "Your friend is in the other room, at the end of the hall. I can take you to see her, once I ask you a few questions."

"I need to see her now," Angelus said, throwing the blanket off himself. His clothes were gone, replaced with a gray nightshirt that fell to the middle of his thighs.

"Like hell," another voice, younger, snapped from the doorway. A boy, probably in his teens, glared at Angelus, a short sword in his hand. "You'll answer his questions first."

"Like hell," Angelus echoed, with several degrees more venom. He took a step toward the boy, but Rom stepped between them, hand on Angelus' chest, as the boy raised his sword. Angelus could tell by the way he stood he didn't know how to use it.

"That won't be necessary, Aaron," Rom said to the boy, voice authoritative and sharp, a voice used to being heard and obeyed.

Aaron seethed, but lowered his weapon. Angelus didn't relax, his fists were clenched and ready to smash the boy's face in if he had to.

"Where is she?" Angelus bit out, eyes cutting to Rom.

"I'll take you to her right away." He gestured with a hand to something on the table. "My wife laundered your clothes. Perhaps you would like to dress first?"

Angelus stepped back, turning to the table. He grabbed his pants and put them on, leaving the nightshirt, and shoved on his boots. Then he strode to the door, Aaron stepping out of his way to avoid collision. Rom kept pace beside him, gesturing to a door at the end of the hallway. "Through here," he said.

Angelus wrenched the door open, but the room was empty except for a bed and some rickety wooden furniture. Angelus

176

whirled on Rom. "Where is she?" he demanded, not bothering to keep his voice down.

"She must have gone outside with my wife," Rom said calmly. "Right this way. There's no need to shout."

Angelus would be the judge of that. He followed Rom out the front door of the small house, and he found himself standing in a little grassy yard, a clothes line stretching across it. And there was Veronica, smiling as she spoke to a woman with silvery hair and a lined face, aged with sun like Rom's, a smile lighting up her own face. Veronica turned when she heard the door open, her eyes locking with Angelus'. Her cheeks were pink, her dark eyes dancing with light. She wore a moss-green dress someone must have given her, though it was too long and the hem brushed the grass.

Angelus almost lost his footing looking at her. Something was squeezing his chest so tight he thought he might die. *She's alive.*

They stepped toward each other in unison, and Veronica closed the remaining distance, wrapping her arms around his middle. Angelus just stood, paralyzed.

"You're awake!" There was relief in her voice, and also something like a laugh.

Angelus let his hands slide over her hair, disbelief making him clumsy and uncertain. "You... you're alright?"

Veronica smiled up at him, stepping back and releasing him. Angelus wished she wouldn't. "I'm fine," she said. "Rom fixed me. I've never been better."

Angelus believed her. She was practically glowing. He turned to Rom in disbelief. Rom nodded, accepting the thanks Angelus couldn't voice aloud.

Placing a hand on Angelus' shoulder, Rom addressed Veronica when he said, "Why don't you finish helping Pauline? We'll join you for dinner in a moment." With the barest pressure, Rom steered Angelus across the grass and onto the street outside the house. For the first time, Angelus took in his surroundings properly. The village was a smattering of short, wide brick buildings, and beyond them were two narrow stone towers that sat several feet apart, forming a passage for people and wagons to come and go from the road. A wall of stone, almost as tall as Angelus, surrounded the perimeter of the village. Even from a distance, Angelus could see armed men milling about the towers. They wore no armor, so Angelus didn't think they were soldiers. Civilians?

Angelus turned in a slow circle, taking in the place. At first, it looked like any village, but closer inspection revealed the glaring difference. Women in small gardens hovered over plants growing alarmingly fast, a small green stem suddenly flowering before Angelus' eyes as though months had passed in a handful of seconds. On the doorstep of a nearby house, Angelus saw a man painting a symbol on the front door with black paint, and it shimmered like heat rising off a street, before the symbol vanished.

"What is this place?" Angelus asked Rom.

Rom smiled. "A place I very much want to protect." He glanced back at where Veronica was still standing, helping the older woman hang clothes on the clothesline. "That's something I believe you understand."

Angelus did. "The fight with Wielders is not mine."

"I believe you. Others might not, not at first. There aren't many who are friendly to our kind, especially not now." Angelus thought of Finn, of Avery and the innkeepers. Allies were rare, but they existed.

"Your friend," Rom said, starting down the street again, Angelus walking beside him, "Was very ill when you brought her here. Do you know why?"

Angelus shook his head.

Rom appeared unsurprised. "Neither did she. I could tell right away, she uses her Magic infrequently. Too infrequently. You have to understand, Magic is like water, and Wielders are like pitchers. So long as the water has somewhere to go, the pitcher never gets too full. But when the water is trapped, the pitcher overflows. The Magic needs an outlet, or it can cause great suffering. Hers manifested physically. I believe it has been for a long time."

Angelus remembered the night he had awoken to her cries, the way she couldn't control her breathing, how tightly she held onto him. She said the attacks had been happening since she was ten years old. How long, he wondered, had Veronica been sick; a secret, perhaps even to herself? But there was also her constant fatigue, the ill pallor to her skin and the dimness of her eyes Angelus had observed the first time he ever saw her, that never seemed to entirely go away. Glimpsing her from a distance, watching through windows, he'd seen her haunted face, how she hid it when Finn was around. But when she was alone— or thought she was alone— her face had been so fragile. Angelus had spent countless nights, lying in the soldiers quarters, wondering why, while a string tugged at something in his chest. Even after

Finn had gone to the castle, Angelus kept watch over the house, far more frequently than Andromeda had instructed him to. He couldn't help it. She was just...

Angelus shook himself, forcing his thoughts back to earth. "How did you help her?" he asked Rom.

"I had to drain some of her Magic. The pitcher is no longer overflowing. But it will fill again, and fast. Do you understand?"

Angelus nodded.

"Have you seen her use Magic before?" Rom asked.

"Once."

"And was she able to control it?"

He recalled the wall of flame, how she'd lost consciousness immediately after, as though she expelled part of her soul along with the Magic. "I... I don't think so."

"And she started to become ill afterward, correct? Probably gradually at first, then all at once?"

Shivers thrilled up Angelus' arms. That was exactly what had happened.

His silence was answer enough, and Rom nodded, looking pained.

They walked in silence for a while before Angelus asked, "How are these people able to practice Magic in the open?" The penalty for practicing Magic was death. Angelus had been there when the law was passed. "Why aren't the soldiers arresting them?"

"I'd like to see them try," came a voice from behind them.

Angelus turned, his lip curling when he caught sight of Aaron, along with a couple other boys his age coming up the road, their shortswords out like badges of honor. Angelus hoped they tripped and fell on them, and learned a lesson in carrying weapons properly.

"If soldiers try to get through the wall," Aaron continued, nodding to the towers, "They'll have a hell of a fight on their hands."

"It hasn't become necessary yet," Rom told Angelus. "But Aaron is right, they won't get far." He continued, at Angelus' surprised look, "After the ban on Magic passed, we fortified this village. No one unfriendly to our kind is getting through. Thus far, our Magic has remained a secret to everyone on the outside."

Cold fear trickled over Angelus, his stomach hardening. Were these people insane? Artemis could send an army to demolish this village if he suspected the residents were Wielders.

Rom smiled, reading Angelus' thoughts on his face. "We have Magic, and weapons, but resistance is our true weapon."

Insane indeed. But also brave.

They walked to the towers, and Angelus saw several armed men, most with swords though there were a few with bows and arrows, talking amongst themselves goodnaturedly.

Could these men fight? Angelus wondered. Could they fend off an attack of trained soldiers? Of monsters?

"You know your way around weapons," Rom said to Angelus. It wasn't a question.

Angelus frowned. "How do you—"

Rom pulled one of Angelus' knives from his pocket, handing it to him. "People don't carry a set of knives like that in their vest for decoration, now do they?"

The corner of Angelus' mouth lifted in the barest hint of a smirk. They certainly did not. "I have a few tricks," Angelus said.

Rom smiled, but Aaron looked unconvinced. "What's a pretty knife against a sword?"

Angelus snapped his wrist toward Aaron, the blade flashing through the air so fast Aaron could only suck in a shocked breath before the hilt was protruding from the building behind him, right above his head.

Rom laughed, delighted, and Aaron stormed off, face red, his friends following behind him.

Angelus retrieved his knife, the blade stuck in the space between two bricks. When he turned around, Rom was smiling approvingly, hands on his hips.

"We could use a man like you," he said. "We always need more able bodies."

A lot of good that would do them, Angelus thought, if Artemis brought his army of creatures here. This fortress, even with the advantage of Magic, couldn't last forever. Not if Mayva didn't return.

"I can't," Angelus said, even as his stomach twinged with regret. "I have my own task to finish." He swallowed. "But... Veronica. Would she be safe here?"

Rom smiled. "If she wanted to stay, there would be a place for her." Something about the way he said it made Angelus think Rom doubted Veronica would want to stay. There was no reason for doubt— after the last two days, if she wasn't eager to get away from him, Angelus would be shocked. She couldn't— wouldn't— choose him over *this*. This place. Her own people, her culture.

"If she wanted to stay," Angelus echoed. *Please Veronica, stay here.* Saying goodbye would be so much easier if she said it first.

ANGELUS hardly saw Veronica that day; Rom took him on a tour of the village, introducing him to residents as a "friend," which Angelus wasn't sure how to feel about. He was no one's *friend*.

He was coerced into spending the night, and Rom invited him to stay for Harvest Festival.

"Harvest Festival?" Angelus asked, gathering up his supplies. He wanted to leave first thing in the morning. He picked up the tattered satchel, frowning at it. The thing was ruined.

"I'll find you another one," Rom said, nodding to the satchel. "Harvest Festival is a holiday we celebrate every year. You should join us. Veronica has already agreed to attend."

He wanted to see her, just one last time before he left the next morning. "Alright."

Rom beamed, and Angelus frowned at him. "Why haven't you asked me who I am? Why are you trusting me?" he asked.

Rom cocked his head. "You saved one of our own. She trusts you, so I will too."

Angelus sat down on the bed. "There's something you should know. It isn't only soldiers looking for Wielders. There's something else."

Rom's brows rose. "And what would that be?"

*   *   *

BY nightfall, the village was bright with torch and lantern light. Angelus followed the procession of men, women, and children as they made their way to an open patch of land, an enormous, roaring bonfire at its center.

Angelus watched the crowd, catching sight of a few armed men bending their ears toward Aaron, who was passing along Angelus' warning to Rom. Soon the entire village would have heard about the creatures coming to find them. One of the men nodded, and disappeared into the night, probably to spread word of the new security measures. Every man who was capable would be armed and on their guard. They were right to fear monsters more than men.

"You asked why I trust you," Rom had said after Angelus told him. He hadn't revealed anything about his identity, only warned of the danger headed their way. "This is why."

He found Veronica near the bonfire, watching a group of girls in white dresses dance together, arms linked, chains of braided flowers in their hair. Music hummed to life, a violin hidden somewhere in the crowd.

Angelus walked toward her, and she raised her eyes to his when she spotted him. She smiled, and Angelus' stomach tumbled down an invisible staircase.

"Are you alright?" Angelus asked when he reached her, bending down to speak into her ear so she could hear him over the music and the chatter of the crowd.

She nodded. "Yes." Peering up at him she asked, "Are you?"

He wasn't listening. He was caught in her scent, in the way her dark eyes sparkled in the firelight. Her hair, usually braided, was down, falling in long dark waves over her shoulders. It looked so soft. It took him a long time to answer, having forgotten her question. "Yes," he finally said, a little too quickly. "Of course."

He glanced around at the growing crowd, more dancers joining the girls twirling around the fire. "What is this?" he asked.

Veronica watched the dancers. They were graceful white wraiths, wisps of pale smoke twirling through the air like a dream, or an old memory nearly forgotten.

She leaned closer to him, and he had to bend down again to catch her voice. Her breath tickled his ear, and his pulse tripped over itself. "Harvest Festival. The fire invites the Goddess to the village, and they dance to ask her to bless their harvest."

"Do you celebrate it?" Angelus asked, voice barely a breath, afraid to ask her anything about her past. She never spoke of it, and Angelus could understand that.

She swallowed. "No. But my mother told me about it."

They were silent for a long time, nothing except the wind and the crackling fire and the violin music filling the space around them.

"Rom said my Magic is what made me sick."

Angelus stilled, waiting. This felt like a dangerous conversation, a secret he wasn't supposed to know.

"He said... not using my Magic was like drinking poison everyday, and believing it's medicine."

"Why don't you use it?" Angelus asked— carefully, so carefully.

Her eyes fell to the fire, a blazing inferno not so different from the wall of flame he had seen her create. "Because it only ever hurts people," she whispered, her face darkening.

I don't want to burn. He remembered her saying those words. She had been ill, feverish, but he thought she still meant them.

"It's ugly," she said with finality.

Angelus looked around at the crowd, at the dancers and the fire. There was so much *life*, the ground itself seemed to pulse like a heartbeat. Sparks from the fire floated up into the air, but instead of disappearing into the night, they hovered around the fire, pulsing in time with the music.

Magic.

It was power. It was life. It filled these people.

It was not ugly. Maybe it could be, but not then, not in that moment.

Angelus leaned toward Veronica, his lips accidentally bumping the side of her ear as he whispered, "I thought it was beautiful."

"What was?" she breathed, not moving, not looking at him as she spoke.

"Your Magic. Your fire. I thought it was beautiful."

Her eyes found his, wide with surprise, but before she could answer, the violin died down and someone shouted, "Praise the Goddess!"

The crowd cheered, faces beaming. Men carried tables, setting them down on the grass so women could set plates of food and pitchers of drink on them. Glasses were passed around, and Angelus retrieved two, one for himself and the other for Veronica. He offered it to her, and she accepted it. Her smile burned more than the alcohol.

He watched her be pulled away by one of the dancing girls, resisting at first, but then laughing when the girl spun her in a circle. Angelus sat down on the grass, a little ways off from the crowd, and watched Veronica twirl, her long hair fanning out around her, the skirt of her gown twining around her legs. He watched, because that was all he had ever done. Watch from afar.

Someone touched his shoulder, and Angelus flinched, badly, jumping to his feet. One of the men he'd seen on guard at the towers earlier took a quick, startled step backward. "Apologies," he said. Angelus was spared the necessity of answering as the man continued, "Rom says you're good with a knife. Help with the patrol of the north-east sector?"

Angelus stole a glance back at Veronica. She was still dancing, laughing with her head thrown back, cheeks flushed from the alcohol, or maybe she was just happy. It made his chest ache.

"Let's go," was all he said.

*   *   *

"WHAT are we looking for?" Angelus asked as he followed three other men through a cluster of trees on the north end of the village, just outside the stone wall. There was nothing but fruit trees clustered around the worn footpaths. One of the men carried a torch, and the firelight turned the fruit into formless black creatures hanging from the branches.

"Mountain bandits have been spotted around here," the man carrying the torch explained. Angelus thought he heard someone call him Cal. "They've been attacking wagons on nearby roads, and even robbing a few small groups of soldiers from the castle. We think they might set their sights on the village."

Angelus frowned. Something pricked at his memory. Thieves. Intercepting soldiers. Then he remembered. Veronica's money from the castle; it had never been delivered. Could there be bandits spread out as far as her village? He hadn't heard anything about bandits, not even while he was in the castle.

Cal glanced back at Angelus. "Is it true you're not a Wielder?"

Angelus let silence be his answer, too tired and irritated to want to speak.

Cal shook his head. "I didn't believe it when Rom told me. There aren't many non-Wielders who are on our side."

Angelus bristled. He wasn't on anyone's *side*.

He didn't answer Cal, just continued walking in silence, eyes scanning the land around them.

"It's clear," someone up ahead called. "You two get back to the festival, we'll finish the patrol and come join you."

Cal nodded, handing his torch to one of the other men and gesturing for Angelus to follow him. By the time they returned to the party, Angelus was restless, the feel of his clothes too much against his legs, his wrists and shoulders. His irritation only grew when he saw Veronica, drink in hand, laughing at something Aaron was saying. Another boy stood on Veronica's other side, eyes clouded with alcohol and a grin clouded with desire.

Angelus sneered, grabbing a drink he knew would only worsen his mood, but he didn't care. He kept his eye on Veronica. She clumsily raised her glass to her lips, and Aaron took hold of her wrist, laughing.

Angelus slammed his empty glass down on the table and stalked toward them. He snatched Veronica's drink from her hand, smoothly pushing Aaron out of the way with his shoulder as he did so. "You've had enough," Angelus said, tossing the contents of the glass over his shoulder. Aaron scrambled backward to keep from being splashed.

Veronica pouted, her cheeks bright pink. "I only had a little," she whined.

Angelus grabbed her shoulder, being careful not to do it too forcefully, and steered her away from the drunk boys, who looked on with disappointment. A satisfied smirk morphed Angelus' features for just a moment.

"You need to be careful," he warned, leaning forward so he could speak quietly to her. She turned, brushing his hand away.

"I was just talking to them," she said, a whine still fixed to her voice, making her sound about fifteen years younger.

Angelus sighed, but before he could speak, Veronica asked, her voice more serious, "Where were you?"

Angelus frowned. "I was helping with a patrol. Why?"

She crossed her arms, looking tipsy and self conscious. "I thought... maybe you left. Without me."

A fist clamped around Angelus' lungs. "No. No, I'm right here."

Veronica stepped closer to him, a little unsteady on her feet, and placed her palm on his chest. "Here," she agreed. "Don't go anywhere."

Angelus stilled under her touch, eyes falling to the place her warm palm connected with his chest.

"I won't be in the way," she promised. "I'm better now. Well, not right now, I think I'm drunk, but I'm not sick. I can keep up. I can... help?" She said the last word like a question, as though she wasn't sure but she wanted to be.

Angelus shook his head. "Veronica, you don't have to worry about that." He swallowed. "But... what if you got sick again?"

She shook her head. "I won't. I won't let it get that bad again, I promise."

Angelus glanced around at the party happening all around them. The bonfire had grown larger, and its proximity heated his entire body. Or maybe that was just Veronica's touch. "You don't want to stay here, with people like you?" It killed him to ask it, but it had to be said.

She pressed her hand into his chest a bit harder, curling her fingers into his shirt. Lightning bolts traveled from his stomach all the way down to his toes. "I don't belong here."

"But you're one of them."

She shook her head again. "I'm not. Not really. I don't fit with regular people, because of my Magic. I don't fit with *them,* because I don't use my Magic." She looked up at him, a sad smile on her face. "They're proud of who they are. I'll never have that. I'll never... fit."

Angelus tipped his head toward her. "But... you fit with me?" He'd meant to say it teasingly, but his voice was too low, too soft.

To his surprise, she smiled a little. "I might."

The bonfire's flames were inside him, burning him alive. All the air had been sucked out of Angelus' body, leaving only fire. And he knew, in that moment, that there was no leaving her behind.

They didn't move, just stood there, looking at each other, and Angelus wondered if she too felt fists crushing her lungs, as he did. He had been stupid to think she was safer without him. No one would protect her like he would.

Her face changed slightly, and she opened her mouth to say something, but froze when a scream suddenly tore through the night, followed by another, and another, until Angelus understood.

Artemis' creatures had arrived.

CHAPTER NINETEEN

A blood-chilling howl, like that of an enormous, deranged dog, tore through the night, getting closer and closer, until three hulking figures could be seen hurtling toward the bonfire on all fours. One of them had something clamped in its teeth, and even as Angelus grabbed Veronica and started running, he could see what it was. A human arm, veins and strings of torn flesh dripping blood.

Angelus couldn't hear or think over the screaming. The only thought in his head was, *get Veronica out.*

Rom was bellowing over the chaos, but his words were stolen by the screams. The wolves launched themselves into the crowd, throwing people, children, out of their way, snapping long sharp teeth.

As he ran, he could feel the ruined identification necklace bounce against his chest. How could they have found him without it?

"Are they here for you?" Veronica gasped, running beside him, her hand crushed in his.

Angelus glanced back. The wolves moved with no formation, no premeditation. They were simply killing, slaughtering. Angelus understood then. This was not a hunt. This was a massacre. Artemis must have learned of this village's existence, and he had sent his monsters to destroy them. This was not like Veronica's village. All of these people were going to die.

Something enormous crashed into Angelus' spine, breaking his hold on Veronica's hand. He hit the ground, his face smashing into the earth so hard his vision blurred. Hot breath scorched his neck, and huge claws pressed down on his arms. It had him pinned, he couldn't get up. It was going to kill him and he couldn't even see it.

Then the weight vanished.

Angelus flipped over onto his back, expecting a monster rearing its ugly head back, ready to tear into his throat, but there was only sky above him. He scrambled to his feet, Veronica appearing at his side and clutching his arm.

"Are you alright?" she screeched, her voice bordering on hysterical.

Angelus couldn't answer. He could only stare as the beast, standing on its hind legs and revealing its vaguely human torso, stretched wide with chiseled muscles covered in thick black fur, snapped its jaws at... thin air. It threw its body against some invisible wall, unable to get through. Then Angelus saw Rom, his hands stretched out before him. A shield. He had created a shield.

"Go!" Rom shouted at Angelus.

For a moment, Angelus was frozen, staring at the gaping mouth full of teeth that had nearly torn his head off. That had been a human. Once. And Artemis had ruined him.

"Angelus!" Veronica's voice brought him back, and, reclaiming her hand, they ran. The streets of the village were mayhem, people running into their homes, or the homes of neighbors, and barricading their doors— flimsy slabs of wood that were no match for those monsters.

"Where's the house?" Angelus demanded, searching for Rom's home.

"There," Veronica panted, pointing.

They hurried inside, bolting the door behind them, as if it would do any good. Angelus ran to the bedroom he had slept in, grabbing the satchel of supplies, the blankets, and the sack of food from beneath the bed. There was a knapsack on the bed, the one Rom had promised to replace the satchel with, and Angelus dumped everything into it and slung it over his shoulder.

"Where are we going?" Veronica asked, her arms crossed as she fought down her shivering. "We have to help them!"

"We can't do anything," Angelus said, leading the way back to the front door.

"So we're just going to leave them?" Veronica's voice cracked softly.

Angelus looked at her pleadingly. "I'm sorry." And he was. But they had to get out. This village was a grave for anyone who stayed.

When Veronica hesitated, Angelus' stomach fell. "Veronica. Are you coming with me, or not?"

Her eyes found his face. "Yes," she said, voice barely audible.

He took her hand, and they ran back out into the night, into the air filled with screams and the streets slick with blood.

Angelus nearly slipped in a thick pool of red, oozing from the broken skull of a young woman laying in the street. She appeared to have been trampled, but Angelus wasn't sure if that had been before or after her head was crushed by an enormous jaw. He dragged Veronica down the street, away from the carnage and toward the towers and the forest-lined mountain road beyond.

And if they encountered a beast on the road? Angelus couldn't think about that, not yet. They had to get out of the village first.

The screaming didn't stop. It sounded like one long, high wail, but it was many, one starting when another ended. The air was thick with the scent of blood, and it made Angelus want to gag. That smell was familiar. The fear, the panic, the screaming of his breath, it was all too familiar.

He remembered the water, the cold lake weighing down his clothes, dragging her body away from him on the current.

Blood. The scent of her blood had clung to her... her body...

Angelus ran harder, faster, and he and Veronica bolted between the towers. He could see bodies lying along the stone wall, explosions of red smeared across the gray stone. He didn't look any closer, just kept running, eyes fixed on the road ahead, and he didn't slow down until the screams started to fade— not because they had ended, but because they were getting farther away. They had been prepared for men, not monsters, to attack.

If we had gotten there sooner, if I had warned them sooner...

Angelus only stopped running when Veronica halted suddenly, jerking her hand free of Angelus' grip and doubling over, hands on her knees, her breaths ragged.

Angelus grabbed her shoulder, scanning the road and the surrounding trees. They could be anywhere. There could be one just feet away and Angelus wouldn't know until it was too late. He couldn't fight them. *He couldn't fight them.*

"Come on," he gasped, almost begging.

Veronica straightened unsteadily, still struggling to catch her breath. Her eyes were wide and shining in the dark. There was the fear Angelus expected, but there was also something else. Something harder. "We have to find her, Angelus." Her voice wavered, choking slightly.

Angelus didn't immediately understand what she meant. Then he realized. Queen Mayva. "We will," Angelus said, and he meant it.

"This can't be for nothing."

Angelus didn't think she only meant the village behind them. "It won't be," he promised.

*   *   *

THE sun was beginning to rise when exhaustion finally claimed both Angelus and Veronica. His muscles spasmed, his eyes itched from fatigue. As the sky began to lighten, they found a patch of grass under a canopy of dense trees and crumpled to the ground, breathless.

Angelus didn't know how far they were from the village, but he couldn't go any further without rest. He didn't bother with a blanket. He laid on his stomach, cheek pressed to the cool, damp ground, and his eyes closed instantly. He dimly sensed Veronica beside him, her breathing strained and exhausted, the same as his. Before he fell asleep, he thought he heard her try to smother a sob.

Angelus' fist curled in the long, wet grass. He could still smell blood. The grass was cold in his hand, sticky and damp, and all he could think of was her. Her hair, wet and silky in his hands. Salt. Blood.

The images clawed at the corners of his mind, reaching black, taloned hands from the shadows, and he squeezed his eyes shut, trying to escape, to banish them. He thought of the letter, her final words to him, and heat burned in his throat. He couldn't think about it, couldn't examine the memories too closely. He had to stay present, undistracted. Veronica needed him. He couldn't be pulled under now.

But he couldn't help but wonder, would he ever stop watching people die?

*   *   *

ANGELUS was underwater. The black water of the lake froze him to his core, jabbing icicles into his veins, but he kept swimming.

"Angelus!" Andromeda screamed, reaching for him, before her head was sucked underneath the surface.

Angelus dove under to follow her, reaching desperately for her hand. She was sinking, an invisible weight pulling her down. He was so close, her fingertips brushing his. But then her eyes changed. In the dimness, her irises burned gold.

And then it was no longer Andromeda reaching for him.

Veronica opened her mouth, as though to cry out his name, but the water rendered her silent. He froze, shocked, and that second of hesitation was all it took. She disappeared beneath the dark water, and she was gone, as if she had never been there at all.

* * *

ANGELUS woke up cold. The forest's thick foliage blocked the sun from reaching him, and he shivered in the dewy grass. The dream had stolen all the air from his lungs, and he could only lay there, unable to reach for the blanket in the knapsack, unable to do anything.

A soft rustle whispered beside him, and he turned his head enough to see Veronica shift in her sleep. Her back was to him, and her braid had come undone, leaving a dark waterfall of hair trailing into the grass. For a moment, for a single heartbeat, he thought she looked like Andromeda. But then she turned onto her back, and he saw her face.

He turned away, squeezing his eyes shut. He reached out, and found her arm. He let his fingers wrap around her wrist, lightly, carefully, so as not to wake her. Even with his skin touching hers, she still felt miles away, and Angelus could only float on a current dragging him further and further from shore.

CHAPTER TWENTY

VERONICA couldn't remember the last time her body felt so light. Her chest, arms, and legs were almost weightless, despite the mountain becoming steeper and the climb tougher. She was keeping up with Angelus, though he was likely still going slower than he would have alone, and it was a little victory despite the unease prickling at her mind. Even that was milder than it might have been ordinarily— she could think about the fear, not just be consumed by it.

But she was still afraid. How long would this feeling last? How long could she put off the Magic? How long until it came back with a vengeance, needing to be released?

She shook her head to clear it, and Angelus glanced back at her. "You alright?"

"Yes," she said quickly. She was humiliated by how much he had needed to take care of her, and was determined never to let it happen again. If she kept needing him, he would eventually understand she was more of a hindrance than a help. And he would leave her behind. He had tried already— he'd wanted her to stay in Rom's village. He had never said it, but she could tell. He'd been planning to leave.

Though, if he had, she would be dead by now.

A terrible chill clawed its way up her spine and over her shoulders, and she clenched her jaw. She could still smell the blood, her throat coated with it.

Angelus' shoulders shifted as he turned back to the trail before them— though "trail" might have been a bit generous. It was a stretch of dirt weaving through the thickly clustered trees; Angelus had been adamant they not use the main roads unless absolutely necessary. Veronica could see a stain of sweat coloring the back of his shirt. The days were still warm, but the nights were getting colder. Last night Veronica had barely been able to sleep because of the cold. It didn't help that their map had been left behind, and they were back to relying solely on Angelus' memory. But he hadn't failed thus far in navigating, so Veronica tried to put the worry to rest.

Angelus stopped abruptly, holding his hand up, and Veronica paused. She didn't hear anything except the birds overhead and the soft hiss of the leaves around them, but Angelus held perfectly still. Images of the wolves flashed across her mind, and the sweat on her skin turned cold.

Angelus lowered his hand, turning back to face her. "We need to get farther away from the road," he said, voice low. "I hear wagons."

Veronica followed as he turned right and moved deeper into the trees. She had no idea how he wasn't utterly lost; everything looked the same to Veronica. No intuition appeared to guide her north, no instinct prompted her to follow one path over another. She was the follower. But she trusted Angelus enough to follow.

The longer they walked, the rockier the ground became, trees giving way slightly to reveal enormous pale rocks and boulders protruding from the ground, forming something like a wall, a few feet taller than Angelus, that blocked the wind coming from the east. It was suddenly much quieter without the wind, and the sound of her breathing was abruptly deafening.

Angelus glanced back at her, and she knew he had noticed the change too. He didn't smile, but his eyes were less hard. She remembered, like an almost forgotten dream, the vision of his smile.

The idea of peeking inside him, whether by accident or intentionally, made her insides squirm. The visions had never come from touching a person before, she doubted she could do it anyway. But still...

"We should stop here for the night."

Veronica had to blink several times before she understood what Angelus said, and to register what he was pointing at. A short, wide opening in the rock wall. A cave. Veronica was short enough to walk inside easily, while Angelus had to bend slightly to fit. She couldn't imagine being that tall, it looked cumbersome.

The cave was completely silent except for their breathing. It was dark, and hard to discern its size, but if it was wide enough for Veronica to lay down and sleep she didn't much care how big it was. Angelus handed her the sack of supplies, and she pulled out the blankets and food.

"Hand me the flint," Angelus said, holding out his hand. "I'll make a fire."

"Is it safe?" Veronica asked. It was probably a stupid question, but Angelus seemed to know what she meant.

"The smoke will be invisible once it's dark." With the heavy cloud cover, the moon would be practically nonexistent, turning the landscape around them black. And with the bottom of the cave sloping down from the entrance, the light of a fire would be mostly hidden.

Veronica dug around in the sack until she found the stones, and handed them to Angelus. He pocketed them. "I'll get some wood."

Veronica's stomach twinged with nerves. Neither of them had gone off by themselves since they left Rom's village. She nodded slowly. "Just... be careful."

He didn't say anything, only stepped out of the cave and disappeared.

Veronica poked through the food they had left, taking out the fruits starting to get soft and brown. She was starving, and it surprised her a bit. Even on the farm, she'd never possessed much of an appetite. But now she was famished, as though something inside her had shifted, making room for hunger. Was that her Magic too? What else was not using it doing to her?

Her flesh crawled, the Magic like insects under her skin.

Not yet, she thought. *I can wait a little longer.*

But what if she couldn't wait? What if she got sick again? *He'll leave,* she thought.

She went still in the little cave. It was so quiet.

Angelus still wasn't back.

Dread filled her chest with cold mist.

She got to her feet, walking slowly to the mouth of the cave. If he wasn't out there... if he was gone... if he left her behind...

She had to clap her hand over her mouth to keep from shrieking when he suddenly appeared, nearly walking straight into her. His arms were full of twigs and dry grass, and he stared at her in surprise, then worry. "What?"

She lowered her hand, shaking her head quickly. "Nothing, you were just gone so long. I thought..." *You left... something happened to you...* She didn't finish.

Angelus set down the branches and grass and turned to her. "You don't have to worry about me, nothing's going to happen to me." He sounded so certain. Or perhaps merely unperturbed. Veronica didn't think he much cared if something happened to him. Dying didn't seem to scare him. Nothing did.

"You better be right." She meant to say it lightly, but her voice held something of a warning. Surprise and confusion clouded his face, but then it cleared. He looked down at the twigs and grass, and said, "You do it."

Veronica blinked. "Do what?"

"Light the fire."

Veronica's eyes widened, and she immediately shook her head. Angelus sat down on the ground, a stubborn set to his jaw.

"Rom said you got sick because you don't use your Magic enough. You're not going through that again."

You're not putting me *through that again,* Veronica thought he really meant. She swallowed. "I... I can't."

"Why not?" The question was hard, sharp, as though Veronica were being intentionally difficult.

Veronica stuck her hands out, palms up, helpless. "I don't know how... how to *control* it. It usually comes out by accident, and it's *bigger* than I know what to do with." She could tell by his face he didn't understand, and Veronica couldn't blame him. *She didn't understand either.* "And the fire... the fire is the worst. I didn't mean to do as much damage as I did." She sighed, closing her eyes for a moment.

Angelus got to his feet and stepped in front of her. "Then try another," he said, his voice softer. "A different spell."

Veronica's breath left her in a hard exhale. "You make it sound like I can do anything. I can't. I never learned. I've only ever used fire."

His brow furrowed in confusion. Of course he was confused. She was a Wielder that didn't know how to use Magic. Veronica agreed, it didn't make any sense. But it was the truth.

"No one taught you?" he asked. "Your family? Anyone?"

Her family. No, her family had not taught her. They said it was dangerous, they had kept her inside, hidden, as much as possible. She could recall their fear, like a heavy, sharp scent in the air. Constant, unending fear. Fear that their daughter would be discovered. Veronica hadn't understood how poorly the Wielders were treated back then— it had been close to ten years, and it had only gotten worse every day. Her parents, she thought, had been afraid of this. What the world was becoming, had already become. So Veronica hid. And she was still hiding. She'd lost her home, her family, but that fact remained unchanged. She had only ever learned one spell, one symbol.

She remembered smoke. Fire. Heat. Screaming. The crash of the ceiling falling down around her, covered in flames that somehow hadn't touched her.

Her pulse began to race, her stomach rolling over and over. Her breathing was growing uneven, panic building in her throat, crushing her windpipe. She didn't realize her hands were shaking until Angelus took them in his, his long fingers wrapping around her palms and spreading warmth into her cold, cold skin. For someone with so much fire trapped inside, she was a painfully cold creature.

"Alright," he said quickly. "Alright. I'm not going to force you, gods." He looked uncomfortable, unsure what to say or what to do. That made two of them.

It would be so easy, for now, to ignore it. But she would become ill again. Maybe it would take a year, maybe it would take a day. But the Magic still wanted out. It didn't care if Veronica was ready or not.

She had to swallow the lump in her throat before she could speak. "I don't want to hurt you."

Angelus blinked in surprise. He shook his head. "You won't. Is that what you're worried about?" His eyes were somehow both pitying and amused, and it only made Veronica feel more pathetic. He seemed to remember he was still holding her hands, and pulled his away, crossing his arms like he was cold. "When you're ready, you don't have to worry about me."

Veronica nodded, releasing a tight breath.

Angelus used the flint stones to light the fire.

*　　*　　*

WHEN Veronica woke up, the small fire was nothing but embers, and when she turned to face the mouth of the cave from where she lay on the smooth floor, she saw the night was a solid, endless black. She also saw Angelus sitting in the cave's mouth, his face turned up to the night sky like he was waiting for something. He had to be freezing, wearing nothing but his boots, pants and the thin black shirt Rom had given him. It was too large for him, making him appear oddly small.

Veronica stood up, taking one of the blankets with her. Angelus didn't react when she sat down beside him, the wadded up blanket in her hands.

"Aren't you cold?" she asked.

He shook his head, but Veronica draped the blanket over his shoulders anyway. He didn't move for a moment, but then he turned his face slightly into the blanket, as though trying to catch some of the warmth with his lips. She could see he was holding something in his hands, and it took her a moment to recognize it. The broken identification necklace. He was turning the blackened glass over and over with the tips of his fingers, the motion slow and hypnotic.

"Can't sleep?" Veronica asked.

Angelus' shoulder twitched in a half shrug.

"Bad dreams?" Veronica knew something about those.

He made a noncommittal sound in the back of his throat.

Veronica folded her hands in her lap, unexpectedly nervous. "I... dream sometimes. About things that haven't happened yet. And then they come true."

Angelus leaned forward, his head turned, trying to look at her face, but Veronica kept her head down. "Do they always come true?"

She shook her head. Not so far, anyway.

"Are they good things?"

She was silent.

"No," he replied for her, sounding disappointed but unsurprised, like he had known all along the future was bleak, but had wanted to be contradicted nonetheless.

"I dreamt Finn dying." She'd never voiced it aloud before, and she felt oddly wrong, as though this were a dirty secret, never meant to be disclosed, something to take to her grave. She didn't realize until she finally said it, how much fear she'd harbored because of those dreams. Did she dream them because they would come true? Or did they come true because she dreamt them?

Veronica drew in a shaky breath. She remembered the fear, the panic, in the dream when she fell with him. When she felt him die. But he didn't just die— he'd been killed.

Tears burned her eyes suddenly, and she couldn't breathe. Finn's golden hair and smiling eyes were a sun that would never rise again. The blackness of the night seemed infinite.

Angelus swallowed, staring out at the night as though wanting it to swallow him. "I'm sorry," he said. "I never said it... but I am sorry."

Veronica swallowed the ache in her throat, a tear running the length of her nose and dripping off the tip onto her clenched hands. She swiped her sleeve across her face, and glanced at the necklace in his hands. "I'm sorry, too. About Queen Andromeda."

Angelus paused his slow turning of the glass in his hands, and Veronica asked quietly, "What was she like?"

"She was..." Angelus trailed off, and Veronica looked up at him. His face was pale, his jaw clenched tight as if he were in pain, but otherwise he wore no expression at all.

"Who was she to you?" Veronica whispered, leaning slightly toward him, as though hiding her words from the listening night.

She expected to see sadness, but if there was any it was choked by the dark, *dark* expression on his face. Anger. It was gone as soon as it appeared, and Veronica could have believed she imagined it. The guilt she had sensed radiating off the letter, the one the queen had written Angelus, came back to her. She remembered seeing Angelus through the queen's eyes. Andromeda had hurt Angelus, and she knew it.

Anger, protective and defensive, surged through Veronica's chest. *What did she do to you, Angelus?*

"She..." Angelus' voice was painfully soft, as though his throat had been reduced to the tiniest sliver, and barely any sound could escape. He shook his head, unable to finish. Maybe he didn't know how.

Veronica's eyes stayed on his face, her chest tight. She reached out her hand, and when her palm touched his shoulder, an image flashed through her mind, like a memory. A young, dark haired girl, perhaps sixteen years old, standing over Angelus, hand outstretched, her face haughty and hard and beautiful, body swathed in pink silk. He had been so struck by her impossible beauty. And then her face changed, haughtiness dissolving into pain, into tears. "Promise," Veronica heard her gasp. "Promise you won't leave me." As fragile as the words were, they still sounded like an order.

She drew her hand back quickly, as if burned. "I'm sorry," she whispered, unsure if she was apologizing for the invasion, or for the pain inside him. His expression did not change, and Veronica thought he must not have felt her Magic touch him. She lowered her hands back to her lap. Softer, she repeated, "I'm sorry."

CHAPTER TWENTY-ONE

THEY set off early the next morning. Veronica didn't sleep well. She didn't remember what she dreamt, but it left her with an ominous, haunted feeling that followed her from the cave and out onto the rocky landscape. Her footsteps cracked like thunder on the pebbled ground, sharp rocks digging through the bottoms of her boots. The soles of her feet were hot and sore, and she tried to conceal a grimace as she walked.

Angelus paused, peering up at the line of trees ahead of them. There were hardly any trees in this rocky patch of land, and the oaks and pines looked like smudges of gold and green in the distance. "We're getting close. The checkpoint isn't far from here."

Veronica heard him, but she didn't immediately understand what that meant. They were almost there. The last place Queen Mayva had been seen, where she might still be.

Almost there.

Excitement mingled with anxiety in Veronica's blood, the hope singing in her veins clouded with the fear this would all be for nothing. If the queen wasn't there, then what? How long could they keep searching? How far away was too late?

We'll find her.

They stopped to eat after a few hours of walking, and Veronica winced as she sat down on the ground, her feet and ankles throbbing. She waited until Angelus left to relieve himself to slip off her boots. The bottoms of her feet were red and raw, tender and bruised. With a groan, she flexed her feet, the muscles seizing.

She rummaged through the sack of supplies, looking for her canteen, hoping some water might soothe her skin, and pulled out Finn's satchel. All of the contents had spilled out the tear in the side, which had grown enormous. It was completely useless as a satchel now, and Veronica's heart panged. Finn had owned the bag longer than she'd known him. She set it down next to her, a deflated carcass of old leather, and rifled through their meager supplies. She pulled out the kitchen knife, which she forgot was there, and set it gingerly aside. Finally she found the canteen, but her stomach fell when she felt how light it was. She hadn't seen any water sources for a while, and the sky was nowhere near rain.

Veronica frowned, observing her surroundings. The large rocks separated patches of grassy area. There weren't many trees, but there were some wild flowers growing wherever they could find enough room.

Barefoot, she walked to the flowers growing between two boulders that were three times as tall as Veronica. She followed the clumps of green to a small slope leading down to a grassy area, where the trees hung low and blocked the sun. Veronica slid down the incline, and at the bottom her bare feet met damp grass.

She listened carefully. Birds chirped somewhere nearby, and she followed the noise until she found a flock of black birds congregated around something on the ground, dipping their beaks low to reach... water. It was a narrow vein that must have branched off of a larger stream somewhere further uphill. Veronica hurried to where the birds jumped around the stream on their tiny legs, startling them into flight. She filled her canteen, then stuck her feet into the water, shockingly cold, instantly soothing her sore muscles. She let out a long sigh of relief. The icy water trickled slowly across her skin, and she sat there until the pain in her feet subsided.

A bit regretfully, she got up and started making her way back to the incline. It was a little harder getting up than down, but she managed to pull herself up. She was barely on her feet before she heard a loud, sharp shout. "Veronica?"

Her pulse jumped, and she looked around wildly. Angelus was standing next to the abandoned supplies, his head whipping around as though trying to catch sight of an insect flying about his head.

"Here," she said quickly, relieved he was alright. He spun around, eyes locking on her as she approached.

Veronica held up the canteen by way of explanation. "Sorry," she said in a rush. "But I found—"

A punch of air left his lungs, and his hands flew up to press against the sides of his head, eyes squeezed shut as though in pain.

Veronica stared at him. "A-Angelus? I'm— I'm sorry—"

He dropped his hands, then sat down on the ground with a long sigh. He didn't look at her when he spoke. "Don't wander off like that." His voice was painfully restrained, almost too quiet in its attempt to sound calm. "I thought— I thought—" His eyes finally found her face, and Veronica was frozen under his gaze, wide-eyed and frightened.

She had been wrong before. There was something he was afraid of.

She knelt down in front of him, reaching out to touch him, but quickly withdrew her hand. "I'm sorry," she said again. "I didn't think. I'm alright, I was just looking for water."

He cleared his throat, a sharp, loud sound, and nodded. He ran a hand through his thick black hair, the gesture strangely wary.

"Just..." He sighed.

She remembered that first night he had been in her home, his tight grip around her wrist. *Don't go.*

"I wouldn't just leave," she said. "I'm not going without you."

He grimaced, the expression disappearing quickly, but Veronica still saw it. He got to his feet, trying, but struggling, to make his face appear normal once more. He regarded her for an instant, then his eyes cut away, and Veronica was left with the strange sense she had done something wrong, though she didn't know what.

* * *

ANGELUS filled his canteen in the stream Veronica directed him to, and they set off again, the sun bright, but cold, where it hung in the sky. With her feet less sore, walking was much easier, and she was able to keep up with Angelus. He seemed impressed by this, not because he said anything, but because of the approving arch of his eyebrow when she matched her stride to his. Or, tried to.

"Wait," Angelus said suddenly, and Veronica stopped. They were walking on a long path of hard packed earth, tall pillars of rock on the left side and a drop off to a gravelly crater on the right.

"What's wrong?" Veronica asked, as loudly as she dared.

He pointed to the path before them. "Those are wheel tracks."

Veronica's eyes widened. "Is this a main road?"

Angelus shook his head, bewildered. "No, we're miles away from a connecting road." It was a dangerous place for a wagon, the narrow path caged in by rocks and trees on the left and a sheer drop on the right. "It's a hidden road," Angelus marveled.

"But then—"

The unmistakable sound of hooves and wagon wheels thundered through the air. There was nowhere to go, nowhere to hide. They were trapped.

Angelus grabbed Veronica's hand and pulled her forward, dragging her farther up the path and into a narrow gap between two rocks. It was barely wide enough for both of them, and Veronica's spine was crushed to Angelus' chest, his hand over her mouth to stifle her rapid breathing. Her heart. Her heart was what had to be silenced— how could the people on the road not hear it?

A topless wagon barreled in front of the crevice they hid in, towed by a dark brown horse, its ribs showing through its filthy coat, mud spattered up its legs. Veronica held her breath, waiting for the horse to topple over the edge, but it didn't. The wagon, full of crates of food, weapons, and blankets, passed where Veronica and Angelus hid, and Veronica shrank back as much as she could when a group of men followed behind the wagon, one of them on a horse but the other three on foot. They wore identical black scarves around their necks.

"Army pigs," one of them crowed, spitting on the ground, and the others laughed.

They disappeared up the path, the sounds of their laughter and rickety wagon still discernible even after they were out of sight. Angelus lowered his hand from Veronica's mouth, but she remained still and silent.

"Bandits," Angelus whispered. "The villagers warned me about them."

Veronica's legs shook slightly as she stepped back out onto the path, feeling instantly exposed and vulnerable. She had always known she and Angelus were not alone on this mountain, but it had started to seem that way. Angelus stepped out after her, his green eyes alert, dancing across their surroundings, his face unreadable, but his body tense and ready. There was a knife in both of his hands, though Veronica hadn't seen him draw them.

"Let's go," he said, waving for Veronica to follow him back down the trail they had come from, and where the bandits had come from.

"Where are we going?" Veronica asked, unable to keep from whispering.

"Their hideout is probably at the end of that path. Besides, didn't you see what they were carrying?"

Veronica frowned, unsure why it mattered. "It looked like food and supplies. Some weapons."

"Military-issued weapons."

Veronica shook her head, still not understanding.

He turned to her. "They stole those weapons from an armory. The checkpoint must be nearby."

CHAPTER TWENTY-TWO

THE checkpoint was exactly as Angelus remembered it. He had toured the bases and checkpoints as part of his training, and though he had only seen this place once, and briefly, it had not changed. A gray stone tower, stationed on a hill of earth with a worn footpath leading to it. It was a simple, straight structure with barred windows all around it, and a flat top with a waist-high wall that, during an attack, served as cover for hidden archers, as well as protection from enemy arrows. The only difference was that it was now completely empty. Angelus could tell right away it was abandoned, and the soldiers were not simply hidden from view, because the windows were smashed and the door hung open, swaying and creaking in the light wind. He already knew before entering that the armory would be cleaned out, but he hadn't been prepared for the complete and utter emptiness. There was nothing left, not a crumb of food or a piece of furniture. The floor was coated in a thick layer of dust, permeated only by footprints. A cold wind blew through the broken windows, and Angelus fought a shiver.

"Those bandits did this?" Veronica's voice was loud in the empty space. Angelus turned in a slow circle, surveying the room.

"No," he said finally. "There's no sign of a struggle. This tower was abandoned long before they got here. They just took whatever was left."

"But why would the soldiers abandon this place?" she asked.

"Good question."

This was the last place Queen Mayva had been seen, the last place a message from her had been sent. And then all communication had ceased. She'd just disappeared. But there was nothing to suggest she had been attacked, or kidnapped. All signs pointed to the soldiers simply walking away. But why?

Angelus climbed the stone steps to the top of the tower, Veronica following behind him. The first room they found was the sleeping quarters, three cots arranged in a line in the small room, stripped of all their blankets. There was nothing but the frames of the cots. The bandits must not have wanted them, or perhaps hadn't been able to carry them.

They stepped back out onto the stairs and continued climbing, until they reached a door in the ceiling leading to the roof. Angelus pulled the rope, a ladder sliding down, barely low enough for Veronica to reach. He climbed up first, and when he was satisfied there was no one on the roof, he beckoned for Veronica to follow.

He helped her up the last rung, making sure she was steady on her feet before he let go of her arm. She looked around with wide eyes. He couldn't blame her; the view over the stone wall was incredible. Miles of endless green, the main roads forming dark veins through the red and green trees.

From this vantage point, there was no way not to see an enemy coming.

"What's that?" Veronica asked. Angelus' eyes followed her pointing finger, landing on a little metal and wood structure sitting on one side of the tower's roof. Angelus' eyes widened.

"That's... where the messenger birds are kept." *Are,* not *were,* because the red-tailed hawks were still inside it. They hurried to the wire enclosure, Angelus opening the door— unlocked— and staring at the cages. They were all full. Not a single bird was missing. They looked hungry and haggard, obediently waiting for their next assignment from masters who abandoned them.

"Why would they leave them here?" Veronica asked, eyes moving slowly from bird to bird. Each looked the same as the last, sharp faces and gray-white plumage with brick colored tails.

"Why would they leave their only method of contacting anyone?" Angelus mused, his curious gaze reflecting those of the birds. "I couldn't tell you."

"We should let them go," Veronica said.

Angelus blinked, surprised, though he had no reason to disagree with her. He reached to unlatch one of the cages, before he realized it wasn't locked. None of the cage doors were locked. The birds could have left, but they simply waited. Veronica and Angelus pulled open the cage doors, but the birds only stared at them, uncertain and expectant. A few of them flapped to the ground in an experimental way, but they didn't go far.

"If they're hungry, they'll leave," Angelus said when Veronica frowned at the birds. It would take a while for them to grasp that no one was coming back for them. They were lost without a master, a task. Angelus wondered if they could survive on their own. They weren't wild animals anymore, they had been tamed, tools dressed up like birds, all of their wildness gone.

Angelus grimaced, and kicked at the birds that had flown to the ground. They spread their wings, startled more than threatened. "Go," he snapped. "They aren't coming back." When the birds didn't move, he sneered, and kicked at them again, harder, the tip of his boot brushing one of their wings. He shooed them out the door until they were outside. "Get out of here!" he shouted.

"Angelus!" Veronica cried. "What are you—"

The birds suddenly burst into flight, taking to the air and circling above the tower, their hoarse, raspy shrieks echoing through the air. One of them shot past Angelus' head, blowing his hair into his eyes and nearly knocking him off balance, before landing on the stone wall. The other birds still swooped through the air, as though stretching their wings after so long in cages, but this one pecked at something on the wall by its feet.

"Angelus," Veronica said, "Look at its leg."

For the first time, Angelus saw a green scrap of fabric caught on the hawk's talons. It stabbed at the fabric with its beak, but it didn't budge from the long, deadly claws. He stepped forward, reaching for it, hesitating, expecting the hawk to bite him, but it just waited, unblinking, as Angelus removed the fabric. Immediately the hawk shot into the air. In seconds, the birds were nothing but specs in the sky, following behind the hawk that Angelus had freed.

Angelus examined the fabric in his hand, rough and dark green. It was frayed around the edges, as if it had been torn from a larger piece of cloth, and dirty with flecks of straw and bits of feather. But the design of an eye, that of some kind of animal, could be made out in the center of it, embroidered with midnight-black thread.

Angelus recognized it instantly. It was part of the same flag he had seen on the tower in Rom's village. The colors were a perfect match, though the exact pattern of the embroidery escaped him. He hadn't gotten a good look at it before. But he was certain it was the same.

He handed it to Veronica, waiting for her to confirm his rising suspicion.

She gaped at it. "This is... But it can't be."

"There's more than one flag," Angelus said. "I think this is the symbol of the resistance."

*   *   *

THE empty armory was the sole room in the tower without a broken window, making it the only place to sleep.

The bolt on the door had been broken, and the door hung open uselessly, unable to close completely. The walls held abandoned hooks and shelves where weapons once rested, sticking out of the bare walls like hands, pathetic and expectant.

Angelus practically threw his blanket onto the ground and immediately laid down, turning onto his side and facing the wall.

He heard Veronica sit down a few feet away. "What now?" she asked quietly.

"We keep looking."

"Where?" Her voice sounded defeated. "There isn't a single hint to where she went."

Angelus knew that, and it made him furious, but he swallowed down his harsh tone. "There's nothing else to be done." It was the truth, loathed as he was to admit it.

"She could be anywhere."

Did she think he didn't know that? Mayva was a ghost, smoke on a breeze blowing in no discernable direction. But he had to find her. Veronica was counting on him. He couldn't fail.

He wouldn't admit that, perhaps, he already had.

He must have dozed off, because he jerked awake suddenly. Something had touched his back in the dark, trembling against him. He turned over, and made out Veronica's small, dark shape beside him. Somehow, during the night, their bodies had moved closer together. It was freezing in the armory, despite the shelter from the wind, and there was no sound except for a tiny whimper.

"Veronica?" He reached for her blindly, his fingers finding what might have been her shoulder. She gasped, and he could feel her shaking under his touch.

"I'm fine," she whispered stiffly. "Just cold."

Angelus shed his blanket and draped it over her. They were practically pressed against each other already, so Angelus lifted the blankets and slid beneath them. Her back pressed against his chest, and he was seized with the sudden desire to wrap his arm around her, to offer her some more heat, but he held still.

She shocked him by turning over, facing him, and curling into him. The tips of her boots bumped against his knees, and her breath tickled his neck, but he still could not bring himself to move. She shivered, and somehow it broke the spell of uncertainty cast over him. Slowly, he slid his arm under her head like a pillow, before carefully laying down, afraid to move too much or too quickly. He braced for her to push him away, but she didn't. Her fingers brushed his other arm, and he grimaced. "Gods," he whispered, taking her hand in his. "Your hands are freezing."

She laughed softly, and Angelus felt the sound deep, deep inside. She pressed closer. "And you're warm," she sighed, her breath trickling down his collarbone. If he moved at all, her lips would touch his skin. His flesh warmed at the idea, his heart thudding faster and faster until he thought it might explode. Her head fit beneath his chin, and he let his right arm drape over her, waiting for her to protest, but she didn't. His hand pressed into her back, and his palm brushed against her hair. Slowly, painfully slowly, he ran the tip of one finger up her braid until he reached the nape of her neck. Her hair was smooth and soft, and he let his fingers linger there for a moment, before his hand fell away. In the instant before falling asleep, he thought he might have experienced perfect calm.

*   *   *

WHEN Angelus opened his eyes, there was a fuzzy, reddish tint to his surroundings. But he could make out a face hovering above him.

"Are you dead?" a girl's voice asked, cold and calm.

Angelus expelled a breath— it was all he could manage.

"Where did you come from? Who did this to you?"

His face and head and chest pounded sickeningly. Resmond. He was gone, really gone, then. He became aware of the straw scratching against his skin. How long had he been there, lying in that stall? And who was this girl who had found him? His vision cleared somewhat, and he tried to focus on her face. She was young, maybe around his own age, but something about her dark eyes didn't match her clear, pale, youthful skin. He had never seen eyes so dark brown, nor so ancient. She frowned at him, not concerned so much as darkly curious.

Self consciousness burned in his stomach and face. He felt abruptly pathetic. With a bloody and swollen face, he must look horrible, and she was so beautiful, in a long pink silk dress, her face sharp and proud, like a siren from an old fisherman's tale. He tried to get up, but couldn't get his arms to support his weight. A hand touched his shoulder, and he flinched away from the contact.

"It's alright." Her voice had changed somewhat, turning a little softer. She withdrew her hand. Angelus managed to prop himself up on his elbows, then push into a sitting position.

"I'll go," he croaked. Speaking made his entire face hurt. He wondered if his jaw was broken.

"Go where?" she asked. By the way she asked it, it sounded as though she knew the answer already.

A black cavern, cold and empty, opened in Angelus' chest. *Go where?* There was nowhere for him to go.

Angelus couldn't speak. But he didn't need to. The girl got to her feet, and though she was shorter and slighter than he was, he felt small when he looked up into her face. A little smirk twisted her mouth, and her eyes flashed. The hand she extended toward him was a mirage in his hazy vision. "Come," she said. "You can come with me."

Angelus didn't hesitate, didn't have to think. He took her hand, and got unsteadily to his feet.

"What's your name?" she asked.

"Angelus," he breathed.

Her smile was sharp as a dagger. "I'm Andromeda."

*   *   *

ANGELUS woke up breathing in Veronica's scent. The raspberry smell had faded, but was still there, lingering on her skin. Eyes still closed, he inhaled, and something tickled his nose.

Slowly, groggily, he opened his eyes. The top of Veronica's head rested below his lips, a few stray hairs brushing his nose. His arms were wound around her, her body flush against his. She, too, had wrapped her arms around him.

He couldn't breathe for one... two... three seconds...

Carefully, he slid out of her arms, sitting up. She didn't stir, sleeping soundly. He allowed himself to watch her for a minute, something hot prodding the inside of his chest, and a swirling sensation fluttering behind his naval.

He wanted to stay, trapped in that moment, for just a little longer. But the desire was overshadowed by a feeling of dread, something cold drowning out the tiny warmth forming in his chest, nestled underneath his breastbone.

He was such a fool. When had anything good ever lasted?

He got to his feet and left the armory without turning back. He didn't think he could go if he did.

CHAPTER TWENTY-THREE

VERONICA understood two things upon waking. The first was that she had not dreamed. The second was that she was alone.

The door to the armory was open, cold air and blueish morning light streaming into the empty room. Veronica sat up, peering around, but Angelus wasn't there. The floor beside her was cold to the touch, though she remembered him sleeping next to her. When did he leave?

She stood, and walked out into the main room of the tower. It was bitterly cold, the wind groaning as it scraped against the jagged pieces of glass remaining in the window frames. She peered through one of the ruined windows, and from between the iron bars fixed to the outside of the window, she could see Angelus standing on the edge of the hill the tower sat upon, wearing nothing but boots and pants, throwing knives. They were like little bolts of lightning, flashing in his hand and then in the blink of an eye protruding from a tree trunk.

She stepped out the door to the tower, crossing her arms to guard against the chill of the morning, and walked toward him.

"Angelus?" she called when she was a few paces away, not wanting to startle him.

His gaze flitted to her long enough to catch her eye, then he faced the tree again, drawing his arm back and throwing the knife. It found its mark in the tree trunk, the hilt pointing accusingly at Angelus.

"We need to keep moving," he said, voice hard. Despite the cold, his back was slick with sweat. How long had he been there?

"Right..." Veronica trailed off. "Are you... Did something happen?"

"The queen is missing and the soldiers deserted their post," he snapped. "That's what happened."

Veronica blinked, surprised. "Right," she repeated.

He took aim again, drawing back his arm. "If they're deserters, they probably went higher up the mountain. The woods are denser— more places to hide."

"Do you think they know what happened to the queen?" Veronica asked.

"They're the only lead we have." The knife sliced through the air, landing next to the previous knife. He was down to his last one, and he adjusted his stance, pointing the blade at the tree, one eye closed, lining up the shot. "If we can't find them, maybe someone in one of the villages around here knows what happened."

Veronica nodded, though he wasn't looking at her. "Alright. I'll pack up."

Angelus didn't answer, too focused on getting his feet in the perfect position. Veronica turned to walk away, but glanced back just as he let the knife fly.

He missed.

*   *   *

ANGELUS found the main road easily, though they kept their distance from it. The bandits seemed to have put him on edge, more than usual, and Veronica couldn't blame him. Even so, he looked bothered by something, but Veronica said nothing to him as they walked.

When night began to approach, they were walking through a wide, grassy space, surrounded on all sides by trees in an almost perfect circle. Though the sun hadn't fully set, stars were already appearing, eager twinkling eyes in the sky. Veronica wished she could be as high as they were, gazing down at the world. The mountains and trees and tragedies of earth must look so small from the sky.

It was starting to get cold already, and Veronica wondered if Angelus would sleep next to her again. But she couldn't shake the feeling his dark mood was partly her fault, and she kept a safe distance while they set up camp for the night. Veronica was just reaching for one of the last bits of food left, a strip of beef tougher than leather, when something moved in the tree beside her. She looked up, and a bird peered down at her. In the growing darkness it was hard to tell what type of bird it was. It wasn't very large, and its entire body was so black it was almost blue. A raven, perhaps. Or a crow.

She glanced back at Angelus, who stood on the other side of the open sphere of earth, trying to reach some sort of fruit he'd found in one of the trees. Turning back to the bird, she walked closer, curious. It was staring at her, and as she got nearer, she noticed a long gash across its left eye, as if something, or someone, had tried to gouge its eye out. Its feathers were ruffled and falling out in places, and even though it was only an animal, there was something cruel about its expression, eyes enormous black holes in its eager, strange face.

Suddenly its beak opened, its neck stretching forward as it cawed at her. The sound was piercingly loud in the otherwise quiet night, and Veronica jumped back, startled, nearly tripping over her skirt as she retreated. She collided with a broad, hard chest. Enormous hands clamped down on her arms and spun her around, and she found herself face to face with a tall, boulder of a man with beady eyes and a black scarf hiding the bottom half of his face.

For a moment, Veronica couldn't scream, she could only stare at the man. Then the fear tore from her throat, too fast for him to cover her mouth. *"Angelus!"*

The man clapped his palm over Veronica's mouth, almost covering her entire face with a single hand. He jerked her into him, pressing her back to his chest and forcing her to walk in front of him, his other arm wrapped around her to keep her hands at her sides. When they faced the opening in the trees, she could see Angelus was on the ground, pinned under another man, this one thin and wiry, landing blows across Angelus' arms, which were raised to protect his face.

He managed to land one punch to the man's face, sending him reeling back, and Angelus was on his feet instantly. But he didn't attack the thinner man. He sprinted toward Veronica and the man holding her, leaving the man with no choice but to throw Veronica away from him in order to be ready for Angelus' blow. It was no use, however. Angelus buried one of his blades in the man's neck so fast Veronica didn't even see it happen. His neck was clean, and then it was covered in blood.

"Run!" Angelus shouted at Veronica as he pulled his knife free. The man fell to his knees, thick hands wrapped around his throat as though he were choking himself.

Veronica bolted for the trees, no thought in her head except to escape. But to where?

"Run!" Angelus shouted again, louder, harder, as though he sensed her fear, her hesitation. She turned long enough to watch Angelus swing his blade at the other man's face, but he ducked before the knife could cut his flesh to ribbons. He, too, wore a black scarf over his mouth.

Just like the bandits from the hidden road.

They had been followed.

Veronica could hear Angelus' pained cry as the bandit landed a solid blow to his stomach. He didn't fall, but he was stunned long enough for the bandit to get close enough to wrap his hands around Angelus' neck.

Veronica looked at her hands. Fire. Fire was all she knew how to create, the only weapon she had, but what good would it do if she couldn't control it?

Sucking in a breath, she reached for the fire inside. It felt hollow and cold and faraway. She drew the symbol for fire.

Nothing happened.

Panic threatened to swallow her. She tried again. Nothing.

She wanted to scream. She was useless. Completely and utterly useless.

So she ran. Not away, but toward them. The bandit didn't see her coming, didn't expect her to jump on his back, wrapping her arms around his neck and wrenching back as hard as she could. He tumbled back, falling on top of her. His elbow rammed into her side and she cried out, the pain blinding, exploding from her side and swallowing her entire body. He turned, face to face with Veronica, and his sharp face hovered above hers.

"Hello, beautiful," he said through a rapidly widening grin. His scarf was gone, and Veronica saw his teeth were stained crimson with his own blood, the left corner of his mouth leaking dark red blood and saliva that dripped onto Veronica's throat, scorchingly hot.

Angelus seized the bandit by the shirt and hauled him back, slamming him to the ground. "I told you to run," Angelus tried to shout, but it came out as more of a desperate rasp. He was slowing down, his energy spent. His hands were empty. The knives were gone.

He was going to lose this fight.

Veronica grabbed one of his knives from the ground. "Angelus!" She threw it, and he caught the hilt, almost missing it, and he gripped it tightly as he ducked a sailing punch. He slashed, but the air was empty. The bandit was dancing with him. Teasing him.

This was not the fight from the village, with spectators and someone to stop them from going too far. Someone was going to die.

Angelus must have known it, because he pivoted another blow then spun away, running for Veronica. In one liquid motion he put his single blade back into his vest and with the other hand seized her arm and dragged her with him, breaking into a dead sprint Veronica could only match because of the fear in her blood. "Run *now!*" he bellowed. "Get into the trees and hide, and by the gods don't you dare leave until I find you. Do you understand?" He stopped abruptly, shoving her toward one of the trees, with lots of branches like a ladder leading up into the foliage, midnight-black in the silvery night. All Veronica could see was the moon reflected in Angelus' eyes, and their breath fogging between them.

Then Angelus lunged forward, and for a wild heartbeat Veronica thought he was going to kiss her as her back smashed into the tree. Angelus screamed, *screamed,* as something hit him from behind. He hadn't lunged for her. He'd been shoved. She was crushed between him and the tree, and the bandit landed blow after blow across Angelus' back. And he was laughing. The bandit was howling with delighted laughter.

Angelus didn't raise a hand to protect himself. He kept her pinned between his arms, one hand coming up to push her against his chest. Protecting her.

He was going to die protecting her.

The bandit's face appeared over Angelus' shoulder, and his insane eyes met hers. He pushed harder into Angelus until Veronica was completely crushed. She couldn't breathe.

He laughed again. He continued to laugh as Veronica slid her hand into Angelus' vest, fingers closing around the hilt of a knife. He was still laughing when Veronica reached around Angelus' side, and stabbed.

His eyes went wide, his mouth gaping in shock more than pain, his laughter turning to a horrible gurgling as he stumbled back, the hilt of the knife sticking out of his chest, nestled between two of his ribs. He fell, folding to the ground. Blood burst from his mouth in a wet cough. If she'd stabbed his lung, he'd be dead soon.

Veronica panted against Angelus' chest. For a moment, he just stood above her, his forehead on her shoulder, before he too crumpled to the ground. Veronica fell with him, guiding him to the forest floor.

"Angelus," she panted. "Angelus!"

"Go," he whispered. "There might be more. You have to hide."

Veronica shook her head, and was surprised to realize she was crying. A loud sob broke free of her trembling lips. "Where are you hurt?" she demanded, running her hands over his chest, his arms. She couldn't see. She couldn't see in the dark. But she felt the blood. Was it his? The bandits? "Angelus," she cried, louder, "Angelus, where are you hurt?"

He didn't answer.

Veronica looked around at the trees, black phantoms closing in around her. "Please," she whispered, though she wasn't sure who or what she was speaking to. "Please, help."

No one answered. No one came.

They were the only ones in the world. And soon it might just be her. Alone.

"Help!" she screamed into the night. "Somebody please... *help us!*"

Something tore free of Veronica's chest, as though her heart had sprouted wings and was making its desperate escape. Pale purple light lit the night, only for an instant, like a shooting star flying overhead, illuminating the dark for a single heartbeat, and as the light dimmed, so did Veronica's vision.

She slumped forward, her head falling onto Angelus' barely moving chest, neither of them aware of the running footsteps coming toward them, or the neighing of horses somewhere beyond.

All Veronica knew was darkness.

CHAPTER TWENTY-FOUR

ANGELUS' body was a temple of pain. Nothing existed except the white film over his vision, and the searing heat in his spine, across his ribs and in his skull. Though his sight returned, slowly, the pain never waned. He grunted at the jolt of agony taking a simple breath shot through his side. He knew that pain. Broken ribs.

The ceiling above him came into focus. No, not a ceiling. The slope of a tent roof, pale gray and shimmering from bright sunlight overhead.

"Are you awake?"

Angelus didn't recognize the voice, and it sent a tremor of fear through him. A face appeared above him. The man was young, though older than Angelus was, with a lot of dark stubble and overgrown hair, falling over his blue eyes. His cheekbones were sunburnt, peeling slightly, and he wore a dirty chestplate over a rumpled white shirt.

"Don't try to move," the man warned. "Your ribs are broken."

Angelus took a slow, careful breath. He licked his dry, cracked lips, trying to speak. "Wh... where..."

"Where's the girl?" the man offered. He appeared relaxed, but Angelus was not calmed, despite there being something strangely familiar about him. "She's alright. She's on her way now." He glanced at something outside of Angelus' field of vision, nodding at someone and pointing.

Angelus bent his arms, intent on propping himself up, but the man put a warning hand on his shoulder. Before he could speak, Angelus swung an arm toward him— a mistake he instantly regretted— knocking his hand away. "Don't touch me." His voice was sharp between his clenched teeth. "I need to see her. Where the hell is she?"

"Calm down," the man said, voice reasonable, but firm. "She— "

"Liam," came a female voice from the door of the tent. The man, Liam, stepped back, and stood straight backed, arms at his sides.

Angelus turned, slowly getting into a sitting position, though his chest screamed in protest, making his stomach roll with nausea.

A tall woman in dark armor stood before the entrance to the tent, where, Angelus saw, there were lines of cots, all empty except the one Angelus sat in. An infirmary tent. The woman's eyes locked with Angelus', and for a moment he could only stare at her. Black hair, eyes dark green like moss, except for half of her left eye, which was so dark brown it was almost black, like the pupil had been punctured and bled into her iris. Her jaw and cheekbones were sharp, her mouth thin and flat.

Just like her sister.

"Queen Mayva," Liam said, startling Angelus. He'd forgotten someone else was in the tent.

The Second Queen of Lavdia waved a hand, and Liam relaxed, sitting down in a chair Angelus only then realized was next to his bed. How long had he been asleep? How long had Liam been watching him, waiting for him to wake up?

"Angelus," Mayva said. Her voice bore no inflection at all, giving nothing away. "It's been a long time."

Angelus didn't make any attempt to bow, or kneel. He just sat, watching her. Her short swords were strapped to her back, crossing over her armor and revealing the hilts above her shoulders. She was exactly the same as he remembered her from the castle. Dark and imposing, a pillar of shadow, like a thundercloud on the horizon, or the mountains at night.

"It has," he agreed, voice slow, testing. "Where am I?"

"When you can stand," Mayva said, turning to go, "I will show you."

"No," Angelus hissed, trying to get to his feet. His knees buckled and Liam caught him, but Angelus pushed him away, hand pressing into the cot's mattress for support. He couldn't control the rising of his voice, didn't understand where the anger was coming from, he only knew it was there, and it would destroy him. "You'll tell me now! Where have you been? What happened—"

Someone burst through the tent flap, nearly colliding with the Warrior Queen. Veronica, her eyes wild and her face horribly pale, followed by two soldiers, made a dash for Angelus. "What are you doing trying to get up?" she demanded, taking his arm and guiding him back to the bed.

He sat, carefully, searching her face. "Are you alright?" he asked quickly.

She nodded, though she didn't *look* alright. She looked like she'd been crying, her eyes damp and swollen, pink rimming her dark eyes.

Fury was a taloned monster in Angelus' chest, trying to claw its way out.

"I'm fine." Her voice was tight. "You're the one that's hurt." She glanced back at the two soldiers who had followed her into the tent, both of them looking harassed and irritated. "They wouldn't let me see you until you woke up."

"How long was I asleep?" Angelus asked, his fingers closing around her wrist, afraid she would leave, or someone would try to take her away. They could try.

"Two days," Veronica whispered. She still wouldn't meet his gaze. Her eyes were on the queen. But Mayva only had eyes for Angelus.

"We'll let you two talk," Mayva said. She nodded for Liam to follow her, and he did. He was taller than she was, but only by a little. They were both stone towers turned to people, their bodies straight and muscular, their movements certain. Their eyes swept their surroundings in an identical way, as though burying anyone who crossed them with a single look.

Mayva was royalty, but she was powerful in a different way than the royals and politicians at the castle. It was the difference between a threat and a promise.

Once the tent was empty save for Angelus and Veronica, she turned to him. With him sitting on the cot and her standing, her face was higher than his, and he had to look up to meet her eyes. He wanted to touch her face, as though to make sure no secrets hid beneath her skin. "What happened?" he asked.

Veronica swallowed, eyes on her feet. "They found us in the woods, after the bandits attacked. They brought us here, to some kind of camp."

"Did you tell her anything?"

"Just that we've been trying to find her. That you have information she will want. Goddess, Angelus, I thought they were going to kill us. Queen Mayva was furious when the soldiers who found us brought us here. But she recognized you. That's when I told her we were looking for her."

Angelus nodded, though his stomach twisted. Veronica had been forced to handle it on her own, while he lay injured and useless. He let his fingertips brush against her cheek. "You did the right thing. It's alright."

Her expression was still tight, but she leaned almost imperceptibly into Angelus' touch, and the beast inside him calmed. "There's something else," she said, stepping back and going to the tent's entrance. She drew open the flap. From where Angelus sat, he could see other tents scattered around, and people milling about, all of them armored, but that wasn't what caught his attention. What he couldn't tear his eyes away from was the banner, hanging from a strip of rope secured between two trees. It was dark green, with two crossed swords and a black horse emblazoned across it.

The symbol of the resistance. It was Mayva's banner.

VERONICA didn't leave Angelus' side, perching on Liam's vacated seat next to the cot. She tried to convince him to lay back down, but he couldn't, his body too restless. Finally, after what had to be an hour, Mayva returned, Liam trailing behind.

"Veronica told me you've been looking for me," Mayva said, getting straight to the point. Her face was coldly beautiful in the way of marble statues or sharpened blades. Precise, deadly, and impossible to read. If she was angry, Angelus couldn't tell. She still wore her armor, though Liam remained in only a chestplate and loose clothing.

"Everyone's looking for you," Angelus snapped. His temper had rushed back through the door along with the queen. Liam and Veronica both shot him identical warning glares, but he didn't notice. "No one knows what happened to you."

Mayva's expression did not change. "I don't believe you came all this way, with a Wielder in your company—" Angelus' lips peeled back to reveal his teeth, an angry retort on his tongue, but he stopped when Mayva raised her hand calmly— "simply because you were concerned for my well being. Why are you here?"

Angelus pressed a hand to his aching ribs, his rapid pulse amplifying the pain, the tight bandages making it difficult to breathe. Or maybe that was his anger. "Andromeda's dead." The words were sharp and acidic, leaving a dead silence in their wake. He wanted her to flinch. She didn't. Her expression remained carefully the same, blank and cold. To anyone else, she would have appeared unaffected. But Angelus, who'd spent a great many

240

years perfecting that very expression of stone, could see the tightening of her mouth, the ever so slight widening of her eyes.

Liam didn't hide his shock. His eyes went from Angelus, to Veronica, to the queen. When she didn't speak, Liam asked Angelus, "How?"

Angelus didn't look away from Mayva. She didn't look away from him.

"She wrote you letters," Angelus spat, not answering Liam's question. "She needed your help." He couldn't keep his voice even, it rose and sharpened with each word. "Every messenger hawk the castle sent out for the last four *months* returned because they couldn't find you. And all this time, you've been *here?*"

"My Second asked you a question," Mayva said, voice just as sharp as Angelus', but her calm was somehow worse than Angelus' fury. "Answer him."

"Artemis," Veronica spoke up, clearly afraid Angelus would only make things worse. She was glaring at him warningly, anger and confusion warring on her face. *What are you doing?* her eyes demanded. "He told me Artemis killed her."

At no point did Angelus and Mayva break each other's gazes. They were both wary predators, waiting for... something. She cocked her head slightly, the hilts of her two crossed swords like black eyes peering over her shoulders. "How do you know?" she asked Angelus, as though it had been he, not Veronica, who had spoken.

Angelus shook his head. "I'm not telling you anything until you explain. What is this place?"

241

He expected Mayva to argue, or refuse, but she merely swept toward the door and pulled the flap away. "Come with me and I will show you."

Veronica rushed to help Angelus as he struggled to his feet. He would have forced himself to walk without her help if he needed to. He gripped her shoulder for balance, and she slid her arm behind his back carefully. Angelus limped forward, making his slow, stiff way to the tent door. Mayva stepped outside, and Angelus followed. The mountain air was frigid, and his chest, bare except for the bandages around his ribs, seized from the cold. He didn't let his face reveal his discomfort. Mayva was watching him closely.

Men and women walked among the tents, at least fifty Lavdian military-issued shelters of identical gray with dark rope. The weapons, too, were the standard, simple steel Angelus was used to seeing in the castle. It looked like any military campsite; soldiers trekking across the land to help settle a dispute, or Queen Mayva herself traveling simply and efficiently. But Mayva had not left the castle with this many people. Where had they come from?

"What is this?" Angelus breathed.

Mayva finally betrayed the slightest hint of emotion. Amusement. It appeared at the corner of her thin mouth, and remained trapped there, unable to reach her eyes. "This is my army," she said simply. "And now that you have seen it, I have some questions I require answers to."

CHAPTER TWENTY-FIVE

THEY were separated for questioning. Liam took Veronica, guiding her toward a tent on the other side of the camp, and Angelus could do nothing but watch. She glanced back at him, once, and nodded as though to tell him she would be alright.

Mayva took Angelus.

He hobbled back to his cot, refusing her offered hand. He was sweating despite the cold, and he thought his ankle must have been sprained because it seared with every step he took, only letting up when he sat down again.

"Your friend tells me you were attacked by bandits." From her tone Angelus deduced she didn't fully believe this.

"We were," Angelus snapped, instantly defensive. He pointed to his bandages. "You think bears did this?"

Her eyes flitted to his chest, moving slowly up to his face. "We've been moving through these mountains for months and encountered no bandits."

Angelus recalled the black scarves around the mens' faces and throats. Strangely familiar, though he hadn't been able to place them. Then he remembered. A man with a black scarf covering his face in the Imperial City, the one that attacked Andromeda's carriage.

The Lawless.

"They weren't bandits," Angelus breathed, his anger momentarily forgotten. "Lawless. It was the Lawless. They must have a hideout in the mountains."

Mayva's eyes narrowed. She looked disinterested, but Angelus wasn't fooled. "I will alert the camp's watch," she said simply, sitting down on the cot across from his, her eyes intent but revealing nothing more. She could have been about to kill him and Angelus would have no warning. That was who Mayva was. She was meant to be enough of a mystery that you were afraid. There were endless rumors surrounding her, Angelus gleaning bits and pieces of the stories the servants whispered to each other, hands over mouths and eyes wide with awe, or fear.

Angelus had heard it all. Mayva killed her first man when she was five, picking up a sword bigger than she was and chopping off his hands, letting him bleed to death. Her armor was made from the charred skin of her enemies. Her heart had been carved out and replaced with steel. She wore her armor, not because she needed it, but to hide the horrid scars her body had accumulated. As someone with his fair share of scars, Angelus always wondered if that last story bore any measure of truth. Seeing her now, however, put the curiosity to rest. Mayva would never hide anything that made her appear strong.

But the other rumors? He didn't know. No one was supposed to know. You were meant to think they were all true, or at least that they could be.

"I want you to tell me what happened," she said. "To..." She hesitated, only for a breath. "To her."

"What *happened?*" Angelus repeated, heat immediately rushing to his chest. "What happened is that Andromeda wrote you letter after letter, asking you to come back. And you never did. And now she's dead. Artemis killed her because she figured out what he was planning."

"And what would that be?"

It was impossible. She didn't betray a single hint of emotion. It was as though Andromeda's death meant nothing. As though Andromeda meant nothing.

Perhaps her heart really had been replaced with steel.

Angelus cut his eyes to the door of the tent. "Looks like you already know."

Mayva got to her feet, pacing in slow, even steps along the end of Angelus' cot. "It wasn't exactly a mystery," she said flatly. "It was only a matter of time before he made a move for more power. And his prejudice against Wielders wasn't something he or his followers ever tried to hide."

"His followers?"

"He's had most of the castle soldiers in his pocket for years. And the Lawmakers—" she gave a soft snort. "They've always been his pawns."

"The Lawmakers are dead," Angelus said coolly. "Artemis killed them. He and Queen Morgeoux are the only ones left in the castle."

Angelus could have imagined it, but he thought he saw her hands twitch, as though about to clench them. He wondered then, what would become of Queen Morgeoux when Artemis was gone? Whose side was the High Queen really on? Could Mayva overthrow her own sister if necessary?

All she said was, "My objective remains unchanged. We will stage a coup, handle this quickly and quietly."

Angelus glanced toward the tent entrance again. "That's where you've been?" he asked, incredulous. "Gathering an army?"

"I don't trust the soldiers in the castle would side with me over Artemis. I needed an army of my own. Loyal to me, and me alone."

"Where did they come from?"

"Some of them came from the castle, most of them are deserters or people from the mountain villages. Wielders and non-Wielders alike. They were eager for a chance to help bring balance back to this country." She gripped the edge of the mattress Angelus sat on, leaning forward. "Now. Why did you come to find me?"

"Because this dispute has spread far beyond the castle. He's attacking innocent people— he attacked Veronica's village. He massacred a village of Wielders. They need your help."

Mayva's expression didn't change. "And what made you believe I was the one to help you?" she asked. "Why not seek help elsewhere?"

"Because Andromeda told me to find you." Angelus was shocked by his own words.

For just a moment, less than a heartbeat, something flashed behind Mayva's eyes. But then it was gone.

Angelus was abruptly exhausted, his anger burned up, leaving him empty. He glanced at the tent door. "I hope you've found people you can trust." He grimaced. "You're going to need them."

"And why is that?"

Angelus' gaze turned to granite. "Because Artemis doesn't just have *people*. He has monsters, *Magic*. I've seen them, we— Veronica and I— have seen what they can do."

Mayva sat back down. "I need you to tell me everything you know."

Angelus' lip curled, half amused. Only half. "Why do you think I've been looking for you?"

Mayva looked at him expectantly. "I'm here, aren't I?"

*　　*　　*

"IF you keep pacing like that, you'll wear a hole in the floor."

Veronica paused, glancing back at Liam where he stood by the tent entrance, his gaze trained on the infirmary tent, where Mayva and Angelus were. Veronica lowered her thumb from her mouth. She had been chewing at the skin along her nail so long it was starting to bleed.

"Why does she need to talk to him?" Veronica demanded. "He isn't a... *a spy*. Artemis wants him dead for what he knows. We've been looking for Mayva for days— weeks, probably, at this point."

"*Queen* Mayva," Liam corrected, his voice for the first time holding a warning.

Veronica folded her arms. Liam had introduced himself as Queen Mayva's *Second,* and though at the time Veronica hadn't understood what that meant, she was beginning to. He was her second in command, her right hand. She had his loyalty, that was obvious, and his respect. But it wasn't just respect in his eyes when he looked at the queen. There was something else, too.

"She doesn't think he's a spy," Liam said, his eyes still on the tent outside.

Veronica walked over to stand beside him, peeking out at the infirmary tent. After a few minutes, Mayva exited, cutting a quick glance toward Liam. She couldn't have seen him inside the tent, but she knew he was there. Waiting for her signal.

Liam nodded to himself. "Come with me. There's someone you should meet."

"Who?" Veronica asked, startled. Someone she should *meet?* She followed Liam out of the tent. He was the same height as Angelus, perhaps even taller, but his presence seemed larger, giving the impression of a giant. Watching him walk through the camp reminded Veronica of the time she saw a stag walking on the outskirts of her village. She'd only been living with Finn, still just an apprentice himself, for about a year, and they had gone together to the village to deliver remedies. Their master Duvar's hands and feet were growing stiff with age, his capacity for walking limited, so Veronica and Finn made all the deliveries themselves. Veronica remembered peering around at the village as they walked together, and at the dense forest separating them from Resh. That's where she saw him. An enormous stag, with a rack of antlers towering above his head, impossibly heavy-looking, but the creature remained tall and proud. He was a giant; from a distance Veronica thought his flank might have been as high as she was tall, and she was aware in a detached, logical sense that if it charged it could kill her, trample her, but she hadn't been afraid. By the time she turned to tug at Finn's sleeve so he would see it, the stag was gone.

Liam reminded her of that stag. Tall and proud, capable, but not frightening. Not like he should have been.

He led her to a small tent on the edge of the camp, strangely distant from everything and everyone else. Liam called, "Tabitha?"

"Come in," a female voice chimed from inside the tent.

Liam gestured for Veronica to enter, following in behind her. The tent was cramped, a pile of blankets in the center of all the... Veronica squinted... *books.* They were piled and scattered all over the tent, pieces of folded parchment poking out of nearly all of them, and still others were held open to particular pages with rocks or other books. Veronica gaped. She hadn't seen a book in what felt like forever. She was abruptly, painfully homesick for Finn's collection of tomes back at the farmhouse, and she fought the urge to claw at the ache in her throat.

A woman rose from where she sat in a corner of the tent, startling Veronica. She hadn't even noticed her. The woman was short, though taller than Veronica, and very thin, with pale skin and large, slightly watery brown eyes. Her hair was shoulder-length and brown, stringy and limp like it needed to be washed. It was hard to tell her age— Veronica didn't think she was very old, but something about her face spoke of too long a life lived in too short a time, but she guessed the woman was in her early twenties.

249

There were dark circles under her eyes, though despite her obvious fatigue she gave Veronica a smile. "Hello," she said. Her voice was soft and light, almost childlike. "I'm pleased to see you well. I'm Tabitha." She offered a thin hand for Veronica to take.

Tabitha's skin was cool and dry like stiff parchment. "Hello, I'm Veronica."

"I know." Tabitha grinned.

Liam nodded to the women. "I leave her in your care, Tabitha."

"Of course." She turned back to Veronica as Liam left, her eyes bright and intent. "I heard you in the woods. Your call was very clear, even from miles away."

Veronica shook her head slowly. "My call? What do you mean?"

Tabitha blinked, confused. "Your call. Your Magic, you sent it out to find help."

Veronica's skin crawled, though she wasn't sure why. "I... I didn't..."

Tabitha cocked her head, thoughtful. "Ah. I wondered. You can't control it, can you?"

Veronica's face burned. Her lack of control was going to be the stuff of legends. "No." She didn't see any point in lying.

To her surprise, Tabitha beamed at her. She reached out and took Veronica's hands in hers. "I can help you."

Veronica's eyes widened. "You're a—"

Tabitha, still smiling, nodded. Her eyes were bright with excitement. "I can teach you how to use it, how to control it. If you wish to learn."

Once upon a time, Veronica would have said no. She didn't want to control her Magic because she didn't want any Magic to control. But now, the image of Angelus fighting the bandits in the woods flashed through her mind, the memory drenched in terror and helplessness. The Magic hadn't been there, and because of that Angelus could have died.

She would never let him be hurt because of her again.

"Why would you help me?" Veronica asked.

Tabitha just smiled, and Veronica felt her heart soften toward the woman. "Because we need more Wielders to help fight."

Veronica was not a fighter. But maybe she could be. For the first time in her life, she wanted to try. That had to mean something. It had to be a start.

"Please," Veronica said. "Show me."

CHAPTER TWENTY-SIX

ANGELUS slept as much as he possibly could, willing his body to heal faster. He barely left the infirmary tent; the camp set his teeth on edge. He wanted to leave that very second, but he could barely walk on his own, and he wouldn't ask Veronica to care for him. Not again. He needed to wait until he could protect her again.

In the days that followed, Angelus barely saw Veronica, but Mayva, who came to the tent nearly every day, and Liam, who usually accompanied her, assured him she was comfortable and well taken care of, and she was free to visit him, unaccompanied, whenever she wanted. She did come, but rarely. She said nothing was wrong.

But everything was wrong. Angelus' skin was on fire with the need to get up and run, to move. Everything pissed him off, every word Liam or Mayva or another soldier said to him, the drafty tent, his aching, broken bones, the banner watching over him and the rest of the camp like a giant green eye.

He didn't know, nor did he care, where the anger came from. He only cared that if he didn't do something about it soon, it would eat him alive.

He looked around the tent. There were several beds, all empty, and he imagined tearing them to pieces, ripping the sheets and throwing the metal skeleton of the cots across the room. His blood hummed, his pulse starting to gallop.

He stayed where he was, taking a deep breath and blowing it out slowly through his nose.

He needed to leave.

*　　*　　*

VERONICA was trying desperately to hide her shaking hands from Tabitha. She smoothed her damp palms over her skirt as she sat on the blanket the Wielder woman laid out for them. The morning was cold, but the thick clothing Veronica had been given to wear— wool leggings to replace her worn stockings, boots lined with deer fur, and a knee-length black coat with buttons down the front— kept the chill at bay.

Tabitha sat down across from her, a small stack of books between them. Most of Tabitha's books were in languages Veronica didn't recognize, but these were just translation keys, and the two of them spent most of the evening poring over them in Tabitha's tent.

"How familiar are you with Wielder history?" Tabitha asked.

Veronica disguised a grimace. "The... basics. The Mother Goddess gave some humans the ability to draw on Her energy, in order to manipulate or create."

"The Favored," Tabitha said, "They were the first Wielders. We are their descendants. These symbols—" She tapped a finger against one of the book's covers— "serve as a kind of gateway. Think of us and the Goddess as separated by a thin veil. Drawing these symbols is like tearing a hole in the veil, letting Her power come to our side for us to use." Tabitha spoke quickly, as though she'd memorized all of this in preparation to explain it. Her eyes were bright and excited; her heritage, her abilities, were important to her, a source of pride Veronica had never shared.

While Tabitha was excited, Veronica felt slightly ill. She hadn't wanted to know these things. She spent years of her life being hidden from it, and then spent just as long trying to pretend it didn't exist.

A *Goddess'* power. It was too much to consider, too much to comprehend. But there it was, flowing in her veins, whether she wanted it or not.

"Some Wielders," Tabitha continued, leaning toward Veronica as though discussing some delicious secret, "Don't need the symbols to focus their Magic. They use sheer mental focus." Her eyes were wide, wider than usual. "Incredible." She shook her head, turning back to her book and pointing to a string of symbols printed on the page. "Each symbol, or combination of symbols, means different things. You said you've used "fire" before, right?"

Used was putting it mildly. Veronica nodded.

"Good, then you already understand it a little. We should start by teaching you some of the basic symbols."

Veronica nodded again, though the idea made her want to shiver. She remembered how sick she'd been before, the fever burning her alive. That was because she *hadn't* used her Magic, according to what Rom told her. She'd been too *full* of Magic. And it made her sick.

"Do you..." Veronica wavered, unsure how to phrase the question. Tabitha waited, patient. "Do you get sick when you don't use your Magic?"

"What do you mean?" Tabitha frowned, confused. "Do you?"

"Yes. Sometimes."

"How often do you use Magic?"

Never, if she could help it. "I've... only used it a few times."

"A few times? In... your life?" She looked dumbstruck.

A blush crept over Veronica's cheeks. She felt stupid. Tabitha knew so much, and she knew nothing. "Yes," she admitted. "I've only ever used "fire," and in my whole life I've only done it twice." Once as a child, and once in the village when the soldiers and wolf had cornered them in the plum orchard.

Tabitha stared at her. Finally she asked, quietly, "Why?"

Veronica didn't want to discuss this with her. She didn't know how to explain it without offending Tabitha.

Because Magic is destruction, it's dangerous, it's power I don't want and can't control. Why would I use it at all?

"Because I never learned." It was the truth, or at least partly. An empty box shaped like the truth.

Tabitha's expression saddened, her gaze turning pitying, and Veronica felt even worse. Tabitha leaned forward and gripped her wrist. "I'll teach you," she promised.

And she did.

In a week, Veronica memorized a few basic symbols, but remembering them was not the difficult part. It was *using* them that Veronica was rubbish at.

She spent hours every day with Tabitha in a cleared space a safe distance from camp, a soldier or two accompanying them for their protection. Occasionally Liam was the one to join them, but only for a little while before he switched with someone else, going back to camp, and to Mayva, Veronica assumed.

Veronica hated being watched, but she did her best to ignore Tabitha and the men while she practiced.

"Try drawing it faster," Tabitha called. She had retreated several steps since they first started that morning, though it had long since proven unnecessary— Veronica hadn't managed to conjure a single flame all morning.

Veronica drew the symbol, faster this time, with her finger in the air. Nothing happened.

Face flushed and sweaty, her hair coming free of its braid, she turned to Tabitha, who considered her as she approached. "Has this happened before?" Tabitha asked, stepping up beside Veronica and staring into the air where Veronica had tried to draw the symbol for fire, as though it was there, just invisible.

Veronica thought of her vain attempt to use fire during the bandit attack. "Yes," she admitted.

Tabitha tapped her foot thoughtfully on the ground. "But you've succeeded in conjuring fire before, haven't you?"

It was not the orchard that Veronica recalled at Tabitha's question. It was an old, faded, gray memory. Smoke. Fire. The room falling down around her. Screams.

Cold crawled inside Veronica's fingers, and she clenched them tightly, as if she could stop the ice from creeping in any further. "Yes." Veronica's voice was flat, empty.

Tabitha's eyes found hers, and Veronica crossed her arms, glancing away.

"I see," Tabitha said, a little sadly. It was like she knew. Veronica's stomach pinched painfully, her back and neck breaking out in a sheen of cold sweat.

"We'll try something else then. We've been at this all day." She stepped back a few paces. "Water," Tabitha called once she was a fair distance away. "You remember the symbol for water?"

Veronica did. She traced the symbol, an odd loop with a line through the center, and as she did a strange sensation came over her. It was like the water that appeared before her came from her veins, like she was bleeding into the air, but at the same time it was as if the blood was not *hers*. Unnatural. The water felt unnatural, even if the act of conjuring it relieved some kind of invisible pressure in her chest.

"That's it!" Tabitha cried from somewhere behind her. A thin veil of water formed in front of Veronica, stretching and rising until it was taller than she was.

Veronica forgot the wrongness. It was beautiful.

Tabitha appeared beside her, beaming, and took hold of Veronica's other hand. She raised her own right hand and held it up in the sky. She traced a symbol into the air, so fast Veronica didn't catch what it was, and the wall of water rose up until it formed a translucent ceiling above them. Then, with a grin, Tabitha drew another symbol and the water turned to ice. It burst apart, and rained down on the ground in the form of snow.

Tabitha released Veronica's hand to stretch both of hers into the air, catching snowflakes in her palms. Veronica looked up, blinking when the flakes caught in her eyelashes.

"Well," Tabitha said with a little laugh, "You have no problem with water."

Veronica recalled the sensation of foreignness, but shook it away. Did using her Magic always feel that way? Conjuring fire in the orchard hadn't.

"Tabitha?" Veronica addressed the sky as she spoke. The snow was gone, and there was nothing but misty gray above them. "I don't understand any of this." It came out like a confession, a shameful fact.

"I know," Tabitha said. "But you will."

*   *   *

MAYVA found Angelus struggling into a shirt that evening.

"Going somewhere?" she asked.

Angelus didn't turn around, mostly because he didn't want her to see the grimace of pain on his face as he lifted his arm to thread it through the sleeve. "If I can walk I don't need to stay in bed," he said, addressing the wall of the tent in front of him.

"Very well," she said, and Angelus turned to face her, buttoning the shirt over his still bandaged chest. "Come with me."

He pushed his feet into his boots and followed after her, annoyed that he could barely keep up. He was winded after only walking a little, but Mayva gave no indication she noticed. It was nearly dark, the air smelling of pine and the mountains and smoke. It was a sharp, clear, natural smell, and Angelus found it rather alluring.

There were so many tents it was like a small village. There were people everywhere, some appearing to be around Angelus' own age, and still others that were older, their hair or beards starting to gray.

"Where are we going?" Angelus asked. The cold air bit into his aching body, but he ignored it, gritting his teeth.

Mayva didn't say anything, just pointed ahead, toward the banner. Liam, sitting on a wooden stool outside his tent, a sword and sharpening stone in his lap, looked up as they passed. He sheathed his sword and followed behind them, inserting himself easily into their midst.

"How is the training going?" Mayva asked over her shoulder.

"She shows promise," Liam said, and Angelus heard a grin in his voice. "Tabitha is an excellent teacher."

They turned, walking between a row of tents until they reached the edge of the camp. A single tent sat a short distance from the rest, occupying the very outskirt of the camp. Not far off, a group of armed men patrolled. There were more than immediately appeared necessary, and Angelus guessed Mayva must have told them about the wolves. Rom's village flashed through his mind, and the hairs on his arms stood up. Would that happen again? If this camp wasn't safe, with an army led by Mayva, then nowhere was safe.

Beside the tent, Veronica and another woman sat. They were all bright eyes and emphatic hand motions, poring over thick books. Veronica didn't look happy, exactly— but there was something different about her. Next to the other girl, she appeared to belong.

Angelus' chest felt as though it had been kicked.

"They've been at it for days now," Liam said from behind Angelus.

Angelus glanced back at Liam, who watched the two women with something close to fondness. It made Angelus' stomach curdle, a sour taste peppering his tongue.

"Veronica has already much improved."

Her name sounded wrong coming from Liam's mouth, too familiar and casual, as if he'd known her forever, as if they were friends. Angelus didn't realize his hands were fisted until his sore arms twinged as though annoyed with him.

"Tabitha is the best Wielder in our company," Mayva said. Her voice gave away no pride, but Angelus thought he sensed it all the same. "Your friend will get the help she needs."

Angelus' gut clenched painfully. *Help.* As though Veronica had some sort of disease.

"She doesn't need help," Angelus bit out, his voice barely louder than the breeze.

Mayva turned her face to his, her expression chiseled from stone, but her eyes for the first time held some heat. "You want her to remain as she was? Sickly and out of control?"

"She was learning to control it," Angelus snapped. "She just needs time."

Mayva gestured to the women sitting on the ground, Veronica's eyes lighting up as Tabitha pointed out a line from one of the books, and she nodded eagerly. "That's what she's being given."

"And what's it to you?" Angelus asked, trying but failing to keep his voice level. "Why do you care whether she can control it or not? You just want another soldier in your army. Veronica is not going to war, not for you, or anyone else."

Mayva's eyes sparked with amusement. "I wouldn't be so sure. I think there's something she wants to protect. Something she'd be willing to fight for."

When Angelus looked back at Veronica, she was already watching him. She got to her feet, her eyes never leaving him, but Angelus tore his gaze away, glaring at Mayva. "She's not your soldier." He turned, walking back to the infirmary tent.

"No," Mayva agreed as he stormed away. "She isn't."

In the tent, Angelus barely pulled on his coat before Veronica appeared.

"What are you doing?" Veronica asked, watching with wide eyes as he attempted, in vain, to thread his arm through the coat's sleeve. It was thick and black, same as the one Veronica and others around the camp wore. He'd found it at the top of a pile of clean clothes Liam brought him, and he prayed to the gods it hadn't belonged to Liam. Somehow the idea of accepting the man's charity made Angelus' flesh crawl. The clothes he'd worn when they arrived at the camp were nowhere to be seen. They were probably ruined and subsequently disposed of, and this made Angelus even angrier, though he knew it was stupid and childish.

"Leaving," Angelus bit out, gritting his teeth until he finally managed to get the sleeve on properly. "Get your things."

Veronica stared at him. Her cheeks were pink from the cold, her hair slightly wind tossed, a lock coming free of her braid.

She looked a little wild, and Angelus was too angry to admit he kind of liked it.

"But... but we can't go. You can't travel, not in your condition. And besides, where would we go? Angelus, we're right where we've been trying to get all this time. It's better than we could have hoped for. Mayva is on our side. Why are you acting like this was all a failure? It wasn't."

"All Mayva cares about is playing the leader. She wants bodies to fight and hands to carry her banner. If we stay here, we'll be soldiers. We'll belong to *her,* is that what you want?"

Veronica's eyes rounded, stunned. "So you just wanted to find her and then... what? Disappear? You aren't even going to try to help?"

"Since when do you want to fight?" Angelus bellowed. He had already been angry, but now he was on fire. "I thought you didn't want your Magic! And now you're, what, learning spells from that woman? Letting Mayva turn you into one of her dogs?"

"I'm not a dog!" Veronica shouted, her eyes blazing, on the verge of tears, but she didn't look sad. She looked angry. Her fire was rising to meet his, and they would either burn everything around them, or choke out and vanish. "You're right, I don't want this. But I *have it,* Angelus. I'm trying to be useful— I'm done staying on the sidelines while people I care about get hurt!"

"Finn is already gone!" Angelus shouted, not caring that it was cruel.

"I'm not talking about him!" Tears appeared on her cheeks like diamonds on her skin.

"Veronica." Liam appeared in the door of the tent, his voice firm and body tense, as though prepared to intervene. As if

Angelus would hurt her. "Let's go. Dinner is ready, and Tabitha wants to keep practicing afterwards."

Veronica swiped her palms across her cheeks, sniffing quietly. "I'm coming." She strode past Liam without a glance back at Angelus. Liam didn't move. He watched Angelus for a moment, his eyes narrowed, then he shook his head.

"It isn't really her you're angry with," Liam said. "Don't forget that." He left Angelus in the tent, alone.

*   *   *

VERONICA stood behind Tabitha in the line to be served dinner. A big burly man with a patch over one of his eyes ladled stew into dishes, and Veronica made her slow way down the line, her eyes still burning, but she willed away the tears. She would not cry.

"Are you alright?" Tabitha asked when they sat down on the ground. There was a large fire burning in the middle of the camp, and nearly everyone besides those on watch were gathered, sitting or standing around the fire as they ate their dinner. Nearest to where Tabitha and Veronica sat was a tall, muscular man with deeply tanned skin and a shorter woman with blonde hair so pale that the firelight made it look white. She laughed at something the man said, but Veronica didn't catch the words.

Wrapping her cold hands around the bowl of stew in her lap, Veronica gave a slight nod. "I'm fine."

"Liam told me what happened," Tabitha admitted.

Veronica said nothing, and Tabitha fell silent.

Veronica took a breath. "Tabitha. Why do you stay here?"

Tabitha blinked, surprised. "Because I want to help. Queen Mayva is trying to bring order back to this country. She stands for the same things the Savior Queen Amora stood for. Equality, safety. I want to see that vision realized."

Her answer was so simple. Veronica wished her intentions were as noble. "I don't have a vision. Not like the queen does. I just..."

Tabitha smiled knowingly. "You want to protect him."

Veronica's eyes widened, her face coloring. "Not— I mean, I don't—"

Tabitha chuckled. "It's alright, I understand."

Veronica wasn't sure she did. Sighing, she turned her eyes back to the fire, on the other side of which Mayva and Liam were talking in low voices. "Is that a good enough reason?" she muttered, more to herself than Tabitha.

"For what?" Tabitha asked, following Veronica's gaze to the fire.

"For staying. Will the queen let me stay here, let me learn from you, if I'm only in it for myself?"

"You aren't in it for yourself. You're trying to protect what's important to you." Tabitha smiled. "I think Mayva understands that better than anyone."

Mayva. Not *Queen* Mayva. Liam was the only other person in the camp Veronica ever heard address the queen by her given name. Veronica understood then that Tabitha was the queen's friend.

Not a dog, she thought, remembering Angelus' bitter words. Here Tabitha was fighting for people like herself, like Veronica, because she wanted to be. It dawned on her suddenly how

264

incredibly brave these people were. They were prepared to go to war if necessary.

For her. For those like her.

Veronica did not think she was brave. But she wondered if maybe someday, she could be.

CHAPTER TWENTY-SEVEN

VERONICA didn't go to see Angelus the next day. She spent as much time as possible with Tabitha, not only practicing Magic, but explaining her dreams, the visions she saw when she touched things. She wasn't sure why Tabitha was so willing to help her, but she was grateful regardless.

"To have the gift of Foresight and Touch is exceptionally rare. I've never met a Wielder who could do both." Tabitha regarded Veronica as though she was an especially fascinating specimen of insect, and Veronica fought the urge to squirm under her gaze.

The afternoon was sunny, and surprisingly warm after so many cloudy, cold days in a row, and they sat on the ground outside Tabitha's tent.

"Do you notice one taking precedence over the other?" Tabitha asked. "Do you use one more than the other?"

"I don't See or Touch on purpose," Veronica admitted. "Every time it's been an accident. But... the dreams happen more often." She focused on the grass beneath her, not allowing memories of her dream about Finn to surface in her mind.

Tabitha flipped open one of her many books. "Wielders who can do those kinds of things are called the Gifted. Not much is known about them, at least not that I've read. But scholars suggest the Mother Goddess gave some people gifts, or talents, that don't require symbols to use."

"Are you one?" Veronica asked. "A Gifted?"

Tabitha's finger, which had been tracking her progress down the page she was reading, paused. She hesitated. "Yes." Her voice sounded normal, but Veronica thought there was something uncertain to her posture. "I'm a Dream Walker."

Veronica frowned. "What does that mean?"

Tabitha looked up from her book. Her finger on the page still hadn't moved. "I can see people's dreams. Change them, sometimes."

Veronica's eyes widened, equal parts horrified and fascinated. "Anyone's dream?"

Tabitha grimaced. "I have to know them, or know of them, and it's easier when I've met the person, or if they are nearby, but yes. Anyone's. There are limitations, of course, there always are. But—"

"That's incredible," Veronica breathed. She meant it. It was terrifying, a gift she would never wish to possess, but it was nonetheless impressive.

Tabitha relaxed visibly, a relieved smile crossing her face. Veronica wondered if she'd been worried Veronica would be afraid of her.

"It took practice," Tabitha admitted. "But it's a valuable skill."

Veronica threaded her fingers together in her lap. "Will you show me how you learned to control it?"

Tabitha nodded quickly. "Absolutely. I'll help you."

Veronica felt an inexplicable rush of affection for the odd, but kind, Wielder beside her. She smiled, and Tabitha's eyes softened.

"Shall we start now?" Tabitha asked.

Nerves tremored in Veronica's stomach. "How?"

Tabitha shifted so she was sitting in front of Veronica. "You only See when you're dreaming, right?" Veronica nodded. "Let's see if you can do it while you're awake. Don't try to look for anything specific, just see if something comes. I'll guide you if you need me to."

"Guide?" Sweat moistened Veronica's spine. *Guide* made it sound as though she were leaving, going somewhere far off and unfamiliar.

"Talk to you," Tabitha clarified, "Make sure you stay focused."

Veronica sucked in a breath, then blew it out slowly, closing her eyes.

"It's alright," Tabitha whispered. Was she whispering? Her voice sounded far away. "Just let go."

There was nothing but darkness behind Veronica's eyelids. Panic was starting to rise in her throat. What if she *did* See? Her visions had always been of death, of separation, of pain. Whatever she was afraid of, she saw it. And it came true.

Please, Veronica thought, or prayed, *Show me something good. It can't all be dark.*

The black shifted, paling, until she made out movement behind a gray haze, like watching the sun through the fabric of the tent roofs. She had no body. She was just floating.

"Tabitha?" she breathed, unsure if she'd actually made a sound.

"I'm here," Tabitha promised, her voice miles away, carried by a wind Veronica couldn't feel. "Can you see anything?"

Veronica couldn't. But she did smell something. Salt water. A bird cried out above her, and suddenly Veronica was standing, barefoot, on a sandy beach, kernels of warm sand biting into her skin.

The ocean. It was a blanket of cloudy blue stretching out forever in front of her. Her heart swelled, overwhelmed, at the sight of it.

She turned, and saw there were two other people on the beach. A small child, his back to Veronica, walked inches from the water, his hair wavy and dark brown. A tall man walked beside him, a hand outstretched to the boy. The little boy wrapped his hand around one of the man's long fingers.

When the boy turned back to Veronica, smiling, the whole world narrowed to his eyes, forest green and sparkling with his smile. Though she knew she'd never seen him before, he seemed familiar. Something about the shape of his face, the color of his hair. And then she realized why she recognized him. He looked like her.

Veronica's eyes flew open, her hands flying up to cover her face. There were tears on her cheeks, though she wasn't sure why, and she panted into her palms, her chest heaving as though she had been running.

"What did you see?" Tabitha asked in a rush. "Did it work?"

Veronica lowered her hands, which shook slightly. She stared at her palms, lying face up in her lap. "I... I saw..."

Something behind Veronica caught Tabitha's attention, and Veronica turned.

Angelus walked nearby, his limp gone but his head hanging low. He turned, almost like he could sense Veronica's gaze. His eyes met hers. Green. Green as the forest all around them.

Veronica turned her head away.

Tabitha peered into her face. "Are you alright?"

Veronica forced herself to speak. "Yes, I'm... I'm fine. I just..."

She glanced back at Angelus, but he was gone, leaving her with her pounding, unsteady heart.

CHAPTER TWENTY-EIGHT

ANGELUS laid in his cot, idly turning the identification necklace over in his fingers, and didn't look up when an unfamiliar male voice barked from the other side of the tent, "Come with me."

"Why?"

"Orders from Her Majesty," the soldier said. "She requests your presence."

Her Majesty. Angelus sneered, but he got to his feet, tucking the necklace back into his shirt. Pieces of the glass had fallen out, leaving a few jagged teeth attached to the gold frame. The point of one of the glass shards pricked at his chest, though Angelus barely registered the sting. His ankle no longer pained him, but his side still ached. A medic removed the bandaging that morning, revealing horrid purple and green bruising. Nothing that would scar, though. For once.

The soldier at the tent door didn't give any indication what *Her Majesty* wanted with him, and Angelus fought the urge to ram his shoulder into the man's as he passed him. These people. What was it about them that infuriated him so much?

Angelus was taken not to the queen's tent, as expected, but to a line of stakes hammered into the ground, where a few horses were tied to them. An enormous black horse took up most of the space, its neck thicker around than Angelus' waist, its midnight mane and tail rippling like flags in the breeze blowing from the north. Angelus froze as soon as he saw it. He'd never seen a horse that big before. It looked like it could trample him if it felt so inclined, and by the way its eyes locked on Angelus, he wondered if it was indeed so inclined.

To his amazement, Queen Mayva appeared around the horse's other side, dragging a brush down its flank. Though she was rendered much smaller standing next to the beast, she did not appear out of place beside it. Her eyes fell to Angelus, and she beckoned him forward. She'd replaced her armor with black leather trousers and a long dark gray shirt, over which she wore a vest made of what might have been blackbear fur, fastened in the front by three silver buttons. Her swords were at her sides instead of on her back, and without the armor she seemed a little more human, and a little less like a force of nature.

"I've reached a decision. You will join me and my company down the mountain. We will be looking for a territory to make our base."

"Then what?" Angelus asked.

"We gather as many as we can. And then we find Artemis. End this war before it can truly begin."

Angelus glanced back at the camp, full of armored men and women. It looked an awful lot like a war had already begun.

"And Veronica?"

"She's training with Tabitha. She wants to help. I won't be the one to refuse her."

"She'll be slaughtered," Angelus snapped, "She's just a girl. She isn't a fighter."

Mayva turned to him. "And you are?"

Yes. But not for her. Not for Mayva. Not for anyone. Except...

Mayva shoved the brush into Angelus' hand, wiping her palms against her thighs. "You'll make yourself useful, regardless." She stepped back, folding her arms, waiting for Angelus to move. He didn't. He did not take orders from her. He would not be her stable boy, while she went off to play the leader.

He expected her to walk away, but she didn't. Instead, Mayva picked up another brush from the ground and started moving it down the horse's flank again. Angelus remained where he was.

"His name is Drom," Mayva said, breaking the tense silence.

Drom.

Andromeda.

Angelus glanced back at the banner, the swords crossed behind the black horse. *This* horse. The cold in Angelus' chest had fingers, spreading out slowly into his limbs, as he began to wonder...

He touched the brush to the horse's side. The beast didn't protest. So Angelus brushed him.

They didn't say anything for what felt like hours, until Mayva spoke. "You will begin training with me tomorrow. Your injuries are healed enough, you need to stay sharp if you're going to be of any help to us."

Angelus looked over the top of the horse's back to see Mayva's face. "I don't need any training. I was a soldier, and your sister's guard, in case you've forgotten."

The barest hint of a smirk. "I haven't forgotten."

*   *   *

THE next morning Angelus found a leather training suit on the floor beside his cot. It was the same as the ones used in the castle during training, the chest piece and leg protectors thick enough to block a wooden sword's blow, but Angelus didn't think Mayva would be using a pretend sword.

Irritated, he pulled on the leg pieces, and slipped the chest piece over his head, securing the leather ties on either side.

There was a soldier waiting outside for him, though the guide wasn't really necessary. A large crowd had gathered in the center of the camp, where the nightly fire was usually lit. But instead of a bonfire lighting the early morning, the gray, overcast sky gazed down on a square of earth sectioned off by four lines cut into the ground, nearly the width of Angelus' foot.

Mayva stood beside it, waiting for him. She was wearing a similar outfit to his, but instead of old brown leather gear, her chest piece was black, patterns of vines and tree branches carved into it. Her swords were once again strapped to her back, and she looked ready for war.

For the first time, nerves tickled at Angelus' insides. This was training, he reminded himself. She wasn't there to kill him.

But it didn't help to remember that she *could* kill him. Angelus was well trained, but Mayva's entire life was battle. That was her role. Her task was perhaps the simplest of any of the queens. Be the last one standing, no matter what.

Angelus stopped at the edge of one of the lines in the dirt, Mayva across from him on the other side of the makeshift arena. Someone handed Angelus a sword, a real one, and he took it, letting it rest loosely in his hand. His pulse was beginning to race, shoulders and hands itching with anticipation, but he wouldn't show it.

Mayva pointed to the ground, and Angelus stepped over the line. She did not. Instead, she gave him an appraising look, then just shook her head a little. Liam stepped in front of her, his blue eyes locking on Angelus' green ones. His leathers were identical to Angelus', and he carried a single sword in his hands. He looked like he knew how to use it.

Without even a glance back at the two men in the ring, Mayva walked away, her hands behind her back, her spine straight and eyes ahead. As though this were a sideshow she'd grown bored with.

Someone in the crowd shouted, "Fight!" and suddenly Liam was lunging for him, his sword a long silver arm cleaving the air. He had Angelus' confusion and surprise on his side, and he used them. The edge of the sword smashed against Angelus' side, pressing the leather into Angelus' bruised side like a fist grinding into his bones. Angelus gasped, nearly dropping his sword, but he swung it instinctively upward, blocking Liam's next attack.

The crowd rustled, excited, eager.

"She said she was training me," Angelus barked at Liam.

Liam grinned. "She is." He lunged again, but this time Angelus was ready. And now he was angry. Was she trying to make a fool of him?

Liam snapped his head to the side to avoid a slashed neck, and Angelus expected someone to stop him, to tell him he couldn't go for the throat, that it was against the rules of this game. But no one said a word. And then Angelus understood. There were no rules.

Mayva's soldiers were trained this way. They fought and they won, or they would bleed.

But he would not be her soldier. He wasn't going to play her game.

Liam raised his weapon again, but instead of lifting his own to block, Angelus straightened, and threw down his sword.

Liam froze, barely keeping his blade from striking Angelus' head. He glanced at Mayva, who stood watching, face impassive, and for the first time Liam appeared uncertain.

Mayva raised a hand.

The match was over.

Angelus was already walking away, tearing at the ties holding the leather chest piece in place. He yanked it over his head and tossed it aside. He heard it hit the ground with a thud, but didn't look back to see where it landed.

No one stopped him as he strode back to the infirmary tent, not even Veronica. His eyes met hers for a single heartbeat, his full of rage and hers wide with shock. In that moment, he hated her just as much as the others.

If she wanted to play soldier with Mayva, fine. He'd let her. But Angelus was done being used. Queens be damned.

CHAPTER TWENTY-NINE

"WHAT happened?" Veronica demanded as soon as she caught up with Liam. He walked beside Mayva, but when he paused to look at Veronica, Mayva did not. She went into her tent, not sparing Veronica a glance.

Liam turned fully to face her, hands on his hips. "Nothing happened, he's fine." He didn't sound happy about it.

"Why did he give up?" Veronica asked. Watching Angelus throw down the sword, and as a result nearly have his head taken off... The image would not soon leave her.

"He didn't," Liam said with a frown. "He's trying to make a point."

Veronica was bewildered. "What do you mean?"

Liam's expression softened. He was so different from Angelus; she remembered his face after the fight she witnessed in the village, when his eyes had been burning, his body still back in the ring long after he walked away. He never truly walked away. But Liam looked like he always did; fighting didn't do to him what it did to Angelus. Whatever that was.

Liam met her gaze, his eyes warm, the corner of his mouth lifting in that reassuring way it did, and Veronica was reminded of something, or someone, but she couldn't place it. "You've been training with Tabitha. He's training in his own way. He's just doing it a bit louder than you."

Veronica still didn't understand, so she only sighed, "Just... don't hurt him."

Liam shook his head. "I'm not the one who's hurting him. I think you know that."

Veronica thought she was starting to.

*   *   *

GOING off with Tabitha to practice in her secluded little corner of camp was a relief to Veronica. No one in the camp could talk about anything but Angelus' spectacle that morning. Some appeared angry, saying his defiance was disrespect thrown in Queen Mayva's face. Others seemed merely amused, as though Angelus were a child that would come around in time.

Veronica read the same page in Tabitha's book three times before she slammed it closed, frustrated. She couldn't focus.

Tabitha glanced up from her own book. "Something wrong?"

"No," Veronica shook her head. "I didn't find the symbol you were looking for. Any luck?"

Tabitha turned the book around so Veronica could see. She tapped a triangular symbol in a long list on the page. "This one.

We can use this, in a combination with a few others, to help you with your fire conjuring."

Veronica stared at her, stunned. "What?"

Tabitha's eyes glittered, eager and excited. "The books say Magic is energy. But I believe it's more complicated than that. Magic is the Goddess' energy, coming through us, but the ability to control that Magic comes from our own energy. What if there was a way to focus our energy, in its entirety, on the Magic? More control. More power."

Veronica barely understood half of what Tabitha said on a good day, and this was not a good day. "Tabitha, what are you saying?"

She thrust the book into Veronica's hands. She was familiar enough now with the basic symbols that she could pick them out of variants, but nothing on the pages Tabitha showed her was remotely familiar. It was like another language entirely. Veronica glanced from the book to Tabitha, shaking her head, still not understanding.

"Don't you see?" Tabitha asked, almost giddy. "If we write some of these symbols on you, it might focus your energy enough so you can use fire. It's just targeting the Magic inside you, drawing it out."

Veronica's stomach pinched painfully. She wasn't sure why— she should have been elated. But the last time she used fire...

"What if I lose control again?" Veronica breathed.

Tabitha smiled at her. "You won't."

"Promise?"

"I promise."

VERONICA met Tabitha outside her tent that night. It felt strange to be there at night— they always practiced together in the morning. She wasn't sure why Tabitha insisted on meeting so late, when most everyone else in the camp was asleep or on patrol, but she was too nervous to ponder it very much.

Huddled in her coat, Tabitha waited outside her tent, a misshapen and featureless ghost.

The moonlight made their breath look like smoke, but Veronica wasn't cold; her back and hands were slick with sweat, and her body hummed with anxious energy.

"Are you ready?" Tabitha asked, her voice barely more than a whisper.

Veronica wasn't, but she nodded. Tabitha led her into the trees, to the spot where they usually practiced, though it was entirely foreign in the dark. The trees enclosing the sphere of cleared space were menacing, anonymous black shapes, the moon directly above them an all seeing, unblinking silver eye. Veronica shivered. "Tabitha," she whispered, then cleared her throat, unsure why she felt the need to whisper. "What are we doing out here? Why couldn't this wait until morning?"

Without answering, Tabitha paused and turned to face Veronica. She drew a symbol in the air, and it transformed seamlessly into a floating ball of light that hovered above their heads, bathing their faces in a soft yellow light. Tabitha reached into the pocket of her coat and drew out a tiny vial of what looked like black ink. "Hold out your hand."

Nerves flickered in Veronica's stomach, but she obeyed. Tabitha knelt on the ground before her, opening the vial and dipping her finger into it, before tracing small symbols across the top of Veronica's hand. Her finger tickled Veronica's skin, but as the inky symbols took shape across her hand, the world began to fade, until there was nothing except her pulse. She was hyper aware of her heartbeat, and something else, a thread pulled taut in her chest, drawing everything toward it. Nothing in the world existed except that.

When Tabitha smiled up at her, Veronica could not smile back. She had no body. She was just—

"Ready?" Tabitha whispered, getting to her feet.

"Ready," Veronica breathed.

Tabitha stepped back, her eyes eager and hands clasped before her in seemingly unconscious anticipation.

Veronica took a deep breath, then released it. Her arm extended, almost as though it were a possessed limb. Somehow, she was not surprised when the fire appeared, crackling to life. It hung in the air, and Veronica held it, slowly withdrawing her hand and willing it to stay.

"Now try to move it," Tabitha encouraged.

Veronica held her palm in front of her. The fiery spiral moved closer, morphing into a ball of flame. It was warm, not hot, when it drew into her palm. It was like holding a candle.

"You're doing it!" Tabitha cried, voice shockingly loud in the otherwise silent night, but Veronica wasn't paying attention. She focused, unblinking, on the fire in her palm. It flickered and swayed. Then Veronica raised her arm, and tossed the flame into the air.

It burst up into the sky, higher than the trees, and spread out in a flash of light before it disappeared.

Tabitha appeared in front of her, grabbing her arms and shaking her, face beaming. "It worked!" she was saying, but Veronica was far away from her body. She was somewhere in the sky above, with that fire, and it took Tabitha shaking her to bring her back.

Slowly, very slowly, Veronica returned. She was exhausted, as if she'd been running. Sensation came flooding back, so fast and with such ferocity Veronica's legs nearly gave out. "It worked," Veronica breathed. She held onto Tabitha's arms to stay upright. "You were right." It was finally dawning on her what had just happened. "Tabitha, you're a genius!"

Tabitha's face was practically glowing, and despite Veronica's fatigue she couldn't help but smile. Tabitha helped her to the ground, where Veronica sat to catch her breath.

"Is it supposed to be like that?" Veronica asked.

Tabitha shook her head. "Like what?"

"Like..." She struggled to find the words. "Like the Magic takes over?" She looked up at Tabitha. "It's... it's supposed to feel that way, right?"

It might have only been the minimal light, but Tabitha's eyes seemed to go strangely blank, emptying of light, though her smile remained. "Of course," she said.

*   *   *

WHEN Veronica could stand without help, she made her way back to her tent. For a moment, she was tempted to go to the infirmary tent to tell Angelus what happened, what she'd done, but she didn't.

The torches in the camp flickered where they were driven into the ground, and Veronica was surprised at how reassuring those little fires were. She walked beside one, and caught sight of the symbols still written on her hand. She lifted them to her face, trying to make them out. They were much more detailed and intricate than the symbols she was familiar with, with artful lines and curves and embellishments. As she observed them, she frowned. What she thought was black ink was actually a deep, dark crimson.

Something uneasy flitted across Veronica's stomach, up into her chest and making a little chill slither up her arms. Raising her hand to her nose, she breathed in. The scent of the forest had masked the smell before, but now, Veronica recognized it. It wasn't ink Tabitha wrote with on her skin. It was blood.

CHAPTER THIRTY

IN the dream, Angelus ran. Whether he ran toward, or away from something, he didn't know. He just ran, his bare feet silent on the cold castle floor. The ceiling above was arched, narrow windows nestled between the many doors occupying both sides of the walls around him. The corridor was endless.

A door slammed behind him, and he whirled. "Andromeda?" he called. There was no one there.

Another door up ahead crashed open, and Angelus lunged for it before it could close. Suddenly he was in Andromeda's bedchamber. The wide bed with red sheets and blankets was perfectly made, the room pristine.

"Where are you?" Angelus called into the empty space. The room wasn't nearly large enough for his voice to echo, but his words carried back to him, bouncing off the walls.

"She's gone," came another voice, directly behind him.

Turning, he found himself face to face with Andromeda. The relief was a physical pain in his chest, making his legs weak. He shook his head. "What? No, you're—"

"She's gone," Andromeda repeated, her voice louder, sharper. Her face shifted, the outline of her body flickering, until she was Veronica. "She's gone," Veronica said, but her voice was still Andromeda's.

Angelus took a step back, then another, shaking his head. "Where is she?" he demanded, hysteria building in his throat.

A hand closed around his shoulder, turning him roughly around. Mayva glared at him, her nails digging into his skin. "She's gone," Mayva said. But it was a man's voice that came out of her mouth. Angelus blinked, and it was Resmond standing before him.

Angelus' knees buckled, and he fell to the ground, shrinking away from Resmond.

"She left you, boy," Resmond sneered. Or was it Mayva? He didn't know anymore. Resmond laughed, and it was just as hoarse and terrible as Angelus remembered. Veronica stepped beside Resmond, and he was Mayva again. They turned away from him, walking together toward the door.

"Wait!" Angelus cried. He couldn't get off the floor. Something was holding his body in place. He looked down at his hands, which had disappeared underneath the black water rising up from the floor. "Don't leave me here!" He would die, he would drown.

Veronica and Mayva were gone, and it was only Andromeda in the doorway. The light from outside the room bathed her in bluish light. She didn't turn back. She walked away and shut the door behind her as the water covered Angelus' face, and his screaming mouth filled with black water the flavor of blood.

When he woke up, he turned to lean over the side of the cot, and vomited. He heaved and heaved, but there was nothing left. His eyes swam, his nose and throat burning. He could still taste the black water in his mouth, still feel it filling his ears.

He sat up, slowly, and everything around him spun around and around. The infirmary tent was empty, a couple of lanterns illuminating the space in a dim, tranquil light.

He was so cold, despite the fact his shirt was drenched with sweat. His teeth chattered violently, and he wrapped his arms around himself. All he could do was sit there, shivering.

"Angelus," came a soft voice. A hand touched his damp forehead.

His head snapped up, and there she was. Andromeda sat on the edge of the cot, peering at him with her head cocked slightly. Her concern was only evident in the slight tightness at the corner of her mouth. "You have a fever," she said, withdrawing her hand.

"I'm fine," he said through his chattering teeth. Andromeda raised an amused eyebrow, but she said nothing. She just got to her feet, and went to the tent door.

"Wait," Angelus gasped, rising from the cot. He could barely keep his footing, the spinning room threatened to topple him over the edge of the world.

Andromeda did not look back. She opened the tent door, and stepped outside.

Angelus did the only thing he'd ever known to do. He followed.

CHAPTER THIRTY-ONE

VERONICA wasn't surprised that Angelus was absent from yet another meal. Worry settled low in her gut as she sat beside Liam on a log before the fire. She stirred the broth in her bowl absently.

The back of her hand was pale and shiny in the fire light. She'd washed away the symbols Tabitha had written there, but she still thought she could feel them.

"It'll get cold," Liam warned, before taking a deep drink of his own broth straight from the bowl.

Veronica blinked, her eyes focusing on the bowl in her lap. She took a few spoonfuls, but it was all she could manage. "I'm going to go see if he wants anything," Veronica said, getting to her feet.

"He's been offered food, he won't take it," Liam said, and he sounded annoyed, not with Veronica but with Angelus. For just a breath, Veronica allowed herself to be annoyed with him too. She had enough to worry about without Angelus refusing to eat. The skin across her knuckles tingled, and she shivered.

"Liam?" she asked, eyes on the ground as she sat back down.

He set his empty bowl aside, looking at her.

"Where did Tabitha come from?"

He seemed surprised by the question, but he said, "She was one of the first people to join Mayva's army. She doesn't talk about it, though from what I can tell she was treated horribly by soldiers in her village when they discovered what she was. We found her in the woods, practically starved to death."

Veronica's stomach tightened painfully. "And... you trust her?"

Liam was quiet so long, Veronica turned to face him. "I do." His expression softened a bit. "If you have something you want to ask Tabitha, ask her."

Something like relief warmed Veronica's chest. Of course, she was being silly. Tabitha was Liam's, and Mayva's, friend. She was jumping to conclusions, being paranoid.

Veronica nodded. "I will. I'm going to find her to practice more."

She stood, setting down her bowl, and started toward Tabitha's tent, her chest a bit lighter. When she reached the tent on the edge of camp, she stepped in front of the tent door and called, "Tabitha?"

There was no answer. She hesitated, then parted the tent flap and peered inside. Tabitha wasn't there.

Frowning, Veronica glanced around. She hadn't seen Tabitha at dinner. She peered around the trees on the edge of camp, the gaps between the trunks like black mouths opening in front of her.

With a strange, inexplicable certainty, Veronica knew Tabitha would not be found in camp.

She stepped into the forest.

In the dark, the sounds of the forest plucked at her nerves, winding her tighter and tighter until she thought she might snap. When she heard a murmur coming from the trees beyond, she froze.

A voice, low and hypnotic, the words unintelligible, was coming from somewhere close by. When Veronica, carefully, silently, crept through to the clearing, she couldn't immediately process what she was seeing.

Tabitha knelt before a circle on the ground, made from thin twigs and dead branches. There was something small and white at the center of the circle. Four knives protruded from the mass, and it wasn't until Veronica crept closer did she understand what it was.

A white rabbit, pinned to the ground by blades. It was shaking, and Veronica, horrified, realized it was still alive. For a moment she just stared at it, but when Tabitha raised another knife and pressed it to the rabbit's stomach, Veronica finally found her voice.

"Tabitha?" she gasped, unable to make her voice louder.

Tabitha was standing and facing her so fast Veronica didn't track the movement. She was simply sitting and then instantly on her feet in front of her.

"What are you doing?" Tabitha demanded, appearing more surprised than angry. Still, the knife in her hand did little to reassure Veronica.

"What am *I* doing?" Veronica hissed. She pointed to the... sacrifice. There was no other name for it. Tabitha's hands were covered in blood. "What are *you* doing?"

Tabitha dropped the knife, as though only just remembering she was still holding it, and extended her red-stained palms out to Veronica. "I can explain."

Veronica only stared at her. The light from the moon above and the single candle at their feet turned Tabitha's face blue-black, her eyes anonymous shapes in her barely-there face.

"The symbols I drew on your hand, I need this in order for them to work."

"And what is *this?*" Veronica swept her hand toward the bizarre, sickening scene before them. The rabbit was no longer moving, though its eyes were open. There was so much blood all around it— she was shocked something so small could hold so much blood.

"A ritual." Tabitha didn't look the least bit concerned, or ashamed. She merely looked hurried, as if she had to explain this all to Veronica as quickly as possible. "Don't look so frightened," she chastised, and Veronica gaped at the lunacy of this request.

Veronica could admit to herself that she did not understand very much about Magic, but she didn't have to in order to know, deep in her bones, that there was something wrong with this. Magic was from the Earth Goddess— it was energy, creation. This was...

"Our Magic isn't unlimited," Tabitha went on, "It might appear that way, but it isn't. We can create, we can manipulate, but there is no way to manipulate the Magic itself. But this—" She pointed to the bloody circle behind her, her eyes wide and bright, almost feverish with excitement— "This breaks every barrier, Veronica. There is a whole new world of possibilities when you can touch the Magic itself."

Veronica's stomach hurt with sudden nausea. There was no wind, not even a breeze, to carry away the thick stench of blood, and Veronica thought she might choke on it. "What... what are you talking about?" But she thought she knew. The symbols written in blood on her hands, the fire coming effortlessly when before it had been impossible. *Touch the Magic.* Tabitha had reached inside her and forced the fire out. A horrible shiver raked its claws over Veronica's body. She felt violated, like something had been taken from her. "You manipulated my Magic?" The idea sickened her, but she wasn't sure why. It just *felt* wrong. Was it?

For the first time, Tabitha looked defensive. She seemed disappointed Veronica did not understand her brilliance. "We need this, Veronica," Tabitha said, a bit of a snap entering her voice. "*You* need this. You couldn't conjure fire without it. I *helped* you."

Veronica stumbled back as though she'd been slapped. She couldn't speak, her throat was coated in the reek of the crimson river at their feet. She'd *allowed* Tabitha to use this Magic on her.

"Magic as you and I understand it isn't going to be enough to defeat someone with the kind of Magic Artemis has access to." Tabitha's voice was rising, angry. "We have to do what it takes to defeat him! We can't let him win just because he's willing to use Blood Magic when we aren't!"

Veronica still said nothing.

"He killed Finn!" Tabitha shouted. "He wants to kill *us!* Don't you want him to pay?"

Veronica froze. She could only stare at Tabitha for a moment before she said, "Tabitha." Her voice was the barest hint of a whisper. "How did you know Artemis killed Finn?"

Angelus told the queen that Artemis killed Andromeda. No one ever mentioned Finn. Why would they have? No one knew who he was.

Except Tabitha.

"Tabitha." Veronica's voice betrayed a breath of fear. She took one step back. Then another. "How did you—"

"You told me," Tabitha said dismissively.

Lie. Veronica never told her anything of the kind.

"Don't walk away," Tabitha snapped.

Veronica realized her feet were moving, backwards, toward camp.

"We need this!" Tabitha repeated, voice growing strangely desperate. "You need me Veronica! You can't fight them without this, without me!"

Veronica ran, never once looking back. Cold sweat made her shirt stick to her back, her fur lined gloves moist against her palms. Her heart was beating so fast it hurt.

She broke through the line of trees, nearly colliding with Liam and two other men following closely behind him.

"Veronica," he said, startled, then relieved. "Is Angelus with you?"

Veronica blinked. "What— no, no he isn't." Her eyes took in the torches they held, their swords or bows in hand. "What happened? Where is he?"

"We don't know," Liam said. "No one can find him. We thought you two left together, we were coming to look for you. Where were you?"

Veronica couldn't answer, but in that instant it didn't matter. Angelus was gone? Her first thought was that he'd been taken, that the wolves must have found him, but then another idea tugged at her, unpleasant and heavy. What if he'd left?

"I was with Tabitha," Veronica said quickly. "I'll go with you, help you find him."

Liam looked as though he was about to argue, but he just nodded. He pulled a hunting knife free from a sheath at his hip and handed it to her. "Let's go."

CHAPTER THIRTY-TWO

ANGELUS stumbled through the dark trees. It was bitterly cold. The moonlight, smoky behind a covering of clouds, illuminated the steam of Angelus' rapid breaths as he crashed through the brush on numb feet. The fabric of his shirt caught on branches as if sharp talons were reaching down from the trees around him. The forest could have been the mountain greenery he'd grown used to, or it could have been the trees around the lake at the castle. The cold, the smell, was the same.

Andromeda danced in front of his vision, disappearing into the trees, a silvery wraith he couldn't catch. The world spun, round and round like a top. Angelus stumbled, his breathing loud in his ears. Cold. He was so cold. He shook violently, barely able to stay upright, reaching for trees and rocks to balance himself. But he kept running. He needed to find her. If he could just catch her—

Is this a dream?

"Andromeda?" he called out in the dark, his voice a thin tremor, strained from the cold. The freezing air speared his chest, making him cough. He couldn't feel his hands, his feet. He tumbled to the side, reaching out blindly, palm raking against the rough bark of a tree. He held onto it as the dark woods around him blurred into a whirl of black and blue.

He'd lost sight of her. Where was she? He had to find her, had to bring her back. Somehow he knew that if he could just find her, touch her, then everything would be alright.

He blinked rapidly, trying to clear his vision and stop the world from spinning.

Where am I?

The woods. The woods by the lake, at the castle. He wasn't too late. He could save her. Hope and relief were a sickness inside him.

But... no. Something wasn't right. These woods were different, colder, darker.

Where am I?

The trees went abruptly silent, as if someone had pressed their palms over Angelus' ears. He couldn't see her, and slowly, distantly, a ringing started somewhere in his head.

He was completely still. He might not have been breathing.

Gone.

No. No, she wasn't gone, she couldn't be.

"I'm sorry," he gasped. Something hot and wet touched his face, like blood trickling from an open wound. He tasted salt. Tears. He didn't understand what he'd done, why she was angry with him, why she would leave and not take him with her, but he must have done something. "Andromeda, I'm sorry. Please come back."

She did not answer.

She did not come for him.

She had always come for him.

"Don't do this," he begged. His legs were slowly liquifying as his body understood, even if his mind couldn't catch up, that there was nothing he could do, nowhere to run, no way to catch her. His knees grew cold and damp where they sank into the wet forest floor. His breathing was a loud, sharp blur of noise in his ears. He clutched his head, pressing so hard his skull threatened to cave in.

Come back. I need you. I don't know what to do. Just tell me what to do.

"Come back!" He might have shouted it, or perhaps only thought the words. "Come back, damn it! *Don't leave me here!*"

It was as though one of his limbs had vanished, left behind and buried at the bottom of a lake as salty as tears.

No. No, no, no.

"Please," he begged, voice like vapor, grasping at the trunk of a tree to help him stand. He stumbled forward in the dark. "I'm not ready yet." The ground grew uneven, and he fell, his ankle turning, and his face smashed into something sharp. A rock? He was blind in the dark. Hot blood smeared over his face, running down from a gash across his temple. The forest spun and swirled, nausea crawling up his throat. His chest was all aching and sharp, terrible spasms.

"He's here!" came a shout in the dark, but it was far, far away.

Hands appeared, turning him onto his back. Blue eyes watched him from above, like two small moons.

"You're alright," Liam said. "Help is coming. Can you stand?"

Angelus didn't answer.

"Can you hear me?"

Angelus' eyes closed, and he never wanted to open them again. Liam picked him up, grunting as he maneuvered Angelus' weight so his stomach was pressed against Liam's shoulder. Liam straightened, and Angelus' feet left the ground.

"You're alright," Liam repeated.

But he wasn't. Angelus wasn't alright.

"Angelus!" Veronica's frantic cry cut through the fog, long enough for Angelus to lift his head. The bonfire blazed in front of them, Liam walking toward it with Angelus still hanging over his shoulder like game brought in from a hunt.

Angelus was suddenly on his back, soft blankets brushing his skin. The tent was so warm after the woods.

"Angelus?" Hands, Veronica's small, thin hands, touched his face. Angelus realized his eyes were open, though he couldn't see anything but blurred shapes and far off fragments of light, as if his head were under water. *"Angelus?"*

He didn't recognize his own name. It didn't belong to him, it was an empty word without meaning.

When darkness claimed him, he did not know, nor did he care, if it was sleep or death.

CHAPTER THIRTY-THREE

LIAM, Mayva, and Veronica were always with Angelus.

Mayva told Liam to take him into her tent, instead of returning him to the infirmary tent, and at first Veronica felt awkward being in the Second Queen's own tent, but worry quickly replaced any sort of self consciousness.

Angelus. Angelus was ill.

It was obvious in the fat, blue veins webbing underneath his eyes and across his eyelids, in his deathly pale color and his constant trembling. It was as if the cold was coming from inside him, an ice chip lodged in his soul that was slowly freezing him to death, despite his fevered skin.

Veronica gave up asking why Angelus had been in the woods last night. No one knew. No one noticed him leave.

Had he been under the influence of some fever hallucination? Had he intentionally tried to leave without her?

Mayva stood a ways off from the bed, eyes on Angelus as though he were a mildly interesting puzzle she'd been presented with. Her eyes were so cold, but Veronica wasn't entirely fooled by this act of indifference. He was sleeping in her tent, after all.

The queen was starting to remind her of another black-haired warrior. Just a little.

Liam gathered a damp rag in his hands, ringing it out slightly before laying it over Angelus' forehead. And Veronica finally realized who he reminded her of. When his expression was soft, his hands working with fragile things instead of weapons, he looked a lot like Finn.

Veronica turned her eyes away.

"Tabitha is probably looking for you," Liam said quietly to her.

A chill slithered up Veronica's spine. She hadn't seen Tabitha since—

"Liam?" Veronica's voice was small. "Do... Do you know what Blood Magic is?"

He blinked at her in surprise. Mayva spoke before he did, her sharp, hard voice a knife blade through Veronica's chest. "It's an evil, unnatural form of Magic." Veronica sensed the queen's heavy stare upon her, but she couldn't lift her head to meet it. "It's taboo, a violation."

There was a heavy silence. Then Veronica asked, "Why?"

"Because it is used to manipulate Magic. To touch another person's Magic... you might as well have touched their soul, and bent it to your will."

Veronica's eyes fell to her hands, clasped tightly in her lap. She could still feel the bloody symbols burning into her skin, and it made her sick. Tabitha had touched her Magic. Had *wielded* her

Magic. Her skin crawled like a million cockroaches were scuttling over her arms and back.

"Why are you asking?" Mayva's voice hadn't changed, but the atmosphere had. It was too quiet, the air growing heavier and heavier by the second.

Veronica rose, unable to meet the queen's eye, unable to answer her question. Not until...

"You're right," she said to Liam. "I think Tabitha is looking for me."

*　　*　　*

IT was early. Dawn had barely arrived, and the camp was asleep. Veronica walked to Tabitha's tent alone, the mountains around the camp deathly silent.

Tabitha's tent was quiet, and she looked up in surprise when Veronica pushed the tent flap open. She was sitting on the ground, legs folded under her with a book in her hands. When her eyes met Veronica's, she closed the book and got to her feet. Veronica stepped into the tent, letting the flap fall closed behind her.

"I want to know how you knew about Finn." It wasn't what she'd planned to say, but the words came out firm.

Tabitha shook her head. "I already told you. You said he—"

"No, I didn't." Veronica was impressed with the evenness of her voice, despite the anger swelling in her chest. "How did you know?"

Tabitha rolled her eyes, scoffing, and brushed past Veronica, letting her arm hit Veronica's as she passed. Veronica whirled, grabbing onto Tabitha's shoulder. Anger pulsed inside her, along with an understanding of what she needed to do.

She tightened her hold on Tabitha's shoulder, and Tabitha didn't break the contact fast enough.

Images swirled like the contents of a cauldron, bubbling and boiling over, some real, and others that felt wrong. Dreams of dreams and lies about lies. There were forests, like the ones around them, but the trees were younger, in the throes of spring, not autumn's chill, and a sense of such desperate fear it was unbearable. She was being chased— someone was throwing rocks at her, trying to hit her as she bolted through the trees. "Witch!" cried voices from behind, children's voices, "Kill the witch!" Then the images shifted, and there were soldiers all around her, raising long metal poles above their heads, and bringing them down on her arms, her legs, her back. "Sing, little bird!" one of them shouted. "Sing! Show us what you can do."

But then there were other things, impossible things, grand carriages pulled by horses, gardens brimming with thorned roses like globs of blood on thick bushes, a throne, washed black by dim candlelight.

And Finn.

Veronica was shocked to see his face thrown in front of her eyes. He was sitting across from her in a carriage, a white physician's robe wrapped around him. And then Angelus was there, and he was smiling, just like in the vision Veronica saw all those weeks ago, when she touched the letter. Queen Andromeda's letter.

And then there she was. Andromeda, tall and beautiful, with terrible dark eyes centuries older than her young face. She was barefoot, and Veronica watched her and a young red-haired girl walking through a dark, moonlit patch of grass. Veronica. Veronica was the girl.

No. Tabitha was the girl.

A scream wrenched Veronica back to herself, her own mind, her own memories, but her head was still full of falsehood. Of dreams that were not her own.

Tabitha was screaming. She'd fallen to her knees and was clutching her head, curled in on herself like she was trying to protect her center from being hit.

Veronica stumbled backward, suddenly afraid, ready to bolt as though Tabitha were some creature that would bite, that would attack.

"What did you do?" Veronica cried. She was still reeling, unsure what had been real and what had been a dream.

Finn's face, exactly as she remembered it, young and handsome, long golden curls and eyes like a sunset, was branded on her mind's eye. A memory. A memory that wasn't hers. But it wasn't Tabitha's either.

"What did you do?" Veronica demanded again, her voice rising, becoming harder, angrier. "Tabitha— *What did you do?*"

Dream Walking. She remembered the words, remembered when Tabitha told her of her strange and rare gift.

Tabitha didn't answer, only sobbed quietly, still clutching her head. But Veronica didn't need her answer. She understood.

Tabitha had gone into Queen Andromeda's dreams.

Veronica watched as Tabitha rolled onto her hands and knees, and when Tabitha looked up at her, Veronica retreated a step. There was fire in Tabitha's eyes, dark, *dark* fire.

Veronica burst out of the tent, but Tabitha was right behind her. Her finger swirled through the air, drawing the symbol for fire, so fast Veronica didn't have time to think, to draw her own symbol, to do anything except raise her hands instinctively. Tabitha roared a single note of wordless fury as she hurled the fire at Veronica.

The fire never reached her.

It burst apart across an invisible shield in front of Veronica. She thought one of the other Wielders in camp must have erected the shield, but the camp was only just beginning to stir, a few people stepping from their tents to investigate the noise. Veronica's hands were still in front of her. She'd drawn no symbol, and yet when she lowered her hands, the shimmering haze disappeared.

"Tabitha!" Liam's voice rang through the early morning air, making both Tabitha and Veronica whip their heads to look at him. He was running toward them, Mayva right behind him. "What in the gods' names are you doing?"

Tabitha, her eyes completely unrecognizable, demented and furious and... scared, shouted, "She attacked me!"

Veronica turned imploringly to Liam. "She's lying!"

"Shut up!" Tabitha shouted at Veronica.

"She used her Gift on Queen Andromeda!"

The entire camp went silent. By then, nearly everyone had gathered around to see what was happening. They all froze at Veronica's words. The sky itself seemed to be holding its breath.

"Liar!" Tabitha snapped, a little too late. "You don't know what you're talking about!"

"She Dream Walked Queen Andromeda." Veronica was speaking to everyone, but her eyes were on Queen Mayva. "I saw it."

For the first time since she'd met the queen, Mayva looked shocked. Her eyes were enormous, her lips slightly parted in astonishment.

"What are you talking about?" Liam spoke first. He'd ventured the closest to the pair of them, silent and ready. To attack? Defend?

But it was Mayva who spoke. "You're mistaken. Tabitha would never do something like that without consulting me."

So Mayva really didn't know. Tabitha had gone completely behind the queen's back.

"Your Majesty," Veronica breathed, "I'm not mistaken. I saw Queen Andromeda in Tabitha's memories."

Tabitha made as if to bolt for the trees, but Liam tackled her so fast Veronica barely saw him move. He pinned her hands to the ground, and Veronica realized it was so she couldn't draw a symbol. She'd been about to attack him, or perhaps Veronica.

Mayva's hand seized Veronica's upper arm, wheeling her around sharply. The shock was gone from the queen's face. There was nothing but anger in her dark eyes now. Veronica had seen Andromeda's face in Tabitha's memories, and the similarities in their faces were incredible. For some reason, Veronica hadn't truly thought of Mayva and Andromeda as having been sisters until that moment, and she understood then just how much grief the Warrior Queen had been trying to conceal.

"Restrain her," Mayva barked at Liam, and two other soldiers went to help him. She turned her icy gaze on Veronica. "What did you see?" Mayva demanded, her jaw tight, though not as tight as her grip on Veronica's arm. She seemed to remember there was an audience of stunned onlookers, and began dragging Veronica toward her tent. She pushed Veronica inside before following. "Tell me," she nearly shouted.

So Veronica told her.

CHAPTER THIRTY-FOUR

THE next time Veronica saw Tabitha, she was chained between two trees well outside of camp. The forest was dark except for the torches Mayva and Liam held, casting their faces in a swirling mix of orange light and black shadow. As Veronica walked toward them, her skin crawled, her stomach twisting as she beheld Tabitha, wild-eyed, wrists bloody from tugging at her bindings.

When Tabitha's eyes locked with Veronica, she shouted at Mayva, "You're taking her word over mine?" Both Tabitha and Veronica looked at Mayva, whose eyes were dark holes in her marble face.

"Veronica never lied to me," Mayva said simply. Her voice was low and quiet, but it still carried, filling the air around them all.

Veronica stepped in front of Tabitha, her hands trembling.

"Don't you touch me!" Tabitha screamed. "You *bitch!* Don't you dare touch me!"

Liam drove his torch into the dirt, the fire swaying with the movement, and stepped behind Tabitha. He gripped her hair so she couldn't move her head. "Do it, Veronica," Liam said. "She can't do anything with her hands and feet bound."

That wasn't entirely true. Tabitha writhed and thrashed against her bonds, but her arms were stretched so wide, her feet shackled to heavy weights on the ground, she couldn't move very much. Her hands, Veronica noticed, were wrapped in cloth, too tight for her fingers to move, for her to draw a symbol.

Veronica reached for her, and Tabitha roared as Veronica pressed her hands to either side of her face. Immediately images rose to meet Veronica's mind, but they were dark and indistinct. It took all of Veronica's focus to sort them, to pin them down so she could understand them.

The first sensation was emptiness, as though Veronica's body were a gaping chasm swathed in skin. No, not Veronica. And not Tabitha. She'd found Andromeda's mind, her memories, trapped in Tabitha's head where they did not belong. Tabitha's memories were tinged in a sort of blue hue that made them discernable from Andromeda's. Andromeda's were... black.

Guilt, shame, pain, it all crashed down on Veronica's consciousness. It was too much. How had the queen bore it?

"Veronica?" Mayva's voice echoed distantly in her mind, and the world was suddenly split in two; Tabitha's gaping mouth and wide eyes, and an image of Queen Andromeda, her gaunt reflection in a large mirror.

"I see her," Veronica gasped. Her mind was tearing in half. Veronica sucked in a breath, and it took several beats for her to be able to speak out loud again. "Tabitha. Show me Andromeda. Show me what you showed her."

Tabitha put up a strong fight, Veronica could feel her shrinking away from Veronica's power, but she reached mental fingers further and further into Tabitha's mind, her actual hands pressing harder against Tabitha's skull.

Finally, the images shifted. Dark caverns and empty dungeon cells rushed by her, until she was standing before a man with black hair, holding a blade above his head. Chanting filled her ears, the language unfamiliar, making the hairs on her arms rise.

The man drove the blade into the chest of the man on a table before him.

Screaming filled her ears, and she didn't know if it was her own scream or if Andromeda, or Tabitha, were screaming in the memory.

"*Kill them,*" came a voice from inside Veronica's head.

And then she was falling, past images and emotions moving too quickly for Veronica to decipher. A blonde woman, sickly and pale but with such beautiful blue eyes that made Veronica's— no, *Andromeda's*— heart ache.

There was so much aching, for places and things, and for herself.

But then everything started to dull. Images of blood, of death, permeated her thoughts.

Death. She wanted it.

She wanted to die.

And why wouldn't she? There was no conceivable end to the pain, no break in the cycle. Hopeless. She'd been utterly hopeless.

Her mind was like smoke, dark and impossible to pin down, to touch. Tabitha found a way inside so easily because of it.

A hand closed around Veronica's arm, pulling her back. Veronica's legs buckled, her body slamming to the ground before Liam could catch her. He crouched over her, gripping her arms. "It's alright," he was saying. His voice was too loud, battering Veronica's ears, which were ringing, ringing, ringing. Her face was wet, and she realized she was crying.

"Queen Andromeda," Veronica choked out, trying to get control of herself as Liam helped her to her feet. "Tabitha showed her what Artemis was creating, she told Andromeda to destroy them. She pretended to be... I don't know who. Someone Andromeda knew, a little girl."

Liam turned to Mayva. She was standing, frozen, staring at them. Her eyes were black and soulless.

"You manipulated her into helping you," Mayva said, her voice deadly calm. "You lied to her, and you put her in harm's way. Why?"

"Because those things were going to kill us all!" Tabitha cried. "She could have done something to stop them!"

"How did you know?" Veronica spoke up. "How did you know about the wolves?"

"You think you're the only one who can see things before they happen?" Tabitha asked.

Veronica's eyes widened. Tabitha could see the future, just like her.

"What did you see?" Liam asked. He looked as shocked as Veronica felt. He hadn't known about this gift of Tabitha's either. Perhaps no one had.

"I saw monsters," Tabitha said, "Monsters created to find us, to kill Wielders. I used the queen to try to destroy them before they destroyed us."

"And you said nothing?" Liam demanded. "To any of us?"

"You would have returned to the castle," Tabitha said angrily. "I saw a way to take care of the problem before it became worse, so I did."

"But you knew what Queen Andromeda was planning to do," Veronica said, shocked and incredulous. "Why didn't you tell anyone?"

"What she planned to?" Liam asked. "What are you talking about?"

Veronica swallowed, her eyes falling to Queen Mayva. "Queen Andromeda... she was going to kill herself. And Tabitha knew."

For a moment the queen didn't move. Then Mayva's fist crashed into Tabitha's face so hard Veronica *heard* Tabitha's nose break.

"You knew?" Mayva breathed as she drew her fist back. "You knew she was in danger and you didn't say anything?"

Tabitha's head hung, and for a breath Veronica thought she was unconscious, but then she spoke, voice dead and choked with blood, "You would have gone back for her if you knew." She spit a mouthful of blood onto the ground. "We needed to stay focused on the plan. We needed to keep gathering more people. She was more useful as a pawn. I needed to be sure she wouldn't mess anything up."

Mayva's hand shot out, gripping Tabitha's hair and yanking her head back so their eyes locked. "You went inside my sister's mind and lied to her so she would further your cause? So she would help you?"

"Us!" Tabitha shouted. "So she would help *us!* I was trying to end this war before it began, to keep those creatures from ever being awakened!"

"That wasn't your decision to make," Mayva snapped. "If I had returned to the castle, I could have saved her. She would still be alive."

"The Mother Queen was beyond saving," Tabitha spat. "Her mind was a black pit no one could have helped her climb out of."

Veronica expected Mayva to hit her again, but she didn't. She released Tabitha's hair and took a step back.

The anger and resolve in Tabitha's face shattered, her face crumbling as she let out a wordless sob. "I'm sorry," she whimpered. "Your Majesty, please don't kill me. *Please.*"

Veronica's stomach turned, her arms and legs growing cold. Would Mayva kill her? Would Veronica watch it happen? Despite what she had done, despite Veronica's horror and revulsion, she couldn't find it in herself to hate the girl chained before her. She pitied her; it was difficult not to, with her bruised wrists and ankles bound, tears and blood and snot running down her fractured face. How much could she hate someone for trying to survive?

When Veronica looked to the queen, she expected to find hate and anger. But there was nothing. *Nothing.*

"Release her," Mayva ordered, and Liam stepped away from Veronica toward Tabitha. He would never disobey an order, but Veronica thought she sensed a hesitation in his gait. Veronica watched, breath held, as Liam freed Tabitha from her restraints.

Immediately she fell to her knees, crawling toward Mayva. "Thank you," she gasped, reaching to touch Mayva's boots.

Mayva stepped back.

"You will be exiled." Tabitha's head snapped up, but before she could speak, Mayva continued, "You will take nothing with you, and you will leave at once. Get up."

Tabitha's body shook with sobs. "Your Majesty, please— I didn't mean to. I'm sorry, please forgive me— Your Majesty, *please!* They'll kill me if they find me, those things will find me—"

Mayva's expression did not change. "You will feel what she felt. Abandonment. No one will help you, no one will come to save you. Your fate will be the same as hers."

Tears burned Veronica's eyes. Not for Tabitha. For Queen Andromeda. Her heart ached and shattered for a woman she'd only ever seen in other people's memories. Alone. So utterly alone.

"Get up," Mayva said again, but Tabitha didn't move, she just laid at Mayva's feet, sobbing.

"Come on," Liam whispered in Veronica's ear. She hadn't heard him approach. His hand touched her arm, a light pressure directing her back to camp.

"I'm sorry," Veronica whispered, though what exactly she was apologizing for she didn't know.

Liam pressed her arm again, leading her back to camp, and leaving Tabitha to her fate.

CHAPTER THIRTY-FIVE

ANDROMEDA'S bedroom was warm.

Angelus stood beside the window, gazing out over the grounds and at the crescent moon above, a diamond pendant hanging from a midnight blue neck.

Andromeda sat at her dresser, pulling a silver brush through her long hair. Silla had already helped her prepare for bed, and her white nightgown hung loosely over her shoulders. Angelus heard the chair legs scrape against the floor, and he turned to see her walking toward him. She joined him at the window, but didn't step out onto the balcony. She looked up at him, and Angelus turned his face to meet her eyes.

He'd been her guard for barely a year, but it felt like forever.

She brushed her fingers over the identification necklace displayed proudly on his chest. He'd received it a few months prior, and that too felt like forever ago. She turned over one side of his vest, revealing the jeweled knives secured there. She gave them to him the same day he'd received the necklace, when his training was complete, and he was still getting used to their weight. She began teaching him how to use a knife shortly after they met, and he loved the subtle secrecy of the weapons. He could use a sword well enough, and his fists and feet even better, but the knives were their secret.

She smiled. It was not her usual, dark smile, however. There was something a little unfocused about her eyes, a struggle to hold Angelus' face. When she spoke, he smelled plum wine on her breath. When had she been drinking?

Her hands traveled down to his waist, and she pressed her palms to his hip bones. Angelus' back touched the wall behind him, and his eyebrows drew together in confusion.

Her fingers curled over his belt. "I just need... a distraction," she whispered, tilting her lips up to his. "Just... do this for me?"

Angelus' hands closed around her wrists, pushing her gently away. He shook his head. "You don't want me," he said, voice calm, "Not in that way."

Her lip trembled, her eyes growing wet. She drew back, her chest heaving. "You— you're my guard, you have to do what I say," she snapped, but the effect was stolen by the sob hitching in her throat.

Angelus shook his head, and stepped toward her. She stilled as his right palm pressed to her cheek, and he gave her a soft smile. "I have to protect you," he corrected her. "From danger, but also from things you would regret. You don't want me that way, Andromeda."

Her face crumpled as a sob filled her chest. He cupped her face gently, so gently, in his hands. Their chests touched when he stepped even closer, resting his chin on the top of her head. Her breath tickled his throat. She did not move, her arms remaining at her sides.

"Sleep," he whispered.

For a moment she said nothing, but then she pulled away. Her hand closed around his. "Will you stay with me?" she asked.

His heart ached. He would. Of course he would.

He nodded.

In her bed, he laid above the covers while she burrowed underneath them at his side. She curled into him, and he stroked his fingers through her hair.

"Promise," she gasped. "Promise you won't leave me."

"I promise."

She shook her head. "I don't believe you. You're only here because you had nowhere else to go."

That might have been true, that first day, when she found him in the stable. But that hadn't been the case in a very long time. His fingertips brushed like a sigh over her arm. "No," he whispered, "I'm here because you're here. And I'll stay as long as you let me."

Her hand fisted in the fabric of his shirt, her face turning into his side to hide her tears. Her chest heaved with a silent sob. "I should set you free," she whispered. "Before..."

He looked down at her. "Before what?"

"Before forever is over."

He brushed his fingers down her arm, then back up, slow, careful, soothing movements. He'd never seen her this upset

315

before. Her skin was so delicate under his fingers, and protectiveness swelled in his chest.

"Forever?" he asked with a smile. That was all he'd ever wanted.

Andromeda didn't answer, and Angelus thought she must have finally fallen asleep.

*   *   *

ANGELUS did not wake up. Waking meant changing from sleep to consciousness, and though his eyes were open, he did not feel conscious. He became slightly more aware, enough to know his ankle and face were painfully swollen. But he had not woken.

Shapes and sounds blurred around him, indistinguishable faces floating above him, empty voices swirling like smoke in his ears.

"She entered the Mother Queen's mind... Tabitha... She's been banished..."

Tabitha. It took him a while to place the name. Then he remembered her, the girl he saw with Veronica, the Wielder.

He was not aware of his body as he rose, didn't hear the faceless medic telling him to lay back down. He reached for the ruined necklace on the table of supplies near the bed, slipping it over his head. He pushed hands away, walking in a blurred, fogged daze out into the cold.

The cold.

It focused his mind, sharpened everything just the tiniest bit, but it made all the difference. He started walking, barefoot, shirtless. There was nothing but the cold.

CHAPTER THIRTY-SIX

THE entire camp was divided into two lines, facing each other in the gray morning. Mayva stood between the divided crowd, Liam at her side, and Tabitha in front of him, hands bound, though no one had ever looked as unthreatening as she did then, her face battered, spine bent, eyes empty.

Veronica hovered beside Mayva, right at the end, and her proximity to Tabitha made guilt swirl in her gut. But there was a flicker of anger there, as well.

The soldiers, Wielder and non-Wielder alike, had been shocked when Liam and Mayva appeared with Tabitha after Liam ordered them to line up. But their faces were masks now— Veronica wished she knew how to hide her feelings the way they could. She felt small and insignificant in her too-big coat, next to these armored men and women. All she wanted was to disappear into the trees around them, but Liam told her to stand there. Why, she didn't know. She felt too visible, on display, despite the fact no one was looking at her, their attention stolen by the limp Wielder before them, her face nothing more than a horrific bruise.

Whispers had traveled through camp already— nothing could be truly hidden in these trees, not with everyone so close together with only tent walls to separate them.

Traitor... She Dream Walked the queen's sister... She could have saved the Mother Queen... Veronica was tired of the voices. She wanted this over with.

She scanned the crowd, not realizing at first that she was searching for Angelus. But of course, he wasn't there. He was still in Mayva's tent. Veronica itched to retreat there, to check on him, to be anywhere but here. She stayed where she was.

No one spoke, and Mayva's sharp eyes scanned the faces around her. The queen was tall and statuesque in her dark armor, her raven hair rippling in the cold wind blowing down the mountainside.

"Traitors," she began, and the wind itself seemed to quiet in order to hear her, "Have no place here. Liars don't belong to anyone, and those of you in this camp belong to this army."

Someone howled their agreement, and several people smirked. They were proud of who— what— they were. Who they belonged to.

These people were hers. Mayva's. And they all knew it.

But Tabitha was no longer one of them.

"Exile," Mayva said, voice clear and loud, though she didn't shout. "Her fate will be exile."

A few of the faces in the crowd twisted, clearly having expected something worse to befall the traitorous Wielder before them.

They wanted her to die for what she did, Veronica could see it on their faces.

Mayva, more than any of them, must want Tabitha dead. So why not kill her? Was this mercy?

Your fate will be the same as hers. Veronica remembered the queen's words from the previous night.

Justice, Veronica decided. Perhaps Mayva was not cruel, or merciful. Perhaps she was merely fair. Respect for the Warrior Queen swelled in Veronica's chest, but there was a bit of fear, too. Queen Mayva understood true and fair punishment, and that was a frightening thing.

Liam pushed Tabitha forward, and she kept her eyes down as she walked between the lines of people. They stared her down, as though they could bury her with the weight of their gazes alone, disgust etched across their faces.

Veronica watched as they walked, Mayva, Liam, and Tabitha, to the end of the line, to the edge of the camp where a watch was posted.

The lines of people began to merge, following behind their queen, her right hand, and the traitor. Veronica followed numbly, watching. She half expected Tabitha to put up some kind of fight, even if it proved to be useless. But she just shuffled forward, one slow step after another. She was defeated. She knew it, and so did everyone else.

"Wait!" someone shouted, and Veronica turned, shocked, as Angelus limped across the grass. His face was so pale it was almost gray, and his torso, bare except for that broken necklace, was slick with sweat despite the cold air. His eyes were hazy, but desperate. Mayva didn't pause, didn't look at him, though a few others did. Veronica rushed to his side, catching his arm, but he kept moving toward the crowd.

"What are you doing?" Veronica demanded, her voice a hiss through her teeth. "You'll freeze out here!"

Angelus tried to pull his arm away from her, but Veronica didn't let go. "I have to— I have to know—"

Veronica put his arm around her shoulders, pressing her hand to his chest to steady him, and they stumbled into the procession, everyone casting him wary glances. They didn't trust him, that much was clear. Not the way they trusted Veronica. Why they trusted her, she didn't entirely understand, but she'd never been subject to these tense, judging stares they now trained on Angelus. Veronica had the wild urge to tell them to leave, to turn away, to leave him alone. But she didn't say a word, just helped Angelus limp to where Mayva stood, right on the edge of camp. Tabitha was the only one not looking at Angelus. Her eyes were still on the ground.

"You went into her mind," Angelus panted. He looked like he was about to be sick, but he pressed on, sweat beading on his forehead and above his lip, "Tell me— tell me she wasn't really going to go through with it."

Veronica stared at Angelus, bewildered. Mayva's eyes went from Angelus to Tabitha, then back again.

Slowly, Tabitha's head tilted up, not meeting Angelus' eyes directly, but her face was high enough Veronica could see a slight smile. "Her fate was sealed," she said simply. "Whether by her own hand, or another's, her grave had been dug for a long time."

Angelus suddenly lunged forward, toward Tabitha, so fast Veronica barely understood what was happening until Liam intercepted him, dragging Angelus back and wrapping a thick arm around Angelus' neck. "Liar!" Angelus shouted, clawing at Liam's arm, but he didn't budge. "You're a liar!"

Mayva turned to the men posted on watch. "If she tries to return to this camp, break her legs and leave her to die."

They bowed their heads, swift, stiff movements that meant their unquestioning obedience.

Mayva nodded to two soldiers behind her, who had been part of the crowd moments before, but stepped forward at the queen's silent order. They grabbed Tabitha by the arms, one on either side of her, and led her unresisting body into the woods.

"No!" Angelus growled, and Veronica's gaze whipped from Tabitha to him. "Bring her back! She—"

"Shut up," Liam hissed in his ear, arm tightening around Angelus' neck.

Loose rocks and twigs popped under Mayva's boots as she strode toward Angelus. He stopped struggling as she approached, spit flying from between his clenched teeth as he panted.

Veronica ran to his side, holding out a hand to Mayva. "Wait, please—"

"Release him."

Liam dropped Angelus instantly, and he crumpled to his knees, one hand pressing against his throat as he choked and coughed. Veronica crouched beside him, prepared to throw herself in front of him if the queen took another step—

Her glare was terrible, the power of an icy ocean behind them. "Get him out of my sight." With a start Veronica understood the brittle, sharp words were for her. It was incredible how her face remained blank, but her eyes screamed out her fury.

"I'm sorry," Veronica gasped. It was only then she realized how terrified she was, how tight every muscle in her body had become, making her voice come out high and thin and breathless. She helped Angelus to his feet, keeping her hands wrapped tightly around his arm, as though he might bolt. He looked crazed and wild enough to try it.

His fevered glare was trained on the queen, but he was a barncat before a lion. "Angelus," Veronica said, voice sharp. "Let's go." She tugged on his arm.

For a long, breathless moment, Angelus and the queen just stared at each other. Then Angelus let Veronica pull him to her tent.

CHAPTER THIRTY-SEVEN

INSIDE Veronica's tent, the floor scattered with some of Tabitha's books, Veronica closed the tent flap and whirled on Angelus. A thousand angry words threatened to burst from inside her chest, but all she could do was stare at him. He was shaking, head to toe, and no wonder, he wore only pants, no shirt or shoes in sight. His eyes were huge, the pupils swallowing all of the color, the stitched up gash across his forehead standing out sharply against his pale face.

"Angelus." She meant to sound more forceful, but her voice was only a strangled breath.

His head jerked sharply in her direction, his neck bent and his shoulders too high, like an animal prepared to bolt, or attack. He was such a wild, untamable creature, and it had never been as clear to her as it was then. "I don't understand." Her voice was still too thin, her throat thick and aching. "I don't understand what's happening. You need to tell me— please just let me help you."

Angelus sucked in a quick, uneven breath. "It's her fault."

Veronica had expected him to shout, but his voice was low, hard, flat, and somehow it was worse than if he yelled at her.

"She left Andromeda there, even though she knew what Artemis was. She abandoned her. It's her fault she's dead."

For a moment, she thought he meant Tabitha, but then she realized he was talking about Mayva. Veronica shook her head. "No, Angelus, Queen Mayva didn't know what happened to her, Tabitha didn't tell her—"

"It's her fault!" This time he really did shout, and Veronica started at the sudden volume.

"Angelus," she tried again, taking a cautious step toward him. Angelus didn't move. Where was he? Where had he gone? The boy in front of her was a stranger.

Come back. Please come back.

"If it weren't for her, Andromeda would still be alive!" Veronica flinched at his shout. "She would still be here, she would still be with me!" His face shifted, the anger turning into something... else. It was like defeat, only worse. Desperation. "I— " he faltered. He shook his head, a tight, jerky movement that looked as if it might break his rigid neck. "I can't. I can't stay here. We have to leave, now."

"Angelus." She spoke softly, stepping right in front of him. He blinked at her, as though surprised to see she had gotten so close. "We can't just leave—"

"Yes we can," he snapped, anger returning to his face, a bit of color rising to his cheeks. "They can't make us stay here!"

324

"They aren't making us stay," she said. "But I... I *want* to stay."

He stared at her, disbelieving. "You... you don't want... to come with me?"

A hairline fracture spidered across Veronica's heart.

"What did she tell you?" Angelus asked, and his voice had lost all of its anger. It sounded like a plea now. "She's lying to you— she's turning you against me."

Veronica shook her head, her fingers closing around Angelus' upper arms. He went rail straight at the contact, his chest heaving, the ruined glass hanging from his neck swaying with the movement. "I will never be against you," she promised. "This is about doing the right thing."

"We have to *go!*" he shouted. "That *is* the right thing!"

Veronica took a step back, letting her hands fall away from his arms. She wasn't going to get anywhere with him, not today. "We can talk about this later, once you've calmed down."

She left him in her tent, even though it killed her to do it.

CHAPTER THIRTY-EIGHT

ANGELUS' body itched and prickled, his mind worn thin, stretched too far and wide. He was on fire. He was exhausted.

Mayva. She'd turned Veronica against him. Her fault, this was all her fault.

Her fault, her fault, her fault.

He went to the infirmary tent to find some proper clothes and put them on, slipping on his coat and lacing up his boots. He needed a weapon— he lamented again the loss of his throwing knives. He'd have to steal a sword. He thought he'd heard someone say Liam housed an impressive collection of weapons in his tent. He waited until nightfall, then went in search of the tent.

The paths between tents were empty with everyone at dinner, and the overcast sky made the ground look blue. It was so cold. Cold enough to snow.

Liam's tent was the same size as everyone else's, only Mayva's tent and the infirmary tent were any larger than the rest, and there was no one to stop Angelus from pulling aside the flap of Liam's tent. And no one to explain what he saw when he did.

Liam was not alone. He stood behind a woman sitting in a chair, slumped forward with her head in her hands. Her shoulders gave a single shudder. Crying. She was crying.

Queen Mayva was crying.

Liam touched her shoulders, leaning down to press his lips against her neck. It was not the intimacy of the touch that surprised Angelus, but the gentleness of it. Mayva and Liam were warriors, castle fortresses given flesh and bone. They were supposed to be unshakable.

But Mayva was human, despite her attempts to appear otherwise.

Angelus remained frozen, still unnoticed by the pair before him. It took several heartbeats before he finally remembered how to move, and he backed away, his hand still raised as though reaching for something.

Andromeda. He didn't know how he knew, but he was certain that was why Mayva was crying.

Her sister was dead.

Her grief made him sick. He had been at Andromeda's side, he had been there when Mayva hadn't. Mayva left her alone, abandoned her. Angelus stayed, until the end. Mayva had not earned those tears. She couldn't mourn a sister she'd cared nothing for.

If she loved Andromeda the way he did, she wouldn't have left. She'd lost a sister, but Angelus lost everything.

Hypocrite. She was a hypocrite.

And Angelus was done with it, with all of it.

CHAPTER THIRTY-NINE

THE night after Tabitha's banishment, the sky looked as heavy and miserable as Veronica felt, as though something behind it threatened to rip the clouds apart in order to be released. The entire camp seemed on edge, the air tense with something akin to anticipation. She didn't understand what was different, she only knew something had changed.

The wind battered the sides of her tent, and she shivered as she paged idly through one of Tabitha's books. The lantern in front of her illuminated the small space, and she held her hands around it for warmth.

"Veronica?" Liam's voice carried from outside the tent.

Veronica glanced up, surprised. "Come in."

She had to give Liam credit for politeness. He was the queen's Second, he didn't have to ask permission to enter her tent.

Liam stepped inside, careful to avoid stepping on the books scattered around as he approached. To her surprise, he sat down in front of her, moving a book aside so he could sit comfortably. Resting his elbows on his thighs, he said, "You haven't been practicing."

Veronica wasn't sure what she'd expected Liam to say, something about Angelus' outburst perhaps, but not this. She shook her head a little. "No," she agreed. "I haven't."

"You know what happens when you don't." Liam's voice was kind, but the words still stung, making her face heat with embarrassment.

"A fat lot of good it does anyway," Veronica muttered.

"What are you talking about?"

Her eyes suddenly burned, her throat too swollen to speak for a moment. When she did force the words out, they were choked. "I can't do it. The fire, the only weapon against those... *things*... it doesn't come. Not anymore. Not without—"

Not without Tabitha. Not without Blood Magic.

Evil. That's what Mayva had called it. *Unnatural.*

What did it say about her, if unnatural Magic was the only way for her to express it?

Veronica looked down at her hands, clenching and unclenching her fists. "What's wrong with me?"

"Something is blocking your Magic," he said. "That doesn't mean there's something wrong with you. It means there's an obstacle you have to overcome."

Veronica shook her head. "I don't understand. I've done it before."

"That's for you to discover." He offered her a smile, and held out a hand to her. "May I see your hand?"

Confused, she tentatively offered her right hand. Liam took it in his, turning her wrist so her palm faced her. He pinched the place between her thumb and index finger lightly, his thumb pressing into a thin vein visible through her skin. "Magic has a pulse," Liam said, "Just like a heart. Can you feel it?"

Veronica shook her head. There was only one beat in her ears, her veins, that she could sense.

"What about me?" Liam released her hand, then extended his own palm toward her. Veronica's eyes widened. She took his offered hand, pressing her fingers to the same spot he touched on her hand.

Warmth spread from his palm into her fingers, something leaping beneath his skin like a bowstring pulled taut. And she could feel it. Like a tiny, warm river flowing beneath his skin.

"You're a Wielder?" she breathed.

His smile was a little sad. "Not in the same way you are. You're Magic is far stronger— my bloodline has been diluted, but yours is much purer. That's why you're so powerful, Veronica."

Powerful? She held in a laugh.

"You can sense the power in me," Liam said. "You need to find it in yourself, too." He let go of her hand, resting his on his thighs. There were several scars across the tops of his hands and fingers, silvery memories of cuts. Veronica wondered where they came from. She opened her mouth to ask, but before she could speak, the tent flap burst open, and a soldier Veronica had seen before, but didn't know by name, appeared, eyes wide. "The queen has been challenged," he panted, as though he had been running, "To the fighting ring."

Liam and Veronica were on their feet instantly.

"What?" Liam demanded. "By who?"

Veronica shook her head, her stomach slowly sinking. "Who do you think?"

*   *   *

FIRE coursed through Angelus' body, burning in his veins and crackling through his limbs. He wore armor, but he did not need it. Rage, blind and pure, was the only armor he needed.

His body shook as he approached Mayva, a crowd surrounding the makeshift arena he had fought Liam in, adrenaline like lightning in his veins. The fire inside was reducing him to a paper-thin shell. He was wild and angry, and weakened by it.

But the anger would win.

Mayva's inky black hair was tied back in a long plait down her back, her head free of a helmet, though Angelus wore one. The rest of her body was armored. She watched Angelus approach, her face as cold and sharp as the smell of coming snow.

Angelus' slow exhale fogged the air.

Mayva's eyes held amusement, but the rest of her face remained cold.

Angelus lunged.

He swung high with the sword he'd been given, going for her face. She blocked him easily with one of her shortswords, the other still strapped to her back, and Angelus felt mocked by it. He put all his strength into the blow, but she only needed half her weapon to defeat him.

He swung again, a wordless shout tearing from his throat.

Mayva jutted her spine back, her stomach disappearing from where the tip of Angelus' blade slashed.

"Why are you angry?" she asked, voice infuriatingly calm.

Angelus didn't answer, only grunted with the effort of his next attack. Form and technique were forgotten— he was feral and bloodthirsty.

"Your stance is sloppy," Mayva barked. "Anger is good, you can use it, but not if it distracts you."

Angelus slashed again, and again.

"Use it," Mayva snapped.

Angelus used it. The tip of his sword screamed against Mayva's chest plate, the first time he'd managed to touch her.

A satisfied smile flashed across Mayva's face before it was replaced with cold concentration once more. "You can't use it unless you understand it," she told him.

He lunged forward again, missing Mayva as she twirled effortlessly out of the way, then pointed her sword at him. "Why," she asked again, "Are you angry, Angelus?"

He roared as he lifted his sword, bringing it down with all his strength, right onto Mayva's waiting blade. The weapons sang against each other as she held the block, her face inches from his. "Why?" she demanded.

"It should have been you!" He drew back his blade, freeing it from her block, and nearly tripped over his clumsy, numb feet as he stumbled back. "You left her!"

Mayva cocked her head, eyes narrowing. Then she nodded, slowly, as though agreeing with some voice she alone could hear. She turned sideways, lifting her sword to point it at him. "Again," she ordered.

Angelus ran forward, intent to stab, to harm, to punch the sharp blade straight through her armor to the stone heart it protected. It should have been her. *It should have been her.*

"It isn't only me you're angry with," she said like a taunt as she danced around his blows, not even a bead of sweat forming on her brow, while Angelus was drenched. "What else? Who else?"

Angelus tore off his helmet, furious with its insufferable heat. It clattered to the ground several feet away. With his face and head free, his breathing came slightly easier, and the cold air threatened to freeze the sweat on his face. "Don't talk about her!" he shouted. "You don't have the right!"

Mayva looked like she was waiting for something. "It's her," she said, almost like a question. "You're angry with her."

"I'm not!" He wasn't. He couldn't be. He could never be angry with her.

Could he?

His eyes burned, and he couldn't see. Andromeda's face swam in his eyes along with the tears.

Mayva lowered her sword, and Angelus hated her for it. "It's alright," she said, so softly Angelus barely heard her over his gasping breaths.

"No!" Angelus bellowed, lunging again, not caring that she had lowered her weapon. It didn't matter anyway, she blocked him easily.

"Tell her, Angelus," Mayva said, and finally her breathing started to come a little faster. "Tell her why."

Angelus couldn't get any sound to come out of his mouth except for a hitched sob he hadn't realized had been building. "She left me," he managed to gasp. As soon as the words were out, all his strength left him. He dropped to his knees, the sword clattering to the ground. "She left me!" He shouted the words at Mayva, at the sky, at the vast expanse of gray-white where Andromeda hid, perhaps looking down on him. Just like she always had. "She promised she wouldn't leave me!"

It wasn't her choice, he thought. She was killed. It wasn't her fault.

But she'd planned to leave him anyway.

He thought of Resmond, leaving him in that stall to die, of Veronica refusing to go with him.

Why?

Why was nothing he did ever good enough? Why did everyone leave him in the end?

He doubled over, long arms wrapped around his stomach as invisible claws tore at his insides. The tips of his hair brushed the dying grass, and the perfume of the black dirt threatened to suffocate him.

Dead. She was dead. She was gone.

She left me.

He would never have left her. He promised her he wouldn't. But she broke her promise.

She broke her promise. She left me.

He bent lower, his hands knotting in the grass as a sob wracked his body. The tears were slow, terrible tears, each one dragged from his eyes by force. Dying, this had to be what dying felt like.

Angelus had broken his promise too. He was supposed to protect her. He was supposed to save her.

This wasn't Mayva's fault. It was his.

"Get up," Mayva ordered. Though Angelus could not see her, he could feel her sword pointed at his head.

Do it, he pleaded to her in his mind. *Just do it.*

A foot slammed into his side, and his breath burst out of his lungs as he fell, curling into a ball as his barely-healed ribs seized. Mayva glared down at him, an imposing thundercloud.

"Please," he whispered.

She kicked him again, harder. "You don't beg," she spat. "You *never* beg." She pointed her sword at him. "Get up," she ordered again. When he didn't move, she drove her sword into the ground, a breath away from his face. "Dead," she declared. "You can't expect mercy on the battlefield. If you stop, if you fall, if you hesitate, then you die."

But dying was what he wanted. In that moment, it was the only thing he could possibly think of wanting.

She kicked him again, this time in the spine, and Angelus cried out, pitiful as a wounded dog.

"Stop!" someone screamed, their voice far, far away. But he still recognized it. Veronica. His eyes peeled open, and he found her face in the crowd, bone-white, eyes rimmed with red as though she had been crying. Liam was gripping her arms, holding her back.

"Stop!" she screamed again. "You're hurting him! Please!"

Mayva gestured toward Veronica with her hand, eyes still pinned on Angelus. "You're going to let her fight your battles for you? Don't be weak."

But he was weak. There was no other word for him.

"Angelus!" Veronica cried. Angelus couldn't look at her. "Get up! Fight back!"

Mayva waited. Liam waited. Veronica waited. The crowd and the wind and the mountains waited.

Angelus didn't get up. He didn't think he could ever get up again.

It took the crowd a long time to realize it had begun to snow.

CHAPTER FORTY

VERONICA waited on the edge of the camp. Heavy, thick snow fell from the sky, which was obscured by dense, swift-moving clouds. Snowflakes dampened her hair and slipped down the back of her coat collar.

Utterly silent, Angelus appeared in the clearing, dressed for travel, with a pack slung over his shoulder and a sword at his hip. Even though Veronica knew this was coming, knowing she had been right still made her whole body ache. She slid down from the rock she'd perched on, and Angelus paused when her feet thumped lightly on the ground. He didn't turn around.

"So that's it?" Veronica asked, her voice oddly strained. "You were just going to leave without saying goodbye?"

The night woods were a black smear around them, midnight-colored paint brushed over a landscape with an unskilled hand. As he turned to face her, the clouds shifted, letting some of the moon's light through, illuminating Angelus' pale face. He looked terrible, like all of the air, all of the warmth, had been sucked from his body.

Angelus dropped his bag of meager supplies, a single sigh escaping him, clouding in front of his mouth. "You don't understand." His voice was empty.

Veronica stepped toward him. "You're right, I *don't* understand. I need you to explain it to me. What *happened?*"

Angelus was shaking his head before she finished speaking. "I don't belong here, Veronica. I have to go."

"Where?" she demanded. "Where are you going to go?"

"Anywhere but here."

Veronica stepped to his side, reaching for his pack. "Fine, let's go."

"No," he said, voice flat and final. "You're staying here."

"No." Her tone echoed his. "I'm coming with you. I'm not letting you go by yourself," she said, her voice rising. It felt wrong to shout in the darkness, as though the mountains around them were sleeping giants they might disturb. They sensed it at the same time, and Veronica lowered her voice slightly, though the words were still sharp and clear, "You aren't leaving me behind."

He shook his head, expression pained, sad. "I don't belong anywhere," he said, voice a strained whisper in the dark. "Or with anyone. I'm a stray, that's what they've always called me. I'll always be that, nothing but a stray." He sucked in a breath, his eyes falling to the ground. "The only home I've ever had was with her, and I lost it. I should have known it wouldn't last." His gaze found hers, and Veronica drowned in the look in his eye, as though he had not only lost one person, but as though Veronica, even as she stood in front of him, was already gone. "They all leave in the end. Every single one of them. They use me, then they leave me. I think they care about me, but then they wind up hating me in the end."

Veronica shook her head, her hands over her mouth to stifle her sob. She remembered the guilt on the letter, remembered Andromeda's memories inside Tabitha's head. So much blackness, so much pain, so much hate. But there was still the flash of Angelus' face, of his smile.

The Mother Queen was beyond saving. Her mind was a black pit no one could have helped her climb out of.

Veronica wasn't entirely convinced that was true.

"She didn't," Veronica said, and her voice was choked with a sob, "She didn't hate you, Angelus. She *did* care about you."

Angelus shook his head. "She suffered so much, and I never knew. She never told me the truth. I should have seen it. Maybe if I had, I could have helped her. But there's just something inside me people can't help but leave behind." He turned, picking up his pack and stepping toward the forest.

"Wait," Veronica cried, rushing forward and gripping his arm. He stopped, but didn't turn around. She wrapped her arms around his middle, her face pressing into his back. He remained perfectly still, his arms limp at his sides. "Please." She gripped him tighter, and images started to swirl before her closed eyes. Andromeda, young and beautiful, and Angelus, hovering in doorways and in corners, watching, always watching over her. He would have done anything for her. It was warmth and light and certainty, overwhelming and pure. It was the way Finn looked at Duvar, the way the village children looked at her.

340

It was how Veronica had felt as a small child, when she looked at her mother.

But amid it all, there was a ghost hovering in the corners of Angelus' vision, a sense of dread, of fear. He always remembered, could never forget, when he had been left behind before. She could see a pair of retreating legs from where Veronica— Angelus— lay on the ground.

Abandoned. Forgotten. Left behind. Alone.

Veronica sucked in a breath, and she could smell Angelus, musky and dark and wild, like the forest and the mountains.

She couldn't lose him.

"I won't," she gasped. "Angelus, I won't. I won't do that to you. I'm not going to leave you behind."

A slow sigh escaped him, she could feel his ribs expand and retract under her palms. "Yes you will," he said simply. "Everyone always does. I'm just saving you the trouble."

Very slowly, he lifted his arms and pried her hands away, stepping free of her hold. He didn't turn around, not once, as he walked away. And then he was gone, disappearing into the night, and leaving her behind.

* * *

VERONICA ran all the way to Liam's tent.

He was the only person Veronica thought *might* help her. She crashed through the opening of his tent, her lungs seizing from the cold air. "Liam?"

Liam looked startled, sitting in a chair before a low wooden desk in the corner of the tent. Queen Mayva was beside him, peering over his shoulder at a roll of parchment spread across the desk surface.

Mayva's expression didn't change, but Liam stood, his eyes wide. "Veronica? What happ—"

"Angelus is gone," Veronica gasped, her voice still choked with tears. She fought them down, battling the white-hot, searing pain in her chest. "He left. Please, you have to help me bring him back."

Liam appeared... torn. His eyes flitted from Veronica to Mayva, just once.

"And why should we help him?" Mayva's voice was sharp and cold, like a steel blade, or the wintry wind outside the tent. It froze Veronica to her core. "He's done nothing but cause problems and disrespect me and my company since he came here." Her eyes narrowed on Veronica. "Why," she repeated, slower, "Should we help him?"

Veronica couldn't speak. *Why?* What gain was there for Mayva in Angelus coming back? What use did the Warrior Queen have for a runaway, a deserter? But that wasn't Angelus— not the real him. That was why she had to find him, to bring him back. Before it was too late. Before Angelus couldn't be found.

Veronica said the only thing she could. "I'll do anything." It was the truth. "Please." Her lips trembled, and the sensation of tears tickled her face. If she'd been able to move, she would have gotten on her knees. But she could only stand there, frozen. "I'll do whatever you want. Just help me bring him back."

Liam watched the queen, something sharp and pained shading his face and pronouncing the shadows under his eyes and across his cheekbones.

For a moment, none of them said anything.

Then Queen Mayva said, very calmly, "You will ride with Liam."

CHAPTER FORTY-ONE

ANGELUS' toes were numb. He walked stiffly through the white-covered brush; the snow was falling fast, and piling steadily on the ground and in the branches of the trees above. It collected in his hair, on his eyelashes, making his vision fuzzy around the edges.

The sun was starting to rise— he wondered what time it was. How long had he been walking? Forever. No time at all.

Veronica's face flashed across his mind, her pleading eyes full of hurt, the melting snowflakes on her cheeks like tears.

An invisible knife slashed across his chest, leaving behind an empty ache. The cold seemed to numb that, as well.

He kept walking.

The dense wood eventually gave way, and in the clearing Angelus could see a partly-frozen pond, surrounded by fir trees covered in feather-like snow. And beyond them, mountains. Blue-white whispers of shapes in the distance, a heavy fog rendering them almost invisible.

He felt infinitely alone then, as though he were the last man on earth.

Until a low growl came from behind him.

*   *   *

VERONICA held tightly to Liam's waist as the horse beneath them galloped through the trees, Mayva's raven hair flying ahead of them like a flag, leading them on. Mayva's horse was an enormous bear of a creature, shockingly black against the white landscape, but the queen had complete control of him.

It was so cold, the wind battering Veronica's face.

"He can't have gone far," Liam said, yelling over the wind and the heavy tread of his horse.

Veronica nodded against his back, though she wasn't sure he felt it through his thick coat.

Liam suddenly pulled the horse to a halt, nearly colliding with Mayva, who had stopped at a clearing. "Do you hear something?" she asked, turning to face them.

Now that they had stopped, Veronica did hear something. The distant but unmistakable sound of branches breaking, and the rumbling that meant something massive was running...

A howl ripped through the air like a blade through silk, and Veronica made out the enormous outline of a four-legged creature bolting toward them. They had no time to react before the beast tore from the trees, and leapt over them, clearing the top of their heads by inches, before it landed on all fours and kept running, disappearing over a shallow ledge leading down to what looked like a huge pond. And there, Veronica could see from above, was the figure of a man running.

"Follow it!" Veronica cried, even as the horses reared up, their ears pinned back and their whinnies shrill.

Mayva didn't question her. She clicked to her horse, digging her heels into its sides. It jolted into a run, and Liam and Veronica followed.

"What is that thing?" Liam breathed.

"A monster," Veronica answered.

*   *   *

THE surge of panic Angelus experienced when he remembered his knives were gone was a sharp and blinding sensation. The sword at his hip was weighty and awkward as he ran, but it was all he had. He couldn't fight the creature at close range, it wasn't possible.

So he ran. The edges of the wide body of water were frozen and covered in snow, and the ice cracked ominously beneath his feet. *Damn it.* He couldn't tell what was frozen water and what was solid ground. Everything was white, white, white.

The wolf was a hundred times worse than Angelus remembered. A hulking, impenetrable mass of black fur and muscle. And its eyes. Enormous, sickly yellow orbs with long black slits for pupils. It was a breath behind him— he didn't dare look back, but he could smell it, sense it, hear it.

"Angelus!"

It was impossible, but Veronica's voice rang out as though from the center of the world.

Angelus slid on an invisible patch of ice. His heart lurched as he lost all traction, he was simply floating until he crashed to the ground.

The beast should have killed him. It should have caught up to him, opened its maw and crushed Angelus' skull in its teeth.

But it didn't.

Instead, Mayva's horse crashed into the beast's side, sending it flying back and rolling onto the frozen surface of the pond. Its enormous body cracked the ice instantly, and it sank down to its neck in the water.

"Liam!" Mayva shouted. "Veronica!"

Angelus stared as another horse appeared, two figures riding atop its ash-gray body. They dismounted, and Angelus watched their hands fly through the air. Instantaneously, the water began to shift, moving as if a current controlled it. Then it rose, arms made of water and ice reaching up over the beast's head and wrapping around its body, a transparent cocoon. It thrashed, twisting and writhing in the water swirling around and around its body.

Dead. It should have been dead. Why wasn't it dead?

He recalled what Andromeda said, a thousand years ago now. *I believe he's made them powerful enough to hold their own against Magic.*

But not fire. Veronica had killed one, burned it to death. They *could* be killed.

The beast went still, even as the twisting water continued to flip its body over and over. But then even that stopped, Liam and

Veronica severing their Magic bond to the water, and the beast crashed down into the pond.

For a moment, they were all still.

Then the monster burst from the water. And ran straight for Veronica.

Mayva and Angelus reacted in unison. Their swords were sheathed, and then they were both stabbing the creature from opposite sides. Angelus shouted with the effort it took to penetrate the thick hide. The wolf spun, rising to stand on its back legs and using its enormous, taloned hands to pull the blades free and toss them away. Blood dripped from the stab wounds, but they appeared to have little to no effect. Angelus remembered trying to stab them, still in their human forms, in the dungeon, how his blade shattered. The Magic that had protected them in slumber was gone, or at least weakened, but a sword was still far from enough to do any real damage.

The world stopped as the creature's yellow eyes locked on Angelus, and he knew he was about to die.

But the creature seemed to... smile. It was a terribly knowing smile, impossible for a real wolf to conjure. It turned to Veronica, a slow, deliberate movement, and Angelus understood.

Veronica first. Angelus second.

Angelus could do nothing, it happened so fast. The creature lunged, and Veronica's scream rattled the frozen landscape. "Mayva!" Angelus bellowed, and she threw her second blade to him. He caught it, and slashed it through the creature's neck. Heat and blood exploded in Angelus' face, the sword tearing a five inch seam into the wolf's neck. Its teeth remained locked around Veronica's leg— but it was surprised, and distracted.

"Fire!" Angelus shouted to Veronica. "Now!"

But it was not Veronica's hand that drew the swirling symbol to conjure the flame. It was Liam, appearing from nowhere, who moved his fingers through the air, creating a fiery spiral in the air that morphed into flame. He threw it at the beast.

There was no slow spreading of flame, no trickling of burning fingers through the creature's fur, lighting it aflame.

There was nothing, and then the beast was a ball of fire. When the flames were gone, there was nothing left of the monster, only ash.

Liam dragged Veronica backward, his hands under her arms. She was untouched by the fire, but her bleeding leg left a trail of red in the snow.

Angelus started to run toward her, but he stopped when Mayva stepped before him. She seemed to simply appear in front of him. Then she punched him in the face so hard he saw stars. The back of his head cracked against the ground, and he found himself staring up at the tower of a woman before him.

She set her feet on either side of his waist and knelt down over him and gathered the front of his coat in her fist.

Her eyes were black and green flames. Angelus fully understood then why Mayva was the Warrior Queen.

"Is this what you wanted?" He had never, not once in his life, heard Mayva shout in anger. But she bellowed in his face, spit flying and eyes wild. With her other hand, she pointed to where Veronica was struggling to stand on her good leg, Liam's arm wrapped around her, supporting her. Veronica's eyes were wide, not with pain, not with fear for herself, but for Angelus. This whole time, she had only ever been afraid for him. "This is what happens when you run away!" Mayva shouted, shaking him roughly until he looked from Veronica to her. "You abandoned her! There are those that would see her dead for what she is, and you left her alone!"

There were a million things she could have said, a million things Angelus thought she would say, but this was not what he had anticipated. He stared at her, unable to speak.

Her other hand joined her first to grip Angelus' coat, hauling him up into an almost-sitting position, his face inches away from hers. Her voice lowered to a deadly hiss, far worse than her shouting. "This is how you justify your pathetic existence. You find what you would die to protect, and then you die to protect it. Don't ever let me see such a blatant display of cowardice again, or I will kill you myself and do the world a favor."

Then she let him fall.

Heat burned behind Angelus' eyes, and he sucked in a deep breath before he rolled over and pushed himself to his hands and knees. Shakily, he rose to his feet. Something inside him was paralyzed, stunned.

Liam was trying to lead Veronica back to the gray horse, but Veronica remained still, watching Angelus.

He didn't move. He just stared back. His eyes slowly fell to the blood on her leg, the torn fabric and skin. His fault. This was all his fault.

He was supposed to protect her. And he had walked away.

Mayva took Veronica's arm, and together she and Liam helped Veronica limp to the horse. Mayva turned back to Angelus. "If you come back, that's it. You aren't leaving again."

Finally, Angelus found his voice. "I won't." And he meant it. Gods, he meant it.

CHAPTER FORTY-TWO

MAYVA waited outside the infirmary tent while Angelus wore a track in the dirt before the door with his pacing. She did not stand directly in front of the tent's entrance, but Angelus understood he was being barred from entering.

After some time, one of the medics, followed closely by Liam, stepped out of the tent with nothing but a nod to tell Angelus she was alive, and that he could go inside.

Mayva stopped Liam as he started to walk away, speaking to him in a low voice. Angelus paid them no attention, hurrying into the tent. Veronica was sitting up in one of the cots, her legs, one thickly bandaged, hung over the side. Her face was ghostly pale, and when she looked up at the sound of him entering, he froze, her eyes stopping him short. He could do nothing except stare at her, unable to move or speak because of the ache in his chest.

Veronica opened her mouth, but Angelus spoke first. "Why did you come after me?" He'd meant to sound angry, but it came out... wrong. It was almost pleading. His knees all at once felt weak. "Why would you do that?"

She held his gaze.

Gods, she was so small, and the bandages and the paleness of her skin only made her appear smaller, younger. He wanted to step in front of her and shield her, though from what he didn't know. *Everything.*

"You could have been killed." His voice was still painfully faint. "Do you realize that?"

She nodded, just once. She did not look away. "You could have been killed, too." Her voice was so much stronger than his, so much more sure.

His legs carried him toward her, and he found himself kneeling in front of her. His left palm closed over her unbandaged knee. "You don't ever put yourself in danger for me." It was an order, but a plea, too.

She was already shaking her head. "I wasn't going to leave you out there by yourself. And if you leave again, I'll come after you again." She managed to sound much angrier than he could. The ache in his chest wouldn't go away; if anything it was getting stronger, more painful.

"Why?" He couldn't shout the word, as he'd meant to. It was just a breath, nothing more.

"Angelus." Her voice cracked, and she looked both frustrated and sad. She covered his cheeks with her palms, cupping his face, tilting his head so his gaze met hers. "I told you— I'm not leaving you behind." Her eyes blazed, and Angelus wondered when these

353

eyes of hers appeared, so full of fire and strength. Had they always been that way?

I'm not leaving you behind.

The ache turned to a lead weight pressing against his ribs from the inside, threatening to blow his chest wide open. Her hands. Her hands against his face, skin to skin. It was the most real thing he'd ever known. He was there, in that tent with her, and it was like the first time, like he had been far away for a long time, trying to make her out from a distance, but now he really saw her, felt her.

He reached up, closing his hands around her wrists. "You could have been killed," he said again, but his voice was fading out. It wasn't a reprimand this time; it was the voicing of a nightmare he hadn't been able to speak aloud before.

"Then don't ever do something like that again. You leave, I'll follow. Where you go, I go."

This close, Angelus could see a ring of gold around her pupils, lighting up the brown of her irises, a hint at the fire hidden inside.

You leave, I'll follow. Where you go, I go.

The pain in his chest was going to kill him. But there was something else forming inside him, something softer, warm and... calm. There had been a storm raging inside him for as long as he could remember. But it was beginning to dissipate.

He dropped his head, unable to meet her fiery gaze. His face pressed against her unbandaged leg, and as her hands slid up over his head, twining her fingers in his hair, he wrapped his arms around her waist, as tightly as he dared. When her lips pressed to the top of his head, leaving a soft kiss in his hair, a sob hitched in his chest.

"I'm sorry," he gasped, barely able to get the words out. "Veronica, I'm so sorry."

"It's alright," she said. Her fingers gripped his hair more tightly. "But don't you ever leave me again."

Tears spilled over Angelus' cheeks, the fabric of Veronica's skirt absorbing the tiny raindrops. "You were hurt because of me. Gods— I swear, I won't ever let that happen again."

Her arms wrapped around him, and he was struck by the way she held him— ferocious and gentle all at once, like she was protecting him. Not as though he were frail, or weak, but as though he were something precious, something worth protecting. Never, not in his whole life, had anyone ever held him like that. "I know," she whispered into his hair.

Her voice stole all the strength from his limbs, while simultaneously lighting wildfires in his chest.

Nothing was ever going to hurt her again, not so long as he lived and breathed.

Her lips whispered against his hair as she said, "I won't let anything happen to you, either. I'm going to get stronger. I'm going to protect you, too."

Angelus couldn't speak. He had fought so hard for such a long time, but never had someone fought equally as hard for him. No one, except Veronica. She wanted him to stay.

She wanted him to stay.

"You aren't a stray, Angelus," she whispered. "Not anymore. Never again."

He finally looked up at her face, and her expression softened when she saw the tears on his face. She wiped them away with her fingers, along with what remained of the beast's blood, gently. So gently. No one had ever been gentle with him before.

She smiled, and Angelus would burn the world to the ground to keep that smile safe.

"I'm home," he breathed, almost a question, but not as much as it would have been before.

"Home," she agreed, tears streaming silently down her cheeks as she pulled his hand to her lips, kissing his knuckles lightly. "Welcome home."

CHAPTER FORTY-THREE

ANGELUS stayed with Veronica, curling his long body around her small one in the narrow cot until she fell asleep. He rose only when hunger and thirst threatened to overwhelm him. He couldn't remember the last time he'd eaten. Carefully, he slipped from the bed, adjusting the blankets so she was well covered before leaving the tent.

Mayva rounded the side of the tent, her eyes far away, and the expression on her face, the thoughtful turn of her head, the sad eyes, made her look so strikingly like Andromeda that his breath faltered, and he stilled.

She paused when she saw him, her expression instantly unreadable. She watched him, waiting, as though she could tell he had something to say.

Angelus swallowed. He spoke first. "I'm sorry."

She was silent for so long Angelus didn't think she was going to speak. Then, finally, she said, in a low voice, "I failed her." He knew who she meant. Her eyes swept over the camp around them, lingering on Liam's tent. "But I will not fail them."

You find what you would die to protect, and then you die to protect it.

"I will fight with you."

Mayva's eyes cut to the tent beside them, then back to Angelus. "For her?"

"Yes." Simple. The truth.

Her dark eyes glittered in the night. "On this we can agree. No one comes before they do."

"They?" Angelus asked, though he knew the answer. Veronica. Liam.

"The only reason you and I are still here. Without them, people like us would burn the world without cause. At least now, we burn to keep them safe." Mayva's smile was deadlier than any weapon of war. "That's what warriors do. We protect what's ours. We protect our home."

You aren't a stray. What was he then?

With careful fingers, Angelus reached into the collar of his shirt and procured the identification necklace. There was hardly any of the glass left, but the gold frame and the chain had remained mostly intact. He extended the necklace to Mayva, and she held out her hand. He dropped it into her palm.

She leveled her eyes on his, that penetrating gaze so much like her sister's. "You fought well," was all she said before she walked back to her tent.

There were a great many things she could have meant. But Angelus didn't think the fight she was alluding to had anything to do with swords or beasts or wars.

You fought well.

Angelus had been fighting for a very, very long time. She didn't say the war was over. Only that he fought well.

Angelus didn't realize until that moment he'd been waiting his entire life to hear those words.

That's what warriors do.

You fought well.

PART THREE

CHAPTER FORTY-FOUR

VERONICA limped and wobbled her way across the infirmary tent, holding onto Angelus' arm for balance.

"You should be resting," Angelus said, scowling down at the ground, watching her feet as though waiting for her to lose her footing.

Veronica shook her head. She'd been resting for a week. While one of the camp's medics' healing Magic had greatly sped up the recovery process, the wounds would need some time to finish healing. She was holding up the army's progress down the mountain, she knew that, and hated herself for it.

If she'd been able to use fire, if she'd been faster, stronger, maybe the wolf wouldn't have had time to attack. Maybe Liam wouldn't have needed to rescue her.

She was restless; it coated her skin like itchy, ashy residue. She wanted to go back to her own tent, to read the books Tabitha left behind. There was no other option; she needed to learn how to conjure fire. She wasn't leaving herself, or anyone else, at the mercy of those monsters.

"Where's Liam?" Veronica asked, slightly winded from limping to the other side of the tent. She wouldn't let her muscles deteriorate, she had to keep moving. Incredibly, none of her bones had been broken, the only evidence of the attack being oddly star-shaped puncture wounds around her upper thigh. She wondered if they would scar.

Angelus rolled his eyes.

"He hasn't come to see me," Veronica pressed. "Is he alright?" He'd told her his Magic was weak, what if he had done too much?

Angelus' expression was pained. "If you're asking me to inquire after his health, you greatly overestimate my compassion."

He helped her back to her cot, and she sat down awkwardly, trying not to bend her leg more than necessary.

"Do you want me to stay?" he asked, and Veronica held in a sigh. She wasn't going to get any information about Liam from him.

"No, I'm alright. You should be training."

Angelus had started sparring with Mayva nearly every day, which had surprised Veronica to the point of disbelief, but so far as she could tell Angelus was participating under his own steam.

He cast a glance at the tent opening, and Veronica forced a smile. "Go on, I'll be fine."

He nodded, though still looked as if he would rather stay. He left the tent, and Veronica waited a moment before trying to stand up again. The wounds around her thigh ached, and with a wince Veronica stood up on her good foot. She limped carefully to the tent entrance, and parted the flap to peer outside. She could see Angelus' retreating form, and the crowded, noisy camp was rendered hazy in the sunlight struggling to shine through a smoky cloud covering. There were several loud cheers as two men emerged from the trees, carrying the carcass of an enormous deer between them, its legs tied around a thick wooden plank the men carried on their shoulders.

Veronica could see, even from a distance, the slow *drip, drip, drip* of the blood running from the arrow wound in its chest.

She stepped out of the tent, walking gingerly on her injured leg. Most everyone had gathered around the hunting party's spoils, and Veronica made it to Liam's tent mostly unnoticed. But Liam wasn't there. His tent was empty, and the bed clearly hadn't been slept in for a while. Days.

Dread slithered down her chest and settled in her stomach. Where was he?

A faint, wet cough whispered from inside one of the nearby tents. Veronica could have imagined it, but years spent as a physician's apprentice had made her far too familiar with that sound to ignore it. She turned, facing Mayva's slightly larger tent, which sat a few feet away. Instinctively she stepped toward it, and when she was just outside the doorway, she heard it again, a damp, heavy cough.

She parted the tent flap.

The tent was dark, the shaft of light the open tent flap offered falling across the bed. Liam sat, propped up on pillows, shirtless and glistening with perspiration, among the fur blankets. Liam was tall, taller even than Angelus, and much more muscular, but right then he looked feeble and small. Veronica stared, uncomprehending, until a hand closed over her shoulder. With a gasp she spun and faced—

"Your Majesty!"

Mayva's eyes were slightly widened, the only change to her usually impassive face, and it was how Veronica knew she was angry.

"I'm sorry," she said hurriedly, letting go of the tent flap and letting it fall closed behind her. Mayva did not release her shoulder. "I just wanted to see if he was—"

"If he was alright?" Mayva asked. Her voice was sharp. "He isn't. Do you know why?"

Veronica shook her head jerkily.

"He used too much Magic when he saved you from that monster. He told you his bloodline was impure, yes? He can't use as much Magic as you can, it wears him down to—" Her eyes flicked to the tent— *"That."*

This was her fault?

"I'm sorry," Veronica repeated, her eyes, to her humiliation, beginning to burn.

He was sick, all because she couldn't conjure fire?

My fault.

"Will he be alright?" she forced herself to ask.

Mayva let go of her shoulder abruptly. "He better be." Her teeth flashed like fangs behind her dark lips, and Veronica understood Mayva would do anything for Liam, just as Angelus would do anything for her. Just as she would do anything for him. "There is no room for dead weight in my company. You need to get yourself under control."

Veronica's eyes burned hotter, as did her face. But Mayva was right. Of course she was right.

"Mayva." Liam's voice, strained with fatigue, sounded directly behind Veronica. He was standing in the entrance to the tent, his skin pale and clammy, eyes bleary, his back hunched slightly as though his stomach or chest pained him.

"Get back inside," Mayva snapped, and Veronica was stunned to hear her speak that way to Liam. She had never heard the queen sound angry with him.

"What's going on?" came another voice. Angelus was making his way toward them, his posture relaxed but his eyes alert.

"Nothing," Veronica said quickly. She stepped out from between Liam and Mayva, and made a break for her tent, which was difficult to do with her bandaged leg.

"What did you tell her?" Liam demanded.

"The truth," Veronica heard Mayva answer.

Angelus caught up to her easily, grabbing her arm to halt her steps. She was so dangerously close to tears, she thought if she looked him in the eye she would start crying and not be able to stop. "What happened?"

"Nothing," Veronica said again.

"What did she say to you? Veronica, what—"

"It's like she said," Veronica snapped, pulling out of his grip and walking toward her tent. "The truth."

* * *

NO one came to Veronica's tent, to her relief. She needed to cry in peace. Then, with a deep breath, she started sifting through the stacks of Tabitha's books. She'd discovered the books in her tent the day after Tabitha's banishment. She didn't know who brought them to her tent, but she had a feeling Liam was at least partly responsible.

Liam.

A fresh surge of guilt crashed over her, and she hurriedly gathered the books she needed, but her eyes were swimming too much to read. She didn't know what she was looking for, anyway. Most of the books were meaningless without Tabitha's guidance.

Why? she thought. Why did the fault in her system have to be so big, so important, and so impossible?

She threw the book she was holding across the tent, where it hit the wall and bounced to the ground with a dull thud. Shamefully, she bent to retrieve the volume. She hadn't noticed which one it was, and when she closed it and peered at the binding, she frowned. The cover was horribly worn and faded— the book must have been over a hundred years old. What was discernible of the title was written in a language Veronica didn't recognize. But she knew which book this was. Tabitha had gotten her Blood Magic symbols from inside it.

She remembered the blood oozing from the deer's chest, the rabbit Tabitha killed, the bloody symbols written on Veronica's hands.

And the fire that blood helped her conjure.

The tent walls began to fade, the world ebbing away. An invisible wall seemed to separate her from everything else. She found her hands opening the book.

Notes were scrawled all over the pages, and Veronica wondered if any of them, or perhaps all of them, were Tabitha's.

She was searching for any symbols she recognized, until.... There. A row of symbols neatly underlined with black ink. She felt their ghosts against the skin of her hands.

Blood. She needed blood.

Her pulse was galloping so fast her heart must have been at risk of exploding. But there was also a warm tingle starting in her hand, the hand Tabitha had written on, starting at the tip of her finger which pressed into the page of the book, and spreading up her arm. That calm detachment Veronica had nearly forgotten was taking over. It was like relief, but different somehow, artificial. There was no emotion attached to the sensation; it was simply a muting of self.

Was this what Blood Magic did? Veronica didn't really care anymore.

Blood.

Find the blood.

Limping back to her cot, she sat down and pulled up her skirt to reveal the bandaging around her leg. With numb hands, she unwrapped the bandage, revealing the wounds which were only starting to heal. Jagged punctures the size of the pad of her thumb formed red-black stars against her skin. One of them, the largest and deepest, pooled with blood when she removed the bandage, the delicate layer of healing skin ripped away with the cloth bandaging.

Veronica stared at it.

Blood. Find the blood.

It was like the blood had been waiting for her. In a trance, she dipped her finger into the wound. She barely felt the sting. She lifted her red-tipped finger to her eyes, gazing at it. The rabbit

Tabitha sacrificed, it had been alive when she'd bled it dry. Would this be enough? It wasn't animal blood, but it was *her* blood. Blood that held Magic already.

"Veronica."

Slowly, Veronica looked up.

Liam stood before her, his face still horribly pale, but he was dressed in his usual dark pants and white shirt. His hair was dirty and overgrown, and his cheekbones were more pronounced than usual.

Her fault. This was her fault.

"I know how to fix it," she whispered.

Liam snatched the book from the bed and slammed it closed. Veronica shook her head as though coming out of a dream. She looked at her finger, at her exposed thigh and the bite marks as if seeing them for the first time. She covered her mouth with her unbloodied hand. "Oh Goddess," she gasped. "Liam, I—"

"This," Liam said, holding up the book. "Is not the way."

She shook her head, hand still over her mouth, eyes flooding with tears that seared her already swollen, sore eyes. Shame rolled through her stomach like nausea. Liam looked at the wounds on her leg. "Wait here," he said, leaving and quickly returning with a roll of clean bandages. She began to rewrap her leg. Now that sensation had come back to her, the wounds throbbed and stung horribly, and she wrapped them tight.

Veronica pushed her skirt back down to cover her legs. "What is wrong with me?" she gasped, pressing her hands to either side of her head. "Liam, what is *wrong with me?*"

Though it clearly pained him to do so, he knelt down in front of her. His eyes were so kind, but it couldn't hide his exhaustion.

"It isn't you," he said. "This kind of Magic... it's hungry, greedy. It will sink its teeth into whoever it can find." He tipped his head to peer into her eyes, trying to read something in her face. "Tabitha used Blood Magic on you," he asked softly, "Didn't she?"

Humiliation colored her face and hollowed out her chest. "Yes," she admitted.

Evil. Unnatural. Taboo. Queen Mayva's words came back to her. Veronica had known, even before she knew what Blood Magic was, what it did, that it was a crime, that it was wrong. A violation of Magic. She could still feel those symbols burning her skin; she was surprised they hadn't left a visible scar.

"I'm sorry," Liam said. "But it isn't the right way. You need to be better than Tabitha."

"But it's the only thing that helps," Veronica said, fighting a sob. "I can't help anyone without fire Magic, and this is the only way to get it out. I'm just dead weight otherwise."

Liam shook his head. "Mayva shouldn't have said what she did. She's just trying to protect me."

"But she was right," Veronica's voice was more sob than it was words. "You're sick because of me. Angelus got hurt before because of *me.*"

"I can help you," he said. "Or... I can try. But we have to do this the right way. It's going to be unpleasant, it's going to be hard. Are you ready for that?"

Was she ready? It didn't matter.

"Yes," she said. "Yes, I'm ready."

CHAPTER FORTY-FIVE

"WHERE the hell are you two going?"

Veronica didn't look back at the sound of Angelus' voice, but Liam did. It was early, the sun barely risen, and Veronica walked with Liam toward the surrounding forest. She was outside of her body, though somehow she was heavy, exhausted, as if she hadn't slept at all. She hadn't, really. She'd dreamt of blood, and of Tabitha, forcing her to drink it.

Liam rested a hand on Veronica's shoulder, making her pause as he addressed Angelus. Veronica's eyes remained ahead, on the line of trees before them. "She's going to be training with me for a while." The last word turned into a cough, which he tried to smother. He was still recovering; he should have been resting, but instead he was helping her.

"I'll go with—"

"No." Veronica's voice was heavy with finality. She wanted to face him but she couldn't. Liam had told her the previous evening what they would be doing, what could happen, and she couldn't bear the idea of Angelus being harmed by her lack of control.

Veronica didn't have to turn around to sense the hurt on Angelus' face. He must have walked away, because Liam wordlessly turned and led her, with a gentle guiding hand at her back, into the woods.

They stopped in the same clearing she and Tabitha had practiced in, and Veronica's heart panged at the sight of it. It felt contaminated somehow, darker than the rest of the forest around them.

"This is Gerard," Liam said, and Veronica blinked, realizing there was someone else in the forest with them. She had seen Gerard around camp, usually in the company of a woman with white-blonde hair in multiple braids, though she'd never known either of their names. Gerard was a giant of a man, tall and wide and heavy with muscle that stretched his leathery, sun-bronzed skin. His eyes were so dark brown that there was no discernable difference between his irises and pupils. "He's going to help you. Is that alright?"

Veronica dipped her head in answer, her tongue too leadened to speak. To her surprise, Gerard extended a hand toward her, and she grasped it, the feeling of dream walking dissipating slightly. He did not smile at her, but his face was not hard. So many in Mayva's company, Veronica thought, were somehow strong and kind at once.

Liam motioned for Veronica to sit down on the grass, and she did. Gerard sat across from her, and Liam remained standing.

"Veronica," Liam said, "Close your eyes."

Veronica obeyed. The breeze was cold against her face, and it tugged at her braided hair.

"Gerard has a talent for healing Magic," Liam said. "He's going to use it to help locate the block keeping you from connecting to your fire, and I'm going to help you clear it."

Veronica nodded. Or at least she thought she did. She was so tired. So heavy.

"Don't fight it," Liam said as Veronica felt Gerard's fingers press into her temple. "Veronica, do not fight it."

The darkness behind Veronica's eyelids shifted, somehow gaining texture and movement, like black waves under a black sky lapping at black shores. She had no body, and she was reminded, distantly, of when she had seen the vision of the boy on the beach. And of when she'd watched Finn fall. The utter blackness that followed.

She gasped, opening her eyes. But it was not Liam or Gerard before her, nor was it the mountain forest she'd grown accustomed to. She was in the plum orchard outside her village, and the wolf was before her, enormous and terrible. Angelus was there, and she wanted to scream at him to run. He was going to die.

Run! she thought, desperate.

And then her hand was moving, tracing the symbol for fire in the air. She hadn't needed to think about it, the Magic rising like a buried instinct. She'd done it. For the first time in almost ten years she'd done it.

The world tilted, and Veronica was falling. Down, down, down into blackness. She landed, unsteady on her feet, in a small room with a tiny window too high for her to see out of. The sunlight was feeble, so gray it was almost white.

Her bedroom. She was in her bedroom, in her parents' home. Before it had burned to the ground.

Instantly fear flooded her lungs. She tried the door but it was locked, or stuck. She banged on the walls. "Let me out!" she screamed. *"Let me out!"*

Already the room was filling with smoke, rising up as though from the floorboards themselves. The room was on fire, and she was going to burn with it.

She should. She deserved it.

Veronica screamed. She screamed in the memory, in the vision, and she was still screaming when she woke on the forest floor. She was curled on her side, and Liam knelt next to her, his hands gripping her arms. "Veronica," he said, shaking her. "Veronica, it's Liam, can you hear me?"

She sucked in a breath. Her chest was a den of vipers, striking and biting and filling her with venom. She pushed Liam's hands away, struggling to get up. Gerard remained sitting where he had been before, watching, but not moving.

Veronica pushed herself to her feet, swayed dangerously, and Liam held her arm to steady her. She wrenched out of his grasp. "Don't touch me!" she shouted. She couldn't control her voice— it was high and loud and wild. "You left me there! You left me there to burn!"

"Veronica." Liam's voice was firm, hard. "It wasn't real. You were never in any real danger. It's only in your mind."

Veronica wasn't listening. She stumbled back toward the trees, back toward camp. She was shaking so badly she could barely walk.

"Veronica," Liam called after her. "We need to finish this."

"I am finished," she barked back at him, clutching her still spasming chest. Though she knew even as she said it, that it was a lie.

CHAPTER FORTY-SIX

ANGELUS heard Veronica before he saw her. He paced restlessly along the edge of the forest that skirted the camp, waiting. Where were they? How far into the woods had they gone?

Then he made out the snapping of branches, and the unsteady footfalls of someone just beyond the line of trees. Veronica emerged, coming out a few yards ahead of him, and he hurried to her side. Something was wrong— her face was deathly pale, her eyes rimmed pink and hands shaking where they lay against her arms, crossed over her chest, as though she were cold.

Worry lanced through Angelus' chest, fast and hard and terrible. "What happened?" He was grabbing her arms, turning her toward him, and he nearly let go of her in surprise when her eyes found his. They were dark; there was no light left in them. There was nothing but—

She shoved his hands away, and Angelus' letting her go had more to do with his shock than any real strength on Veronica's part. "Don't." Her voice was the same shade of black as her eyes.

Angelus could only stare at her, frozen, as she limped back to her tent. Then he went to find Mayva's tent.

The Second Queen glanced up from her spread of maps on the desk before her, raising an eyebrow at Angelus' intrusion.

"This is your fault," Angelus bit out. "What did Liam do to her?"

Mayva's eyes narrowed. Or, rather, they twitched the tiniest bit before looking normal again. "You had your opportunity to train, to learn. Now it's her turn. It's hardly Liam's fault your friend has so much darkness buried inside her."

Angelus' blood chilled. *Darkness?* What darkness? "What the hell are you talking about?"

Mayva cocked her head. "You really don't understand, do you?" Her tone was purely observing, but Angelus' pride still smarted.

"Understand *what?*" he demanded.

She turned her gaze back to the maps, abruptly disinterested in him. "You can either help her, or stay the hell out of her way. I suggest you decide now."

*   *   *

VERONICA couldn't stop shivering.

Even with her coat and boots on, and laying under every blanket in her tent, the shivers wouldn't subside. Her teeth chattered so hard she bit her tongue, and tasted salty blood.

It was as though whatever kept her body warm had been carved out, leaving her hollow. And so desperately cold. She reached for the lantern, pulling it closer, but she was untouched by the little flame's warmth.

Veronica watched the fire in the lantern sway slowly from left to right. Finally, in the solitude of her tent, she allowed herself to cry.

*   *   *

THE village was still burning in her dreams.

The sky was black and red, the ground a carpet of ash and fire. Everything was burning.

Veronica could only watch as the wolves destroyed her home all over again. They tore apart houses, set barns ablaze, reached through windows and tore children through the jagged glass before biting into their legs, their arms, their chests and their screaming faces. Sully, Martha, and so many others were dead all around her, nothing but bloody, tattered remains that enormous flies and rats converged upon to devour.

There was nothing inside Veronica except the knowledge that this was her fault.

The running villagers blurred to indistinct shapes, black masses that dashed and skittered across her vision like shadows. But one person stood in the center of it all. Veronica seemed to be the only one who noticed him.

Angelus was burned and blackened, but still alive, still standing. Then he changed, shrinking into a child. For a moment, she thought it was Angelus, just younger, but then she recognized him. He was the child from her vision, the one with Veronica's face, and Angelus' eyes. He was, incredibly, unscathed, a little dirt and soot-streaked, but uninjured. Veronica reached for him, relieved, but her feet wouldn't move.

Then a wolf appeared behind him, rearing back, jaw gaping.

"Run!" Veronica screamed. He didn't see it. He was looking at her. *"Run!"*

His calm faced suddenly transformed into pure, blind terror. He reached his arms toward her, a silent plea to save him, *save him.*

But Veronica couldn't. She watched as the monster devoured him, leaving nothing behind.

*   *   *

VERONICA woke, throwing herself up into a sitting position, as though she could escape the dream. Her shaking hands covered her face, damp with sweat. Her breathing was loud and shrill in her ears. She'd bitten her cheek, and she dragged her hand over her mouth, wiping away the blood.

Blood.

Did it matter, really, how she controlled her Magic, if she could save them?

It's the only way.

Veronica pressed her thumb and index finger together, rubbing the blood between the pads of her fingers.

It had been so easy, when Tabitha drew those symbols in blood on her hands. The glorious loss of her identity. How she longed for that now. She'd simply *been* the Magic. It wielded her, for once.

It's the only way.

No. It wasn't. If it was, Liam wouldn't have been trying to help her find a different way.

Unnatural. Evil.

There *was* another way. There had to be.

CHAPTER FORTY-SEVEN

VERONICA didn't wait for daybreak.

Liam must have been a light sleeper, or perhaps he'd somehow known she would come, because he opened the flap to his tent as soon as Veronica stepped before it.

"Are you alright?" he asked. His hair was messy, his shirt untucked and unbuttoned at the top. He looked so tired.

Veronica didn't have an answer to his question. "I want to try again."

Liam said nothing. He retrieved his sword and belted it to his hip, then slipped on his boots and coat and followed her to the trees. Veronica glanced around, wondering which tent was Gerard's, but Liam shook his head, as though reading her thoughts. "It'll just be us this time."

They walked into the woods, silent as the night around them.

WHEN Angelus saw Veronica's empty tent, panic seized him. He went to Liam's tent, but it too was abandoned. He was supposed to spar with Mayva, though that was well forgotten now. Angelus practically ran to the sparring ring, where Mayva was strapping on her armor in the misty predawn.

"Where did they go?" Angelus demanded.

Mayva looked at him. He could tell by her lack of response that she was surprised. Liam and Veronica left without telling her, and she didn't know where they were either.

Without a word, Mayva and Angelus both ran to the forest.

*   *   *

VERONICA didn't say a word until she and Liam sat on the forest floor, the sun beginning to rise above them. When Liam reached out his hand to touch her, Veronica leaned away quickly. "You can't," she said. "You haven't recovered yet."

Liam shook his head. "It's fine."

Veronica swallowed. "Are you sure?"

His smile was a worn, exhausted thing. He didn't say anything, only pressed his fingers to her forehead exactly as Gerard had. "Don't fight it," he whispered as Veronica closed her eyes. "Let it run its course. Let it be over, Veronica."

There was no gap between shutting her eyes and the vision, no wandering through her mind. She closed her eyes, and she was instantly inside her old bedroom.

Only now, it was on fire.

Veronica stood perfectly still in the center of the room, taking careful, slow breaths. The reek of smoke was thick and heavy in the air, but Veronica did not choke on it as she had before.

The fire was spreading so quickly, the walls now nothing but shadows. Ghostly flames lapped at Veronica's feet, at the hem of her skirt, more like water than fire, but she did not burn.

She did not burn.

The door to the bedroom crashed open, and Veronica saw her parents. Her father, tan and muscled from working the fields, and her mother, with her thin face and eyes that always looked just a little frightened. They wore identical horror-stricken expressions. They coughed and choked on the smoke Veronica remembered so clearly, she could smell it even in the memory. A beam in the ceiling cracked, crashing to the ground in an explosion of sparks. Her parents jumped backward at the same time she did, hands up to protect their faces. She wanted to scream at them to get away, to get out of the house. They were going to die.

And it was all her fault.

She'd broken their one, sacred rule.

Never use your Magic, Veronica. Never.

She'd found her mother's Magic book, a secret kept even from her husband, and Veronica's young and curious hands had stolen it away to her room, tracing symbols with her fingers. Veronica recalled the relief, short lived as it had been, as though something caged had finally been set free.

Through the fire, through the smoke, Veronica's mother reached for her. That was all Veronica could ever remember. But now, she saw her mother's finger was tracing a symbol in the air, even as her clothes caught fire.

An invisible wall slammed into Veronica, and she was shoved back, what remained of the wall crumbling as she crashed through it. And then she was gazing up at the sky, breathing clean, smokeless air.

A shield. Her mother, who never used her Magic, had made her a shield.

Never use your Magic, Veronica. Never. They can't find out what you are.

Her mother, who Veronica always thought hated her for what she was, had saved her.

And then she died. And it was all Veronica's fault.

"Veronica!" The voice was far away, but it cut through to Veronica's mind. Liam. Liam was calling her name. She became aware of her body once more, but when she opened her eyes, the fire was still there, the smell of smoke still lingering.

It was because, Veronica realized, she was on fire.

CHAPTER FORTY-EIGHT

VERONICA was trapped inside a ball of fire, the flames the same orange-gold as the sun, burning just as bright, streaks of purple like lightning cutting across the mass of heat. She couldn't breathe. Her face was wet, and she realized she was crying.

She killed them. She killed her parents.

My fault, all my fault.

I'm sorry, I'm so sorry.

But what did it matter how sorry she was? It changed nothing. She killed them. Her mother, her father, they were dead, because of her.

Fists closed around her chest, cutting off her air, crushing her from the inside.

My fault. All my fault.

The flames around her grew bigger, higher, and there was no way out. She was a prisoner in a cage of her own making.

"Veronica!" Liam bellowed from somewhere beyond the fire, but she couldn't see him. "It wasn't your fault!"

Yes it was. It was her fault. She'd always known it, deep down. It was the image of her mother creating the shield that she could not accept. She'd told herself so many times her mother hated her. Maybe it had been easier to believe that.

But she had saved Veronica. Maybe she'd known it was too late to save herself. But she hadn't even tried. She'd used what was left of her life to save Veronica's.

Veronica fell on her hands and knees, the pain in her chest, the weight inside her threatening to drag her down through the earth and into nothingness. She was buried alive, even as she was burning.

"I'm sorry," she sobbed. "I'm so sorry."

Then, impossibly, she felt a hand close around her arm. She dragged her eyes up, and saw—

"Veronica!" Angelus screamed. "Get up, now!"

His clothes were catching fire, his skin burning. He was reaching through the flames to get to her. He'd joined her in her fire, and he would burn because of it.

His eyes were wide and desperate, their green color retreating to reflect the gold inferno around them.

Veronica took hold of his hand, and he pulled her free.

As soon as Veronica was beyond the fire's touch, it vanished. There was nothing but a patch of burned grass as evidence the fire had been there at all.

Angelus collapsed onto his back, Veronica landing on top of him, arms clinging to his neck. His chest crashed up and down against hers, his breathing heavy and loud.

He wrapped his arms around her tight, *tight,* as she sobbed.

"It's alright," he panted, smoothing a hand down her hair. "You're safe now. It's alright. I've got you."

"I killed them," she sobbed, so hard her words were nearly lost. "It was my fault."

"No," he breathed, "It was an accident."

"I'm sorry," Veronica wailed, crying harder than she'd ever cried before in her life. She'd never let herself mourn them, never let a tear fall for either of her parents. "I'm so sorry— *I'm so sorry.*"

"I know," Angelus panted. She could feel his hard exhales against the top of her head. "You're forgiven. Veronica, you're forgiven. It was an accident. Do you understand? You didn't mean to."

It shouldn't have changed anything. The world was not different now that she'd said the nightmarish words out loud. But the weight in her chest lightened, a bird once made from stone finally free.

My fault. I'm sorry. I didn't mean to.

Please forgive me.

I love you.

I'm sorry.

Angelus held onto her impossibly tighter, nearly crushing her, as though he was afraid she'd vanish. He should have been pushing her away, trying to get away from her. But he wasn't. He was holding her like he would never let her go.

Slowly, very slowly, she began to relax in his arms, her breathing starting to come a little easier.

She was warm. She was so, so warm. Like a fire had been lit inside her.

No. Like a fire had been uncovered inside her.

The Magic was free. And so was she.

CHAPTER FORTY-NINE

WHEN Angelus picked Veronica up and carried her back to camp, Liam and Mayva both stepped aside to let him pass. Veronica was tiny in his arms, curled up in a ball and burrowing into his chest. Her breaths still hitched with small sobs, but her expression was clear. When he touched her inside the ball of fire, he'd glimpsed images, memories, of a burning room. He'd understood, all in the span of a second, what she was seeing, as though he were the one remembering, as though she had somehow let him inside her mind.

His heart seized as he looked down at her. He forced himself to speak. "Do you want to go back to your tent? You should rest."

She shook her head, her cheek rubbing against his chest. "Take me somewhere else."

So Angelus took her somewhere else.

He walked and walked, the forest thickening and darkening the further they ventured, until he found an enormous tree, the trunk several times wider than he was. He adjusted an unprotesting Veronica so that her legs were wrapped around his waist, and her arms around his neck. Chest to chest, he reached up and started to climb. The burned skin of his hands stung at the contact of the rough bark, but he kept climbing. Stopping at a thick branch, he sat down, legs dangling over either side of the limb, his spine pressed to the tree trunk, and Veronica curled into him. Angelus didn't say anything, he just ran his fingers over her hair, down her cheeks, wiping away the last of the tears.

After a moment, Veronica whispered, "Angelus?"

He loved the way his name sounded when she said it. It sent a warm, trickling sensation down into his stomach, like a sip of alcohol.

"Why did you come to my village?" Her voice was quiet, almost timid. "When you were hurt. Why did you come to me, and not someone else?" She glanced up at his face, but just as quickly looked away. "Why me?"

He bit the inside of his cheek, hand whispering down the back of Veronica's head, her hair smooth against his palm. "Because... it felt safe." He wasn't sure where the words were coming from, but they didn't stop. "I was supposed to watch Finn, those were my orders, but you were always there." Working in the herb garden, taking care of patients, teaching the children to read. She reminded him of a fire burning in a hearth, warm and inviting and... "I thought you felt... safe."

He remembered the soft kiss she'd pressed against his knuckles. *Home.*

He'd known, somehow, long before they ever truly met. She'd felt like home, like all Angelus had ever wanted.

Her palm was pressed against his chest, like she was trying to find his heartbeat, and his skin tingled at the contact, even through the fabric of his shirt, some of the material blackened and crisped. She had to feel the warzone his heart was turning his chest into, but she didn't move away. "Safe," she repeated. "Do you still think that? After—"

"Yes." Though his voice did not rise above a whisper, it was still fierce, sure. "I'm not afraid of you."

He felt her exhale with her entire body.

"Why did you do it?"

He didn't have to explain what he meant. "I couldn't save you before," she said softly, "When that wolf was going to attack you. Or from the bandits. You've saved me so many times, and I couldn't do anything for you."

"That's not true," he said. "You saved us in the village."

"But I wasn't in control. I could have hurt you." Angelus shook his head, but she continued, "I can't be weak anymore. I'm never letting anyone get hurt for me ever again."

Angelus smiled, slow and soft, though she couldn't see his face.

She ran her hand down his chest, stopping at his ribcage. The jagged scar there was numb to her touch, the feeling in that patch of ruined skin having long ago abandoned him. "I couldn't save you from this either. But I will. From now on, I will." She looked up at him, and her smile, small and sad and brave, lit a fire in Angelus' chest. "I'll keep you safe."

Angelus pressed his lips to the top of her head, feather light, barely a kiss and more like the memory of one. "It's not your responsibility to save me." But he was smiling as he said it.

She straightened, hands wrapping around the back of his neck, pulling him closer. "Yes it is," she whispered. "Yes it is."

And then she kissed him. It was every fire she'd ever created, every fight Angelus had ever won, every mile of forest traveled and every inch of the mountains around them, all wrapped up in that one touch. She exhaled against his mouth, and a piece of him died.

The whole world became nothing but this. Her hands in his hair, his palms hot against her back, her breath in his mouth, and both of their hearts burning until there was nothing left of either of them, nothing but pure white flame the color of the fresh, fallen snow.

CHAPTER FIFTY

AS soon as Veronica and Liam were both able to ride, the company packed up camp and made their way down the mountain.

Angelus walked beside the horse Veronica had been given to ride, the reins in his hand. Veronica couldn't help noticing how his eyes darted around the trees on either side of their path. He couldn't know Mayva's eyes were doing the same. Veronica knew they were both watching, waiting, for wolves.

Veronica nudged Angelus' shoulder with her foot, and his attention was instantly back on her. His eyes found her face, and she gave him a smile. She saw him relax, just a little. One of his hands settled on the back of her leg, and she felt grounded by the touch.

They walked from sunrise until sunset, setting up camp by the light provided by the Wielders in camp, including Veronica. Liam gave her an approving smile as she held the symbol for "light," a blending of two triangles Veronica discovered in one of Tabitha's books. It glowed a soft white-yellow above them and illuminated the ground so a few soldiers could set up their tents.

"When you're finished," Liam said to her, "Come to Mayva's tent. Angelus is already there."

Surprised, Veronica nodded.

When she reached the Second Queen's tent, Liam, Mayva and Angelus all hovered over a map spread out on the table in the center of the room. Veronica had never seen such an intricate, detailed map of Lavdia before, and she stared at it as she approached. She knew Lavdia was a small country, but spread out on the table, it seemed like the whole world.

The others looked up when she entered, and Angelus stepped to the right to give her room next to him. His fingers brushed her hand, a secret, silent greeting.

"Veronica," the queen said, looking Veronica in the eye as she spoke to her. "Thank you for coming. You two—" she glanced between Angelus and Veronica— "Are the most recent travelers from below the mountain. You're more familiar with the situation in the villages than any of us. We need a place to set up our base, somewhere not too close to the Imperial City or the castle, and somewhere that will welcome our cause."

"My village," Veronica said at once. Whatever was left of it, at least. "It's right on the border, with nothing but woods on the west side."

"Sympathizers?" Liam asked. He was still pale, his eyes tired, but his voice sounded as it usually did, steady and calm. He'd been completely drained after using his Magic on her.

Veronica overheard him and Mayva arguing about it inside the queen's tent. "She's worth the risk," she'd heard Liam say, "She's more powerful than I'll ever be. You *need* her."

Veronica opened her mouth, slightly self conscious with all eyes fixed on her.

"There's no way to know for sure," Angelus said, answering for her. She squeezed his hand in wordless thanks. He pointed to the village on the map, a cluster of drawn houses with dense ink trees alongside them. Veronica watched Angelus draw a circle around the village with his finger, his neck bent over the map, his other hand on the hilt of the sword at his hip. He appeared older, somehow. "But it's small, spread out with lots of land around it. The Imperial City is maybe a day's journey by horse."

"They'll help us," Veronica added quickly. They had to. The villagers and farmers, her friends, neighbors, would help them, she knew it.

"It's perfect." Liam was speaking to all of them, but his words seemed to be directed at Veronica more than the others. His way of thanking her, perhaps, for volunteering her home to them.

Nerves fluttered in Veronica's stomach— she wasn't sure if they were unpleasant nerves or something else, it was just energy with no direction, nowhere to go.

They spoke for a while— or rather, Veronica listened to the others strategize— before Angelus slipped his hand into Veronica's, a wordless invitation to leave with him. Liam and Mayva said nothing, not even glancing up from their map as Angelus and Veronica left.

Lower down on the mountain, there wasn't as much snow, but the wind was still freezing. Veronica didn't feel it, not with

Angelus' hand in hers, warm and dry and so much larger than hers. Her sigh formed a soft cloud in front of her. When she looked up at Angelus, however, the reassurance she felt was not reflected on his face. His expression was drawn, tired and tense.

She squeezed his hand. "What's wrong?" she asked softly.

Angelus stopped walking, eyes moving across the hastily assembled camp, then pulled her toward the trees. The forest they camped in was thicker and denser than before, and it didn't take long for the trees to darken the sun. Angelus led her away from the camp, until the sounds were muffled, and they were as alone as they could manage.

"What's wrong?" she asked again, voice a whisper.

He spread his fingers across her neck, drawing her forward into a kiss. "I want to take you away from here," he whispered, then smiled faintly when she opened her mouth to speak, shaking his head. "But I know that isn't going to happen."

"Maybe it would have," she admitted, "Before."

He cocked his head. "What changed?"

She thought of the camp, of the villages, of the visions of a little boy with green eyes, of Angelus' warm palms on her skin. "The world got bigger."

His smile was a little wistful, his eyes dropping to her jaw, where his thumb traced delicate lines back and forth. "My world is still small."

She couldn't help a smile. "I know."

He sat down at the base of a thick tree, taking her hand and pulling her onto his lap. Her legs were on either side of his, their chests brushing, and her face felt hot, her skin tingling. The only thing that calmed her was his expression, his wild eyes somehow tamed, his mouth softened. For her, only for her.

She leaned forward and pressed a soft kiss to his collarbone, where a burn had mostly healed. He tipped his head back, exhaling slowly as he closed his eyes. She smiled against his skin. His palms brushed over her sides, settling on her hips.

"May I ask you something?"

Veronica looked up, and found his eyes locked on hers. She nodded.

"Have you... *Seen*... anything about what happens next? If this coup will work? Anything?"

The truth was, Veronica hadn't. She'd waited every night for the dreams to come, but they didn't. She shook her head. "No. I haven't. But I also haven't tried."

Angelus frowned. "You can try? I mean, you can See on purpose?"

"Only... once." Her face warmed, and she continued, "I'm not sure I want to know."

Angelus' brow furrowed. "What?"

"If we're going to fail... I don't want to know. I want to keep believing... we could win."

She remembered the boy from the vision, walking on the beach, smiling at her. She remembered the dream in which she watched him die. Two potential futures.

A choice, she realized.

Fight, or surrender.

Perhaps if someone had fought for her as a child, the world would be a very different place.

"I want a better world," she whispered.

Angelus' smile was made of stars. "Then we'll make one."

CHAPTER FIFTY-ONE

ANGELUS stayed beside Veronica's horse as they traveled. Walking back down the mountain was strange, like walking through a memory, the dark forest eerily familiar. Veronica seemed to think so too, because she held up a hand to indicate she wanted him to stop. He tugged the horse's reins, and it halted.

Veronica looked around. "This place is... familiar."

"Is this—"

"The village," Veronica said, at the same time Angelus thought it. "Rom's village, it's near here, isn't it?"

Angelus had to take a second to orient himself, but then he nodded. He pointed down a left-leading path. "That way."

Several people both on foot and on horseback had paused behind Veronica, and Liam called from up ahead, "Is everything alright?"

Veronica didn't answer. She slid off her horse, making a clumsy landing Angelus kept from turning into a fall. She still limped slightly, and Angelus kept close behind her. He too ignored Liam calling after them, and soon heard others starting to follow.

The towers were still there, though the banner was gone. Just for a moment, Angelus could pretend it was the same as they had left it. But the smell of blood, the sound of screaming, came rushing back to him.

Veronica walked as if in a dream toward the village, and Angelus followed. When they stepped between the pillars, there was nothing beyond them.

The houses were burned to the ground, nothing but charred black smears on the ground where they had once been.

And there were bodies. Rotted, decayed, ruined bodies. Everywhere. They were *everywhere.*

Veronica crumpled to her knees, and Angelus could only stare out at the carnage. All the breath was gone from his lungs, and he was simply empty.

All of this, he thought, because they were Wielders? Because of Magic?

He looked at Veronica, and something hot slashed across his airless chest. He remembered the wolf's teeth around her leg, the intent to kill in its eyes.

This would never be her fate. He'd die before she was a ruined corpse on a makeshift battlefield like this, or anywhere else.

A crowd of soldiers had gathered behind them, standing a little ways off as though out of respect.

Mayva stepped beside Angelus, followed closely by Liam. "What is this place?" she asked.

It took a beat for Angelus to find his voice. "A Wielder village. They took us in, helped us. And those creatures killed them."

Liam sucked in a breath. Mayva was silent.

"They had your banner," Angelus told Mayva.

Her expression did not change, but her eyes hardened. Angelus realized then that Queen Mayva never knew her banner was being used as a symbol. He wondered if they chose it because of Mayva, or if it had been for a quieter, subtler reason. To communicate with others, to disguise themselves under a banner of Lavdia that no soldier would ever know was meant to represent something more. Or was it because it was the symbol of a warrior, and that was what they were all trying to be. More like her.

She turned to her soldiers. "We will bury them," she said. She turned back to the carnage before them and said, quietly, just for Angelus, Veronica, and Liam, "We owe them that much."

CHAPTER FIFTY-TWO

ANGELUS expected to travel down the backroads he and Veronica took up the mountain, but Mayva led them down the main mountain roads, past villages and farms and clusters of wide-eyed people. She was the Warrior Queen, after all. She had no reason to hide. This was her country, and she seemed to be making a point of reminding them all of this.

Nevertheless, being out in the open set Angelus' teeth on edge. He stayed well concealed within the army's ranks, away from eyes that might recognize him from wanted posters. But the anticipation was painful— every branch snapping in the trees around them sounded like a wolf hot on their trail, every moment spent where he didn't know where Veronica was, even if it was only a second, felt dangerous.

When they made camp for the night, the scent of death still in his nose, Angelus walked restlessly among the tents. It wasn't nearly as cold at night now that they weren't high up in the mountains, but there was still a biting chill in the dark. He was exhausted. They'd buried hundreds of bodies. It should have taken days to bury so many, but with Mayva's army, and with Magic, it had taken a day. A few of the Wielders in Mayva's company drew symbols in the ground, causing the earth to part under where the corpses lay, pulling them inside a mass grave. Those without Magic dragged bodies into the hole they created. Angelus didn't think he'd ever forget the smell.

He paused outside Mayva's tent. It was the only one with a light coming from inside. The queen perhaps couldn't sleep either.

Angelus parted the tent flap, and saw Mayva kneeling on the ground, hands pressed together before her, her back to Angelus. She wore no armor, only a pair of brown pants and a sleeveless gray shirt that left her shoulders and arms bare. Angelus stared at the scar visible across her right shoulder, the ruined skin as white as snow, carving a slanting line that slashed down and across her spine, disappearing into her shirt. Angelus' own scars were nothing to this, not even the one across his chest. A wound that deep, that massive, should have killed her.

She glanced at him, then turned away again. She said nothing, but Angelus sensed her invitation. He stepped up beside her, and noticed for the first time the small wooden figure before her, depicting a woman in a wolf headdress, a crow resting in her open palms, as though ready to take flight.

Angelus didn't understand. It was the crow, really, that made him finally realize. The Earth Goddess.

Angelus stared at the queen, but her eyes were closed, her head bowed. After a moment, Angelus knelt beside her.

"You worship the Earth Goddess?" It shouldn't have been so strange, but he had only ever known Wielders to worship the Earth Goddess. Lavdians acknowledged many gods, and this goddess was not among them. It was the first time he'd thought of the Wielders' abilities as part of a religious practice. Magic, he supposed, had to come from somewhere.

"I pray every night for protection." She opened her eyes, lowering her hands and sitting back on her heels. "But tonight... I've asked for their souls to find rest."

Angelus blinked, and saw the mountains of dead bodies once more.

"Are you..."

"A Wielder?" she glanced at him. "No. But it shouldn't matter one way or the other. That's why no one knows about this, except Liam." She nodded toward the carving.

"I won't say anything," Angelus said quickly.

She gave him a slight nod of thanks. "I don't want people to think I've chosen a side. I'm not for Wielders, or non-Wielders. I want only what our founder wanted. Peace between the two." Her dark eyes found his face, and Angelus was frozen under the intensity of her stare. "The only sides are those who stand by the founding principles, and those who want to destroy them."

Lavdia. A place where everyone was supposed to be free. How far they had strayed since their beginning.

"Why does it matter to you?" he asked softly, with no coldness, just curiosity.

Her eyes glittered with amusement, and she looked so much like Andromeda that it made Angelus' chest hurt. But not as much as it might have before. It was only grief, now. "I am queen," she said simply. "Perhaps I did not want to be, but I am. And I have a responsibility because of that. The Savior Queen, Amora, our first queen, made this country a promise. One of freedom. I intend to keep it."

The words to the old folk song came back to him. *Three crowns, that together band, did free the Magic, across the land.*

This wasn't about Magic. Not entirely. Of course it wasn't. Artemis was using Magic, somehow, wasn't he? This was about freedom.

"How noble," he said dryly, and to his surprise, she gave a little huff of laughter.

"There are two sides to every coin. There is my birthright. But there is also what I've chosen."

"And you've chosen to fight."

She leveled her marble gaze on him. "I've chosen my family. And my home. Same as everyone else in this camp."

That's how she had built an army, Angelus thought. She only told them the truth, that their home, their families, their freedom, were in danger. And they chose to fight. Every single one of them.

"I never knew," he said softly, more to himself than the queen. "I was right there, in the castle, at the center of it all, and I never understood what was happening. This country... it never felt like my home, like something I needed to protect." His world had been so painfully small. It still was, in many ways, but it was slowly getting bigger. He thought of Veronica's village, of Rom's, of the hundreds of dead bodies he helped bury only a matter of hours ago. The world was so much larger than he'd ever imagined, so much more than the castle, than the little seaside town he'd been born in, the place that after so many years he still missed in a strange, almost imaginary way. It both thrilled, and terrified him.

Mayva raised an eyebrow. "What about now?"

Home. This could be his home, if he fought for it.

"Now... everything's different."

I want a better world.

Mayva could make that happen. He believed it.

She stood, looking down at him. "You said you would fight with me. Will you still?"

Angelus rose to his feet. "I will. Your Majesty." And then he bowed, his spine bending and his hand coming to rest over his heart. He couldn't remember the last time he addressed royalty this way, and somehow, this time, it felt different. He looked up. "But I have one condition."

Her hands were on her hips, though she appeared slightly amused. "And what would that be?"

"I want to kill Artemis." Angelus' voice was smooth, even. "If it's me and him, I want to be the one to kill him."

Mayva just smiled. "Only if I don't get to him first."

*   *   *

ANGELUS lost count of the days, so he was shocked when the landscape began to flatten, and he realized that the mountains were behind them, not around them. And when they reached the border forest, Veronica gasped. His gaze flew up, eyes following where hers were trained.

Her village was on the horizon. She was home.

CHAPTER FIFTY-THREE

ANGELUS had half expected the village to look the same as the day they left— burning houses and screaming villagers, soldiers and monsters on the prowl.

But it was... calm. Peaceful. The houses Angelus could see as they approached the village bore no evidence of ever having been on fire. In fact, most of the buildings looked almost... new. Doors of dark, clean wood adorned most of the homes. And where there once had been cracked windows and old clothing, there was clean, unblemished glass and colorful dresses and animal skin coats.

The village was almost unrecognizable.

It was also completely silent. Angelus couldn't place what sound was missing, until he remembered the skeletal dogs that had wandered the streets, aimless and hungry, whining and barking. There wasn't a single dog in sight, when before they had been everywhere.

Mayva, Liam, Angelus and Veronica walked at the head of the procession, Mayva's army following behind. Though there weren't many of them, they were impressive, swathed in armor and readiness. A few doors opened, curious eyes peering outside, and even more people watched them from behind windows, but no one came outside until they reached the center of the village, a circular space all the surrounding shops and houses faced, like a round target marking something vital and unprotected.

When the people did file out onto the street, their faces were impossible to read, and Angelus had the strange sensation they were bracing for something. The air was charged like the sky before a lightning strike.

Angelus expected excitement, cheers. Reverence for their queen. He waited for their knees to hit the ground, for them to bow to the Warrior Queen, who protected them, who kept them safe.

But not a single person bowed.

A man stepped forward. Angelus recognized him as the metalsmith. His wife stood in the doorway of their shop, face tight and anxious. "To what do we owe this great honor?" he asked, addressing Mayva. He didn't sound honored at all.

Mayva watched him, not speaking for a moment, but assessing, reading the expressions around her with simultaneous intensity and care. Before she could speak however, Veronica stepped toward the metalsmith. Angelus instantly reached to pull her back, but Mayva shot him a single look. He froze, his heart pounding furiously in his chest. There was something *wrong* here. Warnings whispered across his skin, prickling at his neck.

"Euric," Veronica said, addressing the metalsmith. He stared at her as though noticing her for the first time. His hard expression didn't change, except for a slight narrowing of his eyes, and the tiniest twitch at the side of his nose. Disgust.

"Veronica," he greeted her stiffly. "I'm surprised to see you return. Given the circumstances under which you left."

Veronica paled, and Angelus' hands balled into fists.

"I'm sorry," Veronica breathed. "But I brought help." She waved a hand toward Mayva and her company, toward Angelus. "The queen is here to help us, all of us. She—"

"We don't need her help," Euric practically spat. "You, and your kind, are not welcome in this village. Leave at once."

Veronica looked as if she'd been slapped.

Angelus couldn't hold his silence any longer. "Her *kind?*" he demanded. "Who the hell do you think you are?"

Euric's eyes swiveled to Angelus. "I have been appointed leader of this village by the High Queen. Her law is the only law we obey. We will not house traitors." His eyes went from Angelus to Veronica, and this time he didn't even try to smother his disgust. "Especially not if they are *Wielders.*"

There was something strangely familiar about the way he said "Wielders" that pricked at Angelus' memory. Someone else had spoken that way, with disgust and contempt, and Angelus had been consumed with the same surprise and confusion then as he was now.

Artemis. This man sounded just like Artemis.

Angelus' eyes swept over the village once more, taking in the new clothing the people wore, the repaired buildings.

"He's been here," Angelus whispered to Mayva, leaning toward her but keeping his eyes on Veronica and Euric. "Artemis. He got to them first."

Mayva was suddenly standing in front of Veronica, having moved so quickly Angelus barely registered it. He grabbed Veronica's arm, ready to push her behind him should the exchange turn ugly. Uglier.

"As Second Queen," Mayva said in a loud, commanding voice that sent a ripple of silence like a layer of ice water over the villagers. "I am claiming this village as a war camp." She drew one of her swords from the sheath at her back and drove it into the ground. "Here is where we will set up our base. My soldiers will—"

"The High Queen has outlawed their Magic!" Euric snapped, his forcibly calm mask shattering completely, his eyes going wide with what might have been desperation, or fear. But it was not fear of Mayva. There was something, or someone, that scared him more than her. "We will alert the High Queen at once!"

Mayva drew her other sword in a slow, tantalizing threat. Angelus carefully pulled Veronica behind him as some of Mayva's soldiers started to close in like wolves. "You will obey the queen before you."

"Your status has been revoked by the High Queen," Euric said, "For siding with enemies of our country, the people who killed our Mother Queen! You have no authority here."

Angelus flinched. Of course. Of course Artemis was using Andromeda as a martyr. His blood hummed, sick rage burning in his chest like acid.

All eyes fell on Mayva, waiting.

"Lavdia no longer acknowledges you as a queen— We obey the new order!" Euric looked almost mad, his eyes huge and his face pale.

"No," someone shouted from the crowd of villagers, "We don't!" An old woman stepped forward, limping slightly, using an old cane to keep her balance. "You're a coward, Euric! And you do not speak for me!"

"R-Roberta?" Veronica stammered.

The woman, Roberta, smiled at Veronica, revealing several missing teeth. "Hello dear," she said. She turned back to Euric. "You won't chase these people out, Euric. They belong here as much as you do, as much as any of us."

Angelus didn't think she was only talking about the army.

"Be quiet!" Euric bellowed, stepping toward Roberta as though intent to strike her, but Liam was before him instantly, blocking his way.

"Crazy old hag," someone else in the crowd snapped. "She's probably one of them!"

Several things happened at once. Veronica screamed as someone punched Roberta right across the face. The old woman hit the ground, dead weight, and the villagers surged forward as the army drew their weapons. It was as if a dam had collapsed, letting in a tidal wave.

Angelus hauled Veronica to the door of the metalsmith shop, shoving her inside as people screamed, the riot like a wildfire engulfing the whole of the village square. Angelus didn't even know who was fighting against who. There were villagers fighting each other, Mayva's soldiers trying to separate them, while still other villagers went for the soldiers. They didn't get far, being unarmed and untrained, but they were angry, animalistic fury proving to be somewhat of a match for sharpened steel.

"Enough!" Mayva shouted.

A few of the Wielders in Mayva's army stepped free of the immediate crowd, hands sweeping out in front of them as they drew symbols in the air. Invisible walls erected between the soldiers and the villagers, the latter beating their fists against the shields and emitting purple sparks where their skin touched the Magic wall.

Mayva, eyes wide and hair yanked mostly free of its braid, glared around at the people surrounding her. "Lock it down," she ordered. "No one gets in or out of this village without my order. I want protective shields up, now."

Her soldiers obeyed without batting an eye, and the streets were slowly cleared of the beaten and bloodied villagers.

Mayva turned to the doorway of the shop where Angelus and Veronica stood, frozen, and for a moment the queen and Angelus just stared at each other.

"I'm sorry," Veronica gasped, her eyes bright with unshed tears. "I'm sorry. I-I didn't know. I didn't..."

Angelus' eyes were locked on the queen. "What do we do now?"

Mayva turned her face away, watching the villagers. She said nothing, but Angelus could read the words on her face. *I don't know.*

CHAPTER FIFTY-FOUR

VERONICA'S uninjured leg bounced as she sat in a chair next to Roberta's bed in the old woman's small, one room home. Roberta slept silently, the slight rise and fall of her chest the only sign she was alive.

The left side of her face was bruised and so badly swollen her eye all but disappeared in the folds of angry red flesh. The skin had broken under her left eye, and the dried blood made her face look bone-white. Veronica tried to look anywhere but at the old woman's face. Her eyes fell, unfocused, to one of the walls, on which several strings of beads hung from the ceiling in long rows.

"This is all my fault." Veronica's voice cracked.

Angelus, standing beside her chair, gripped her shoulder. "No, it isn't."

She turned her red eyes upon him. "I should have never told Queen Mayva to come here. I never should have left in the first place."

Angelus shook his head, kneeling down in front of her. "Even if you'd stayed, you couldn't have stopped any of this. Artemis lied to them, and they believed him. If you'd stayed, he would have killed you. There's nothing you could have done."

She leaned forward, resting her head in her hands, elbows on her knees, and fought back a sob. "What are we going to do?"

Angelus pressed a kiss to the side of her head, but before he could answer a small voice croaked, "Don't cry, dear."

They both turned to Roberta, whose good eye was open and fixed upon them.

"Roberta," Veronica breathed, relieved. She reached forward and took the old woman's veiny, withered hand. "I'm so sorry."

Roberta tried to shake her head, and winced. "It's best you got out when you did. Those... *things* turned this village upside down, looking for anyone with Magic. They didn't find anyone, but soldiers came everyday to speak to Euric and others. Then things started changing; the border guards all left, and overnight soldiers from the castle were repairing buildings, bringing new clothes, clearing out the stray dogs, and cleaning the streets. Then they just left."

"Artemis bought off the villagers, then," Angelus said.

"They're scared," Roberta said, "they're convinced Wielders are to blame for everything." She looked at Veronica. "They told us you were a Wielder, that you left to join the Lawless." Roberta slipped her hand from Veronica's grasp to press it to the younger woman's face, smooth and unblemished compared to Roberta's wrinkled and battered flesh. "But I knew you were one of the good ones. I've known it for a long time."

Veronica's eyes went wide. "How did you—"

Roberta smiled. "Now that's a question for another day."

But Veronica sensed something warm jump, just a little, beneath Roberta's palm, as though Roberta allowed it to appear before it was gone. Before it was hidden.

Their eyes locked, and Roberta only smiled.

*   *   *

VERONICA leaned against Angelus as they left Roberta's house. Gerard, who Mayva assigned to guard the place, nodded to them as they stepped out into the cool night. The sky was a pale, dying blue. Worry weighed down Angelus' chest when he looked at Veronica, her face pale and eyes wide, horror and sadness warring on her thin face. Betrayed. Her village had betrayed her.

Anger surged through him. He didn't care about the village, whose side they were on, but for Veronica's home to be turned inside out, to want her gone...

"Don't," she breathed.

Angelus paused his steps, peering down at her. "What?"

"Don't blame them. They're scared."

"I don't give a shit if they're scared," Angelus growled. "They can't treat you this way, treat the other Wielders this way." Something tripped in Angelus' chest, a strange, uncomfortable sensation. Unfair, he thought. This was all so unfair.

He wondered, in a far off part of his mind, if this was how Finn had felt, before.

Veronica said nothing.

Angelus sighed, exhausted. "It's late," he said. "You should sleep."

Veronica turned slowly to face the east side of the village, eyes following the narrow dirt road stretching into the dark. "I want to see it first," she said. "I want to know... if there's anything left."

*   *   *

THE dark road smelled like home. Damp, fallen leaves gave off a sweet perfume of decay and winter's approach. Going from the snowy mountains to this place, barren of snow, was like stepping back in time. A thousand memories flooded Veronica's mind as her boots crunched on the gravel path she'd walked every day for years. Home. She was home. The village may not want her back, but this gravel road, Finn's house, the herb garden, the barn and the little creek, they had missed her.

Angelus' hand tightened around hers, and for a moment she didn't understand why. But then she saw the house.

The door hung open on its hinges, torn drapes reaching through broken windows like arms waving in warning. The herb garden, once lush and green and teeming with life, was a trampled mess of snapped plant stems and torn leaves, hoofprints pressed into the dark dirt as though soldiers came through on horseback, not noticing or perhaps not caring about what lay beneath their feet.

"Veronica," Angelus breathed, half question, half warning.

She pulled her hand free of his, and walked, as if in a dream, toward the house, eyes stuck on that door. It looked how her heart felt, kicked in and ruined.

Her home. They had violated her home.

Finn's home.

Broken glass crunched under her feet as she stepped over the threshold, and all the air escaped through the shattered windows.

The empty shell of a building was unrecognizable. The furniture, little as there had been, was broken and scattered in pieces around the room, like a skeleton picked clean by vultures. Plant entrails spilled from smashed pots, pages from Finn's herb books and journals torn free of their binding and rippling in the wind coming through the open door and ruined windows.

The kitchen was looted, all of the food gone and most of the utensils stolen, except for the basket of Veronica's soap making supplies. It sat on the small stool beside the back door, exactly as Veronica had left it. It was that— the first familiar thing in this empty, strange place, that hit Veronica like a blow. This had been her home. This was not the wrong house, this was not a mistake.

She sucked in a hard, sharp breath, her chest aching, screaming. But she didn't cry. She wanted to cry, perhaps it would relieve the pressure in her lungs, but she couldn't.

A hand touched her arm, tentative and firm at once. Angelus said nothing, just watched her, as though waiting for... what, Veronica wasn't sure.

Veronica opened her mouth to speak, to tell him she was alright— if she wasn't crying, that must mean she was alright— but no sound came.

She pressed her hand to the wall, trying to steady herself. Images flashed before her eyes before she could realize her mistake. *No,* she begged. She didn't want to see.

But she saw. All of it. Soldiers crashing through the front door, turning the place upside down searching for her, for Angelus. There was no anger there, however. They didn't break anything, or steal anything, they simply trampled and searched. It was after they left that the first rocks came through the windows. Villagers. Villagers came and broke her home, took what was hers. They reeked of rage, a black, chaotic cloud of unorganized anger seeping from them as they... punished her. Punished the house, for housing a Wielder, for protecting someone as dirty and tainted as Veronica.

Veronica tore free of the images, her hand pressing over her mouth to stifle her rising sob. She bolted down the hallway, to Finn's room.

If they had touched it... if they destroyed what was left of him...

Veronica pushed open the bedroom door, and froze.

Finn's bed was torn apart, the straw filling of the mattress scattered like gold dust across the floor. The wooden frame of the bed had scratches and hunks missing from it, like someone took an ax to it. But worst of all were the books. Ruined pages torn from their bindings settled on the floor like snow, cold and lifeless. For a wild, insane moment, Veronica felt as if Finn had died in this room, that he'd been murdered right here, and this room was his corpse.

Angelus' hand closed around her arm, pulling her back and steering her out of the room. She reached out, toward the bed, as

418

though to say, *Stop! Wait!* As though they were still there, in that room, and she could stop them.

"No," she gasped, trying to push Angelus away as he dragged her to the front door. *"No."* She was crying. She didn't know when the tears started, but they wouldn't stop. "They took him," she sobbed. "They took him!"

"He was already gone," Angelus said, voice hard, harsh. He was angry. With her? No— with them. With this house, the room behind them. With everything. "I shouldn't have let you come here— it's too much, especially after today. We need to go."

"He's gone," she cried.

Angelus cupped her face in his hands, forcing her eyes to meet his. "Yes, he is. But you're still here. *I'm* still here."

For how long? How long would they last? How much longer did the world have to be this way?

"We have to fix this," Veronica said, voice still thick with strangling tears. "I can't keep... living like this."

She didn't mean the house. Angelus seemed to understand. He pulled her into him, wrapping his arms around her. "We will," he said. "We will."

CHAPTER FIFTY-FIVE

IT felt wrong to be home, but not be able to *go* home. To sleep in a tent instead of inside her house, when it was less than a mile away.

Angelus slept soundly beside Veronica, but she couldn't sleep. The old weight was creeping back into her chest, bricks slowly piling up, one after another, a slow and terrible construction that would crush her beneath it. For the first time in months, she felt like she had for such a long time. Alone, and fragile.

Slowly, carefully, she slipped from under Angelus' arm. He didn't stir. He was exhausted from walking since before sunrise, and everything else that turned the day into a defeat. Veronica was exhausted too, but not tired. Her body did not crave sleep, but some other form of relief.

She pulled on her boots and coat, then slipped into the night. The wind had died down, and the stillness was disconcerting. It was cold, but without the wind, it was tolerable underneath so many layers. She walked, no destination in mind, just needing to relieve some of the tension in her muscles. She'd often paced the house when she couldn't sleep, trying to be quiet so as not to wake Finn.

The shops in the town square were dark and abandoned. The villagers were still confined to their homes, a guard posted outside each door, Veronica passing a few of them as she walked. She tried to catch their eyes, but they didn't seem to see her.

The tents were clustered close together in the center of the village, all of them dark except Queen Mayva's. For a moment, Veronica considered going inside, though for what purpose she wasn't sure. To ask her if she was alright? A stupid notion. Of course she wasn't.

She wandered until she reached the edge of the shield around the village, the invisible wall growing hotter as she drew near it, like heat radiating off a fire. Veronica spread her bare hands before it, drinking in the warm energy, being careful not to touch it. A few birds had attempted to fly through it, and their corpses lay on the ground where they'd plummeted out of the sky.

Veronica's absent gaze traveled over the horizon, the forest like a cloud of black smoke consuming the land beyond. It took a moment for her eyes to focus, and another for her to discern the pinprick of light emerging from the trees, swaying slightly from side to side. Lanterns. Veronica watched, stepping as close to the barrier as she dared, the heat nearly unbearable. She squinted into the dark to see what was coming. *Who* was coming.

Hulking, four-legged figures emerged from the black forest, getting closer and closer, though their gait was unhurried. The shield before her shuddered, as if in warning, sensing the danger beyond. Veronica retreated a step, but then she was frozen. She watched as the wolves, six of them, approached the village, led by another that walked on two legs.

The world around Veronica shifted, tilting slightly forward, and Veronica stumbled, trying to stay balanced, and when the ground righted she was standing near the edge of the forest, and the wolves were mere feet from her. She saw now that the wolf walking on two legs had one of his hands around the back of a woman's neck, dragging her forward, her hands bound behind her. Her dress was tattered and filthy, her face covered in cuts, some fresh, and others scabbed.

It paused, and the creatures following behind it stopped as well, heads tilting and noses turning up into the air, trying to smell what was amiss.

Their leader slowly turned his head from side to side, sniffing the air. The woman in his hold slowly looked up. Directly into Veronica's face.

Tabitha's eyes widened in horror, in realization, and then something pushed Veronica back, sending her tumbling into darkness.

*   *   *

VERONICA woke with a start, sitting bolt upright, clutching her chest, which seized painfully, as though she really had been breathing in the cold night air.

Angelus startled awake, reaching for her in the dark. "Veronica? What is it? What's wrong?"

Veronica didn't answer. Trembling, she got to her feet, pulling on her coat over her nightgown. She was freezing, ice chips surging through her bloodstream. Her teeth chattered, rattling her skull, as she squeezed her eyes shut, then opened them, trying to focus her vision.

Angelus stood before her, bending to peer into her face, his hands closing around her upper arms as though worried she would collapse. "A dream? A vision?"

"Yes," she gasped. "I... think so?" Hysteria was building in her throat. "I don't... I don't know how to tell, I don't know when it's a dream and when it isn't—"

Angelus drew her to him, pressing her into his warm, hard chest. Veronica breathed him in, the world starting to settle around her, some of his heat creeping into her bones. "Shh," he soothed, soft and low. "It's alright."

Veronica shook her head. "No, it's not. They're... they're coming."

CHAPTER FIFTY-SIX

ANGELUS and Liam walked the entire perimeter of the village, following the circle-shaped Magical barrier that, Liam told Angelus, formed an invisible dome over them. Nothing was getting in or out.

Something crunched under Angelus' boot, and he looked down at the corpse of a crow.

"Careful," Liam warned, pointing to Angelus' right. "Don't get any closer to it."

Angelus couldn't see the shield, but he sensed the heat, and he took Liam's word for it and backed up a bit. He stayed on Liam's left. Better he get charred than Angelus.

"Did she say where she saw them?" Liam asked.

Angelus convinced Veronica to share what she'd seen with Liam and Mayva, and she begged them not to say anything to the others. She was scared of being wrong, Angelus knew, of causing a panic when there was no reason to. But Mayva and Liam both listened to her, possibly giving her more credit than she'd given herself. Mayva remained in the village square with Veronica, and Angelus and Liam agreed to go together to inspect the shield.

"She only said she saw them coming from the forest," Angelus answered, gesturing toward the wall of green along the western border. It was dense, dark, and utterly still.

Liam turned in a slow circle, surveying their surroundings. "The barrier hasn't been tampered with," he said. "There's no one out there."

"Will it hold?" Angelus asked. "If they do come?"

"Magic is only as strong as the one that wields it," Liam said. "And we have the strongest. Nothing is bringing this barrier down." He nodded in the direction of the village. "Let's go. You can tell Veronica we found nothing."

They returned to the village square, the people in their homes casting them seething glares from their doorways and windows. Angelus glared right back, adding an extra layer of disdain. They turned away first.

Angelus and Liam parted, Angelus going in search of Veronica and Liam going to report to Mayva. But before Angelus could reach Veronica's tent, his eyes fell on the metalsmith shop. Loathed as he was to have anything to do with Euric or his business, he needed weapons. The sword at his hip was the only weapon he had, and his chest felt too light without the weight of his vest and the throwing knives it held. He was far too exposed, too vulnerable. He had no money, but perhaps he could trade the sword for a weapon more suited to him.

He went inside, hand on his sword hilt. Ready, if necessary.

Euric's wife stood behind a wooden counter, but otherwise he was alone in the low-ceilinged shop, which held a layer of dust over almost everything in it. Angelus supposed it made sense, if Artemis bought off the villagers and was taking care of their needs, there wasn't much use for a shop like this now.

As expected, there weren't many weapons on display, but the knives he'd seen so long ago, when he first came to this shop with Veronica, were still there.

Euric's wife fidgeted where she stood, her eyes on the ground, and Angelus walked up to the opposite side of the counter, picking up one of the knives without looking at her. The knives were longer and thicker than the ones he preferred, but they would have to do. There were eight in all, the sheaths all held together with straps of dark leather Angelus realized was meant to be worn across the chest. Angelus took all of them and the chest holster and placed them on the counter. His contempt had to be visible on his face, but he kept his mouth shut.

The woman only stared at the knives on the counter between them for a moment, then she shook her head, pushing them toward him. "Take them," she whispered. She kept her eyes down, her hair falling over the sides of her face like a curtain.

Angelus didn't move immediately. He asked, voice low, "Did you go to Veronica's house?"

She knew what he meant.

The woman shook her head, fast and hard. "No," she breathed. Finally she looked up at him. Her face was older than Angelus remembered. "I never wanted any of this," she said.

"But you did nothing to stop them."

She was silent.

Angelus took the knives, and left the shop without a word.

*   *   *

ANGELUS found Veronica sitting alone in her tent, a blanket around her shoulders, as she paged through one of the books she'd inherited from Tabitha. She was so focused on what she was reading that she didn't seem to notice him open the tent flap.

"Veronica?"

She blinked, eyes meeting his. He entered the tent, setting his new knives down on the ground before sitting across from her, the book between them.

"We didn't find anything," he said. "No sign anyone tried to get through the barrier. Liam is confident it will hold, regardless."

Veronica shook her head slowly, not like she disagreed, but like there was something she couldn't quite remember. "Tabitha is smart. She had an understanding of Magic, of how to use it, unlike anything I've ever seen before. She could manipulate it so easily." Her eyes found Angelus', and his heart sank at how pale she was. Despite this, however, he couldn't help thinking she was still miles from the scared girl he'd watched from afar so long ago. This Veronica was scared, but she was also brave. *Because* of her fear, she had learned to be brave.

Something surged up in Angelus' chest, overwhelming, stealing his breath. He reached forward, gripping her wrist. "She's not getting in." His voice was hard, sure. No one was going to touch her, hurt her. And when she met his gaze, and she smiled at him through the tremor of fear in her eyes, he was sure. He was sure in a way he'd never been sure of anything in his life. Veronica was not just something to protect. She was *his* to protect. And he was hers.

Her fingers closed over his hand, still gripping her wrist, her skin warm against his, and something in his core unraveled. She lifted his palm and pressed it to her lips. "Either way," she said, "We fight."

"Always," he agreed. "Always."

CHAPTER FIFTY-SEVEN

TABITHA was in Veronica's dreams.

Veronica didn't know what she had been dreaming about, or if she had been dreaming at all, before Tabitha came. There was only the two of them, sitting across from each other on the floor of the forest where they'd practiced together. Tabitha looked as Veronica remembered her, face and clothing clean, and Veronica could almost forget the scraped and beaten face she saw in her vision.

"What do you want?" Veronica asked. She wasn't surprised to see Tabitha. She'd wondered when she would appear, not if.

"You've come a long way," Tabitha mused, as though she hadn't heard Veronica speak. "So you did it then? Used Blood Magic?"

Veronica shook her head. "No. I'm not like you."

Tabitha half grinned, half grimaced. "Do you think I wanted this to happen? It wasn't my choice. *You* got me banished, and those monsters found me." Her voice hardened, rising to a shout. "They forced me to use my Magic to help them find you! They'll kill me if I don't!"

Veronica shook her head again. "Help them? Help them kill us, you mean?" Veronica's voice was rising. "You aren't saving anyone Tabitha, not even yourself. You're going to kill your own kind!"

Tabitha sneered. "And whose fault is that?"

Veronica rose. "Yours." She began to walk away, deeper into the forest, to the edge of the dream.

"I didn't want this, Veronica!" Tabitha shouted after her.

Without looking back, Veronica said, "Neither did I."

*   *   *

THE first scream came at nightfall.

The camp was silent, and just as the sun slipped below the horizon, an ear-splitting shriek rang out from one of the tents.

For a moment, everyone was frozen. Then Mayva turned from where she stood beside the fire, warming her hands alongside a few of her soldiers. Her eyes scanned the faces around her as she began to walk toward one of the tents. She pulled aside the tent flap, Angelus, Liam and Veronica following close behind.

A young woman with several tight blonde braids was on her knees, clutching the sides of her head as though trying to keep it from tearing apart.

"Sylvia?" Mayva breathed.

"Your Majesty," Sylvia sobbed, and Veronica felt suddenly nauseous. "Something... something's inside my head. It's in my Magic." She looked up, eyes pleading.

A horrible chill thrilled over Veronica's entire body.

She remembered Queen Mayva's words from what seemed like another lifetime. *To touch another person's Magic... you might as well have touched their soul, and bent it to your will.*

Sylvia sobbed harder, her fingernails clawing at her face as if something were crawling under her skin. "Get it out," she gasped. Then she screamed, *"Get it out!"*

Tabitha. What have you done?

Another scream tore through the village square, this one male. Gerard crumpled to the ground beside the fire. Mayva didn't move, only stared at him as he bellowed in pain, hands gripping his skull.

"The shield!" Sylvia cried. "Someone's attacking the shield!"

Veronica gripped Angelus' arm. "They're coming," she gasped, all the feeling and color slowly draining from her face. Her hands and feet went cold, her chest still, as though her heart had forgotten how to beat.

"No," Liam said, gaze turning to the trees. "They're here."

CHAPTER FIFTY-EIGHT

ANGELUS grabbed Veronica's hand and dragged her into her tent, where all of their weapons and supplies were. He put the leather knife holster over his head, threading his arms through the contraption so the knives rested across his chest in their sheaths, and then secured the sword Liam had given him around his waist. "You need to get out of here."

Veronica shook her head. "I want to help."

Angelus glared at her. "No, you aren't ready." He grabbed her arms and shook her slightly. "Get out of here now!"

The tent flap ripped open, and Liam appeared, face tight and eyes alert. "We need you," he said to Angelus. "Get to the front of the line, now."

"I'm coming too," Veronica said, grabbing her coat and putting it on.

"No," Liam said before Angelus could say anything. "Go and warn the villagers, do whatever you must to get them out."

Angelus expected her to argue, but she nodded. If this was because she had finally seen reason, or because the howling was growing louder, the ground beginning to shake like a landslide was hurtling toward them, warning them they were all out of time, Angelus did not know.

Would she be safer this way? He'd known all along she wouldn't just leave, no matter how much he wanted her to, and for an instant Angelus couldn't decide if he loved or hated this about her.

Angelus stepped closer to her, and her shoulders straightened, clearly ready to argue again, but he only wrenched a knife free from his holster and handed it to her. "As soon as you can, go to your house and wait for me there. I'll find you." Her small hand wrapped around the hilt of the knife. Angelus pulled Veronica to him and kissed her, brief and hard. Her eyes were blazing when he stepped away, and he decided. Her bravery was something he loved. "I'll find you," he repeated, softer, a promise, and let his forehead rest against hers just for a moment. Then he followed Liam out of the tent, and they ran together through the village square until they reached Mayva, who stood at the front of a wall of her soldiers. Angelus always thought her company had been numerous, but looking at them now, they didn't look like nearly enough.

"They've broken through the shield," Mayva said from atop her horse, and Angelus didn't know if she was talking to him or all of them. "Those with Magic, focus your efforts on keeping them from the village. Use fire, it's the only effective weapon we have against them. Everyone else, protect the Wielders."

Angelus ran a hand over his chest, feeling the ridges of the sheathed knives. They were all he had, but what were they against those creatures? He turned back to see the men and women behind him, and made out a figure running from the center of the village to the houses. Veronica.

Angelus' eyes rose to the sky. *Gods,* he prayed, for the first time in his life, *Let her live. If no one else here lives, let her survive this.*

Then the beasts appeared, charging toward them, and Angelus had no time to think of anything else. He palmed two blades, as ready as he could be. He looked up at Mayva, and she met his eyes. She nodded, once, and then they charged just as hard, just as ferociously, as the monsters.

*   *   *

THE soldiers Mayva stationed outside the homes of the villagers were gone, called to battle, and many of the villagers had already left, their houses abandoned and their silhouettes visible on the east-running road. Veronica didn't know if they were evacuating, or simply ran off as soon as the soldiers disappeared, unaware of the danger outside.

"Get out!" Veronica shouted, banging on the doors. "You have to get out! Run! Take the east road!"

Darkness was quickly swallowing the sky, and Veronica could barely see ten feet in front of her, but she ran down the paths between homes, relying on memory more than sight, Angelus' blade gripped tightly in her hand. When she came to the house of an elderly couple, she went inside and helped them out the door, but she couldn't stay with them long, needing to move to the next house. When she reached Roberta's, she didn't bother knocking, just hurried through the door.

"What's happening?" Roberta asked, rising unsteadily from her bed.

Veronica picked up Roberta's coat, pushing it toward her. "Artemis' wolves are here, we're under attack. You have to get out."

Roberta smiled sadly at Veronica, even as she allowed her to help her into her coat. She pressed her palm to Veronica's cheek. "I'm not getting far on these old legs, my dear."

Veronica fought back her tears. "You have to try— they'll kill you. I've seen what they can do. Roberta, *please.*"

Roberta limped out the door, shaking her head. "I'll help you warn the others."

Veronica couldn't argue, she was too frantic, the darkening sky like a hand closing slowly around her throat.

"Go," Roberta urged her. "I'll warn the people on this side of the village."

Veronica ran back the way she'd come, banging on every door she came across. Most of the houses were already empty, but a few villagers remained. Some of them left after Veronica's warning, others refused. One man spit on her when he opened his door.

Veronica kept running. She could hear screaming and howling, the horrible, horrible howling. She'd never forget the sound for the rest of her life.

The east road was soon full of the retreating figures of villagers, and the village itself was nearly empty. Veronica hurried the evacuees along, making sure children found their parents and the elderly had someone younger to assist them in walking through the dark. When she caught sight of the farmhouse, she paused. Angelus told her he would find her there. Could she wait? Was he there now? If he wasn't, she decided, she was going back to find him. She might not have known how to fight with her hands, but they would need her Magic.

She stepped through the doorway. The wind of the previous night had blown the broken glass across the floor, and it piled in the corners of the room like ashes, or snow. Walking to the kitchen, Veronica peered carefully around, but the place was empty.

Something creaked inside the house.

Veronica froze.

For a moment there was dead silence, but then she heard it again. The soft whine of door hinges, then quiet scuffling. Angelus wouldn't have hidden. There was someone else in the house.

Veronica turned, very slowly, toward the hallway, Angelus' knife tight in her grip. She stepped soundlessly into the hallway, her ears straining... There. In Finn's bedroom. The door was slightly ajar. It could have been the wind that made the door creak.

The scuffling sounded again.

She crept forward, knife at the ready, the fingers of her other hand ready to draw a symbol if she needed to, though she wasn't convinced she would be fast enough.

Veronica ripped open the bedroom door.

*   *   *

MAYVA never called for a retreat. There was no option to retreat. Angelus couldn't help but wonder if there *had* been a choice, would she have taken it?

He would likely never know.

Shoulder to shoulder with Liam, who was conjuring fire with shaking, pale fingers, Angelus had his sword out and ready. Gerard and the other Wielders had managed to kill one wolf, its motionless body engulfed in flame, but they were tiring quickly. And the wolves kept coming. Angelus flinched when he heard a scream, turning just long enough to see one of the beast's jaws was clamped around a female soldier's leg, throwing her into a thick tree trunk several feet away as though she weighed nothing. She did not move again.

There were too many of them, far more than Veronica said she saw in her vision. A dozen? Maybe more.

In the distance, near the trees, Angelus could make out a lone wolf, standing on its hind legs, enormous hand clutching a small human arm in its grip. Tabitha. She and the wolf watched the battle, unmoving.

Two wolves bolted for Angelus and Liam, who tried desperately to draw a symbol, but he wasn't fast enough. Angelus pulled Liam down, shoving him to the ground as the wolves lunged, jumping straight over them and running toward... The village.

No.

Angelus seized Liam's arm and hauled him to his feet. He swayed, badly, and a wet cough punched out of his mouth. Blood smeared at the corners of his lips. His Magic, weak to begin with, would be entirely depleted soon.

"We're getting killed out here!" Angelus had to shout over the clash of swords against claws, the shouts and the roars and the howls. Louder than any of it, though, was Angelus' heartbeat.

Liam, still holding onto Angelus' arm for support, coughed again, blood dribbling down his chin. "I know," he panted. Those two words fell like stones in Angelus' stomach.

Angelus wanted to shout at him, to tell him to get Mayva while he found Veronica, and retreat, to get the hell out before they were all killed. But he could see that desire reflected in Liam's eyes. He didn't have to say anything.

But there was no choice. Retreat was no longer an option. There was nowhere to go, no way to run without being hunted, no path to take that didn't mean leaving someone behind. Fighting was the only choice. That's how it had always been.

If you come back, that's it. You aren't leaving again.

You find what you would die to protect, and then you die to protect it.

Angelus' grip on his sword tightened, just as a piercing howl, almost like a scream, came from behind Angelus. He whirled, and stared as one of the wolves that had run to the village... retreated. For a moment Angelus didn't understand what he was seeing. The wolf was simply backing up, slowly, and then Angelus saw the small cluster of people standing before the creature. They carried torches, and swung them at the wolf, who snarled at them.

Villagers.

"What are they doing?" Angelus demanded, not realizing he'd spoken aloud.

"Fighting," Liam gasped from beside him. His face had gone from white to gray, but even so he managed a bloody-lipped smile.

It wouldn't make a difference, would it? There were still too many of them.

But fighting was all they could do.

A roar boomed across the battlefield, and Angelus turned to see that the wolf that had held Tabitha was now a tower of fire. And Tabitha's rathe-like figure was sprinting away from it. Where she was going, Angelus had no idea, but he couldn't worry about her. Three more wolves were slowly circling him and Liam.

"There are too many," Angelus gritted out.

"I know," Liam said. "I know."

*   *   *

VERONICA was frozen, staring at—

"M-Mary? Sully? Martha?"

The three children, huddled together on the floor, stared up at Veronica with wide, terrified eyes. "What are you doing here?" Her shock, and then relief at seeing them alive, were instantly buried under a wave of panic. She grabbed Martha, who clutched her ragdoll like a lifeline, and hauled her to her feet, Mary and Sully following as Veronica hurried them down the hall. "You have to get out— Where are your families?"

"My papa's staying to fight," Sully declared proudly, even as his voice wavered slightly. "He told us to hide here."

Veronica was stunned. There were villagers staying to fight? *With* Mayva?

It isn't all of them, she thought. *There are still good people left.*

Veronica wrenched Martha down the hall, Sully and Mary following after. Mary, Veronica noticed, was clutching a short, dull-looking dagger. Frightened as she was, she'd been ready to defend the other two children.

"Mary," Veronica said, pushing Sully and Martha toward her, "Get them out— go out the back door and run to the road. Find your families, anyone you know, and stay with them."

"We're staying to fight!" Sully said, balling his tiny hands into fists.

"No," Veronica snapped, "You—"

A piercing howl tore through the night— close, far too close. They'd broken through Mayva's line. They were coming.

Angelus, she thought. *Goddess, let him be alright.*

"They promised," Mary said in a soft, dazed voice. "They promised the monsters wouldn't come here, not if we did what the soldiers and Euric said."

"They lied," Sully snapped, looking angrily at Mary. "Of course they lied! They hate us!"

Another howl echoed from outside the house. Veronica clutched the blade in her hand— it felt so small and pathetic in her palm. If it came to a fight, Magic was her only real weapon.

The howling didn't stop. It got closer and closer and louder and louder until—

"Run!" Veronica shouted at the children, shoving them toward the back door. She barely got the door open before a massive crash sounded behind her as the frame of the front door, and most of the wall around it, gave way, and one of the wolves snarled at them. Veronica threw her hand out— behind her, at the children, a shield bursting free of her palm and pushing them out the door. Just like when Tabitha tried to attack— the Magic simply came, as if it was an extension of some survival instinct she couldn't control.

It left her wide open to the creature's attack.

She screamed as its teeth closed around her shoulder, and the thing landed on top of her, hundreds of pounds of muscle and teeth and sweat-slicked fur.

Her finger traced the spiraling symbol before she pressed her palm into its chest, willing fire to emerge. The creature let her go, jumping backwards as a red burn the shape of Veronica's hand seared across its chest. It was such a small mark compared to what she knew she could do. The shield— the shield had drained too much of her Magic, her energy. She couldn't fight, not like this. She scrambled to her feet, clutching the blade in her hand, her breathing shrill in her ears. The house quaked, as though a gust of wind would bring it to its knees.

She began to draw the symbol for fire again, praying she had enough energy left to conjure something, anything. The creature lunged for her. She ducked out of its way, and it crashed into the kitchen wall.

She tried again, and the burning symbol hovered in the air between them for a moment, before it burst into a wall of fire, just like forever ago in the plum orchard. The creature screamed as it was swallowed by flame, and Veronica dragged herself from the burning house, nothing left inside of her. She had managed to destroy yet another home with her own fire. Her Magic was gone, depleted. When would it come back? She needed it *now*. She couldn't fight without it.

She crashed to the ground in front of the house, coughing and choking on the ash in her lungs, the house quickly turning to kindling behind her.

A huge hand closed around the back of her neck, dragging her to her feet. A wolf bared its long, sharp teeth at her in a smile.

"The Master said to keep one alive," he said, his voice more growl than anything, the words barely distinguishable. "You'll do."

He threw her to the ground, her skull smashing into the earth. Her vision dimmed and tunneled until there was nothing but darkness as endless as the night.

CHAPTER FIFTY-NINE

THE village was a sea of red.

Angelus had never seen so much blood— it was on his skin, in his hair, under his nails. He could feel it in his mouth, in his ears. Hysteria was beginning to build inside him, but he fought it down. A deep gash, a clawmark, ran down the side of his right leg, and he half limped, half dragged himself to a pile of skin and clothes he realized was still breathing. He'd expected one of Mayva's soldiers, but this man was a villager.

"My son," he gasped. "Where is my son?"

Angelus passed him by, knowing there was nothing he could do for the man, even as he cried out, *"Sully?"* in a feeble, dying breath.

The village was on fire. Magic fire, as well as fire from the torches villagers had lit to use as weapons, had spread everywhere. Homes and shops were burning. Soon there would be nothing left.

There was no one standing. No one except Angelus, if his unsteady gait could be considered standing, and Mayva, who stood in the middle of it all, like a statue, and Angelus could imagine her, and the tragedy around her, as one of the paintings in the castle. *The Lost Battle,* Angelus thought it would be called.

Drom, her horse, was nowhere in sight, and Angelus wondered if he too had perished. Mayva's eyes found his, and he limped toward her until he was beside her. Her face was blank, gray-white like the ash falling down around them. It settled on the grass, in the open mouths and unseeing eyes of the dead soldiers, villagers, and Wielders around them. There were two wolf corpses, blackened and burned, among them. Only two.

It was the same as Rom's village. It didn't matter that they'd had Magic on their side; there were just too many of them. Angelus should have been dead, Mayva too. But then the creatures... stopped. A howl had ripped through the air and they fled, like dogs answering a summoning call.

"Veronica," was all Angelus could say. "I have to find Veronica."

Mayva said nothing, only turned and followed him as he limped slowly, painfully, to the road.

Angelus heard Mayva's steps halt, and turned to see what she was gazing at. An old woman, her head torn from her body in a mess of blood, veins and muscle, lay in pieces on the ground. She'd been killed, torn apart, and feasted on. Her ribcage hung in broken shards over her ruined torso. Angelus didn't recognize her. She was just a body. Then he saw the swelling on her face, saw her open, dead eyes, and he knew who she was. Roberta. She stayed behind, or perhaps simply hadn't been fast enough to get away in time.

And now she was dead.

Laying not two feet away from her, was Tabitha. Where Roberta's body was ruined, Tabitha appeared shockingly unharmed, despite the empty eyes that told Angelus she was dead. She looked as though she'd simply fallen down, dead, but Angelus could see blood in her hair. The back of her skull was smashed. She must have died instantly. Who or what killed her, Angelus didn't know, and he never would.

Angelus reached for Mayva's hand, and pulled her forward. She did not resist as he led her through the wreckage, and joined him in searching the faces of the dead. Searching for Veronica, and Liam. Angelus hadn't seen him in what felt like hours. Was he—

"Help," came a moan from nearby, a female voice. Angelus and Mayva turned toward the noise, and then they saw her. Sylvia, her blonde hair soaked red with blood, was pinned beneath what might have been part of a wall from one of the village houses, as though it had fallen on her. Or been pushed by a great, hulking body.

"Sylvia," Mayva gasped, as if she couldn't believe it. Angelus crouched down to heave the wall up, but only managed to lift it a couple of inches, his wounded leg screaming in pain. Mayva seized Sylvia by the arms and dragged her out from under the wreckage. Angelus let go, and the mess of broken wood planks clattered noisily as they hit the ground, producing a cloud of dirt and ash that burst up into the air.

Sylvia, incredibly, got to her feet. She clutched her side, but her legs appeared mostly uninjured.

"Have you seen Liam?" Sylvia asked, wincing.

Mayva went perfectly still. "I thought he went with you."

Sylvia shook her head. "He said he was going to look for you."

Everyone had been scattered, separated, formation and strategy forgotten and replaced with survival instinct and desperation.

Mayva didn't move. She didn't appear to be breathing.

"What about Gerard?" Sylvia asked, eyes pleading.

Mayva shook her head slowly. "Gone," she said, voice barely audible. "They're all... gone."

If they found no one else alive, Sylvia, Angelus and Mayva were all that was left of the army. Everyone else was gone, wiped out in the blink of an eye.

"I'm going to find Veronica," Angelus said. "Go look for Liam."

Mayva's eyes flashed with what might have been gratitude, before she took off running, Sylvia at her heels.

Angelus dragged himself down the east road, stopping only when he saw the smoke.

The house— Veronica's house— was on fire.

He couldn't run, but by the gods he tried.

"Veronica!" he roared. He didn't see her, didn't hear her answer him.

No...

Something moved in the dark, a shapeless black mass in the light from the blazing house. For a perfect, absolutely perfect moment, he thought it was her. But it wasn't. The form was too small as it came nearer, and was joined by two even smaller figures.

Children.

Angelus limped closer to them. Two girls and a boy, faces streaked with ash, except where their tears had cleaned tracks down their cheeks, moved toward him like phantoms.

"Where is she?" Angelus gasped. His leg was burning, the pain growing more and more intense with every step he took. "Where is she?" he repeated, louder.

The older of the two girls looked up at him. Her eyes were empty. "They took her," she said, voice as empty as her eyes.

Angelus shook his head, uncomprehending. "Veronica," he said, loudly and clearly, as though the children might have misunderstood who he was talking about. "Where is Veronica?"

The girl held out her hands to Angelus. In her palms lay his dagger, the one he gave Veronica, and something else. He took it, his hands shaking, and realized what it was. Veronica's red hair ribbon.

"They took her," the girl repeated, her voice breaking. "They took her."

CHAPTER SIXTY

VERONICA did not emerge from sleep as she usually did, like breaching the surface of a still pool. She was thrown into consciousness, all at once, first sleeping and then wide awake.

She gasped as she sat up, a sharp pain lancing through her left shoulder. When she touched it, she felt thick bandages.

For a moment she was relieved. She'd been injured, and was in the infirmary tent. She'd been taken to safety, her wounds tended to. She was safe.

But as her eyes adjusted to the darkness around her, she realized she was not in a tent. She was in a cage. A cell. Three walls of stone, the fourth a series of thick bars made of rusted metal.

She rested her feet on the cold ground. They were bare.

Standing slowly, she walked to the bars. A faint light lit the hallway in front of her, and she could make out more cells on either side of her, stretching on for eternity.

A tall, thin ghost of a figure appeared at the end of the row of cells, walking toward her. Veronica stared, unmoving, as a woman stepped in front of her. She was atrociously thin, and strangely... *faded*-looking, like the edges of her form were frayed somehow. Her eyes were large and dark blue, and her mane of blonde hair fell to her waist. Her dress was white, and embroidered with gold thread that formed a leafy pattern across the skirt.

"Hello," the woman greeted Veronica with a smile. Though she was taller than Veronica, and most likely older, Veronica had the strange impression she was being spoken to by a child. There was such innocence in the woman's face, and despite her sickly appearance, her smile was kind and genuine. While Veronica was sure she'd never met this woman, she couldn't shake the idea she had seen her somewhere before.

"Where am I?" Veronica croaked, her throat painfully dry.

"You're in the castle." The woman beamed. "You'll be safe here."

"Why am I here?"

The woman leaned forward, her forehead almost touching one of the bars separating them. Her eyes were round and bluer than the sky. "Artemis wants to see you."

All the blood drained from Veronica's face, shooting down her body until it soaked into the floor. "Artemis?"

The woman nodded. "Don't worry. He protects us," she said.

"Us?" Veronica whispered.

She smiled again. "My sisters and I."

And then Veronica realized where she had seen this woman before. A memory. Queen Andromeda's memory. Blue eyes. Blonde hair. *Sisters.* "You... You're..."

"My name is Morgeoux." The High Queen of Lavdia grinned eagerly at Veronica. "Have you seen my butterfly?"

END OF BOOK TWO

ACKNOWLEDGEMENTS

Thank you Lord, for keeping your promises. *Soli Deo Gloria.*

Thank you Ben, for never letting me get away with anything.

Thank you Daisy, for being the best friend I could ever ask for. You make me better, in every way. You earned the dedication of this book, truly.

Many thanks to the alpha/beta readers of this book: Ben, Josh, Sania, Anabel, and Meghan, for making this book better, and for all of your honesty and love.

To the book reviewers and bloggers that helped spread the word about this book, as well as *The Heir,* I am tremendously grateful. I wouldn't be here without your kindness and enthusiasm.

A special thank you to the readers who loved *The Heir,* and stalked my Instagram and blew up my inboxes, begging for the next book. You kept me going. I'll never be able to thank you enough.

To my incredible editor, Ricki, thank you for all of your support, and for being a grounding voice in the chaos of writing, editing, and publishing. Getting to work with you is a privilege.

To my writer tribe, Jordyn, Moriah, Josh, and Nix, all of my love and gratitude. You're so much more than just "Writer Friends." Blessings, each and every one of you.

And thank *you,* if you've come this far with me. I'll see you in the last book.

Made in the USA
Middletown, DE
21 September 2022

10935337R00269